"What a fantastic story! Set in the majestic Zion National Park, *Through Water and Stone* is an engaging novel about family, secrets, and self-discovery. Karen Barnett's vivid writing and heartfelt characters always pull me in on the first page. And the mystery! I couldn't put this down until I discovered every secret alongside Talia and Blake."

—Misty M. Beller, *USA Today* best-selling author of the Brothers of Sapphire Ranch series

"With vivid historical detail, compelling characters, and a gripping story, the novel centers around the identity of an abandoned baby and the secrets passed down through generations. A must-read for fans of historical fiction and anyone who values the deep connections that shape our lives."

—Suzanne Woods Fisher, best-selling author of *Capture the Moment*

"*Through Water and Stone* is an immersive story set against the untamed beauty of Zion National Park. Barnett expertly weaves a tale that is gentle and tender yet as powerful as floodwaters in reaching into the heart of love and family. This book should top the to-be-read stack of every nature-loving reader who longs for adventure."

—Amanda Cox, award-winning and best-selling author of *Between the Sound and Sea*

"There's nothing quite like opening a book and falling into the story, which is exactly what happened with *Through Water and Stone*. The characters drew me into the plot and held me. I couldn't turn the pages fast enough, but when I knew I was nearing the end, I didn't want to leave my new friends. I felt every emotion and pull of a muscle. This is a book you'll want to share with every booklover you know!"

—Eva Marie Everson, CEO of Word Weavers International and best-selling author

National Park Novels

When Stone Wings Fly

Where Trees Touch the Sky

Through Water and Stone

THROUGH WATER AND STONE

A Zion National Park Novel

KAREN BARNETT

Through Water and Stone: A Zion National Park Novel

Published by Kregel Publications, a division of Kregel Inc., 2450 Oak Industrial Dr. NE, Grand Rapids, MI 49505. www.kregel.com.

Cataloging-in-Publication Data is available from the Library of Congress.

ISBN 978-0-8254-4853-9, print
ISBN 978-0-8254-7171-1, epub
ISBN 978-0-8254-7170-4, Kindle

Printed in the United States of America
25 26 27 28 29 30 31 32 33 34 / 5 4 3 2 1

To all who proudly wear the green and gray.
Thank you for all you do to protect our parks
and the people who visit them.

He says, "Be still, and know that I am God."

—Psalm 46:10 niv

1

Zion National Park
May 15, 1948

Henry welcomed every new sunrise at Zion National Park as each one thrust his past another day behind him. Dawn crept along the steep canyon walls of Navajo sandstone, bringing its oranges and reds to life as he guided his horse along the trail leading to the Virgin River. How many more Utah sunrises would the pair of them see together?

As they passed the sleepy lodge, he attempted to banish any thoughts of the future—or the past, for that matter—and instead let the juniper-scented air root him in this quiet moment. He longed to think of nothing but the clatter of Duck's hooves and the chirping songs of the morning birdlife. The "sweet-sweet-sweeter-than-sweet" notes of the yellow warbler set the tone for the day far better than a bacon-and-egg breakfast.

Still, reality pressed in. He couldn't delay a decision about the new posting much longer. Alma would likely appreciate the cooler climes of the Grand Tetons, but wrenching his wife from this spot would take more than a written order from his superiors. It would take a word from God Himself. Since the Lord hadn't responded to a single one of Henry's pleas since his son's disappearance, he wasn't sure how to present this particular request to the Almighty.

The memories rushed in like the flash flood that had stolen his joy—his heart. Henry closed his eyes against the familiar ache. His fellow rangers still didn't know how to act around him, their laughter dying away when he entered the room. As much as he loved Zion, he needed a new beginning. Every path held a reminder of what he'd lost.

Alma would demand to stay put for the same reason. The river now flowed in her veins, the icy cold grief carving an impassable chasm through their marriage. Some part of her must be clinging to an irrational hope that one day he'd walk in with their infant son safe in his arms. She wouldn't leave Zion until they could put him to rest.

But the Virgin River refused to give up its dead.

Nine months gone. The thought tightened around his throat like a noose. He couldn't ask her to forego hope, not when he hadn't figured out how to surrender his own guilt.

After the horrors of fighting in the Philippines, moving to this place had been like coming up for air for the first time in years. The cliffs of Zion Canyon had wrapped around him and his little family, shielding them from a world spun out of control. The isolation had given him a place to heal. Until the rain fell and the water rose.

"'The Lord gave, and the Lord hath taken away . . .'" Henry's throat closed, choking off the verse's final phrase: *"Blessed be the name of the Lord."* Perhaps someday—in a new place—he'd be able to give voice to Job's words.

The truth settled over Henry. Leaving would be a mistake, at least until God gave them certainty on the matter. As much as it hurt, he needed to decline the transfer request.

The dun horse swiveled his ears toward the stream, shying a couple of steps to the side and dragging Henry back to the present. Tightening his grip on the reins, Henry stood in the stirrups to scan the riverbank. A mewling cry lifted the hairs on his arms. Likely a wounded critter of some sort. Best to let nature take its course.

The bleat sounded again, the final long quaver tugging at his heart. He nudged the horse forward, Duck's hooves clattering against the rocks. Stopping just short of the footbridge, he scrutinized the bank until an almost imperceptible shiver in the reeds caught his attention.

The breeze tickled the grasses all along the waterline, but something seemed different in that sheltered spot below the span. Whatever was there couldn't be large. Perhaps a weasel had captured itself some breakfast, and the sounds were nothing but the dying gasps of a desert cottontail.

Henry leaned forward, squinting against the glare. The noise lifted again, barely audible over the sound of the river. His father had chided him more than once for being too soft, and the long-distant scolding still triggered a wave of shame. Even so, he couldn't resist answering a call for help, no matter how softhearted it made him appear.

He slid from Duck's back, his boots landing with a muted thud on the trail. He dropped the reins and picked his way to the river's edge, the bridge throwing cool shadows over the surface of the water. A few more steps brought him to the low bank, and he used his toe to pull back the veil of rabbitbrush rather than risk a hand to an injured animal.

A leather hatbox sat in the dirt. Its lid lay flopped behind it and skewed to one side. A section of a wool blanket spilled out, its wide stripes matching the Utah Parks Company's distinctive pattern for the Zion Lodge. The remnants of a picnic lunch? He nudged the box with his foot, considering the likelihood of uncovering a skunk or an angry ringtail cat. The squeaking cry brought Henry to his knees in an instant. He pulled the edge of the coverlet aside, and the mewling doubled in speed and volume—almost as if he'd somehow freed the plaintive sounds to rise to the heavens and summon the help of the angels. The reddened face of an angry newborn glared at him, an almost accusatory look in its eyes.

The moment stretched endlessly as Henry struggled to make sense of what he was seeing. *A baby. Alone.* Images of his own son crashed through his brain, his heart thumping so hard he could feel it against his ribs.

Don't be ridiculous. Henry sat back to gather his senses. He studied the water both upstream and down, hoping for something—anything—to explain how this child came to be in this unlikely spot. Reaching down, he brushed a finger against the infant's cheek, its skin clammy. The baby wailed, extended an arm from the coverings, and shook its balled-up fist.

"A fighter, eh? What happened to you, then?" Henry tucked the blanket back into position. "Where's your mama?"

Duck nickered from the trail, rousing Henry from his reverie. Sliding his hands under the box, he lifted it from its hiding spot. "A child lost. A child found. Lord, what are You doing?" Bracing the container against his chest, Henry climbed the bank with careful steps. No matter how the child came to be here, getting him someplace safe and warm had to take priority.

Someplace far from the river's greedy grasp.

• • •

Alma swished her fingers through the fragrant soap suds. The water had long gone cold, the breakfast dishes cleaned and stacked on the drainboard. But still she remained at the sink, a single verse echoing in her heart: *"My soul thirsteth for thee, my flesh longeth for thee in a dry and thirsty land, where no water is."*

She lifted her gaze to the dusty windowpane and the canyon walls beyond—layers of sandstone, deposited and hardened over time, much like her own spirit. Cast aside by the floodwaters, she'd become another rock in the landscape.

With a sigh, Alma dried her hands on a flour-sack towel and turned to survey the kitchen. Park housing left much to be desired, but she'd finally taken her paintbrush to the small dinette. The dainty Swedish flowers and leaves she'd painted along the trim did little beyond giving her something to do. Most of the rangers' wives entertained themselves with tittle-tattle, park activities, or minding their children. Alma had no desire to help arrange picnics or plan out the new information center. And her child?

She pressed fingers to the bridge of her nose. *Lord, forgive me.*

Retrieving her paint set from the table, she eyed the tall cupboard beside the sink for her next project. The traditional Swedish *kurbits* designs—fanciful plants heavy with colorful flowers and gourds—were said to bring luck to a household. The motif had been inspired by the plant God had provided to protect Jonah from the desert sun. Maybe it would shield her as well.

The familiar tap on the door tightened the muscles along Alma's back and neck. Before responding, she took a moment to gather the strength necessary to face the chatty young woman waiting on the porch. With a deep breath, Alma swung the door open. "Mattie, what a surprise."

The younger woman's laugh was like a songbird's trill. "I only have a minute, Mrs. Eriksson. I'm heading into Springdale for some supplies. Do you need anything?" Mattie swept inside, her aqua-blue crepe dress a colorful change from the housekeeping uniform she often wore. "A friend of mine is feeling poorly, so I thought I'd pick up some ginger ale and such."

"I hope it's nothing serious." Alma reached for the pad of paper she kept on the corner table. How many items could she ask Mattie to purchase before it became an inconvenience?

"She'll be fine, I'm sure." Mattie tucked her small pocketbook against her hip. "Did you hear about the baby that was discovered this morning?"

Alma's pencil bounced off her toe and rolled across the floorboards. "Wh-what baby?"

"Your husband found an infant near the river, not far from the lodge." The woman's gaze didn't waver. "It was in a basket—or something—hidden under the footbridge. Who would abandon a newborn out in the cold where some coyote could come snatch it? Shameful."

"Was he alive?" Her heart fluttered in her chest as if newly awakened.

"Oh—I'm sorry." Mattie's brows pulled together. "I-I didn't think. It was just such a humdinger piece of gossip." She touched Alma's wrist, slowly shaking her head. "Dear Mrs. Eriksson, forget I said anything."

Alma yanked off her stained apron before tossing it and the notepad onto the table. *Not likely.* "I'm going to the ranger station."

"You really don't want to—"

"I need to see the baby for myself." Alma retrieved her straw hat from the coat-tree.

"I don't know what good that'll do." Mattie chewed her lower lip. "Henry's going to get steamed over this. I'm supposed to be helping, not upsetting you."

How long had Mattie been calling Alma's husband by his given name? Alma studied the woman as a sudden chill descended into the recesses of her stomach. The girl was as young as Alma had been when she and Henry had first met. "I don't need your help. And I don't want anything from the market." A sour tone had crept into her voice, but she didn't attempt to soften it. "You can go now."

Mattie backed a few steps before turning and darting out the door. Would she report back to Henry or try to lie low in town until the fireworks were over? Either way, it wasn't any of Alma's concern.

That child was.

• • •

Light spilled in the window of the ranger office as Henry clunked the telephone receiver back in its cradle and turned to Fred. "The sheriff won't be here for a few hours. He's busy with an emergency call over in Hurricane."

Fred's brow wrinkled as he stared down at the hatbox and its sleeping occupant sitting in the middle of his desk. "So the babe just stays here? Should I get one of ladies from the lodge to keep an eye on it? Or maybe we could drive it to the hospital in St. George."

Standing up, Henry sighed and stretched his back. He'd hoped the sheriff would take possession and get this pint-size distraction out of the office before too many people became aware of its existence. "Give Ernie's wife a call. They have two little ones. Maybe Maureen can help. But not a word to anyone else." His whole day had dissolved into chaos. He'd asked the other rangers to keep the news under their hats for the sake of the investigation—but in reality, he didn't want all the rangers' wives crowding into his space to coo over the foundling. Maureen could be discreet.

Alma especially couldn't hear about this. She'd been through enough. They both had.

Henry rubbed a hand over his eyes. He needed to get back to the site. There could be evidence out there showing who had stashed this innocent baby under the bridge. And why.

"I'll find Maureen." Fred grabbed his hat from the hook by the door. "Will you be all right here alone?" He tipped his head toward the box. "What if it starts squawking?"

"I think I can handle it. I am a father. Or . . ." A lump settled in his throat, and he reached to loosen his tie. "Or rather, I was."

The other ranger withdrew from the room, his footsteps echoing down the hall.

Right on cue, the infant stirred, a tiny, grunting cry breaking the silence.

Henry held his breath. One thing he remembered from his days with a newborn—don't rush in too soon or it was all over.

The rumpled blanket shifted, the whimper intensifying into a full-blown squall at a rather impressive pace.

Henry walked over and took hold of the box, jiggling it lightly. "Sh, no crying, Mister."

The baby's round eyes locked onto him as the forehead crinkled. In the next heartbeat, the lips parted and the cherub emitted a long warbling wail complete with pitiful chin quivering. It was followed by a gasping intake of breath and a secondary vocal assault.

"Now, don't do that." The cries punctured Henry's soul. With shaking fingers, he patted the blanket roughly in the area of the babe's stomach.

A bare foot kicked through the wraps, the toes flexing as the child continued to fuss.

Henry tucked the covers back around the squirming form, only to have them upended again. Jaw tight, he squared his shoulders and slid both hands under the infant, lifting him free from the leather case. As Henry cradled the bundle to his chest, the familiar sweet smell demolished what was left of his defenses. He groaned and patted the soft back. "I can't tote you around all day, small fry, but I've got a nice lady coming to care for you. You'll like her."

When the fuzzy head bumped against his jaw, Henry's eyes blurred. He jerked his gaze back to the window, blinking hard. He needed to clamp the lid on his emotions or he'd be of no use to anyone, least of all this tiny fellow. He bounced gently on his toes, the swaying motion coming back to him a bit too easily. "There, now."

"Henry?"

Henry turned at the sound of Alma's voice. The tender expression on her face tore further at the hole in his chest. How many times would he fail to protect her from heartache? "Alma, honey, don't come any closer. You don't need to see this." He held up a hand as if the baby were some gruesome accident scene rather than a perfectly formed miniature person.

She ignored his warning and crossed the room to stand beside him. The flush on her cheeks drew him back to when he'd first laid eyes on her, a girl not quite eighteen in the front row of their small Scandinavian church.

Her lips parted as she stared at him holding the child. "You look . . ." Tears pooled along the lower lids of her pale blue eyes. Alma shook her head as if scattering the thought. "Wh-whose?" She laid trembling fingers on Henry's sleeve and her other hand against the infant's back.

"Wish I knew." Henry studied his wife. After months of barely speaking to him, she didn't seem capable of more than one or two words at a time right now. Then again, he was struggling to find something to say himself. "Why are you here?"

"Mattie stopped by."

He should have known better than to let that young woman walk out of his office after learning of the morning's events. The biggest gossip in the park had gone straight to Alma. "I didn't mean for you to hear it that way." He lifted his voice over the half-hearted fussing.

Alma slid her palm under the swaddled form. "Let me."

If only Fred were still at his desk. With another ranger at the ready, Henry could have held on to the vestiges of common sense and steered his wife away from this danger threatening them both. "I don't think it's wise." But he could never resist her any more than he could keep water from flowing downriver. After a moment's hesitation, he released the weight into her grip. "Maureen Harper is coming to take care of it until the sheriff arrives."

"It?"

"Him."

She cupped her arms around the boy and angled away from Henry as if she and her husband were performing a well-rehearsed dance step—one perfected during the many long nights with their own colicky infant.

"The mother might show up to claim the child. If not, he'll go into state custody. He's not ours—not our responsibility, I mean." Words were starting to flow at last. "We can't keep him here."

"Mm-hmm." She bounced the foundling gently in her arms, her attention fixed.

The little one latched his eyes onto her, his mouth opening round and wide into a massive yawn.

"Alma, don't get . . ." The gentle sound of his wife's humming hushed the words on his lips. The Swedish lullaby "Byssan lull" filtered through the quiet office. This wasn't going to end well.

Voices echoed from down the hall, and Henry willed them closer. "Maureen is here, Alma. She'll take him now."

"Maureen already has two children to look after." Her expression hardened, as if daring him to take the babe from her arms. "If the mother turns up, you know where to find me. It would make more sense to search for her rather than settle for temporary caregivers."

As Fred and Maureen appeared in the doorway, Alma straightened her shoulders. "If you'll excuse me, I have a can of evaporated milk waiting at home. I am sure this little boy is hungry."

Maureen lifted her brows as Alma disappeared down the hall. "You'd best find that mother fast, Ranger Eriksson, or your wife will be knitting booties."

2

Palo Alto, California
Present Day

THE MOUNTAIN LAKE shimmered in the early morning light, the sky above the glaciated peaks stained with the colors of dawn. Talia Eriksson sat back in her ergonomic desk chair and studied the scene on her phone. The epic panorama called to her soul. "Seriously, Jasmine. You have the best job."

Her friend's giggle sounded from just off-screen. "That's what I'm telling you, Tal. You should try it. Drew and I drove up here at three a.m. and snatched an hour of sleep in the parking lot before hitting the trail." Her face came into view, cheeks pink from the cold and shoulders clad in a puffy, insulated parka. "We're about ready to start, and I knew you'd get a charge out of seeing the behind-the-scenes setup."

"You're so right. I'm adding that spot to my bucket list." Talia leaned an elbow on the desk. "I'm surprised you have a signal out there."

"Me too. I'm going to pop my cell on the tripod so you can watch. Drew's going to take the photos with his SLR." Her head turned. "You ready, babe?"

Talia couldn't hear his response, but it must have been an affirmative because Jasmine set the camera so it faced the action before stepping away and walking to the viewpoint. She gave Talia a cheery wave, then struck a cheesy pose with her hands in the shape of a heart.

Her husband stepped closer, the side of his technical pants coming into view and causing the camera to briefly refocus.

Talia propped the phone against her pot of faux succulents and squinted at the familiar silver lettering on Drew's rear pocket—the logo of one of Zeta's biggest competitors. Jasmine and Drew had done a brand deal for them just last month. How much of the couple's gear consisted of freebies sent to them by marketing companies? He strode forward to shift a fallen branch out of the way of his shot.

Jasmine stripped off her coat, grabbed the waistband of her fleece hoodie, and pulled it over her head to reveal the newest ZetaWear sports bra in Moon Mist. The color stood out nicely against her bronze skin. She tossed the outerwear to the side before slipping her baggy sweatpants off the matching bike shorts. "Whoa, brisk."

Rubbing her arms, Talia shivered in sympathy. Her friend was going to freeze her booty off.

Jasmine jogged in place, clapping palms across her toned arms. "Let's do this." She laced her fingers through her long dark hair, pulling it loose from the messy bun and letting it cascade over her shoulders.

Talia lifted her voice to be heard better on the speakerphone. "How cold is it?"

"Not too bad." Drew answered from somewhere nearby. "Around forty. It might get to sixty later, but we like to shoot when the sun angle is still low."

Jasmine made a face. "I don't mind suffering for my art. But I'd like to get done before the wind picks up. Where do you want me?"

Thank goodness for image-editing software that could touch up flushed skin and airbrush away goose bumps. Talia had studied Drew and Jasmine's portfolio. They were talented at highlighting products and making scenes look inviting no matter the weather. That's why she'd brought them on as brand ambassadors.

"Not too close to the edge." Talia bounced her knee in a burst of nervous energy. She'd heard too many stories of influencers taking risks for the "perfect shot."

Jasmine took a few steps closer to the cliff before finding a good rock to sit on. "Don't worry. Drew's really talented with lens compression. The view will look closer than it really is." She wrapped an arm around one knee and let the other leg dangle while she stared contemplatively off into the distance. "How's this?"

The rapid-fire sound of the camera shutter supplied the answer.

A similar rapping on Talia's doorframe drew her attention away.

ZetaWear's designer, Sydney, stood just inside the office. "Got a minute, doll?"

"Come on in." She waved the woman closer, eyeing the stack of fabrics she had draped over one arm. "I'm watching the shoot."

Sydney dropped the samples on the desk and crouched to see. "Nice. What a view." Her brows furrowed. "Can she pull her hair over her shoulder? You can't see the asymmetrical straps. That's the best part of this design."

Jasmine tugged her hair forward and swiveled away from the lens so her shoulders were exposed. "How's that?"

"You know what would be really fun?" Sydney's tone pitched upward as it often did when she was overly excited. "What if you did some yoga positions? Like a warrior pose? Or a handstand scorpion? Can you do that?"

Talia ducked her head to avoid rolling her eyes. "Syd, that's not the vibe we're going for. We want people to think, 'Hey, I want to sit there and enjoy the sunrise like her.' If she does a bunch of difficult moves, people won't imagine themselves in the image. Besides, who's going to hike up to a mountain lake to do yoga?"

The designer frowned. "Me. I totally would."

Yeah, she probably would. Talia took a sip of her chai latte. "Remember, we're trying to evolve our brand positioning away from the image that ZetaWear is only for yoga or the gym. That's the whole point of this promotion." She and Sydney had been battling over this for months now.

Sydney straightened and picked up one of the textile samples. "That's what I wanted to talk to you about. We're tweaking the blend for the upcoming national park line."

"Hold on a second." Talia lifted the cell. "Hey guys, I've got to run. I can't wait to see your images. Please text me your best ones before you post anything. And stay safe out there." She waved to her friend before ending the call and turning to the designer. "All right. What's up?"

"We're going with this updated polyblend. It will save a fortune and give us the capital needed to license the *artwork*"—her nose wrinkled—"you're wanting us to include."

Talia's heart jumped. This collection had been her first foray out of marketing and into design work. The bland, oatmeal color of most of ZetaWear's products had never appealed to her, so she'd suggested a line of athletic wear that sported park-themed graphics—the Grand Canyon's colorful rock layers, the brilliant hues of Yellowstone's Grand Prismatic Spring, the misty blues and greens of the Great Smoky Mountains. "You're going with the artist I recommended?"

"She agreed to let us use the illustrations on spec. We'll see how they look."

"You won't be sorry. Hikers will snap them up."

Sydney pursed her lips. "So you say, and Josiah wants to test the market. This fabric isn't as soft as our yoga line's, but it should hold the ink better. And it's significantly less expensive. If we're going this direction, I don't want to sink a fortune into it."

The dismissive tone set Talia's nerves on edge. "Not everyone cares to twist their body into pretzels in the name of fitness, and we all know getting out into nature is good for one's mental health."

"Whatever." Sydney handed the samples to Talia and turned to leave. "We should have some photo-ready prototypes tomorrow. I'm sure your little hiker buddy won't mind redoing the shoot."

Talia didn't bother to reply, just picked up the swatch and ran it between her fingers, listening as the designer retreated down the hall. The polyester felt slick, almost more like a nylon swimsuit than the feather-soft yoga wear the company had built their reputation on. Maybe once it was washed and sewn into a garment, it would be more appealing. And the nature designs would draw in the exact customer group she'd been drooling over for years.

Her phone vibrated. Lifting it, she skimmed the text from Jasmine.

> Heading back. Here's a preview, but we'll do some post-processing to punch up the light and color. Next time you're coming with me. Start living your bucket list, girl!

Two photos popped into the feed. In the first one, Jasmine sat with her back to the camera, her legs crisscrossed in front of her. The line of sight drew the viewer's eyes first to the fashionable ZetaWear asymmetrical straps on Jasmine's slim shoulders and then to the sunlit mountain lake beyond. The second shot was nearly identical, except Jazz had swiveled to grin at the lens and flash her signature peace sign to her followers.

Talia's throat tightened as she dragged her gaze back to the colorless office. It wasn't often she got so sucked into a marketing image that she experienced the same discontent she sought to provoke in customers—though in her case, it wasn't about wanting cute athletic wear.

She missed being on the trail. Before his retirement, her grandpa had been the chief ranger at Zion National Park, and his passion for nature was woven into her DNA. National park road trips had consumed every summer vacation until her mother's breast cancer shredded the fabric of her family. With Mom's death, everything Talia knew unraveled.

Her dad had married a woman from church a year later. As happy as she was for him, Talia couldn't help feeling like her tight-knit family had all gone their separate ways, reduced to little more than memories and unfinished scrapbooks. How did one make memories alone?

The only things holding her together now were her many to-do lists.

Lately her baby brother had blown up Talia's inbox with photos of his little family's adventures in their self-converted Sprinter van. But she had no time for such luxuries. The only traveling she'd done in the past two years included business retreats at spas and airport conference centers. When had she last felt dirt under her feet?

As her mind wandered, Talia's hands found their way back to the swatch, running the stretchy polyester through her fingers. Every company had its own proprietary blend, each claiming to be an improvement on the competition's—softer, stretchier, more supportive, moisture-wicking, and antimicrobial. That last word still creeped her out. She preferred not to think about microbes or what technology might be used to prevent them from taking up residence so close to her skin. She opened the bottom drawer of her desk and dropped the textiles inside with countless others Sydney had dumped on her over the past two years.

Checking her watch, Talia groaned. She needed to prepare for this morning's online presentation. She was scheduled to talk with a collection of fitness magazines about ZetaWear's current collection. She should make Sydney do it, but the designer was still pouting.

Opening her planner, she scribbled the name of Jasmine's mountain lake onto her ever-expanding wish list and tucked the folded sheet inside the cover flap. Flipping past multiple bulleted to-do notes, she found an empty page and jotted down an agenda for the meeting. She was accustomed to writing press releases, not conducting live interviews where she was expected to answer questions on the fly. She'd hate to get the facts wrong or—worse—completely blank on the product line's colors. *Opal Blush, Moon Mist, Seaglass Veil, Fawn Whisper.* More washed-out pastels and neutrals.

That would change soon. A shiver traced its way up her arms.

An hour later, Talia checked her lipstick in her phone's front-facing camera before she clicked into the online meeting and greeted the small collection of journalists. After reading her prepared spiel and then answering a few questions, she thanked them for coming. There should have been more excitement, but what else could she say? Nothing about this line was particularly a departure for Zeta, and she didn't dare hint at the upcoming national park styles. Not yet.

Each of the reporters signed off until only one remained.

The woman cleared her throat. "Hey, Talia—can I ask an additional question now that it's just you and me?"

Talia's finger hesitated over the X that would terminate the online call. She drew her hand back. "Of course." She glanced at the woman's nameplate. Lissa James looked vaguely familiar.

The reporter offered a well-controlled smile, not flashing a hint of teeth. "Many athleisure companies have tightened their belts in response to the declining economy and rising prices, often cutting corners with fabrics and their environmental impact. Can you speak to Zeta's commitment to providing a greener product—especially since you're entering the crowded outdoor-recreation market and pitching garments to customers who might care a little more about the future of the planet?"

Talia's stomach tensed. "I'm so glad you asked, Lissa." Her favorite stalling technique gave her a moment to recall the well-rehearsed company position on such topics. "Here at ZetaWear, the earth is a top priority. That's why a portion of our profits from this line will be set aside to support nonprofits dedicated to protecting our public lands and promoting environmental stewardship. We fully intend to put our money where our mouth is."

Lissa leaned closer to her camera. "But what of the production itself? Are we talking about any natural fibers? Renewable resources? Zeta's patented polyblend is a closely guarded secret. How can customers be sure you're not contributing to the problems of textile waste and microplastics in our waterways? Not to mention the air pollution caused by production."

They had faced these accusations before, and Talia had written out heavily nuanced answers she insisted every employee memorize, even though the process left her uneasy. "ZetaWear is committed to reducing waste at *every* step of production. We ensure our suppliers share our commitment and goals. In fact, we're one of the few fitness wear companies with a direct recycling program. On our website you can find—"

"Quite admirable. But our testing shows some disturbing facts about your products." The reporter's expression grew steely, her carefully sculpted eyebrows drawing low over her eyes. "I'd like to get your take on it before we go public with our—"

"Why don't you send me what you've gathered." Talia knew better than to get pushed into a corner, the prickling on the back of her neck reminding her to guard her reaction. "Then we can look it over and give you a response."

"—contains forty times the safe limit based on California standards." The woman hadn't even stopped for a breath. "Significantly higher than most of your competitors. Did you know how quickly bisphenol A can be absorbed through the skin? In minutes. And how many of your customers wear sports bras for hours on end—not just during a workout, but all day? The underpaid seamstresses in the sweatshops are at risk, and so are those who buy and wear your product. I'm sure you're aware that bisphenol A has been implicated in various cancers, fertility issues, type 2 diabetes, and cardiovascular problems."

The oxygen in the room dissipated the moment the reporter mentioned cancer. Talia thrust away the memories and sat forward, pinning Lissa with a glare. "You know we'll need to review this data before I can make a comment. Forward it directly to me, and I'll take it to my staff for consideration."

"I'll do better than that." She folded her hands on the desktop. "I'll forward it to the Department of Public Health. You don't need to give me a comment on the study right now. That's not exactly what I'm asking."

"It's not?" Talia reached for a pen. This was not going well. Likely this Lissa James had nothing new, but Talia still needed to prepare a company response in case the news was inflammatory enough to catch the public's attention.

"No. What I want to know is this." She smiled as a dark gleam appeared in her blue eyes. "Are you wearing the product right now?"

A totally inappropriate question, but the chill swept over Talia even before she jabbed the button to end the call.

Of course she was wearing it.

She'd worn Zeta's activewear nearly every day since she'd accepted the job. Everyone here did.

• • •

Zion National Park

The merciless afternoon sun beat down as Blake Mitchell propped a foot on a rock and braced the citation book against his knee. He lifted his gaze to peruse the canyon laid out below them, the spectacular walls of the Great White Throne rising on the far side. The teen standing in front of him deserved to sweat, and there was no place more beautiful to do so.

The kid shuffled his feet and refused to meet Blake's eyes. Maybe there was hope for him.

"I'm not sure what you were thinking, carving profanities in the sandstone." Blake kept his voice steady as he filled out the form. "Not everyone wants to see your artwork. This park belongs to all of us." The lecture made him sound like a grumpy old man. But even though the class B misdemeanor could earn someone prison time and hefty fines, Blake knew how the courts looked on these things. Likely as not, the boy would walk with probation and community service. Hopefully one brush with the legal system would be enough to jar him out of his self-absorbed mindset.

It had taken twice for Blake.

Scowling, the teenager took the slip of paper and jammed it into his pocket. "I wasn't hurting nobody. Just some dumb rocks."

Sure—this time. It was next time that Blake worried about. He returned the kid's license and watched him slouch back to his friends.

In Afghanistan, he'd witnessed juveniles plant IEDs and strap on suicide-bomb vests. Getting hassled about a little graffiti wasn't the worst thing that could happen to a kid.

As Blake descended Kayenta Trail toward the Grotto, he studied the mighty red rock cliffs that towered above the Virgin River. After the convoluted grace journey that brought him to this place, he never wanted to take a minute for granted. As long strings of hikers passed, climbing the trail toward the Emerald Pools, he made sure to give each person a welcoming smile.

In the parking area, Interpretive Ranger Alder Clark leaned against Blake's white Tahoe, relaxed as ever. "There you are. I heard the complaint back at the visitor center. You located the boys, I take it?"

"Pocketknife in hand. Kid bought it at the gift shop, can you believe that? I don't think he meant any harm, just a sixteen-year-old trying to impress his buddies and not considering the long-term consequences."

"Who does at that age?"

It felt good to have made a friend in this new place, and having dinner last night with Alder and his family had cemented it. "Your oldest is about that age, isn't he?" Blake asked.

Alder ran a hand over his hair before replacing the iconic flat-brimmed straw hat worn by most of the rangers. "No, he's just tall for his age. Chase is in middle school. He hasn't hit that 'my friends know better than my folks' stage yet. But I'm sure it's not far off."

"Maybe you'll get lucky. He seems like a good kid." A great kid, actually. Blake had watched Alder and Katie interact with their three children last night, and they'd struck him as the perfect family. But what did he know? He came from a long line of failures. Pursuing a family of his own never seemed worth the risk—though if all children were as fun as Alder's, he might have considered it.

His policy had been to bail on relationships before reaching the "deep conversations about the future" stage. Or conversations about the past, for that matter. It was safer for everyone that way. Blake had made it to almost thirty without getting seriously entangled. That wasn't likely to change anytime soon.

"Kids have to find their own paths." Alder shrugged. "My dad says parenting is a long series of goodbyes. At first, they're a hundred percent dependent on you. But once they take those first steps, they're walking farther and farther away. By the teen years, they're learning to be independent. Good parents need to stand back and let them."

Blake unlocked the Tahoe and opened the driver's side door. "Sounds like you had a great dad."

"The best." His friend leaned his lanky frame against the government vehicle. "What about you?"

"Polar opposite, I'm afraid. Lived fast. Died young." He choked back the bitter taste climbing his throat. This discussion was getting into dangerous territory.

Alder's brow furrowed. "That's rough, man. I'm sorry."

Blake started the engine to get the SUV cooling. "No worries. I'm glad you and Katie have it figured out. Maybe I'll learn something from you."

"We're far from perfect." Alder chuckled. "I lost it with Chase the other day over a stupid homework assignment he'd lied to me about finishing."

Blake studied the ranger's good-natured face. He suspected Alder's version of losing it was radically different from what he'd grown up with.

"That's not what I wanted to talk to you about, though." Alder dug a pair of sunglasses out of his shirt pocket. "Last week you said you're looking for a new place to live."

Blake retrieved his water bottle from his pack. It was only May and the temperatures were already climbing. What would it be like in July? "Yeah. They put me in temporary housing when I arrived, but someone else is scheduled to be in there next month. I've been looking, but the prices are ridiculous."

"Hurricane is a bit of a drive, but Katie and I have a little mother-in-law cottage out back. We'd originally planned to use it as a vacation rental to help with the mortgage, but it's been too much of a headache. We can't take those kinds of chances with the kids around. It's tiny—just a studio. That's why Katie had me invite you over. She wanted to scope you out."

Blake's heart jumped. "Are you kidding me? I'll take it."

The corner of Alder's mouth lifted. "I haven't even mentioned the rent."

"I'm sure we can come to an agreement."

After a quick back-and-forth, they settled on rent and a move-in date. In Blake's mind, he was already throwing his belongings into the back of his beat-up Subaru. The dormitory housing, complete with rodent infestations, had left a lot to be desired. Having his own space—no matter the size—sounded like heaven.

"Hey, you've got Mondays off, right?" Alder asked. "Chase and I were thinking of going to Kolob Canyons to do some hiking. I know he'd love to have someone who's not his old man along. He couldn't stop talking about you last night."

Blake scratched his jaw. "Me? Seriously?"

"Former soldier and law enforcement? You're basically his hero. But the poor kid's stuck with geology-geek Dad. I'll have to remember not to bore him with science facts while we're hiking, otherwise he might try to trick you into adopting him."

Blake had never had anyone look up to him before. That would take some getting used to. "I hope I don't let him down."

"Not much risk of that. Not unless you start telling dad jokes and listing off the different kinds of sedimentary rocks."

"I don't think I even know any dad jokes."

"Well, you're good, then." He headed for his car but stopped halfway across the lot. "Oh—and watch out for Katie. She's already putting together a list of single women for you. I know all of Katie's friends." He grimaced. "If you're smart, you'll find yourself a girlfriend before she gets a hold of you."

A girlfriend? Blake slid into the driver's seat and cranked the AC. Maybe the rodents hadn't been so bad.

• • •

Palo Alto, California

Talia folded her legs under her on the small green sofa in her apartment. The sudden movement sent the damp towel wrapped around her head slumping to one side. Adjusting the computer on her lap, she slid the towel free and ran fingers through her hair before clicking onto yet another website. After her meeting, she'd approached Josiah, the company's chief operating officer, about the reporter's claims. He'd laughed them off as clueless fearmongering.

For some reason, that felt less than reassuring.

The moment Talia got home, she'd jumped in a hot shower, soaping and rinsing every inch of her skin. Twice.

Afterward, she'd gotten busy researching the presence of BPA in workout clothing and taking detailed notes. It would be her job to battle this negative publicity and find some way to spin it to ZetaWear's benefit. Evidently it wasn't just microplastics. Studies indicated that many of these garments also contained unhealthy amounts of toxic chemicals.

She tightened the belt of her terry cloth robe and considered the company's next move. Rather than giving the accusations any credence, she needed to design a campaign to deflect attention and keep customers focused on the positive aspects of their products. *Keep 'em buying.* A hard lump settled in her throat.

What she needed was a list. Uncapping a purple felt tip, Talia brainstormed words she could use. *Movement, fitness, health.* She scratched a line through the last word. Might be problematic. She added several more: *flexibility, strength, stylish, independent, unique.*

Unique? Just last week they'd filmed a video with a group of models striking yoga poses on a sandy beach. The images had been beautiful in their simplicity and elegance, but unique? Hardly. Every woman in the shoot had the same long, lean body type. She'd insisted they include two minority women and a wheelchair athlete, but Sydney refused any talk of plus-size models. Even the sand had been raked until it was uniformly clean and inoffensive. Sanitized nature, ideals of how women should look and behave, and Zeta's subdued colors—it all promoted a myth of perfection the world would never achieve.

Selling a fantasy was the keystone of good marketing.

Talia switched to a green pen, adding color to the bullet points. Everyone knew that buying a simple sports bra and spandex shorts wouldn't provide all the answers, especially not for those who lounged around in their stretchy garments while bingeing on pizza and Netflix. The comfortable illusion was a great deal easier than true change.

But what if their fantasy worlds put them at risk for cancer? She'd struggle to live with herself if her actions led anyone down the torturous path her mother had walked. The oncologist had been unable to explain the cause of Mom's illness, telling Talia there were all sorts of potential triggers.

The world was never again the safe place she'd imagined.

Talia's phone buzzed, jarring her from the dark spiral. She retrieved the device from the coffee table. An unfamiliar number rolled across the screen. Just in case it was work-related, she clicked open the new text message.

> This is Lissa James. Sorry I came on so strong earlier. I wanted to get your attention. Are you open to talking privately? If not, I'll leave you alone.

A half-choked laugh burst from Talia's throat. The audacity of that woman. How had she even gotten this number? Talia tossed the cell on the sofa and glanced at her dinner sitting forgotten on the coffee table. The square of lasagna had dried and cracked around the edges. She scooped up the small disposable tray and walked it to the microwave—after all, doomscrolling wasn't getting her anywhere. It shouldn't be too hard to find a way to spin this development in ZetaWear's favor. Chances were, they'd sell more clothes than ever before.

More people wearing their poison-laced fabric.

The thought sunk its claws into Talia's already strained nerves. Setting the container on the counter, she grabbed a cup and held it under the tap. Cold water spilled over the rim of the plastic cup she'd treasured since she was five. She locked eyes with the Hello Kitty emblazoned on the side. When had BPA-free cups become standard?

This is ridiculous. She couldn't start second-guessing everything around her because of one reporter's allegations. Even so, she dropped the lasagna in the trash and reached into the cupboard for a glass.

The cool water soothed both her throat and her emotions. Hurrying back to the living room, she grabbed her phone and tapped out a quick reply.

> This is unprofessional. Please contact me at the office only.

She refrained from adding an angry emoji before pushing Send, then blocked the number. The cell vibrated in her hand, and she nearly dropped it. "You've got to be kidding me."

When her grandfather's name lit up the screen, she laughed. Talia pressed the phone to her ear. "Pops! How are you?"

"Hiya, kid. I wanted to be the first to wish you a happy birthday tomorrow. How's my best girl? Should I sing you 'Ja, må hon leva' like your *gammelfarmor* used to?"

The image of her silver-haired great-grandmother singing the Swedish birthday song brought a flurry of memories as sweet as pink-frosted cupcakes. "Thanks, Pops, but then I'd have to sing right back at you, and nobody needs to hear that." Their shared birthday had always been a source of joy for Talia, making her feel special among the crowd of grandchildren. She clicked on the speakerphone before setting the device on the kitchen counter and opening the freezer for the pint of pistachio ice cream she'd stashed there yesterday—another birthday tradition. He'd be eating vanilla. "I'm glad to hear your voice."

"Right back at you." He went silent for a moment. "You sound tired. Are you working too hard?"

Pops never missed anything. Talia pried the lid off the container and dug the tip of her spoon into the icy green goodness, but it was too firm to give way—kind of like her mood. "It was a rough day." A rough week, really. She sighed. How long had it been since she'd taken some time off? "I think I need a vacation."

"My door is always open. You know that." His smile was evident in the lilt of his voice. "I'm just rattling around this big house alone. It's a shame."

"I wish I could come." Zion Canyon would be the ultimate escape from the stress of this job. She could almost picture herself hiking the Scout Lookout trail, the spring sunshine warming her shoulders. Just the thought of it melted some of the tension from her muscles.

"But I have a big product launch coming up and there's been a bit of drama—you know, like always."

"Life is full of drama. Don't let it get the best of you." He chuckled. "Though that's easy for the old retired guy to say."

"You're not old. You're the youngest seventy-something-year-old I know."

"And you're the oldest almost-twenty-six-year-old I know."

Talia's heart lifted at their long-standing exchange. They'd been teasing each other as long as she could remember, and she missed their easy banter.

"Well, don't let it get you down," he added. "You're too young for gray hair. Leave that to us senior citizens."

She sank onto the barstool. "I'm not sure why I'm doing this job anymore. I'm tired of trying to convince people to buy stuff they don't need or want." She paused, pondering how much she should share. "Today I learned that the clothing our company makes might actually be harmful. Chemicals and microplastics and all that nonsense." She used the spoon to scrape off a sliver of the ice cream and pressed it to her tongue.

"Have you brought it to their attention?"

"They don't seem concerned. Now I'm trying to figure out how serious it is." She set down her spoon, determined to wait for the thaw.

"You have a big heart, Talia. I know you'll do the right thing."

After ten minutes of chatting with her favorite birthday twin, she wished Pops a happy birthday and good night before hanging up.

Talia stared at the phone screen for a long moment, her spirits finally settling onto a steady path. She needed more information than the internet was willing to provide. Maybe going to the source wouldn't be the worst idea.

She unblocked the number from earlier, then hovered her thumb over the screen for a long moment before touching Call. It connected almost instantly, providing no time for her to change her mind.

"Talia?" Lissa's voice pitched high, her surprise evident.

Talia ran a hand over her forehead. "I-I shouldn't be talking to you."

"I'm glad you called. I didn't mean to harass you at home, I just thought it might be easier for you to talk away from listening ears."

"Just to be up-front, I am loyal to my employer, but I would like to know more about what's going on. What can you tell me?"

For the next hour Talia scribbled down notes faster than she ever had back in business school. The more Lissa detailed the research, the darker the picture became. There seemed little question that the executives at ZetaWear knew exactly what they were doing. Industry professionals had done a shrewd job of covering up the information and pointing the blame elsewhere. Now a small group of people—including Lissa—was determined to shine a light on the situation.

"You could join us, Talia," Lissa entreated. "Give us an insider's view on the athleisure industry, and together we'll blow this story wide open."

Talia dug her fingers against the knotted muscles in her neck. "I have to confess, I'm concerned. But I'd be out of a job—maybe even my whole career—if I shared corporate secrets." ZetaWear had hired her right out of grad school, taking a huge chance on an untested beginner. Could she turn her back on them now?

"There are employment laws protecting whistleblowers. Zeta wouldn't be able to retaliate."

Talia swirled the spoon deep into the carton of ice cream, now the consistency of soft serve. One person's whistleblower was another's traitor. She didn't want to be either. How had this day become such a tangled mess? "Let me sleep on it. If I'm going to blow up my career, I need to be certain."

Lissa's sigh carried through the phone speaker. "Of course. I understand." She paused. "I'm sure you'll do the right thing."

The echo of Pops's earlier statement reverberated in Talia's soul. What was the "right thing" in a case like this? She finished the call, returned the carton to the freezer, and headed for bed. It was going to be a long night.

3

Zion National Park
May 15, 1948

ALMA STIRRED CORN syrup into the evaporated milk and water on the stovetop. Seeing the cherub nestled in the crook of her arm made her heart stutter. She hadn't held a baby since her own son went missing nine months earlier, but the weight of this tiny bundle felt right. So right.

"I don't know where you came from, little one. But I know how it feels to be lost and alone." She reached down and tickled the infant's nose. "And somehow you found me. Two lost souls."

He stared back, lazily sucking on the drooly fist jammed against his mouth.

She looked from the pan to the clean glass bottle waiting on the countertop, walking through the steps in her mind. She used to do this with one hand, but for the life of her, she couldn't remember how. Turning off the burner, she adjusted the funnel and carefully poured a few ounces of the liquid into the bottle. "There we go. Not so hard, is it?" She even managed to fasten the nipple on top and test the temperature on the inside of her wrist all without putting down her young charge.

Those steely blue eyes never seemed to leave her face, almost like he was afraid to look away. It was a feeling she understood.

She directed the nipple toward his mouth. "You're going to like this."

The singsong tone of her voice sounded artificially sweet, as if she'd doused herself with corn syrup as well. "The label on the can says it's 'recommended by doctors.' Not sure if that means it's tasty, though." She tickled the baby's lower lip with the rubber nipple. "Come on, you must be hungry."

Had the child's mother let him nurse before placing him beside the river, or had he been lying there ever since he'd arrived in the world? She set the milk down and carefully unwrapped the baby boy. No, his skin had been washed clean and the umbilical cord had healed. That meant he was at least . . . what? . . . a week old? She cast her mind back, trying to remember how long that had taken with Edward.

The baby's face pinched, and he squalled a protest at the indignity of being examined. The tremulous cry and quivering chin tugged at Alma's heart. Whatever happened, today he needed a mother—if not his own, then a stand-in.

She wrapped the swaddling tight around his little body and tucked him back into the crook of her arm. "No more dillydallying now. You need to eat. You're much smaller than my son was at birth. Maybe you arrived a little early?" Alma tickled his lip again, until the mouth opened just enough for her to slide the nipple in.

After a couple of false starts, the infant latched on and set to draining the Pyrex bottle, making soft gurgling noises as he did so.

The magnetic pull of his gaze weakened Alma's knees. She sat on one of the kitchen chairs. The Lord placed a survival instinct deep in the heart of every creature, and it was that thirst for life that triggered infants to suck long before they understood the purpose of hunger pangs.

The babe's eyes drifted closed even before his mouth released its grip on the nipple. A trickle of milk remained at the bottom of the bottle, but Alma set it to the side. Shifting the warm bundle to her shoulder, she patted a few gentle circles on his back and was rewarded with a soft burp.

She'd like nothing more than to sit here and hold him while he slept, but there was so much to be done. Walking to their bedroom, Alma laid the infant in the center of their double bed and added a pillow on either side. He was far too young to roll, but there was no sense in taking any chances. Henry could retrieve the bassinet from the attic later.

The hatbox lay at the foot of the bed. She slid it close and pulled out the piece of wool blanket that had been wrapped around the newborn. The cut edge was relatively smooth, as if it had been trimmed with a nice pair of sewing shears. She folded the coverlet and laid it to the side. Henry might want to look at it later. The box's silk lining seemed clean and in good condition. She ran her hand along the smooth fabric to make sure nothing else was there—a pacifier or, even better, an identification bracelet. Her fingers brushed against a hard lump wedged under the lining. After locating a loose seam, she managed to pry out the small item.

A padlock? The cold brass piece nestled in her palm. She turned the small lock over in her hand. It was too big to belong to a suitcase, but rather small for most other uses—maybe two inches high, with a little door that slid over the keyhole. Alma squinted at the letters etched on the surface. *H-C-H.*

Certainly nothing a baby would need. She dropped it into a wooden box on the dresser. She'd need to remember to show it to Henry when he came home.

She'd already pulled a few of Eddie's things from her hope chest, but most would need to be washed. Alma shook out a crocheted yellow sacque with wide white piping on its matching bonnet, the sweet garment bringing tears to her eyes. Her mother had sent it for Eddie months before he was born. She pressed the fabric to her cheek, her heart quivering at the mingled scents of cedar and baby powder. Laying it aside, she then added a handful of rompers, shirts, and a blue gown with mitts. The foundling had come wrapped in nothing but a diaper and blanket. Perhaps the mother hadn't had time or money to prepare other garments.

Alma would make sure he had everything.

• • •

Henry leaned one arm against the front desk of the Zion Lodge as his stomach growled. The steamy fragrance of tomato soup filtering from the restaurant upstairs was sheer torture. A dozen or more tourists milled about the spacious lobby, laughing and chatting with one another. None of the women looked suspicious—at least no more than normal. He'd never fully understood the female persuasion.

Life would be much easier if they were all like Alma. She had a gentle manner about her, like those wispy clouds that hugged Zion's cliff tops in the winter.

A redhead with a fur stole exited the small shop to his right, a paper-wrapped package clutched in her leather gloves. As she glanced Henry's way, she graced him with a wide smile before exiting the lobby. Her trim waist certainly didn't hint at a recent pregnancy.

Was this what his investigation had devolved into—scrutinizing women's midsections?

Henry directed his attention back to the desk, relief stealing over him when he spotted the clerk making his way back with a large book.

"Ranger Eriksson, I'm sorry." Elmer Dawson, the hotel manager, set the ledger on the counter. "Several families with children checked in this week, but none with a newborn, as best as I can tell. And only one guest checked out early this morning—Mr. Edwin Miller, an older gentleman traveling alone."

Henry's mind spun through the possible scenarios. "She may have given birth here. Or smuggled the infant into the lodge, I suppose. And there's always a chance that she hasn't left yet. That would be good. Maybe she'll come forward."

Mr. Dawson's brows rose. "And maybe I'm the king of England. If a woman is deplorable enough to abandon her own child, I can't imagine she'd become maternal overnight."

Henry drummed his fingers on the counter. There was too little to go on. He hadn't been trained for this sort of thing. What was he supposed to do—forbid anyone from leaving the park until he could examine them? This wasn't an Agatha Christie novel. He needed a plan. "What about your staff? The maids? Waitresses?"

Dawson's thin lips drew back from his teeth. "The Utah Parks Company only hires single ladies of high moral standards. None with children."

"You may not have realized she was expecting."

The hotelier straightened to his full height and smoothed the front of his fine suit jacket. "Impossible."

"I should speak to them regardless."

"Do as you must, but I believe you're wasting everyone's time, Ranger. If a woman could do something like that, the baby's better off without her."

The coarse words rankled. Though there were plenty of reasons a mother might be forced to abandon her baby, reuniting them seemed better for everyone. And Henry needed answers fast, before Alma was swept away—this time in a flood of her own making. "Please keep a record of everyone who checks out today and any stray details you notice about them. Ask your staff to do the same."

"We always keep precise records, Ranger Eriksson." Mr. Dawson shot him a withering look. "Today will be no different."

Shaking his head, Henry climbed the stairs to the restaurant to interview the waitresses and dishwashers, who seemed to be a constantly revolving staff of giggly young women.

Fred walked out of the kitchen, gripping a fried donut in one hand and swiping crumbs from his uniform with the other. "There you are. I spoke to the head waitress and the cook. Total bust there, boss. No married women and no pregnant girls. In fact, all the ones I saw were as thin as rails. I can't figure why, since they're always dishing out this swell food."

Henry tried to ignore the smattering of sugar on Fred's chin. "Probably has more to do with being on their feet for hours on end." He peered into the empty dining room, where a lone busboy cleaned the tables. "Do you think it's possible one of the girls was pregnant without it showing? When my wife was pregnant, she wasn't all that huge. She carried it rather high until the last few weeks."

"When my sister had her twins, she was as big as an ocean liner. We started referring to her as the *Queen Mary*."

Henry caught another whiff of the lunch special he wouldn't have an opportunity to sample. "Why don't you go down to the lobby and keep watch. If the mother was a guest, I imagine she's going to hightail it out of here today—if she hasn't already. I'll talk with the head housekeeper and see what she knows about the cleaning staff."

Fred cleared his throat. "Is there a chance the baby isn't connected to the lodge at all? She could have been at the campground. Or someone from town who decided this was a better place to abandon an infant than a church doorstep."

"I have Rogers and Nelson scouring the campground, and Sheriff Moody will take point in areas outside the park." The enormity of what lay ahead pressed down on Henry. The what-ifs were springing up faster than rock squirrels at a picnic and disappearing just as quickly. "We need to focus on the most likely answers first. The baby was wrapped in a section of a lodge blanket. Chances are the woman has some connection to this place. So we start here."

"Got it." Fred folded arms across his barrel chest. "If a lady skulks her way through the lobby heading for the door, I'll detain her." His lips scrunched as he thought. "How am I going to recognize her?"

Henry blew out a long breath. "I wish I knew. Use your instincts."

"Assuming I've got any."

Leaving Fred and crossing the lawn, Henry studied the grounds. To better fit the landscape, the architect had opted for a dispersed layout instead of a single large hotel. The central building contained the lobby, restaurant, auditorium, and gift shop. Flanking the structure were a variety of cabins and two staff dormitories. It would be a simple matter for the woman he sought to disappear from any of these buildings without anyone being the wiser.

He needed more eyes. Maybe he could put Mattie's strong gossip-seeking skills to work.

He could still feel the weight of the infant in his arms. Maybe Mr. Dawson was right, and forcing a mother to take an unwanted baby wouldn't be in the child's best interest. Would the woman get jail time for abandoning her child?

Too many questions. Zero answers.

He nearly collided with the head housekeeper as she stepped out of the laundry building with an enormous bundle of folded bedding. Henry put out a hand to help her balance the load. "Let me help you with those."

Mrs. Whyte peeked out from her stack of blankets, the characteristic Zion stripes wending their way through the stone-colored wool. A frown pulled at her face, but she maintained her grip. "Thank you, Ranger, but I'm quite accustomed to the work, and I don't want the younger maids to get any ideas."

Henry stepped back. "I can respect that. But I do need to speak with you."

Her lips pressed together not unlike the neatly folded woolens. She darted a glance down the path behind him, then tipped her head the other direction. "Follow me, please."

He trailed after her past a neat row of identical cabins. He'd visited the lodgings only a handful of times during his time in Zion, usually checking on disorderly guests.

She led him to one of the nearby duplex cottages. A wooden cart waited outside the door, and she dropped most of the blankets onto it.

Tucking the last two under her arm, she opened the door and disappeared inside.

He hovered on the threshold, unsure whether to follow her or wait where he stood.

"Ranger Eriksson?" Her voice rang out. "If you want to speak to me, you'd best do so now. I've got six more cabins to clean after this one."

He poked his head inside. "Are you sure it's appropriate for me to be in here? I need to ask some questions about your staff."

"I believe that badge gives you access." Mrs. Whyte ran a dusting cloth over one of the windowsills and didn't turn her head from her work. "The foundling—I assume you think it belonged to one of my girls?"

Henry lingered just inside the doorway, not wanting to proceed further than necessary. She might hand him a broom. "I don't know who it belonged to. That's what I'm trying to figure out."

She moved on to the next window. "All my young ladies are top-notch, hired from the best universities."

"That doesn't mean one couldn't have slipped. I imagine even respectable girls sometimes find themselves in trouble."

Mrs. Whyte scowled as she tucked the rag into her belt and reached for a broom. "Not the ones who work for me. Now the entertainment staff? I can't speak for them. You know what they say about those theater types." She attacked the floor with renewed vigor as if sweeping away the dregs of society.

He backed a step lest she run the wicker straws across his boots. "Do you always service the rooms? I thought your position was to manage the maids, not do the work yourself."

"I fill in here and there, when someone is sick. We're short-staffed, plus we've had a bit of the flu running through our ranks. I've also had two maids quit this season, and there hasn't been time to find suitable replacements. Young people today can be so flighty. In my day, if you committed to a job, you saw it through."

Henry retrieved a notepad from his shirt pocket. "You have girls sick in bed today? Which ones?"

The housekeeper stilled, the first time she'd stopped moving since he'd laid eyes on her. "It's not what you think."

"Of course not." He pushed a smile to his face. "But I'd like to check on them regardless."

The streak of gray running through her hair made her look a bit like a cornered skunk. "I'll do the checking. They're my responsibility, and I won't have a man tromping through the women's dormitory and upsetting everyone. There's been enough drama of late."

"Such as?" The kind that leaves a helpless babe under a bridge?

"Just the usual. Summer crushes and the petty jealousies that arise. Broken hearts and tears. But the maids look after one another." She shot him a pointed look. "They're good girls. No immoral behavior is tolerated."

Mrs. Whyte didn't seem the motherly type, so Henry couldn't picture someone going to her for life advice. It might be better if he asked Mattie to spill about her coworkers. "I'll need you to take me to see any of your staff who didn't report for work this morning."

"I have five more rooms, then—"

"The cabins can wait." Henry folded his arms. "Unless you'd prefer I go alone."

Mrs. Whyte echoed his posture, not one bit intimidated. "You'd have to get past me first."

They could have used her in the infantry.

After a short standoff, she sighed. "Fine, we'll go now. But if we have guests complaining about not being able to get into their lodgings on time, I'll send them to you."

• • •

The baby had refused to stay settled on his own, even after Alma retrieved Eddie's bassinet from the attic. After multiple unsuccessful attempts to lay him down, she'd situated herself in the rocking chair and sung through "Be Thou My Vision," and "Tryggare kan ingen vara"—"Children of the Heavenly Father"—before the baby finally drifted into a deep slumber in her arms.

She closed her eyes, too, the gentle rocking motion soothing her soul. Even though he already slept, she sang "God Leads Us Along" softly to herself:

> In shady, green pastures, so rich and so sweet,
> God leads His dear children along;
> Where the water's cool flow bathes the weary one's feet,
> God leads His dear children along.
>
> Some through the waters, some through the flood,
> Some through the fire, but all through the blood;
> Some through great sorrow, but God gives a song,
> In the night season and all the day long.

A knock at the door shattered the moment. She pushed to her feet, tucking the baby tight against her body. They'd made it only a few steps when the caller rapped his knuckles against the wood a second time, even louder than before.

The infant startled, his arms flinging out to each side. The delicate skin on his forehead accordioned into a series of ridges, and he began to emit a now-familiar bleating cry.

"Shhh, it's okay. I'm sorry. So rude." She bounced him gently as she hurried across the room.

Yanking open the door, Alma pointed a finger at the man standing on the porch. "You stop that. Right now."

The heavyset fellow lowered his hand, his fingers still curved into the best beating-down-someone's-door position. "Sorry, ma'am. I didn't mean to upset you." The man's star-shaped badge glinted on his wide chest, much shinier than the shields worn by the Park Service rangers. "I'm Sheriff Albert Moody from Washington County. I'm looking for Ranger Eriksson. Your husband, I presume?"

Alma swallowed hard, clutching the little one a bit more snugly. "Did you try the ranger station?"

He ran knuckles across his jawline as if checking for nonexistent stubble. "Yes, ma'am. He wasn't in his office, so I thought I'd check here." He focused on the baby. "Is this the foundling? Or yours, perhaps?"

She hooked her wrist protectively around her charge. *Mine. He's mine.* She bit back the words and forced a nod instead. "This is him."

Sheriff Moody removed his hat. "Kind of you to look after the little sprout. May I come in?"

Her palms grew damp, and she rubbed her free hand along the edge of her cotton skirt. "Ranger Eriksson isn't here."

A smile toyed at one corner of his mouth. "I understand. But I'd like to examine the child. It should only take a minute. I could do so out here, if you prefer."

The infant whimpered, either in response to the man's impertinent suggestion or Alma's viselike grip.

With a sigh, she stepped aside and allowed the man access to her kitchen.

He walked to the table and picked up the ragged blanket she'd stacked with the other items needing to be laundered. "Is this what he was wrapped in?"

"Yes. But I don't know any of the other details. You'll need to speak to Henry."

Sheriff Moody ran his fingers down the cut edge.

The baby's cries had grown quieter, his eyes falling closed between each murmuring fuss. She swayed in time with the trembling in her arms and legs—perhaps a little too fast for optimum comfort.

The man turned toward her. "Do you recognize it?"

"The blanket? It's from the lodge. That's the pattern housekeeping uses for the guest rooms."

He laid it back on the table and advanced toward her. "May I?" He spread his hands in front of him.

Alma tightened her hold, backing a step. "I've just gotten him settled. Now's not a good time. He needs rest after this terrible ordeal."

Sheriff Moody halted, his lips pressed tight beneath his bristly mustache. "I see." His eyes traveled across the baby. "You dressed it, then? What can you tell me about its appearance?"

As if the child were the suspect. "It's a boy. Clean, other than a soiled diaper. Not much hair, but it's dark in color. It's hard to say if it'll stay like that." Her own son had been born with dark hair that lightened over the weeks that followed. Would Eddie have been blond, like his father?

"Eyes?"

She startled. "Blue. But most babies' are."

He rubbed a finger beneath his nose as if to chase off an itch. "Bruises? Sores? Abrasions?"

"How can you think such a thing?" She patted the infant's back, the horrifying idea wedging in her gut like a rock. "No. He's perfect."

His stare didn't falter, as if the man had seen more of life than he cared to share. "I don't want to injure your fine sensibilities, ma'am, but this baby was left out for the coyotes. It's obvious whoever tossed it aside like so much trash held little regard for his safety."

She closed her mind to the memories of the day the river tore Edward from her arms. "I don't believe it was like that."

"Then how do you see it?" He returned to the table. Picking up the hatbox, he turned it over in his hands.

"The mother placed the child carefully, where she knew my husband might find him."

"Your husband specifically?" He met her gaze. "Ranger Eriksson."

"Or one of the others. But he rides that path most mornings." Had the woman left the babe specifically for Henry? Perhaps even for her?

The gentle weight of the sleeping infant nestled against her chest—her heart.

"On the phone, he said it was newly born."

"No. Not today, anyway." She jutted her chin. "A few days ago. Maybe even a week or more. The umbilical cord has already fallen off, but probably not long ago."

He frowned. "I see. That complicates matters, I'm afraid."

"How so?"

The sheriff replaced his hat. "That baby could have come from anywhere."

Another rap on the door interrupted them. Thankfully the babe slept on, likely exhausted from the day's constant activity. She strode to the door. How many people would show up on her porch today?

As Alma swung it open, Mattie barreled in—all smiles and sunshine. "Mrs. Eriksson, I heard you took charge of the foundling. Do you need anything? I still haven't made it into town, so I could pick up diapers—" Her attention landed on the sheriff standing by the breakfast nook and her posture stiffened. "Oh, I'm sorry. I didn't realize you had company."

"Sheriff, this is my friend, Mattie. She's a maid for the Utah Parks Company."

The young woman's slingbacks appeared frozen to the floor.

His brows lifted. "At the lodge?"

"Yes, sir." She turned back to Alma. "I'm sorry to interrupt. I should scoot. Should I buy anything for you?"

As if she could piece together thoughts at this moment. "Maybe another container of evaporated milk and corn syrup. And some washing powder. The diapers I found in our closet . . . they could use a good scrub. They haven't been needed in some time." She ignored the jab of pain the words brought.

Mattie nodded. "I'll be sure to grab some. And if you think of anything else, I can go back tomorrow."

"Let me get you some cash." Alma crossed the kitchen to the drawer where Henry left grocery money for her.

"You can pay me later." The maid darted a glance at the imposing form scrutinizing them from a few steps away.

"Have you seen Ranger Eriksson?" Alma asked. She needed to get this man out of her kitchen. "The sheriff needs to speak with him."

Mattie fiddled with the aqua-colored silk scarf tied about her hair. "Not since earlier this morning, but I heard he was at the lodge talking to the staff about"—she lowered her voice to a whisper—"the sit-u-a-tion." She touched Alma's arm. "God intended for you and Henry to find this baby. I have to believe that."

Sheriff Moody cleared his throat. "I'll check for him there. Thank you, ladies."

As the man departed, Mattie exhaled and leaned back against the kitchen counter. "How is little Billy doing?"

"Billy?"

Mattie shrugged, a smile toying at the corners of her red-painted lips. "We have to call him something, don't we? Do you have an idea for a name?"

Alma pulled back the edge of the blanket to gaze at the sleeping infant, his long lashes forming a perfect line along his pink cheek. "My father's name was William." The softness of his skin against her hand sent a wave of warmth through her. "Billy." Her heart clung to the name, drawing it in like a breath.

The younger woman stepped closer. "He looks content."

"It feels right." Alma adjusted his weight on her forearm. "Like he was meant to be here."

"God has a plan." Mattie's fingertips grazed Billy's head. "And He's doing great things."

4

Palo Alto, California
Present Day

TALIA ONLY HAD a few hours before her presentation, and today—more than ever—she needed to be prepared. Her queasy stomach wasn't helping. Tossing her jacket over the chairback, Talia powered on her computer and started an off-site backup. If she ended up unemployed after the meeting, she'd need access to her portfolio. A new email from Sydney popped into her notifications. The designer had included an attachment detailing the fabric and illustrations for the new line. The finished products would arrive in time for the meeting so she and Talia could show them off to the board.

Talia sat down and opened the document. She'd never paid much attention to the fabric details in the past, other than to look for SEO keywords to use for promotion. Skimming through the specifications, she picked up her coffee for a quick sip. *Fabric: Polyester-Cotton-Spandex blend.* Among the confusing graphs, one showed the bisphenol A concentration—easily twice what Lissa had said their previous blend contained.

She choked, the hot liquid burning its way down her throat. The bottom of the cup smacked the table and droplets of macchiato splattered onto her white blouse. Snatching a tissue, Talia dabbed at the spots. If this top was ruined, she'd be stuck wearing Zeta product for the rest of the day. Yesterday, that wouldn't have bothered her. But now . . .

She opened the drawer and retrieved the swatch Sydney had left behind. The fabric smoothed under her fingertips, just the right amount of comfortable and supportive stretch. Ideal for wearing right next to the skin. Her stomach twisted. This morning she would stand in front of the board and pitch the marketing plan for this line. She'd written the proposal days ago in hopes that Josiah would approve it for this week's meeting; per usual, Sydney had taken her part right down to the wire. Can't rush "creative genius."

Talia hesitated for a moment before forwarding the fabric report to her personal email. Company cheerleader or whistleblower—which would it be?

The computer chirped, signaling the backup was complete.

A brisk rapping on her door made Talia jump. She closed the laptop.

Sydney breezed inside with a bundle of Mylar balloons and an oversized envelope with Talia's name on it. "Happy birthday! We'll have cake at the meeting, but I thought you'd like these in here." She flashed an artificially whitened smile as she set the overly festive bundle in the corner. "We all signed the card, of course."

"Thanks." Talia eyed the silver balloons decorated with pink cats in various yoga poses. It seemed pretty obvious who had picked them out. "You're sweet."

"And I have the prototypes." She walked back to the hall and retrieved a vintage picnic hamper. "You knew I'd come through, didn't you? You're going to *die* when you see them. They're super cute."

Talia swallowed hard, rising from her seat. "Sydney, we need to talk."

"I know, I know." She released an airy laugh. "I really cut it close this time. But pitching these is going to be a snap. The artwork alone will sell them." She placed a hand on her hip. "I realize I fought you on this, but I'm not too proud to admit when I'm wrong, and boy was I off about this one. Women are going to throw money at us. Maybe we should do a limited number and let the scarcity drive the excitement even more."

"I'm not sure—"

"Oh, I haven't shown you yet. Silly me." She dropped the basket on top of Talia's desk and flipped open the lid. Instead of sandwiches and lemonade, stacks of sports bras and matching shorts filled the gingham-lined container. "Aren't they gorgeous? I thought this would be a fun, outdoorsy way to display them."

All of Talia's protests died in her throat. She'd seen the sketches, but the final artwork stole her breath. Arches, Glacier, Yellowstone . . . She picked up a pair of shorts, the watercolor designs of Zion's sandstone cliffs bringing tears to her eyes.

Pops's park. The playground of her youth, where she'd learned that the beauty of nature could instill not only peace but a longing for spiritual understanding, like its name implied. The image reminded her of Gammelfarmor sitting out on their patio with her paints, capturing the light as it traveled across the cliff faces.

She cleared her throat, blinking hard. The resolve she'd woken with this morning faltered. "Stunning."

The designer shrugged. "I wish I could claim the credit, but I just ran with your vision." She lifted a Grand Canyon design from the basket and placed it on top of the pile. "This is my favorite. Think of how good it'll look on social media."

I've created a monster. It had taken forever to convince this company of the power of social media marketing, but now they were all in. By next season, these designs would rule the internet, and every nature-loving woman would want a set. Multiple sets. Talia lifted another pair of shorts, dotted with images of the Bass Harbor Head Light at Acadia National Park. "These are darling."

"Are you ready for the meeting?" Sydney raised her brows.

The meeting. Talia glanced at the clock. Fifteen minutes. "I'll be there soon. I'm going to use the restroom first and make sure I'm presentable."

Sydney scooped the garments back into the wicker basket. "Once these are displayed, no one's going to be looking at you." She flashed a final grin before scooting down the hall toward the conference room.

As Talia unplugged her laptop and slid it into her bag, she paused to study the family picture sitting on the corner table. Pops's face beamed at her, standing out from the crowd of aunts, uncles, and cousins. On a whim, she dug her phone from her purse and dialed her grandfather.

He answered quickly, as if he'd been waiting for her call. "Hiya, kid! Twice in two days. What did I do to deserve that?"

"Years of unconditional love." She rubbed her forehead. "I just wanted to say happy birthday again. And . . ." A lump tightened in her throat. "I-I'm off to demolish my career. Wish me luck?" She tried for a lighthearted laugh, but it came out as a strangled squeak.

"Oh, sweetheart." His voice warmed her through. "You know I'm proud of you, whatever happens. I'll be praying. I'm sure He'll lead you to the right thing."

Talia swung the bag over her shoulder. "If I get fired, can I come crash with you?"

"Always."

• • •

Zion National Park

Blake jammed the heavy sweatshirt into his pack and zipped the bag closed. The cool morning air had lingered through the long downhill stretch to La Verkin Creek, but now that they'd been on the trail for a few hours, the heat pressed in. When Alder had suggested a hike with his kid, Blake had expected an easy day, not an almost-fourteen-mile march. The sweat trickling down his spine reminded him of Air Assault training, minus the 50-pound ruck.

Chase stopped on the path ahead, a wry smile turning his lips. "You coming?"

"As fast as I can." Blake hoisted the bag over his shoulder. He'd neglected his conditioning since leaving the military, and now he was paying for it.

Alder paused to wait. "Be nice to your elders, Chase."

The kid grinned. "How does it feel to be old and feeble?"

Blake doubled his pace, determined to catch the cocky young man. "That's it. I'm going to toss you in the river when we get back."

Chase's giggle had that youthful ring. "You wouldn't dare."

"Watch me." Blake glanced at the boy's father. Alder stood some twenty yards away, staring up at the rock outcropping beside the trail. "You doing all right?"

"Yeah, yeah." He gestured at the wall, his eyes narrowing. "I think these colorful bands are Shnabkaib Members of the Moenkopi. A gypsiferous shale." He touched the rocks embedded in the cliff.

Chase spoke in a low voice. "Watch out. Dad's got his geology face on. We could be here all day while he tells stories about inland seas, shales, and sandy limestones." He shook his head. "Let's go. He'll catch up."

"Don't you think it's cool that your dad knows this stuff?" Blake surveyed the cliff, seeing nothing but bunches of rocks in varying shades of orange and gray. He couldn't imagine having all of Alder's knowledge tucked away in his brain. He'd probably want to tell everyone too.

"I guess, but if you show the slightest interest, he won't quit talking about it. He could be happy just hanging out in this one spot, and we'd never get to the waterfall."

"Hm. Can't have that. Okay, let's go." Blake followed the kid down the path.

His friend continued talking to the rocks, seemingly oblivious—or perhaps unconcerned—that Blake and Chase were abandoning him.

"So geology isn't your thing." Blake focused on Chase. "What gets you excited?"

The boy shrugged—the typical language of a middle schooler.

"Cars. Video games. Anime." He waited until Blake drew alongside him. "So—you were in the army? Ever shoot someone?"

The question hit Blake like a rock from the sky. Only a kid would lob such a point-blank question. "It's not something I talk about."

Chase's face fell. "Makes sense. I guess." Obviously he was hoping for a good story.

Good rarely coexisted with shooting, except maybe at the range. One would think a teen growing up in a world of school violence would get that. Perhaps with their Park Service life, his parents had managed to shelter him from such horrifying realities. "How long have you guys lived here?"

"In Zion?" Chase played with the nylon straps dangling from his pack. "About three years. We moved from Yosemite, and we were in Lassen before that. Mom and Dad met as seasonal rangers at Craters of the Moon, but I never lived there."

"Craters of the Moon? Where's that?"

"Idaho. They took me there last year. It's pretty cool, like one big lava flow. But please don't get Dad started on lava flows."

"You've seen a lot." Blake had never stepped foot in a national park until just after boot camp. Some of his buddies talked him into a backpacking trip in the Smokies before heading to advanced individual training. It had rained the whole trip, but he'd still been blown away.

"Not as much as you, I'm guessing." The kid raised his eyebrows, obviously still angling for some juicy information.

"You've seen stuff worth remembering. All I've got is a load of memories I'd just as soon dispose of." Blake shrugged off his pack and dug for the granola bars he'd stashed this morning. "Getting hungry?"

"Can't." The boy frowned at the bar in Blake's hands. "I'm allergic to peanuts. And I can't eat gluten."

Blake jammed it into his pocket. "Sorry, man. I didn't realize." Evidently kids were far more complex in this generation. He'd need to remember that.

"It's okay. Mom packed fruit and gluten-free cookies. She always makes sure I have safe stuff to eat. I think she worries I'll feel left out, but it doesn't bother me nearly as much as it does her."

Blake pushed away thoughts of his own mom. After enlisting, he'd had no desire to go home to LA. He hadn't even called her since returning stateside two years ago. Maybe if she'd been a little more like Chase's mom, they'd still have a relationship.

No, he couldn't lay that at her feet. Mom had done her best. If a few dietary sensitivities had been his only issue, she could have handled it. But as she was fond of pointing out, he was too much like his dad.

That riverbed dried up ages ago.

Alder loped up behind them, out of breath. "At this rate we'll be there before lunchtime."

A lizard skittered across the path, darting under a scraggly tree root on the opposite side. Chase took off after it.

Grabbing a swig from his water bottle, Alder grinned at Blake. "I hope he's not talking your ear off."

"He seemed worried that you'd do the same. You two are more alike than you think." Blake took off his ball cap and ran fingers through his hair. "Don't Katie and the girls like to hike? Where are they today?"

His friend chuckled. "Katie would leave us all in the dust. She's brutal. Long-distance runner, canyoneer, alpine climber—you name it, she's done it."

"But she's not search and rescue? I know she said she was in the interp division."

"Oh, she's a science geek too. Katie's got a doctorate in herpetology."

Blake nearly spit out his water. "Herpe-what?"

"The study of reptiles and amphibians." Alder shook his head slowly. "Not sure how she fell for a rockin' guy like me."

Chase reappeared from the brush. "Dad, don't start."

Alder flashed his son a crooked smile. "She'd probably say I *rocked* her world."

The boy whacked him on the arm with a water bottle. "No more. You promised."

Blake shook his head. "I think I'm starting to understand what you meant about the jokes. Is that a requirement of fatherhood?" He couldn't remember his dad ever cracking one. At least not one that could be repeated in polite company.

The middle schooler rolled his eyes. "No. It's just him."

• • •

Palo Alto, California

The beaming faces around the table told Talia she'd hit it out of the park—or maybe *into* it would be more appropriate. The slogans, the marketing plan, and Sydney's samples caught everyone's attention. The executives jumped at the park theme. Any more enthusiasm and they'd be waving sparklers and singing "This Land Is Your Land."

One last surprise awaited them.

Decked out in the Yosemite spandex, Sydney clapped her hands for attention. "I think we all need to thank Talia for this brilliant idea. It's going to be an exciting couple of months as the park line goes into production. I can't wait to see these designs splashed all over social media and then on the trails across America. Who knows—maybe I'll even don a pair of hiking boots." She flashed her brilliant grin. "I'm sure we'll hear many more fantastic ideas from Talia in the future."

Goose bumps lifted along Talia's arms. She gathered a deep breath and took a cue from Pops. *Lord, please . . . give me the right words.* "Actually, I do have a few ideas I'd like to discuss." She forced her attention away from Half Dome. Maybe Yosemite's rounded monolith hadn't been the best choice of graphics for a sports bra. "One that I think we should address right now, if you don't mind, Sydney."

The designer's smile faded as she looked down at the agenda.

As all eyes turned to Talia, she shifted in her seat, the large conference chair suddenly feeling a bit too throne-like. "I'd like to discuss the fabric Zeta has been using; specifically, the reports about the new blend."

Josiah sat back, placing the cap on his pen with a loud click. "I believe you and I discussed this yesterday, Talia. And I don't think now is the time or place to—"

"It's the perfect time, since this affects everyone here." She surveyed the room. Several of her coworkers leaned forward in their seats. She'd caught their interest—but for how long? "We're a company that espouses fitness and health. And yet the fabric we've been using for our product has been shown to contain harmful substances that can lead to significant health problems. I think we owe it to our customers to take another look at how we're doing business."

Josiah's eyes narrowed behind his black Gucci frames. "Production and textiles are not your wheelhouse. Why don't you stick to playing on Instagram and leave the manufacturing details to the people who know what they're doing?"

Sydney sat down with a thump, her skin paling. So much for team dynamics.

Talia gestured toward the stack of samples. "If ZetaWear is going to use my ideas and marketing plans, I think I deserve five minutes to point out a few flaws with our manufacturing. Especially if our product is putting both our customers and our manufacturing partners at grave risk. Not to mention the publicity nightmare this could become once the media takes hold of the issue."

He scowled. "You've got five minutes."

The crackling energy in the room flashed Talia back to her childhood. A thunderstorm had boiled up while her family hiked in the Rockies, and they'd fled pell-mell for the relative safety of the tree line.

In this boardroom there was nowhere to hide.

Talia took a quick sip of water, then retrieved a stack of papers from her bag. She passed a stapled packet to each person around the table. "I've been investigating a situation an outside party brought to my attention, and I think it's a valid concern." She avoided looking at Josiah or Sydney. "If you study the graph on the first page . . ."

The minutes ticked by as Talia detailed what she'd learned about the chemistry of polyester and spandex, and how ZetaWear and other companies were ignoring current research data in favor of profit. The meeting grew quieter as she talked, the pressure building as everyone leafed through the pages.

She'd hardly gotten through half the data by the time the clock marked its fifth minute, and a single glance toward the chief operating officer made her think better of continuing. "You can read the rest on your own time. All I'm asking is that we thoughtfully consider our company's actions and responsibilities. With a targeted marketing campaign, we can divert attention from this problem and make this new line a wild success." She met the executives' eyes one by one. "But is it the right thing to do? We have the ability to create a safer, *greener* product for our customers. It would cut into our profit margin, but a better product would also set us apart from the greedy corporations that care only about their bottom lines. I think it's time we decide what sort of company we want ZetaWear to be. One focused only on profit, or a *family* who cares about those who wear our garments and the world in which we live."

Josiah stood, drawing everyone's attention back to him. He picked up the packet and tossed it back toward Talia. It landed on the table and slid to a stop. "We do need to discuss this topic. But before we do so, I think you should leave."

In conspicuous silence, Talia gathered her things and headed for the door. She'd done everything she could to make them listen. Now all she could do was wait.

She didn't have to wait long. Ten minutes later, Josiah was at her office door, his face stony.

Talia's stomach tightened. What was it people said about juries? If they come back in quickly, it always means a conviction?

He clamped a hand on her doorframe and leaned in. "Pack. Your. Stuff." The words dropped like three clumps of pigeon poop from the sky. "I want you out by end of day."

Talia slumped back in her chair. "I should have expected that."

"You gave me no choice."

Oh, he had a choice. They all did.

As Josiah walked down the hall, Talia let her gaze wander over the mementos she'd used to make the small space her own. Framed photos, potted succulents, a couple of bobbleheads. Not much to show for two years of hard work.

The bundle of Mylar balloons floated lazily in the corner next to the massive card Sydney and the others had signed.

Happy birthday to me.

5

Zion National Park
May 15, 1948

HENRY HOVERED IN the dormitory's stairwell as Mrs. Whyte spoke to the maid who hadn't reported for work due to illness.

The young woman balled both hands into the collar of her green terry cloth robe and drew it close to her neck. "I'm so sorry, Mrs. Whyte. I've not been ill like this in years. I was coughing all night." The smudged circles under her eyes and red nose corroborated her story. "Dodie said she'd cover for me."

The bulky robe, belted at the waist, did little to disguise her petite frame. If this young woman had recently given birth, he would never guess. He moved closer but remained well behind the girl's supervisor. "You've been here all morning?"

She turned her bloodshot eyes to him. "I've been in bed since the day before yesterday. You can ask my roommate. Why? Has something happened?"

The head housekeeper shot him a look before turning back to her young charge. "Nothing you need worry about, Phyllis. We were only concerned for your welfare."

Phyllis clasped a hand to the pink hairnet holding her curls prisoner. "Jeepers, I thought you were coming to sack me." Her laugh dissolved into barking coughs as she retreated into her room.

Mrs. Whyte gave Henry a grim smile. "There, see? My young ladies are clean as a whistle. We can visit the other two who are ill if you feel the need to drag them from their beds as well."

Henry led the way down the stairs and out of the women's dormitory, his steps quicker than they'd been on the way in. He hadn't considered hiring a female ranger before, but he could see the use now. A man had no business interrogating half-dressed young women in their lodgings. "I'd appreciate it if you would speak to the others. Please observe them carefully. I know it's difficult to think poorly of your employees, but someone abandoned that newborn. It's important we run down every possibility."

Mrs. Whyte turned to face him, clamping both hands on her hips. "I find it offensive that you assume one of my girls is at fault simply because they work for a living. Countless ladies travel in and out of this park every single day. I will speak to the girls, but you need to promise me that you're turning over every rock—not just my staff."

"Trust me. I want to find this woman, wherever she's hiding. That baby deserves better."

Henry exchanged a few final words with Mrs. Whyte before starting back to the central lodge building. His hope for an easy solution faded with each passing moment.

Sheriff Moody stood at the front desk, riffling through the guest ledger. He glanced up as Henry approached. "Ah, there you are. Quite a situation you've got."

"I'm glad you could come." Henry gestured to the book. "I've already read through that. It's not terribly helpful."

"How far back did you go?" The man flipped a few pages. "Your wife said the baby might be a week old, or more."

Henry clenched his jaw. "You've been to see my wife?" The last thing Alma needed in her fragile state was an outsider on the doorstep.

"I was looking for you. But since you weren't in, I took the opportunity to inspect the foundling." He ran a hand over his chin. "Curiously, she suggested someone may have left the infant for *you* to find."

Henry studied the crowded lobby, his skin crawling. "Let's take this elsewhere." Too many people knew about the situation already. The more staff and guests who knew about the case, the less chance they had to keep this quiet. It was probably only a matter of time before newspapermen descended on the park.

Henry led the way to the parking area. "Alma and I have yet to discuss it, but it seems plausible the box may have been positioned so I would find it."

"What makes you say that?" The sheriff frowned. "It wasn't sitting on your doorstep. Hiding a hatbox in the reeds by a river is taking a big risk. You could have ridden on past."

"That's true." Henry went over the scene in his mind. "But if she—"

"Or he."

The insertion threw him for a moment. "Whoever left it, if that person wanted the baby to die, they could have easily tossed him in the river or left him out in the desert. Instead, they chose a sheltered spot along the footpath."

"One he or she knew you would be passing."

"Perhaps. But many visitors walk that trail every day."

Sheriff Moody stopped next to his glossy black Ford and folded his arms. "Both you and Mrs. Eriksson have said that you believe the person knew *you* would be the one to find it. I think the hotel maid said something similar."

So he'd spoken to Mattie too. "I wouldn't read too much into what she says."

"Look, Eriksson." The man's brows drew low over his eyes, his face grim. "I don't appreciate anyone wasting my time. If you know more than you're letting on—like you've been consorting with a young lady who then found herself in a family way—then you need to be straight with me. I don't believe in playing games or being party to another man's personal shenanigans."

The air rushed from Henry's lungs. "Are you insinuating that I'm somehow involved in all this?"

"I'm flat out asking you." Moody thrust his thumbs through his belt loops.

"No. Absolutely not. I would never—"

"I've heard rumblings about your wife being a borderline recluse. No one could blame you if—"

"I'd blame me." *God would blame me.* His stomach rolled. "And my wife has been grieving. She can't be expected to attend tea parties and social gatherings. If there's anything you need to know, come to me. The park's rumor mill isn't exactly reliable." He and Alma had been its favorite target for the better part of a year. And when he'd quietly slipped Mattie a few dollars to spend some time cheering Alma up, the whispers had multiplied.

"I simply need to know you're trustworthy."

"I called *you*, remember? The child was found inside national park boundaries—that makes it our investigation." He took a deep breath, pushing away his growing irritation.

"Gets sticky, doesn't it? As you're aware, the power over custody and child welfare is reserved for the state." Sheriff Moody shook his head. "I've already contacted the state welfare office, and they'll send someone from Salt Lake City to take custody. In the meantime, I can transport the little guy to the hospital in St. George for the night."

Henry splayed fingers and thumb against his forehead. His original thought had been to get the baby out of here as soon as possible, but now that Alma was involved, *sticky* seemed like an apt description. "Why don't we leave things be for the night? My wife and I are well situated to care for him, and there's a chance we'll locate the mother quickly. Then we can avoid the needless complication."

The sheriff pulled a notebook from his pocket and flipped it open. "Even if we locate the suspect, the babe won't be returned to her until the courts approve. Do you have any leads?"

Henry bristled. This man was about as easygoing as a rattlesnake. "I have a ranger interviewing campers and another watching the lobby for guests leaving. I've been questioning staff—particularly the supervisors. It's a close-knit group here. Someone will dish, in time. We've got the situation well in hand."

The sheriff clapped his notepad shut and jammed it into his pocket. "All right, I'll leave the investigating to you—for now. But if you're going to defend your turf, I can do the same. I'm taking custody of the foundling and delivering it into state hands. Tonight." His mouth settled into a grim line. "And if he ain't yours, you got no reason to protest."

• • •

Alma sat on the front porch, rocking Billy in her arms as Mattie paced back and forth, chattering like one of those little song sparrows. The young woman had delivered a handful of provisions from the store, sweetly adding a few of Alma's favorites without being asked. The sight of Henry's favorite tea had startled Alma for a moment, but she pushed any suspicious thoughts from her mind. Today wasn't the day for doubts.

"And when Eleanor was turning down the beds, the fella came in and landed a pinch right on her backside. Can you imagine? So rude. I'd snap my cap." She rolled her eyes. "She scooted right out of there, not even bothering with the pillows or the towels. And you want to hear something shocking?" As usual, Mattie didn't wait for Alma's reply. "The man's wife reported her for not finishing the cabin. So Eleanor got both a pinch and a write-up. It's a bum rap, I tell you."

Alma murmured agreement, her eyes fixed on the baby's rising and falling chest.

"He must be getting heavy." Mattie crouched in front of them, the smell of her lilac perfume carrying on the evening breeze. "Do you want me to take him for a while?"

"No, we're fine." Billy's tiny fist had closed around Alma's index finger in his sleep. Moving it would break her heart.

"I'll get that adorable little baby bed from your room. You can lay him down out here in the fresh air. I read in the newspaper that it's good for little ones." She disappeared before Alma could think of a reply. One nice thing about Mattie was that Alma never needed to worry about carrying on a conversation. It just happened.

By the time Mattie reappeared, Alma had risen from the rocker. Her friend was right. Alma's own mother had often left little brothers and sisters to nap in the fresh air. After all, *Mor*'s hands were usually too busy to be holding sleeping babies. And Alma had been much the same with Eddie. His little basket would sit in the sunny front window while she worked in the kitchen, the sound of running water providing a soothing background for his slumbers.

Mattie looked completely natural as she bundled the wicker bassinet out to the porch, setting it in a sheltered corner where they could both keep an eye on it.

Alma walked two slow laps around the front porch before stopping next to the bed. "I suppose he needs to get used to it."

"Are you keeping him, then?" Mattie picked at the edge of her sleeve. "I do hope so."

"I-I don't know." She lowered him into the bassinet, keeping one hand on his back for several moments to make sure he'd stayed asleep. The idea of keeping the baby had been flitting around in her thoughts all day. Would Henry be willing? He'd been such a good father to little Eddie. He might not feel the same devotion for a stranger's child.

"You have so much love to share." Mattie edged closer. "I mean, who would be better suited? Plus, Henry—I mean, Ranger Eriksson—he's the one who found him, after all. I think it was meant to be. God in action, right here and right now. You're like the Egyptian princess drawing the baby out of the river."

"I didn't pull him out, and I'm certainly no princess. God would never choose me for such a task." Not after what happened last time. Alma wrapped her arms around her middle to compensate for their emptiness.

Mattie gave a soft nod, her expression steady and kind. "You're a daughter of the King. That makes you a princess."

"You don't . . ." Her words scattered as she spotted her husband walking the path toward the house, the broody sheriff on his heels.

Mattie spun to track Alma's line of sight. "And there he is now." Her words slowed as if it dawned on her that this might not be a social call. She touched Alma's wrist.

Henry's rigid stance and furrowed brow spoke volumes. It wasn't often that Alma saw the uniform more than the man she loved, but today he seemed to be wearing it like a shield.

Alma planted herself in front of the bassinet, balling her apron in her fingers.

"Ladies." His focus skittered over to Mattie before returning to Alma. "You've already met Sheriff Moody, I hear?"

Alma swallowed, the uncertain tone in her husband's voice so abnormal for him. "Did you find the mother?"

"Not yet." He climbed the steps and placed a hand under her elbow, gently steering her a few feet away. "But, Alma, the sheriff thinks it best—"

"No." Her body went cold. Alma moved to duck past him only to collide with his chest. "No, he's not taking him."

Mattie scooted in front of the baby's bed, spreading both arms like a stage actress preparing for an announcement. "Gentlemen, Billy is sleeping. I'm sure you don't want to wake him and cause a fuss."

Henry's soft grip on Alma's arm held firm. "Billy?"

"We needed to call him something." She parroted Mattie's words from earlier.

He nodded. "Well, be that as it may—"

"Billy is staying here with us. He's been through enough." She forced her voice to be calm. "I have the necessary items to care for him and nothing but time. This is a good, quiet place for him to wait until higher-ups decide what will happen."

The sheriff joined them on the porch. "I'm afraid it's already decided. According to the law, abandoned children are wards of the State of Utah, not the federal government. As such, I need to deliver the foundling to the state hospital."

Mattie squared her shoulders, a rock between the men and the bassinet.

Alma scrambled for an argument. Emotional pleas might work with her husband, but she doubted they'd make a dent in this burly man's armor. He was all business. And yet, it was all she had. "This isn't about law, Sheriff. It's about a boy's life. He's not a prisoner to be transported. He needs the loving comfort that only a woman's arms can provide. He's found that here."

Ignoring her, the sheriff moved forward, like a bobcat ready to spring.

Henry's hand tightened before Alma could manage a step. "Mattie, step aside."

Alma's throat squeezed. She yanked her wrist against Henry's fingers, but they held tight.

Mattie didn't budge, her arms forming triangles at her sides as she laid hands on her hips. "Are you a religious man, Sheriff?"

"Not when I'm at work, missy."

She landed a palm on his chest to stop his forward advance. "God placed Billy in Alma and Henry's care for a reason. Scripture says to look out for the fatherless, and this little fellow is pretty close to an orphan right now. Who are you—or the State of Utah—to overrule God? You know what happens to people that get in the Lord's way?"

"Miss, throwing the Bible at me isn't going to change my mind." Even so, the sheriff's ruddy complexion had paled a bit. "Now stand aside." He elbowed past her and clasped the wicker handle as Billy's eyes fluttered open.

Alma held her breath. If Billy cried, it might rend her heart in two. They'd have to mop her up off the floorboards.

Even Sheriff Moody seemed to hesitate when the boy's eyes latched on him, but it only lasted a moment. He lifted the bed and tucked it awkwardly against his chest. Turning to the two womenfolk, he gave a soft nod. "Just so you know, I *am* a religious man. And a family man. I've got four of my own at home." He cleared his throat. "But I also have a job to do." He leveled his gaze at Mattie. "You don't speak for God. None of us do. Thankfully we do have a direct line to Him, and I think we should all be using it on this little fellow's behalf."

Numbness spread through Alma. "If God cared, He wouldn't have taken this boy's mother from him. Or my own boy from me. What sort of God gives and takes on a whim?" She finally twisted her wrist loose from Henry's grip. "I'll gather Billy's things."

The canned milk and corn syrup Mattie had purchased still sat unopened on the counter, beside the box of Eddie's clothes.

Billy had been in her life for less than a day, but somehow he'd already claimed a substantial chunk of her heart.

6

Springdale, Utah
Present Day

"Pops!" Talia pushed open the door to her grandfather's house while juggling an awkward armful of luggage. "Hey, Pops, I'm here. You home?"

She dropped the bags in the entry and took a deep breath, relinquishing the tension of the past weeks like a snake shedding its skin. Like in many homes of its era, the door opened onto a small landing, which was just wide enough for a coatrack and a narrow table scattered with keys and junk mail. From there, one short flight of stairs led up to the living area, the other down to the lower floor. Another choice in the long line of decisions that seemed to define her life right now. Pops's sense of humor was evident in the wooden sign he'd painted and hung on the wall, which read "Choose Wisely."

Had she? She'd never written *be unemployed* or *live with my grandfather* on any of her life lists.

The sounds of a televised baseball game and the squeak from Pops's easy chair in the upper living room gave away his location. She bounded up the steps. He met her at the top, a napkin spilling from the neckline of his Utes sweatshirt and a grin lighting his face. "There's my girl. I didn't hear you drive in. You're early."

Throwing her arms around her grandfather, she caught the mingled scents of pizza and nachos. Ever since Gran passed, Pops's diet had consisted of all the salty snack foods she'd never allowed in the house. Talia would get on him about that later, but right now she just wanted to melt into his hug. "I rolled out of bed early and hit the road. Are we winning?"

He chuckled. "Not looking good. Arizona is already up by three." He gestured to her pile of belongings on the landing. "Let's get you settled. You want the nice guest suite, or are you still set on the old rumpus room?"

"You know I prefer the basement." All the grandkids loved the sprawling lower level, with its threadbare sectional, pool table, and view over the desert backyard. The guest room had been reserved for the adults. Even if she fell neatly into that category now, some habits were difficult to break. "I'll take everything down in a minute. Can I grab some water first?"

"Of course. Make yourself at home."

As he returned to his chair, she ducked into the small kitchen. Opening the cabinet, Talia reached for one of the glasses decorated with a red *Dala* horse. Gran had loved incorporating hints of Pops's Scandinavian heritage and her own Spanish roots throughout the home and garden. The cupboard contained an eclectic mix of both, so the tumblers with the whimsical red horse design sat beside a stack of hand-painted blue Cordoba plates. Gran had been gone for a few years now, but in moments like these, it seemed like she was just in the next room. Perhaps that's how the journey to heaven felt—like stepping from one room to another.

Shaking off the thought, Talia filled the glass from the tap.

Her heart soared at the view of the familiar red rock cliffs in the distance. They were only a mile from the front entrance of Zion National Park. The property values in the gateway town had shot up in recent years. It boggled the mind to think what her grandparents' modest home on twenty acres must be worth now. But Pops had lived his whole life here, and he wasn't ready to trade it for life in the city anytime soon.

"When do you start work?" His voice trailed in from the living room.

"Monday morning." After her job-ending tailspin from ZetaWear, taking a seasonal position at the park's gift shop was either career suicide or exactly the reset she needed. She pushed away any thoughts that went beyond her immediate future. She needed to detox from stress, not add more.

Talia added ice cubes to her glass before heading over to join her grandpa in front of the boxy old TV. "What happened to the flat-screen Dad got you for Christmas? He thought you could mount it on the wall over the fireplace."

"I looked over the instructions, but it's too 'smart' for me. I put it downstairs. Maybe you can figure out how to hook it up."

"It's not that hard. We can install it here if you want."

"This one's fine. We get along." He dug into his bowl of chips. "New isn't always improved."

She settled into Gran's glider rocker and sipped the glass of water. When had she last sat and watched a game? Work had demanded every ounce of her energy.

Nothing was stopping her now. No career, no plan, no life.

She glanced at her grandfather, kicked back in the recliner with a half-empty bowl balanced on his lap. Pops had always been her anchor. A place to find her feet again.

"There's a box of stuff I want you to look through when you get a chance." He gestured to a wooden box on the coffee table. "I've been trying to clear out the storage space downstairs so you'll have some shelves. That came from your gammelfarmor's retirement home after she passed. Jewelry and some other bits and bobs. I don't think anything's valuable, but you might like them anyway."

Talia sat forward and ran a finger across the painted roses on the lid. Her great-grandmother's memory lingered in the delicate folk-art designs adorning several family heirlooms. "I really should learn to do this. I bet there are YouTube tutorials I could watch."

"She'd have loved showing you herself. She used to teach classes at the lodge, back in the day."

Opening the lid, she sorted through the keepsakes, laying each on the table. "These are gorgeous, Pops. The old forties and fifties costume jewelry is a vibe now."

"My father used to say how happy he was that she wasn't the type of woman who asked for diamonds. It's tough to afford such things on a park salary, as I well know." He settled his attention back on the game. "Take what you want. Your great-aunt went through it a couple of years ago and didn't have any interest."

After selecting two vintage necklaces and a pair of funky rhinestone clip-on earrings, Talia pulled a small padlock from the box. The tarnished brass spoke of years of use. She dug through the small chest but couldn't find a key. "Do you know what this is to?" She held it out to her grandfather.

Pops glanced her way. "No. I remember seeing it among her things, but I don't know its story. Lost to the sands of time, I guess."

She fiddled with the lock, the antique igniting her imagination. The heart-shaped body fit neatly in her palm. Though worthless without a key, the item whispered of mysteries and cryptic puzzles. Maybe she could hang it on a chain or something.

Arizona scored another run and Pops groaned. Maybe this was the real reason Talia rarely bothered with sports—her favorites always lost. "I think I'll go put my stuff away. Holler if they turn it around."

"Will do. Let me know if you need anything."

Talia picked up the jewelry and padlock before trotting down the stairs to gather her bags. Flicking on the basement light, she dropped everything onto the sagging single bed in the corner. The ancient bookshelves along one wall beckoned her with well-worn paperback novels and boxes of board games and puzzles. The familiar items welcomed her in like so many old friends. The green-and-pink-striped sectional oozed with nineties charm.

Walking to the sliding glass doors, she grinned. This view was the best part. As a kid, she'd often spread her sleeping bag right here on the rug and stare out at the night sky. She'd awaken to the sun cresting over the sandstone monoliths and spreading a riot of colors down their sides. It was her safe place to hide from the world.

Or perhaps a doorway into another.

Talia's phone vibrated in her hoodie pocket. She pulled it out and skimmed through the notifications. Sixteen new emails—mostly automated replies from job-hunting websites. Josiah had sent a creepy personal email casually asking her out since there was "no longer any conflict of interest." Her stomach turned. That assumed there was interest to begin with.

The current message was from Lissa, begging Talia to join a new nonprofit she'd formed to seek environmental transparency in the apparel industry. Talia tossed the phone onto the sofa.

The news of her "breakdown" had gone viral in the fitness world, ruining any opportunity she would've had to jump to another athleisure company. Even so, she didn't have the heart to turn on ZetaWear. When forced to choose between fight or flight, Talia opted to duck and run. She wouldn't have made a good soldier.

Eventually she'd have to face what went wrong, but for now she was content to shelve her problems with the aging paperbacks. A few months. That's all she needed.

Talia flopped on her bed and pulled her planner from her tote bag. Opening it to an empty page, she started a new list.

• • •

Talia pressed on the accelerator, the small Volvo shifting gears as it started up the hill toward Zion Lodge. It seemed odd to drive through the park by herself instead of arriving with her family, but she'd get used to it. Pops had offered to drive her to work, but being dropped off by the retired chief ranger might bring unwanted attention. Besides, she wasn't a little girl anymore.

He'd grinned at that. "You were never a little girl, Tal. You've always been an old soul. You take the world more seriously than it takes itself."

But now, driving alongside the Virgin River with the stunning red canyon walls all around, she wished she'd accepted his kind offer. It might have kept her heart from kicking along at double its normal pace. The nerves were silly. Her last job had come with a private office, a rotating collection of premium activewear, and a mountain of stress. This job paid minimum wage and required her to wear a stiff maroon polo shirt with "Zion Lodge" embroidered on the front. It was practically a vacation.

Talia slid her window open, letting the breeze toy with the ends of her hair as she caught up to the park's shuttle bus. She slowed down to accommodate its ponderous pace. A pre-recorded spiel warbled from its audio system while park visitors held out their phones toward the passing scenery. "Keep an eye on the weather and make sure that you are not in the river when there is a possibility of a flash flood. Flash floods can kill; don't let it happen to you."

Glancing at the clock on her dash, she drummed her fingers against the steering wheel. *I should have left earlier.* She hadn't factored in the time needed to stop and show her employee badge to enter the canyon, plus wait on the shuttles. And then there were the countless electric bikes to maneuver around.

Tailgating a bus wasn't a good way to start her day.

The disembodied voice from ahead gave her hope that she'd lose the slow-moving vehicle. "This is the Court of the Patriarchs. Depart the bus here for a trail to a scenic viewpoint . . ." The brake lights flashed as it veered into the turnout.

Talia gunned the engine and swerved around the shuttle, intent on getting clear before it released a collection of tourists more concerned with views and maps than watching for cars. The open roadway beckoned, nothing between her and the lodge. Her mind sped too. She still needed to find the employee parking and get herself to the gift shop before her shift started.

An official-looking white Tahoe sat at the far end of the shuttle stop, and the sight sent a wave of cold perspiration across her skin. "Oh no. No, no, no, no, *no.* Not today."

On cue, the SUV lurched forward, lights flashing.

So that's how we're playing it, God? She tapped her brakes, careful to flick on her turn signal before steering her car to the side of the road. Her palms grew damp. She'd never been pulled over in her life. Not even in college, when she regularly raced to campus minutes before a class started.

She bit her lip and glanced at the rearview mirror. The park vehicle sat behind her, lights still flashing. Unlike her, this guy was in no hurry.

After several minutes had ticked by, the shuttle bus rumbled past. As its PA system detailed the story of Zion's Paiute name, *Mukuntuweap*, people swiveled in their seats and pointed their cameras at her.

Someday she'd laugh about this. Talia slumped forward, lowering her forehead to the steering wheel. What would she tell her new boss? Losing this job on top of the last one would be a fun addition to her growing résumé of failures. She might have to resort to playing the "Hey do you know my grandpa" card.

The crunching of gravel caught her attention, and she jerked her head up, swiping fingers under her eyelashes to remove any moisture gathering there.

The ranger removed his sunglasses and stared down at her. "License and registration, please. Do you know how fast you were going, ma'am?"

Ma'am? Talia suddenly felt much older than her twenty-six years. "I-I don't." She dug through her wallet, sliding out the card and passing it to him before reaching for her glove box for the rest of her paperwork.

"I'm sorry, I was trying to get around that infernal— I mean, I was running late for work." She slammed her mouth shut as she handed him the documents. *You have the right to remain silent, idiot.*

His focus dropped to her work shirt. "At the lodge?"

"Yep. First day. Great start, right?" She forced herself to look up at the man. His forest-green eyes caught her so off guard she felt her mouth fall open. *Come on, Lord. That's not playing fair.*

"Food service? Housekeeping?"

"Gift shop."

Unimpressed, the ranger turned his attention to the notebook and jotted down a few lines. "We take visitor safety seriously. If you expect to hold on to this job, you'll need to be more cautious."

"Yes, sir. Usually I am. I was in a hurry—not a good reason, I know." Talia took a deep breath to settle her nerves before she said something even more stupid. Lifting a hand to block the sun's glare, she studied the man as he continued writing. His gold name tag read *Blake Mitchell.* Had Pops been retired too long for the younger staff to know him? This guy looked to be under thirty, the faint lines on either side of his eyes suggestive of too much time in the sun even though the ranger hat cast a shadow over his rugged face. "If you're writing me a ticket, do you mind if I call the lodge to let them know I'm going to be late?"

"I'm issuing a warning, not a citation, Miss Eriksson." His concentration didn't waver from the form. "But I'm happy to give you an upgrade if you prefer. And you won't get a signal here—not until you hook into the Wi-Fi at the Lodge. Would you like me to radio ahead and let Myrtle know you've been detained?"

"Um, no." Talia shifted in the driver's seat. "I suppose I can explain when I get there, Ranger Mitchell." If he could throw her name around, she could do the same.

He smirked. "Tell you what—I'm heading that way. I'll escort you. I'd love to see her reaction."

"That's really not necessary." She pressed her lips together to keep from scowling at him. Today might be the worst first day on record, and having this guy witness more of her humiliation was not high on her list of preferences.

He passed her the notepad. "Sign."

Talia took the pen from his hand and scrawled her name on the official document.

He tore off a sheet, added it to her ID and registration, and extended the assortment to Talia. "If you don't mind waiting a moment, I'll pull out in front of you and lead the way."

She did mind, but whatever. "Sure." As he sauntered back to his vehicle, Talia stuffed her license in her wallet, then folded the warning slip until it became a square no larger than her thumbnail.

Several minutes passed.

The obnoxious red flashers on top of the ranger's Tahoe still pulsed away in her rearview mirror. Talia slid her damp palm along her pant leg and laid her head against the headrest. With her engine off, she could hear the trickle of the river. A young buck, velvet still clinging to his antlers, wandered through the cottonwoods that clustered about the water source. Her heart slowed as she watched the animal dip its head to nibble at the plants.

From ZetaWear to Zion. She needed the solace this canyon provided—the steady, solid rocks standing in sharp contrast to the constantly changing river. She'd been pulled along in the current for far too long.

The SUV rolled up beside her, Ranger Mitchell leaning over to the open passenger window. "You coming?"

Talia jerked back to the present, started her car's engine, and followed him. At least he'd doused the lights. The guy might be set on leading this little parade, but Talia would like to arrive at work with the least amount of fanfare.

• • •

Blake parked his SUV and watched Talia Eriksson scamper into the lodge. Sure, the escort might have been overkill, but she seemed the type to speed off once she was out of his sight. Likely as not, the young woman would fling the blame at him for delaying her instead of admitting she was already running late and had been driving recklessly. But if there was one thing the gift shop manager couldn't stand, it was employees who put their own needs before the park's or the visitors'.

He switched off the Tahoe's engine, quiet draping over him like a blanket. For most of his life—growing up in Los Angeles, followed by eight years in the army—peace and quiet had only ever come in snatches. He soaked in every bit of it he could. Schools would be letting out next month, and that meant hordes of visitors and the standard human chaos that accompanied crowds.

Blake lifted his travel mug from the cupholder before hopping out and locking the vehicle. He'd been thinking about a latte all morning. The café's offerings weren't the best, but they were a significant improvement on the toxic waste masquerading as coffee in the Emergency Operations Center. The glass doors of the Zion Lodge swung easily as he pushed through, tucking his cup under one arm and waving to the front desk staff. The gift shop was just to the left of the lobby, and the recipient of his traffic stop seemed to be receiving her second lecture of the day. Myrtle's aged shoulders looked even more hunched than usual, and though she barely reached the height of Talia's armpits, it was the younger woman who appeared to be cowering.

A jab of guilt caught him in the gut. Poor woman. This wasn't a good way to start the season. He should have radioed ahead and not made her wait so long.

He veered left and stepped into the store. "Hi, Myrtle. Everything okay?"

The woman's scowl transformed, the tension in her face easing into the bright smile she reserved for him—or so the lodge staff claimed. "Hey, good lookin'! What are you doing here?"

If Talia's eyes widened any further, she'd resemble a cartoon character.

He turned his attention to Myrtle. "Don't be too cross with Miss Eriksson. I delayed her on the road. There was a problem with a shuttle, and I stopped traffic until we could get it sorted." It wasn't a lie, exactly. He had stopped traffic, after all. Or one driver in particular.

Myrtle clamped a hand on her bad hip. "Nice try, Blake. Noah was by a minute ago and said you had pulled someone over down the road. I knew right away it must be my new recruit."

At that statement, the seasonal employee lowered her head and seemed to study her shoes.

Well, he'd made an effort. "I'm sure it's just first-day jitters. I had them myself a couple of months ago, and it was your friendly face that got me through."

"Flattery will get you everywhere, Ranger. Fine. I'll let it pass. This time." Myrtle turned back to Talia, the storm clouds returning. "But if I hear of you speeding on park roads again, I'll give your grandfather a piece of my mind. I'm sure he taught you better than that. Don't think you can get away with things just because of who you are."

The hairs on Blake's arms prickled. *Because of who she is?*

Talia nodded. "No, ma'am. I never would think that. I'm very grateful for this opportunity."

"As you should be. Most of the staff was hired months ago. You're fortunate one of them washed out and left me in a bind. Your call came at the right time, and since you're ridiculously overqualified, it was a no-brainer. Most of our staff have hardly run a cash register before, much less organized a display."

"I'm happy to help in any way I can."

Blake edged toward the door. "I should let the two of you get to work. I'm off to the café for some rocket fuel. Can I get you anything, Myrtle? A latte? One of those gooey cinnamon rolls?"

She winked at him. "No more of your sweet talk, Blake. You know I'm a married woman."

Their banter had become his favorite part of the day. He turned to the new employee. "What about you, Talia? Coffee?"

Talia glanced from Myrtle to him, uncertainty radiating from her brown eyes. "No—no, thank you. I'm fine."

His offer probably sounded awkward after their earlier interaction. He'd be tempted to sneak her one anyway if guessing a woman's coffee weren't more precarious than crossing a minefield. Maybe another day.

Myrtle refolded a red T-shirt on one of the displays. "Go on with you, Blake. Save your flirting for those of us who appreciate it. I've got to get Talia up to speed."

He lifted his cup in farewell and headed for the outdoor café. So, Talia Eriksson had an important grandfather. This demanded investigation.

7

Zion National Park
1948

HENRY RECLINED ON the bed, watching as the wide-eyed infant chewed furiously on a damp fist.

The baby had remained in state care for less than a week before the judge signed the order approving Henry and Alma's petition for temporary custody.

And in the five days since, Henry's life had turned upside down.

Midnight feedings, diaper changes, fits of colic—he'd forgotten how much work the tiny creatures demanded.

But during those late-night hours, the boy overran the fortifications Henry had erected around his heart. The combined tactics of cuteness and sleep deprivation made Billy unstoppable.

Alma walked in, a pile of clean diapers over one arm. "I just ironed that uniform shirt and now you're getting it all rumpled again." A vague smile pulled at the corners of her mouth, as if she hadn't quite gotten the hang of the expression. "And you're going to be late."

"I'm leaving now." Henry stood and then smoothed the wrinkles from his uniform.

Alma folded the white cotton into neat squares and added them to the wicker basket on the dresser top. "I filled a thermos with coffee. It was a long night, so I'm guessing you're going to need it today."

Approaching his wife from behind, he slid his arms around Alma's waist before pressing a kiss to the back of her neck—a maneuver he hadn't dared attempt in months. The subtle fragrance of lemons clung to her skin, beckoning him like a honeybee to a fresh blossom. Henry brushed his lips against her skin a second time. "You smell good. New perfume?"

Her soft laugh melted him. Turning in his embrace, she leaned into his chest and cupped a hand behind his back. "Curdled milk, perhaps? It's been a rough morning."

"I think I'd recognize that. This is fresher. Citrus."

"Dishpan hands. I need to remember to use the gloves when I wash the bottles."

He snagged her palm and squeezed it. "Less romantic than perfume, perhaps, but I like it." He needed to get out of here soon or the fellows would send a search party. He leaned in and kissed her again.

Alma drew back a few inches. "Not in front of the baby."

Henry glanced at Billy, who was still trying to cram a fist into his mouth. "The boy's not even a month old. I don't think he minds."

She ducked her head, hiding a smile.

He touched a finger to the tip of her adorable nose. "I have to go, anyway. Try to get some rest today."

"I'm taking Billy to the picnic at the Grotto this afternoon."

"With the rangers' wives?" He tried to keep the surprise from his voice. She hadn't participated in any of the social events in months.

"I want to show him off a little. Don't you think everyone should meet our . . . our Billy?"

Our son. He'd almost slipped a few times himself. The attorney had cautioned them against thinking of the boy in those terms until the adoption proceedings were final. "It's a good idea. Everyone wants to meet our newest honorary ranger. Fred was even talking about making a badge for him."

"Mattie is going to come over and help me pick out something to wear. You know she has a keen eye for such things." She picked up a brush from the dresser and smoothed her blond hair, patting the loose curls into place. After checking her reflection in the mirror, Alma turned and finally offered him a full smile. "Now scoot."

A comfortable warmth spread through him. His life had truly turned upside down.

But in the best way.

• • •

Alma fought to slow the irrational pounding of her heart as she sat cross-legged on the picnic blanket. The gentle breeze rustled the leaves of the Fremont cottonwoods, their massive limbs blocking the glare of the afternoon sun. Despite the tranquil scene, she'd scanned the river repeatedly since she and Mattie had arrived. The water level hadn't changed, and Henry had assured her there was no sign of storms in the weather forecast. Not here in Zion, nor anywhere upstream.

But only God chose the weather.

Several children played by the stream's edge, looking for bugs and lizards among the rocks.

Alma studied her hand resting on top of the sleeping baby. Her Scandinavian complexion had never fared well in the Utah sunshine, but lately her skin had become nearly translucent. Ghostlike. If she weren't careful, she'd fade from existence.

Billy deserved as much fresh air and sunshine as they could give him.

She lifted her face and forced a deep breath, the air sweet with the scent of sage and pine. The only way she'd get past this terror was to force herself into the heart of it.

Mattie joined Alma, handing her a plate before joining her on the blanket. "I got you a few things. You should eat."

The odd combination of items on the dish amused her. The Wednesday picnics with the rangers' wives used to be the highlight of her week, with each woman bringing whatever cold cuts and leftovers they had on hand. There was an unspoken rule that no one should go out of her way to cook. "That was kind of you."

"There's some rhubarb pie on the table. I can get you some of that, too, if you'd like. Or some lemonade?"

Alma took in the cluster of women gathered around the table. After the initial greetings and cooing over Billy, they'd given her space. But returning to the self-imposed desert where she'd hidden her heart for much of the past year—that would be a mistake.

She ran a finger through Billy's feather-soft hair. *He'll be fine.* "I'll get it. You'll watch Billy?"

Her friend's eyes brightened. "You know I will."

Alma passed him to Mattie and stood. Children rushed about, playing tag in the afternoon sunshine, their laughter echoing around the picnic area. She took another deep breath, then pointed herself toward the ladies crowded around the food.

A hush fell over the group as she drew close. Sue Barton hopped up from a camp chair, her dark hair pulled back in a long braid. She'd arrived late and had yet to greet Alma. "Alma, it's so good to see you. How's the little one?"

Is that what they'd been talking about? "Billy is doing well. He's growing so fast."

Sue took Alma's arm and drew her into their circle. "Have you met Patsy?" She gestured to a young woman cradling an infant in her lap. "Her husband is Ranger Hayes, the new man working over in Kolob Canyons."

Alma nodded to the newcomer. "It's nice to meet you. How old is your baby?"

Patsy drew the blanket back from the baby's face. "She's just two weeks. I probably shouldn't have her out yet, but I couldn't wait to introduce Sharon to everyone."

Alma smiled. "Billy is about the same age. The days go so fast."

The younger woman beamed. "I feel like everything is a blur. But that might be the lack of sleep talking. Is your—um—is Billy sleeping very much?"

With the age-old topic of sleeping patterns introduced, the tension lifted, and the women shared stories and parenting tips. Attention drifted away from Alma, and she reached for the pie server and dished a tiny sliver onto a plate. Maureen Harper's pies were the best.

Her stomach tightened. The Harpers had brought a lemon meringue the day after the search was called off.

"Alma?" Sue took hold of her elbow. "You look flushed. Here, sit down." She guided her to a camp chair.

Alma dropped into the rickety seat. "I-I'm just not used to being out in the sun."

"It's going to be a scorcher this week. George and I have talked about moving back to the Rockies. We came here to be closer to my Paiute relatives, but I know he misses the mountain air and can't help longing for it when the weather gets too warm."

Alma's heart rate slowed as she thought of home. "I still pine for Minnesota on occasion."

Sue nodded. "But I can't imagine my kids growing up anywhere else. They love it—especially playing with their cousins and the children here. Just think, Alma—Billy will be climbing aboard that yellow school bus before you know it." She gestured toward Patsy and the new baby. "And Sharon too."

Alma allowed herself another glance toward Mattie and Billy. "I'm not ready for that."

"Of course not. But when his turn comes, you'll be thrilled to send him off for a few hours a day. I'd never get anything done otherwise. Oh—" She leaned forward, a glint in her brown eyes. "Did you hear that movie crew might be coming back? The last picture did so well they're talking about filming another one here in the canyon. Westerns are all the rage."

Alma forced her attention back to the conversation. "I haven't been to the pictures in ages. We never go anymore."

Maureen moved to join them as if attracted by Sue's mention of the film. "You didn't even go to see *Canyon Shadows*, Alma? That's too bad. A few of the lodge staff had walk-on roles. You must remember how gaga everyone was for the movie stars."

It seemed like a lifetime ago, but it had been just after the flash flood. "I remember Mattie talking about it."

"Her and all the other single girls." Maureen laughed. "To tell the truth, several of the rangers' wives were making excuses to visit the lodge to catch a glimpse of Gary Legend and Victoria Reel. They were clearly an item, regardless of what the scandal sheets said."

"Maybe I'll get to see them this time."

Mattie rose from the blanket, Billy propped on her shoulder, and walked toward the river's edge, where one of the kids stood crying, clutching her elbow.

Don't take him over there. Alma's pulse ratcheted upward. She eased out of the chair, using her free hand to make sure the rickety thing stayed put. She had to get Billy away from the water. "I should check on my son."

Sue looked up. "He's fine. Mattie has him. It's sweet that Ranger Eriksson hired her as a mother's helper."

Maureen nodded. "I wish my husband was so thoughtful."

"She's not . . ." A bead of sweat worked its way down Alma's back as she watched Mattie take the little girl's hand and walk her back toward one of the moms sitting at the table. Her stomach uncoiled. "Mattie's a friend. She likes to help."

Maureen swatted a fly away from the knee of her pedal pushers. "I could use a friend like that. A single woman with no children to monopolize her every waking moment? Though I'm not sure I'd want a girl like her so close to my husband. He might start thinking about replacing me with a younger model."

"Henry isn't like that." Alma reclaimed her seat as Mattie handed the little girl off to her mother for a kiss and a bandage. "He's a good man."

"So is my Ernie." Maureen took a sip of water. "But he wouldn't be a man if he didn't look."

Mattie joined them, the pink glow in her cheeks nearly matching the flowers on her dress. "I-I should be going. I have a shift this evening, and we always gather to sing a number for the tour bus when they depart at three." She passed the baby to Alma, helping to get him settled against her shoulder. "I need to change into my uniform."

Maureen pursed her lips. "Such a pity. But then, you wouldn't want to soil that lovely frock when you're scrubbing those guest cabins." She walked down to the river, likely to check on her own two girls.

Alma rested her chin on the top of Billy's fuzzy head, breathing in his warm scent. "I wish you could stay."

"I don't belong here. This picnic is for rangers' wives, and I'll certainly never be one of those."

Sue sat forward in her seat. "You're always welcome. You and any of the lodge girls. The more the merrier."

"You're so kind, thank you. I'll pass the word." Mattie leaned down and touched the tip of Billy's nose. "Be good for your mama, Billy Boy."

Alma swallowed her jitters. She relied on the young woman far too much. It was time to stand on her own feet. "Thank you, Mattie. I don't think I'd have had the nerve to come if you hadn't talked me into it."

Mattie smiled. "You're stronger than you know, Mrs. Eriksson."

8

Present Day

TALIA STACKED THE souvenir mugs three deep, adding new ones in the gaps. A stitch of tension had lodged behind her eyes, and she already regretted refusing the park ranger's offer of caffeine. Why hadn't she thought to fill a travel mug this morning?

Memories of Palo Alto's Cafe Venetia flooded her mind, the sounds of hissing and gurgling and the taste of their delicious tiramisu. She'd probably passed one or two drive-through coffee places this morning, but she'd been so nervous about her first day it hadn't crossed her mind to stop. Now she paid the price.

She pried open a carton of shot glasses, the park's name splashed across each one in colorful letters. These would look incredible in the window, where they'd catch the light, rather than stashed away on this shelf unit.

Across the room, Myrtle showed off a collection of board books to a woman toting an infant in one of those trendy, boho-style baby wraps made by WoollyBearCub. The company specialized in all-natural fibers. Talia made a mental note to add their name to her list of potential future employers. Then again, she knew even less about child-rearing than she did about yoga.

Myrtle gave the young mom a quick hug before reaching for a second book. The manager might be gruff with her employees, but she had a tender touch when it came to sales. Such a change from ZetaWear.

Obviously, this store was Myrtle's baby.

It might be better to keep any suggestions for improvements to herself for now. Talia added the glassware to the shelf beside the mugs. *From MBA graduate to shelf stocker.* Wouldn't her Stanford professors be proud?

It hadn't been the best morning, but tomorrow would be better. After all, she wasn't here to further her career. It was a reset. That was all.

After her mother's death, Talia had buried herself in the constant grind of school, then work. And now, at twenty-six, all she had to show for her dogged work ethic were a couple of degrees, student loans, and a closet of fitness clothing she was afraid to wear. Scrolling through her friends' social media had been the closest she came to adventures: Mia backpacking through Latin America, Emily and her husband restoring an Italian villa, and Chris working as a climbing guide in Yosemite.

Her college boyfriend had done the craziest thing of all. Holden had married the next woman he'd dated—a single mom of twins. His feed was littered with pictures of chubby-cheeked toddlers, and he tagged every post with #instafamily. Whether that stood for *instant* or *Instagram-worthy*, she wasn't sure. Did it even matter?

Adventures, families, purpose.

What was on her account? Photos of sports bras.

Talia never even got a dog because she figured she wasn't at home enough to take care of one.

The souvenir glasses made a musical clinking as she set the final one in place. The stress would fade eventually. Thankfully, beyond the gift shop's windows lay an entire canyon of adventure and beauty. Maybe God had "set her in place" too. Sydney could keep the national park–decorated spandex. Talia had the real thing.

After carrying the empty box to the back, she picked up a crate of guidebooks. Good thing there was an employee discount—she needed one of these to help fill out her Zion wish list. She set a copy aside. There was enough time to unpack several more containers before her break. Then she'd pay for the book and sneak away for a caffeine jolt. The café must be worth a stop if it was attracting good-looking rangers in for a refill.

Did Myrtle flirt with all the men or just him? It wasn't something one saw in the workplace much anymore, and the idea of Myrtle being forced to take a sexual harassment course made laughter bubble up in Talia's chest. The woman had to be close to Pops's age.

By midday, Talia had stocked multiple shelves and recorded the inventory of all the T-shirts they had in storage. It was crazy to think how many shirts this shop must sell each day to demand that many boxes. She'd never been on this end of sales before. Maybe she'd learn a few things this summer that could help her career after all.

Myrtle closed the cash register and glanced at her watch. "Why don't you go take your lunch, dearie? I'll take mine at two. I can see you're dying to get out of here."

Talia folded the last two shirts and added them to the crate of mediums. "I can wait if you wanted to go first."

"No, I'm not hungry yet. I had a big breakfast."

After grabbing her insulated lunch bag from the backroom, Talia pushed through the lodge's large front doors. The weather today was perfect, and if she ate quickly, she might have time for a walk before she needed to be back. She ordered her coffee and then found a bench where she could eat her sandwich and salad. The sunshine warmed her back as she studied the cliff face opposite the lodge. Somewhere up there was the trail to Angels Landing. She'd scribbled down the name on her bucket list years ago after seeing some of Jasmine's pictures. Flipping through her new guidebook, she browsed the information, then squinted at the view again. Which of those ramparts was it?

"Did Myrtle get rid of you already?" The male voice caught her by surprise.

She jerked her head around to see Ranger Mitchell walking toward her, a grin on his face.

"I made it to my lunch break." She waved her empty container. "But the rest of the day is still iffy. What about you? Pull over any more panic-stricken seasonals?"

"Not today." He dropped onto the seat beside her. "One smash-and-grab over by the visitor center, then helping some parents search for their lost child."

"A lost child?" Her heart stuttered. "Did you find them?"

"Yes. In the restroom. Nine times out of ten, they're in the restroom. But it's the tenth one you have to worry about."

She took a sip of her almond-milk latte. "I remember my grandpa saying something similar."

"About that." Blake took off his hat and set it on the bench beside him. "I asked around. I didn't realize you were Zion royalty."

She nearly choked on her drink. "Hardly."

"Bill Eriksson is pretty much a legend, or so I'm told."

"Well, he's a legend to me. But I'm a nobody, at least here at Zion." And she was pretty much persona non grata in the athleisure world now. Talia pushed away the thought.

"So you're here for a summer job. Are you a college student? Or a teacher, maybe?"

She tucked her empty salad bowl in the bag. If she were going to get a walk in, she'd best not let the nosy ranger delay her any further. "Neither. I needed a fresh start. Now, if you'll excuse me, I'm going to stretch my legs for a bit."

"Don't let me stop you." He stood too. "Just don't get lost. I don't want to have to explain to Myrtle why you didn't make it back for your shift."

She pulled the bag over her arm, trying to avoid studying how the gray sleeves clung to Blake Mitchell's biceps. The uniform was notoriously unflattering, but this guy wore it well. "If I do, you'll know where to find me."

He gave her a quizzical look.

"Nine times out of ten, right?"

His laugh trailed after her. "Don't be number ten."

• • •

She was already a ten.

Warmth flooded Blake at the rogue thought, and he shook himself like a wet dog. He didn't need distractions. Best to keep his eyes—and his heart—to himself. He checked his watch and groaned. His schedule had him back at the Emergency Operations Center at 1300, but it was already five minutes past.

If his years in the army had drilled anything into him at all, it was punctuality. If someone wasn't where they were supposed to be, people got hurt. He'd never been able to rid himself of the sense of duty, and to be honest, he wasn't certain he wanted to. Blake jogged for his vehicle, doing his best not to alarm visitors. NPS wasn't military, even with all the trappings of the uniforms and badges. It hadn't taken him long to learn that the preferred demeanor in this agency was a laid-back and professional one, unless the situation called for more. People were here to relax, and tightly wound staff didn't portray the right attitude.

He walked into the EOC fifteen minutes later and headed straight to the chief ranger's office. Hal Martinson had taken Blake under his wing as a favor to a friend—Blake's former staff sergeant. Now Martinson sat hunched over his desk, his shoulders curving toward the computer screen. He drilled a single finger at the Return key over and over.

Blake hesitated in the doorway. "This a bad time?"

The man's eyes flicked toward him briefly. "Just going through the reports for yesterday's incident in the Zion–Mount Carmel Tunnel. The amount of paperwork generated from one motor vehicle crash would surprise you."

The gruesome scene flashed into Blake's mind a little faster than he'd have liked. "It was pretty brutal."

"Motorcyclists rarely win when they cross with pickups at high speeds." Martinson pushed back a few inches from the desk as if the physical distance might provide some relief. "On a lighter note, I heard you had a traffic stop earlier." His lips quirked.

Blake sank into a chair. "Word travels fast. Evidently her grandfather was a ranger?"

"Bill Eriksson was my predecessor, and let me tell you—I was stepping into some pretty big boots. His father was a Zion ranger too. Their family has quite the legacy here."

"I'm glad I didn't cite her, then."

Martinson swung a hand dismissively. "Bill wouldn't want special favors. That man was a stickler for rules. He'd probably have ticketed the presidential motorcade if they were speeding. But a traffic stop involving his granddaughter? That makes for an entertaining story. When I run into him at the grocery store next, you can be sure I'll give him a hard time."

Great. Blake would have trouble showing himself in town after this. "How did she end up working for the concessionaire?" The woman's offhand comment about fresh starts had clung to his thoughts since she'd walked off. If anyone was the king of new beginnings, it was him.

"Bill told me she was some hotshot marketing guru in California but hit a rough patch. She's come out this summer to get her head on straight."

"Great place to do that."

"Especially if you've got a free place to live. Most of the lodge staff are crammed into dormitories, but I'm guessing she's bunking in with her grandpa. He's got a sweet setup in Springdale—been in the family for years."

With so many of the local accommodations being transformed into luxury condos, prices had skyrocketed. For Blake, landing the apartment at Alder and Katie's? It had God's fingerprints all over it.

"Actually, it's those dorms I wanted to talk to you about," Martinson said.

Blake sat forward. "The concession ones?"

The chief nodded. "We're often getting calls—noise complaints, domestic disturbances, and so on. But we've had reports lately of an unknown male lurking about and making people nervous. They usually see to their own there, but I think we should up our presence in the area. Swing through several times during each shift, at random intervals. It'd make the place safer and keep the pressure on anyone looking for trouble."

"We can do that. Do you think it's an employee or a visitor?"

"Likely an employee. Visitors don't get back there much, and the reports have been sporadic, so the guy has been around a while. That's assuming it's the same one."

"Description?"

"It's all very vague. 'Guy in the shadows' sort of thing. But we want to keep it that way. I'd prefer to be ahead on this one. Might just be some guy out vaping or something."

Blake retrieved a notebook from his pocket. Another good reason for Eriksson's granddaughter to be living outside the park.

9

1949

"LET'S START AGAIN, shall we? A fresh start is good for the soul." Alma spread a clean piece of brown paper on the picnic table in front of Mrs. Jacobs. The lodge guests watched as Alma fanned her paintbrush, drawing it along the paper in a gentle C shape—a flourish that would eventually become a leaf. "It's not that hard. Just keep the brush moving."

Mrs. Jacobs bit her lip as she dabbed paint across her practice sheet. "I'm not sure I'm going to master this. I feel like a child learning to finger paint."

Even Alma had to agree that the older woman's green smudges looked more like grass stains than fine art. "It takes some practice." She traded brushes with the woman, guiding her hand into a better position for the technique. "Before you know it, you'll be painting flowers on everything. You should see my kitchen cabinets."

One of the other lodge guests leaned across the table for a better view. "My Norwegian grandmother's house was like that too. I'd forgotten how lovely it was. She painted a rocking chair for me when I was a little girl. I wish I still had it."

"Maybe you'll make one for your own grandchildren," Alma said. "This type of folk art has been handed down in Scandinavian families for generations."

Mrs. Jacobs traded the green paint for the burnt orange. "This seems out of place here in Zion. I'd think you'd be teaching Indian pottery or something."

Alma picked up a few of the discarded brushes for cleaning. "My friend Sue demonstrates Southern Paiute basket weaving on Saturdays. It's beautiful. I'm learning some of her techniques, but I'm not qualified to teach it."

Miss Hood moved around to the far side of the picnic table, reaching for a tube of paint. "I love how you're using the colors of the canyon."

Alma smiled. "When I was younger, I used more blue and gray tones, but now I'm drawn to the oranges, rusty reds, and yellows." The sunset colors found in the massive sandstone cliffs almost seemed a part of her now. She slid one of her wooden boxes in front of the young woman to show some sample flowers. "And in addition to the traditional Swedish *kurbits*, I've incorporated many of the flowers we find here in Zion. The Indian paintbrush, the columbine, and the sacred datura. These splashes of color in the desert are a reminder of God's grace even in the midst of desert times."

Mrs. Jacobs's frown blossomed into a gentle smile. "Like Psalm 23. 'He maketh me to lie down in green pastures: he leadeth me beside the still waters. He restoreth my soul: he leadeth me in the paths of righteousness for his name's sake.'"

"Exactly." Alma reached for a tube of blue paint, preparing to demonstrate the next stroke. *Still waters.* He'd gifted her still waters ever since Billy had arrived in their home. For almost a year now, she'd basked in the joy of being a mother again. And her heart had turned back to Henry in ways she'd not thought possible.

But how long would peace last?

"When you're ready, we can try an S stroke." She waved the ladies in closer so they could see what she was doing. "Pull the brush toward you instead of pushing it. It's always easier to control when you're drawing it in." She loved the way the bristles slid through the pigment, moistening the surface of the paper.

Mrs. Jacobs lifted her head. "Ranger—how long have you been standing there?"

Alma straightened. The sight of Henry brought a touch of heat to her face. He'd been the one to suggest she offer her services at the lodge, but he'd never come to witness her class in action. "Did you need something?"

"I just wanted to spend a few minutes watching my beautiful wife do what she loves." He nodded to them, then continued along the sidewalk.

Alma ducked her head as the ladies tittered.

Mrs. Jacobs focused on her paper. "You're very fortunate, Mrs. Eriksson."

Adding the pile of brushes to the cup of water, Alma watched as Henry strode toward the corral. "Yes, I am."

• • •

Henry guided Duck along Wrangler Trail toward the Court of the Patriarchs. A trail crew had been working on removing fallen rocks, and checking their work seemed like a good excuse to get out of the office. The horse bobbed his head, likely annoyed at having had his afternoon nap interrupted. Duck was getting fat and lazy lounging with the rental horses. Henry needed to get the animal out more.

The afternoon sun heated the canyon like a brick oven, and the light breeze provided little relief. By the time he reached the tree cover by the river, the back of his shirt was damp with sweat.

When he arrived, most of the work crew were guzzling from their canteens, but they'd already relocated a good portion of the rocks. He reined Duck to a stop. "Wow. I didn't expect that to go so fast—especially in this heat."

The foreman took off his wide-brimmed hat and swiped a forearm across his brow. "The men decided to push hard for an early day. There's a dance in Springdale tonight. You heard?"

"I tried to talk Alma into it, but she's not ready to leave the baby for an evening."

The man shook his head. "You can retire those dancing shoes. Next thing you know, you'll have another on the way."

The well-meaning gibe landed like a dart to Henry's stomach. Early in their marriage, they had talked about having a whole passel of kids, but evidently God had other plans. They'd only had one pregnancy in five years, and the Lord had seen fit to take Eddie home. Billy was an unexpected blessing, but it seemed as if he might be the only one. "Yeah, well, we'll see."

One of the men in the group sat up, cupping a hand over his eyes for shade. "Is that thunder?"

There were no clouds in the sky. Henry turned to survey the canyon as Duck jostled, jerking against the reins in Henry's hand. The animal had never liked loud noises.

A plume of dust rose from the base of the Sentinel, isolated at first but spreading fast. Henry's pulse quickened. "Rockslide."

The men jumped to their feet, jockeying for the best view.

The foreman turned to Henry. "Think anyone was down there?"

"It's close to Sand Bench Trail. I'd better head that way and check it out. Can you take the crew back to headquarters and tell any rangers you see to meet me out there?"

"We could help," he offered.

Henry scrutinized the team of men, sweat-stained and weary. "You can take volunteers, but don't force anyone. They've already put in hard work today."

He loped Duck toward the scene. The column of white dust expanded toward Henry as the cloud of pulverized rock spread down the canyon like wildfire smoke.

Within minutes he was enveloped, the grit filling his mouth and lungs. He choked and spat as the powdered dust swirled around them. After slowing Duck to a walk, Henry yanked a bandanna from his pocket and pressed it over his mouth and nose. He squinted into the cloud. "Hello? Anyone there?"

A man and woman stumbled toward him. Even with the woman having a white scarf clutched over her head and pulled tight to her mouth, Henry could see tears washing narrow paths down her face.

The man gripped her arm, helping her along, and gestured behind them. "The rest of our party is back there. We got separated. A big chunk of the mountain fell. Nearly crushed us." He pulled a fedora from his head, a swath of clean skin evident above his brow line.

"Are you hurt?" Henry dismounted.

The woman shook her head, coughing. "Just frightened. And worried about our friends."

After giving the couple instructions on how to get to the road, he led his horse further in toward the slide. He'd thought about asking the visitors to take Duck back to headquarters, but he didn't know what type of grisly scene might lay ahead, so there was a chance he'd need the horse's help. The cloud of debris was thinning as it spread, the breeze doing a good job of dissipating the dust, though plenty still hung in the air.

They'd been fortunate in recent years that all slides had occurred far from the trails. Visitation had ballooned with the end of the war, and every additional tourist meant another chance for someone to get hurt.

He lifted his gaze toward the Sentinel, scanning for evidence of where the slab might have come loose, but he couldn't make it out in the hazy air. Was the cliff face still unstable? He didn't have time to think about it as three more people stumbled out of the haze.

Henry hurried over. "Is everyone all right?"

One man took off his knapsack and shook sand from its creases. "Yes, we were under an overhang. The rocks themselves went right past us, and for a minute I thought the whole mountain was coming down."

"Never in my life . . ." The second fellow stopped to spit, clearing his throat. "Never in my life have I seen boulders bounce like that. When they hit the ground, they launched up before continuing downslope. I thought we were going to die."

Henry pulled down his kerchief. "Did you see anyone else?"

The third man shook his head. "No, we were the only ones back there. Us and the couple of friends up ahead. Did you see them? I think they must have been clear when the slide happened. We were hanging back to get pictures of the views."

Henry spent the next hour checking the trail, searching for any sign of additional hikers but finding none. Three rangers joined him, and they began pushing debris from the trail.

After shoving another chunk over the side, Henry stopped to survey the scene. The gritty taste in his mouth dragged him back to the Battle of Manila. He hauled out his canteen and swished the chalky texture from his mouth, gagging as the memory hit like an artillery shell. The visceral reaction caught him off guard.

He slung the canteen strap over his saddle horn with a shaky hand, then threaded his fingers into Duck's coarse mane. Henry lowered his head to the horse's shoulder, closed his eyes, and took a couple of solid breaths. *Relax. No one was hurt.*

After his time overseas, he could have worked at a desk for the rest of his life, his family safe at home. Instead, God had led them to this place. He could almost hear the words Alma often sang to Billy. "*God leads His dear children along.*" Raw beauty and wilderness came at a steep price.

"You okay?" George Barton's voice pulled him from his thoughts.

Henry opened his eyes. "I'm fine. Just relieved."

"The heat's getting to everyone."

Sure. The heat. "I think we can call it a day. As long as nothing else comes down, I'm satisfied with how things look out here."

George pulled off his hat and slapped the hard brim against the palm of his hand, raising a cloud of dust. "Good. I could use a bath."

"And a beer." Ernie Harper shouted from across the way, shoving another slab of stone to the side of the path. "Maureen's probably beside herself. I told her I'd be home at four today. Of course, she'll have heard what happened."

The image of Alma waiting at home made Henry's throat tighten. At least she'd been at the lodge when this happened, so she wasn't alone. She had finally started coming out of her self-imposed cocoon. Hopefully this wouldn't drive her back into hiding.

• • •

Alma didn't bother to knock on Sue's door. She burst through, her heart pounding with the need to lay eyes on her little boy. "Sue? Billy?"

Her friend rushed to meet her. "Sh, Alma. The kids are sleeping."

The relative quiet in the Bartons' small cottage only amplified the buzzing in her ears. Stopping in the middle of the floor, Alma pressed shaking hands to her lips. "I-I heard . . ."

"I know. We all heard it. Sounded like a clap of thunder." Sue stepped to Alma's side and wrapped both arms around her. "But we're safe. Billy is safe. It was far away, up the canyon."

The pressure of her friend's touch slowed Alma's galloping pulse. She'd realized the rockfall wasn't right here, yet her body had reacted like the world was ending. Evidently she'd turned into Henny Penny. "You must think I'm crazy, but I need to see him."

"Of course you do. Just take a few breaths first." Sue's voice remained slow and even. "You don't want to scare him. And you're not crazy. You're a mother."

A mother. Alma's throat squeezed. Yes. She was. "I-I'm fine." She backed out of the embrace and lowered herself to Sue's settee, right next to a pile of folded laundry. "Henry and George—they must be out there."

"Yes, I imagine so." The woman's brow crinkled. "But it'll be okay. You'll see. Now let me make you a cup of tea. You look as if you could use it."

As her friend disappeared into the kitchen, Alma tiptoed to the bedroom door. Peering through the crack, she saw Sue's two girls curled up on the double bed, asleep. From the light filtering through the sheer curtains, she could see Billy's form in the crib in the corner. He slept on his stomach with his knees tucked and his rear end in the air, like he did at home.

Easing the door open, she stepped inside and crossed the floor, stepping lightly to prevent any squeaks on the old floorboards. She managed to reach the side of the crib without waking any of the children, then laid her hands on the wooden railing that kept her rambunctious boy from toppling out.

Billy's cheek rested against the mattress, his tiny lips moving rhythmically as if he were eating in his sleep.

The rise and fall of his back sent a wash of needed peace through her chest. *One, two, three, four.* She counted the slow inhalations, each one far more soothing than a cup of Lipton.

The moisture gathering on her lower lashes took Alma by surprise. She used the tip of her ring finger to dab her eyes. She couldn't let Sue see her like this. The woman probably already thought she had a screw loose.

Billy was safe. He'd never been in any danger.

"Alma?" Sue's whisper came from the doorway.

Alma backed away from the crib and pussyfooted out into the hall. "I'm sorry," she whispered. "I needed to see him."

"I know."

An elegant tea service was laid on the low table by the sofa, including a little carafe of milk and a bowl of sugar cubes with a baby spoon tucked inside.

"Oh, this is beautiful." Alma sighed. "I wasn't expecting anything quite so fancy."

Sue chuckled. "It's George's mother's set, all the way from England. When we moved, she insisted I bring it to Zion. She said there would be days when we needed a touch of elegance amid the wilderness—not to mention the runny noses and skinned knees. Don't you agree?"

"I often feel a bit like Alice down the rabbit hole." Alma took a seat and picked up one of the delicate flowered teacups.

Sue lifted the teapot. "We live in a dangerous and fallen world—and I'm not just referring to the tumbling rocks. Thankfully the Lord watches over us still." A smile creased her round face. "And as the Psalmist says, surely goodness and mercy shall follow us all the days of our lives."

Alma held the cup out for her friend to fill. "I'd like some of each, please."

10

Present Day

TALIA WAITED AT the register as an older couple leafed through a display of bookmarks on the front counter, picking out one for each book in their stack. The woman added the items to her growing pile. "Fifty years, can you believe it?"

"Congratulations." Talia smiled. They were the cutest pair, like characters from that Pixar movie with the balloon house. "How did you meet?"

A dimple appeared in the lady's lined cheek. "We were both working as climbing guides at Rocky Mountain National Park. I know that's hard to believe looking at us today. We spent the last fifty years climbing peaks all around the globe. Now we're happy to still be able to hike. I have friends who do nothing but sit in their chairs and watch *Wheel of Fortune*."

Her husband handed her a magnet, then pushed back his oversized sun hat, revealing a pair of startling blue eyes. "We need a new one for the refrigerator, dear. Our Zion magnet is pretty shabby."

"Well, so are we." She pushed the sizable stack of merchandise toward Talia. "I think that'll do it for us."

Talia rang up everything, wishing the sweethearts had time to share more of their story.

Chatting with the customers rescued what could have been a very boring job. There were ones she could do without, sure, but many of them were utterly fascinating—like these folks.

With the purchases stowed in their daypacks, the couple walked to the door and pulled out a single set of purple trekking poles. She took one in her left hand, he used the other in his right, and they joined hands in the middle like it was second nature.

Talia's throat tightened. *That's what I want.*

Myrtle popped out of the backroom. "If you don't grab your lunch soon, there won't be another chance until three or four o'clock."

"I'll go now." Talia grabbed her lunch bag and water bottle from the cubby and slipped them into her backpack. A brisk walk would give her the energy to get through the afternoon.

Strolling past the horse corrals, Talia headed for the footbridge. The cottonwoods leaned over the trail, forming a cooling pocket of shade along this stretch.

As Talia meandered along the path, more ambitious hikers strode past on their way to Angels Landing or the Emerald Pools. Someday she'd join them.

But if she weren't careful, the days would slip away along with her wish list. Pops had recommended not hiking alone, but her coworkers from the gift shop—Myrtle excluded—seemed more into weekend parties and rock climbing.

Reaching the midpoint of the bridge, Talia paused to watch the river flow past. In the short time she'd been here, the water had already started seeping into her parched soul. The sandstone cliffs were what made Zion spectacular, but it was the water that breathed life into the canyon.

"Hey, there's my speed demon now." A male voice called from the far end of the span.

Talia straightened and cupped a hand over her eyes.

Blake and another ranger walked toward her. With a grin, Blake gestured to his colleague. "Talia—Noah Collier. Noah, this is Talia. She works with Myrtle."

Noah chuckled. "Poor girl."

Talia shrugged. "She's growing on me. Or me on her, maybe."

Blake nodded. "Myrtle will give you a hard time at first, but once you pass her tests, you'll be best friends."

"I suppose that's true at many jobs," Talia said. "You find your role and learn the pecking order." Though she stood by her decision to confront ZetaWear, she'd probably been mistaken to throw the research in Josiah's face during a meeting. Lesson number one—don't embarrass your boss.

Noah checked his watch. "I'd better head out. I've got a meeting at one."

"Right. See you, man." Blake crossed his arms, seemingly content to stay and chat.

Talia stepped aside as another hiking group passed. Did Blake have a hiking partner? She couldn't imagine asking him such a question, but then, he seemed friendly enough . . . when he wasn't pulling her over. "What sort of adventures are you off to today? Rescuing more wandering children?"

One corner of his mouth lifted sweetly as he gazed out at the river. "Nothing so exciting. We were on an injured hiker call, but it wasn't severe enough to require extrication. I'm waiting to make sure she and her party make it back safely."

"You didn't walk down with her?"

"She was embarrassed enough having two rangers hovering for what turned out to be a mild sprain. I thought I'd give her some space so she didn't push herself too hard."

"That was kind."

"Turns out not every woman wants to be rescued." He shrugged one shoulder.

"Swooning in front of a guy is rarely as romantic as it seems in stories."

"Swooning?" He chuckled.

"That's what my mom called it when I . . . well . . . fainted." And here she thought they'd gotten all their awkward out during their first meeting.

Blake's brow tightened, and he turned to stare at her as if he might have to scrape her off the bridge deck. "You do that often?"

She leaned against the handrail, enjoying the sound of the water moving below their feet. "I had a heart condition as a kid. If I got too excited or overheated, it'd cause me to face-plant. When I was seventeen, it was corrected with a surgery." One her mother hadn't been there for. The procedure had fixed the technical problem, but her heart still missed her mom with every beat. "You don't want to be that kid, trust me. A guy in high school liked to jump-scare me to see if I'd fall over like a goat in one of those viral videos."

"That's horrible." He grimaced.

"Thankfully, it never worked for him. But yeah, not romantic in the least." And if she said "romantic" to this guy one more time, she'd have to crawl under a rock. Instead, she checked her watch. Half her lunch break was already gone. "Hey, I need to get my walk in. I hate to be rude, but . . ."

"Oh, yeah. Sorry." He stepped to the side. "You should have said something. I wouldn't want to get you in trouble with Myrtle. Again."

She laughed. "I'll just tell her that her favorite ranger detained me. Although I'm not sure I'm ready to meet Jealous Myrtle."

"She's like regular Myrtle, but feistier."

Talia took a single step away, but the man's magnetic green eyes drew her back. "You could join me, if you want."

He ducked his head, rubbing the back of his neck. "I— That's a nice offer. But I'm on duty."

Heat crept up her cheeks. Of course he was. She gestured toward his uniform. "And here I thought you were wearing the outfit for style points." *Shut up. He's going to think you're hitting on him.*

And there was that sweet smile again. "Enjoy your walk, Miss Eriksson."

• • •

Blake turned his gaze back to the river rather than watch Talia walk away. Gripping the firm railing helped ground his senses. He'd never been particularly chatty, but every time he encountered this woman, he lost his mind. As soon as Noah had left, Blake was done for.

Good thing he'd drawn the night shift for the next week. Crossing paths with her seemed unlikely if he was cruising parking lots at oh-dark-thirty. Maybe then he could excise her from his head.

She only asked you on a walk. Get over yourself.

His injured hiker finally hobbled into view, leaning on her friend's arm. She pulled a crimson Alabama ball cap lower on her forehead and shot him a shy smile. "Y'all didn't have to wait on me." Her accent washed over him like honey, transporting him back to his days at basic.

"Hey, I'm taking a little break to enjoy the scenery." He wasn't lying. Not entirely. "But I'm glad you made it back. Best get that foot elevated when you can."

"I'll do that. Thanks."

Instead of following her to the lodge, he peeled off toward the parking lot. Martinson had asked him to drive past the employee dorms again this afternoon. Rangers had cruised through each of the previous nights, but the chief thought a stepped-up presence during daylight hours would keep trouble at bay.

Blake had heard more than enough horror stories about concession staff in national parks—domestic fights, drugs, assaults, even the occasional hate crime. These low-wage, high-turnover roles in the restaurants and lodgings seemed to draw a volatile mix: adrenaline junkies, bored college kids, international students chasing a dream—all dropped into tight quarters with little oversight. Most were probably harmless. Probably. But it only took one spark to light the whole mess on fire. The concession group claimed they did background checks, although Blake had his doubts. They needed warm bodies, not clean records.

National parks were expected to contain predators—just not the human sort.

Driving through, Blake studied the outside entrances, the shrubs, the parked vehicles. Everything looked quiet in the bright afternoon sun.

Two young guys with packs and ropes blasted out one of the doors, laughing as they descended the steps toward the parking area. A twenty-something woman waved to them from a Jeep parked at the far edge of the lot. "Finally. I've been waiting for forever!"

The men tossed their gear in the back and clambered inside.

Blake eased his SUV forward and pulled in alongside them. "Hey there. Heading out for some climbing?"

The woman swung her head toward Blake, jaw tightening as she spotted the official vehicle. "Canyoneering. We've got a permit to run Keyhole Canyon. It's late, so we'll only get a few hours in."

"You work at the lodge?"

Her eyes narrowed. "You need some ID?"

He pushed an easygoing smile to his face. "No, nothing like that. I was told that there was some trouble around here last week. I wondered if you'd heard anything."

The guy in the seat beside her chuckled, running a hand through his reddish whiskers. "There was a wild party over in Cottonwood. I can't believe I missed it." He jabbed a thumb toward the guy sitting behind him. "Ethan and I camped out at Kolob Canyons so we could hit the Namaste Wall early."

Ethan's tousled hair made him look like he'd just rolled out of bed. "That was a sick climb, bro."

The woman kept her focus on her steering wheel, giving Blake little more than a dismissive shrug.

Did the topic make her nervous, or was it him? He kept his tone casual. "No matter. Let us know if anything comes up again. Have fun. I've heard Keyhole's incredible."

Ethan leaned forward to talk over the woman's shoulder. "Yeah, dude. That's what we heard too. Can't wait to see it."

Putting his Tahoe into reverse, Blake gave them a little wave. "Wish I was going with you. Watch out for each other."

"Always." The girl lifted her eyes, finally meeting his gaze. "And thanks."

The guy in the rear seat made some crack that made the girl frown. She jammed the Jeep into gear. The tires spun, tossing gravel as she steered the vehicle out of the parking area.

Blake backed into a spot and jotted down the Jeep's license number in his notebook. Something about the woman's expression felt off, but he wasn't sure why.

He rapped his fingers on the wheel, thinking about the plans those three had ahead of them. It had been too long since he'd done any rappelling—and even then most of it had been from a Black Hawk helicopter. Putting those skills to work in a slot canyon had been one of the main reasons he'd applied to Zion instead of another park, but he'd yet to try it.

Alder had mentioned that Katie was into canyoneering. Maybe they'd let him tag along sometime.

His mind wandered back to Talia, picturing her in a climbing harness and helmet.

Blake blew a long puff of air between his lips. He seriously needed this woman out of his head.

• • •

Talia guided the vacuum over the wood floor, scanning for any remaining slivers of broken glass. Nearby, a mother cradled a sobbing preschooler against her shoulder as she spoke with Myrtle. The manager wore her best grandmotherly face but flashed Talia a glare as deadly as any of the shards.

Emptying the canister into the trash, Talia sighed. She'd been working on the shot glass display earlier, loading the shelves with extra stock so they didn't have to continually replenish them. But she hadn't anticipated the brute force of a four-year-old bruiser rampaging through the shelves.

Crouching, she slid the remaining glasses a bit further from the edge, not wishing for a repeat of the earlier scene.

Myrtle was going to fire her. She could feel it.

How am I not even cut out to be a gift shop clerk? Nothing in her marketing classes had prepared her for juvenile bull-in-a-china-shop situations. The best she'd had was a course on advertisements for children. But getting a child to *want* something was simple. Apparently she'd needed an ad about not running in crowded shops.

Myrtle reappeared, her eyes looking more tired than usual. "That was a disaster. What if they had clobbered him on the head? That mom might have sued us."

"I'm so sorry." Talia moved a few more items just to keep her hands busy. "I stacked them too close to the edge."

The older woman walked over and studied the display. "I should have seen it coming. Maybe we could add a plexiglass lip to this shelf. Or a wooden railing?"

"It might help for the future." Talia crouched and examined the underside of the shelf, trying to picture how they could attach something. After years of living in earthquake country, she knew a few things about rattling glassware.

"If you ask me"—Myrtle lowered her voice—"that mother should keep a firmer hand on her child."

Talia glanced up, surprised. Typically Myrtle reserved that attitude for her workers.

"This is a dangerous place. If it hadn't been a drinking glass, it might have been a rockslide on the trail, or a fall. Parents need to keep an eye out for their little ones—especially precocious tykes like that. I could tell you tales that would curl your hair."

Straightening, Talia shifted a few more items. "I've heard people say most parents hover too much and don't allow their children enough freedom to explore."

"There are appropriate times and places for that. And I don't think the middle of our store is the best spot for a child to learn independence." She rolled the vacuum toward the storeroom.

Maybe this was Talia's opportunity. She followed the woman. "We could move the glassware over to the shelves on the wall. Those are much more stable."

Myrtle tipped her head to view the section Talia was pointing to. "What would we do with those books? And the jewelry?"

"We could display the books more centrally. And the jewelry over by the register. That way we can keep a close eye on the merchandise. Jared told me that several necklaces grew legs yesterday."

"You've put some thought into this." Myrtle surveyed the space. "Let's try it." She lifted her wrist to check the time. "Wait until morning, though. I don't want to be here all night."

"I could stay—if you don't mind me working alone. That way we're not making a mess during shop hours." Talia pressed her hands into her pockets, her fingers itching to get started. "I think I could have it done in a few hours."

The manager frowned. "All those heavy stacks of books, though."

"I'm stronger than I look." Talia kept her voice light. She didn't want to scare the woman off the idea. "Is there a problem with me working in the store after closing?"

"Not if you keep the doors locked. The lobby will still be open. But I don't like the idea of you driving home after dark. Wouldn't your grandfather worry?"

"I'll text him. I don't think he'll care."

A smile lifted the corners of Myrtle's mouth, her brown eyes crinkling. "The store could use some sprucing up. We haven't done it in years."

"I have several ideas I'd love to work on." Talia held her breath.

"Ideas, hmm?" The older woman turned to face her. "I thought you might. You've been like a caged tiger ever since you first walked in here."

Baby steps. Remember what happened in your last marketing meeting? Talia crossed the room, toward the shirt table. "I thought we could move the T-shirts over to the—"

"No."

Talia stopped in her tracks. "To the shirts? Or no to all of it?"

"Just do it. If you ask me, then I'll have to think it over. We'll never get anything done." Myrtle laughed, a sharp sound that seemed too large for her tiny frame. "I want results, not suggestions. Your grandfather insisted you had creative talents like your great-grandmother. So far, you've been a grave disappointment." The words were harsh, but a twinkle in her eye softened their delivery. "Let's see what you're made of."

Talia's heart pounded. "You're giving me free rein?"

Myrtle raised a finger. "For one night. But don't get carried away. I don't want to show up in the morning and find out you've transformed this place into an ice cream parlor or something."

"I wouldn't dream of it." As she scanned the area, a few more ideas took root. With a little effort, she could open up the center of the store and make the overall space more welcoming. What they needed were displays that invited shoppers to meander through the shelves and tables rather than just grab a single item and head to the register.

"And if I hate it?" Myrtle raised a brow.

Talia's breath caught. "Then . . . I'll put everything back where it started and never say another word."

"You got it." Myrtle snatched her coffee cup from the counter and headed for the door. "I'll be back in five. Don't move anything. I don't want you to start until closing."

Talia began a list. By tomorrow morning, this place would be a showpiece. She had one opportunity to impress Myrtle, and she wasn't going to miss her shot.

11

1951

THE CHOCOLATE BROWN and dark orange walls of Zion's famous Temple of Sinawava rose overhead as Henry held out a hand to his wife. "You can do this." He'd already lifted three-year-old Billy to his shoulders and stepped one foot into the Virgin River. The cold water rushed around his ankle, the current tugging gently. If she'd take a few steps into the river, this day would be worth celebrating.

Billy grabbed Henry's new straw Panama and plopped it onto his own head, the motion jostling them both. Henry gripped Billy's knee with his free hand. "I believe in you, Alma."

Her hesitant smile didn't erase the panic in her eyes as she looked from him to the Virgin River. She'd done so much better in recent months, getting outside and letting Billy play with the other children. But this was still one place she never went.

The river did more than etch the ancient layers of rock. It brought life and refuge to the flora and fauna clustered along its banks. While a second chance at motherhood had reawakened his wife's spirit, she wouldn't be complete until she allowed herself to step back into the water—into life.

On hot days, the cold water was a blessed relief for most visitors. Several parties were thigh-deep in the current, using walking sticks to keep their balance.

"One step at a time," he said. "That's all you need to do."

His encouragement got her moving, albeit slowly, like a child learning to walk. His heart soared as they managed to get knee-deep into the flow. Once Alma overcame this, there'd be no stopping her. It was little wonder she was terrified, after what she'd experienced. The flood lived large in his memory too. "You're doing well."

"It's nothing but a quiet Sunday stroll." Her voice lifted over the sound of the current. "Just like everyone takes."

"That's my girl. Cracking jokes in the face of fear."

She met his eyes for a long moment before turning to Billy. A tender smile softened the lines of tension around her mouth. "Are you wearing *Pappa*'s new hat?"

Henry stood taller. "Of course he is. Someday he'll wear a ranger Stetson, like his dad."

"Ranger Billy Eriksson." She tweaked the boy's toes. "It has a nice ring to it. But he might have other ideas when he gets a little bigger."

Henry released his wife's hand. He lifted Billy free from his shoulders and down into his arms.

Billy bounced and flung his arms wide, the oversized hat tumbling free.

Alma snatched at the Panama before it could escape, stumbling and pitching forward onto one knee. She crushed the hat against her chest, bracing herself on one of the smooth boulders just below the water's surface.

"Are you all right?" He crouched, touching his wife's shoulder.

She remained frozen. Her eyes slammed shut.

Henry's heart stuttered. He lowered himself to his knees beside her. "Alma?"

Billy reached. "*Mamma* okay?"

She opened her eyes and pulled Billy to her chest. "I'm okay, sweetheart." She swiped a few tears away before letting Henry guide her back to her feet.

As soon as his mother had calmed, Billy squirmed like a fish on a line.

Henry intercepted his son. There was no way Alma would permit the child to walk back to the bank on his own. Better to get them both onto solid ground.

Still, even with this hiccup, she'd made incredible progress today. "You're going to be all right, Alma. I promise you. We're all going to be fine."

"You can't promise what isn't under your control." She brushed her wet sleeves.

She was right, of course. But he'd do anything God would allow him to do to set things right. He placed his free hand under Alma's elbow. "Let's get you home."

She nodded, sniffling and leaning against him.

They set a slow pace along the one-mile trail that paralleled the waterway. In time she'd be able to enjoy the river again. But not today.

When they finally approached the roadway, Alma halted and locked her hand on Henry's arm.

Sheriff Moody blocked the path ahead, radiating authority like heat off sunbaked stone. "Ranger Eriksson, Mrs. Eriksson. I need to have a word with you."

• • •

The hot breeze rustled the shrubs along the edge of the parking area, the scent of juniper filling the air.

Alma balanced Billy on her hip and forced herself to stay still. The sheriff could be here for a million reasons that didn't pertain to her son. *Lord, You lead me beside still waters.*

She'd taken to whispering the psalm to herself over the past few years. Immersing her heart in God's promises often helped chase away her anxious thoughts.

The silly promise her husband had made was nothing in the face of God's will. The war. The flood. Even Billy himself. They were all in

God's hands. And she was getting better at trusting Him. But she still had a ways to go.

She tightened her grip on Billy's back and angled slightly behind her husband.

Henry shook Sheriff Moody's hand. "Good to see you, Sheriff. Is this official business? I'd prefer to see my wife and son home—we're still a bit damp after an unexpected dip."

The sheriff's grim expression spoke volumes. "I think you both might wish to hear it."

Alma bit her lip, fighting against a wave of panic. "I should put Billy down for his nap soon."

"It won't take long." He gestured to the nearby bench. "Why don't you take a seat, Mrs. Eriksson. That little fellow has grown a lot since I last laid eyes on him. He must get heavy."

She took his advice and settled Billy on her lap. He immediately fussed to get down, sliding over her knees and trying to reach the ground with his little cowboy boots. Their guest had probably fewer than ten minutes before her son dissolved into a tantrum. The only times he was content were when he was moving, sleeping, or eating.

Henry stood beside her. "Go ahead and put him down. I'll chase, if need be."

"Not this close to the river." The words jumped from her mouth before she could stop herself. She never liked to contradict her husband in front of others.

"I'm right here, Alma. He's not going anywhere."

She let the boy slide from her lap. Fear coiled in her belly like a rattlesnake preparing to strike.

Billy trotted to his father, grabbed onto his leg, and stared at the sheriff with wide eyes.

"You'd best say what you came to say," Henry said. "Does it have to do with our son?"

The sheriff grunted assent. "I'm afraid so."

Alma raised fingers to her lips. "You located his mother? After all this time?"

The man turned toward her. The sympathy in his eyes would be her undoing. "We're not sure. But I got a phone call from a reporter in Salt Lake City, asking about the Zion foundling."

The word pierced Alma's heart. "Don't call him that. He's our son. The judge said so."

"I'm sorry, Mrs. Eriksson. I meant no disrespect."

Billy took a few steps and crouched, his eyes fixed on a large Jerusalem cricket sitting on a rock.

"What did the reporter want to know?" Henry said.

The sheriff continued. "He'd been researching an abduction case—a baby stolen from a hospital in Salt Lake. Police followed up, but the case went cold."

The words sent a chill through Alma. The parents must have been beside themselves. "How can someone just walk out of a hospital with a baby?"

"She was dressed as a nurse. Said she was taking the baby to see the doctor. The woman disappeared and was never seen again." Removing a notebook from his pocket, the sheriff opened it and skimmed over something written within. "It was an hour or two before the hospital staff realized what had happened."

Henry swooped Billy up in his arms as if the story had struck a chord with him as well. "I'm sorry to hear that. But what does that have to do with us?"

"It happened two days before you discovered Billy under the bridge. The reporter is surmising that he may be that couple's child."

Alma glanced at her son, now resting his head against his pappa's shoulder, thumb in his mouth. "It can't be. Why would someone abduct a child then abandon it here? It doesn't make any sense."

"I'd have to agree with my wife, Sheriff. This is far-fetched. The reporter is reading too much into the timeline."

"I feel the same." Moody hitched up his pants. "But I thought it best that I warn you now, before this story goes any further."

Alma stood. "Further? What do you think is going to happen?"

Moody shook his head slowly. "He's a reporter. They can be as relentless as bulldogs. If the story triggers public outcry, it could get picked up by other papers." His attention flickered between Alma and Henry. "I imagine he's going to want to talk to you both."

Henry shook his head. "I'll speak to him. But he's not coming near my wife or my son. They've been through enough."

"Be careful." Moody tore out a page of his book and passed it to Henry. "Watch what you say to him."

Henry jammed the scrap into his pocket. "Thanks for the warning."

• • •

Crickets chirped a deafening melody as Henry rocked his son in the darkness. The porch chair made a gentle squeak against the floorboards with each motion. Billy had finally dropped off against Henry's shoulder about twenty minutes ago, but Henry hadn't the heart to return the little boy to bed.

Sleep had evaded Henry anyway. He'd lain awake for hours, his body as still as the sandstone cliffs even though his mind swirled and eddied. Billy starting to fuss had given him an excuse to rise and take the child outside.

He patted Billy's back in time with the rocker's motion, the boy's weight against his chest bringing tears to his eyes.

That day when he'd first found the hatbox, he'd sensed their lives were about to change. But like this? No one had expected this.

Lord, what are You doing?

He'd been asking the same question his entire life. Henry lowered his cheek to his son's hair and let the tears fall. The telephone call earlier that day had not gone as he'd hoped.

The reporter, Marshall Peterson, had grown surly when Henry refused his request for an interview. "You're a father," he protested. "How would you feel if your baby was torn from your arms, never to be seen again?"

"I know *exactly* how that feels." Henry had forced the words through gritted teeth.

The line grew quiet for a moment, but the reporter pivoted and continued pressing. "Then you understand what these parents are going through. Would you deny them the chance to see the child? To determine if it might be their son?"

"He's not their son. All signs point to an unwed mother trying to escape a desperate situation. She couldn't care for her baby, so she placed it somewhere we'd find it. And we've given him every bit of love a child deserves. Now you want to walk in here and—"

"I'm not trying to cause trouble, Ranger. I just want answers. The family deserves answers."

"They won't find them here."

"Even discovering he's not their son would be some comfort." Peterson's voice had softened. "It would close one door and help us focus our search elsewhere. Let me come photograph the child."

"We're trying to give him a normal life, and you'll turn it into a circus. We don't want this sort of attention."

The reporter had dropped the bomb at that point. "I'm sorry, Ranger Eriksson, but this attention is coming for you, like it or not. You can cooperate and have some level of input on what I print, or I can write what I see fit."

Once again, the floodwaters were surging toward his little family. And like before, there was nothing he could do to protect them.

The screen door squeaked open. "Henry?"

He shifted in the seat. "We're here. Billy had a bad dream, but he's sleeping now."

Alma's bare feet hardly made a whisper as she crossed the porch toward him, her white nightgown fluttering in the soft night breeze.

He swept the back of his fist across his eyes. “I was hoping you could sleep a little longer.”

She ran a hand along his shoulder, the touch mysterious in the dark. “I can’t sleep when you’re not there beside me.”

The sweetness of the moment almost made tears spill anew. When had he become such a softy? Shifting Billy to the opposite shoulder, he pulled her onto his knee. The flowery fragrance of her hair settled around him. “I love you, Alma. Both of you.”

“And we love you.” She trailed her fingers down the back of his neck. “Let’s tuck Billy in. There are still a few hours until dawn.” She placed a kiss on his cheek. “Come to bed, Henry.”

The distant sound of a fox’s bark echoed through the night air.

He’d meet with the reporter tomorrow. Tonight, he’d spend every moment enjoying the blessings God had given him. “Anything you say, Mrs. Eriksson. I’m all yours.”

12

Present Day

THE NIGHT AIR filled with the sound of popping gravel as Blake rolled slowly into the parking area and switched off the Tahoe's headlights. He backed into a spot and cut the engine. Resting his elbow in the open window, he scanned the side of the staff dormitory. An overhanging lamp shone at the end of the long building, illuminating the doorway with a pool of greenish-white light. A few windows flickered with a warmer glow, suggesting staff members were up late.

They'd gotten another report of someone lurking about the buildings yesterday, so he was here on "deterrent duty." After all, his white SUV with its Park Service logos was about as discreet as a polar bear in the desert. Blake pulled a granola bar from his glove compartment and tore open the foil wrapper. Not the best stakeout food, but it was easy. If this were the movies, he'd have a good-looking partner and pizza.

Then again, in a movie, he wouldn't be hanging out in a deserted parking lot in a national park, watching for suspicious characters.

With the engine off, the quiet of a Zion night pressed in—punctuated by cicadas and tree frogs. Somewhere in the nearby building, music played, the repetitive bass line the only piece that carried out this far.

After twenty minutes, Blake fought to keep his eyes open. He'd be better off patrolling and then swinging back through for another loop in an hour or so. It didn't make sense for him to sit here all night.

As he reached for the ignition, movement in the rabbitbrush on the far side of the lot caught his attention, and he stilled. The scruffy branches shook a second time.

Blake eased the Tahoe's door open, thankful the dome light was switched off. Stepping down to the pavement, he swept a hand across his uniform shirt to dislodge any crumbs, the solid bulk of the duty vest reassuring.

He could still remember his trainer telling him that with the NPS, one never knew what they'd face on a callout. This could be anything from a marauding raccoon to a drugged-out psychopath with a death-by-cop wish. Variety kept the job interesting.

Blake rested his hand on his sidearm, just in case.

Leaving the door open, he eased around the driver's side, determined to put eyes on his suspect. He slid a flashlight from his duty belt. Back in the military, he might have had night vision at the ready, but that wasn't standard issue for a ranger. Crouching, he leaned around the bumper for a better look.

The foliage sat motionless now, and all sounds had stilled, except for the thrumming bass in the distance. Blake questioned his original assessment. He wouldn't put it past his brain to invent some excitement. He'd never been good at sitting—

A few yards away, a clump of sagebrush swayed.

Probably just the breeze.

Only . . .

He glanced around. None of the other vegetation was moving. Just the one.

Was it large enough to obscure a person determined to remain unseen? Maybe. Motion closer to the doorway drew his line of sight over to the building. The metal door opened, depositing two young women into the night, their laughing voices jarring the solitude of the evening.

Blake directed his focus back to the shrubs, scanning for additional movement. An animal would likely flee at the disturbance. A person bent on misdeeds—it was anyone's call.

The women chatted as they walked toward the lodge, blissfully unaware of how the bouncing glow of their phones would make them easy targets. At least they seemed to be using a buddy system of sorts, and they'd reach the other building in a few short minutes.

The shrub to his right twitched again, drawing his attention back to the darkness. Blake lowered himself along the edge of the vehicle and peered at the far side of the lot. Whoever was moving was doing a fine job of staying out of sight as they drew closer. With the women out of earshot, Blake had a good opportunity to bring this to a head. He switched on his flashlight and directed it toward the vegetation. "Hey there. Park Service. Show yourself."

The motion ceased.

He probably should have called for backup. Placing a hand on his holstered weapon, he kept his eyes locked on the scene. "Show yourself."

The sound of a vehicle coming up the road complicated matters. Blake held his position and his breath.

The shrubs whipped apart as a small creature launched through the beams from the approaching pickup. The impossibly long ringed tail was the last thing to disappear as the animal vanished into the night.

Blake exhaled, slumping against his Tahoe for a moment. He'd hoped to someday see one of these elusive members of the raccoon family, but this wasn't how he'd imagined it going down.

As the white truck rolled to a stop, Blake couldn't resist a chuckle. Clicking off his light, he approached his coworker.

The window slid down, revealing Noah's bearded face. "You all right, man?"

"Just checking on things. I thought I saw something back in the brush, but it turned out to be wildlife."

Noah smirked. "I saw. You do know where you are, right? If something's moving in the undergrowth, it's probably a critter."

Fatigue crept over Blake as the adrenaline emptied from his system. "You never know for sure."

"You checking for the creeper?"

"Yeah." Blake rested his hand on the edge of the open window. "I didn't realize you were in this part of the park tonight."

"Just swinging through before heading to the campground. Good thing too. I mean, those ringtails can be unpredictable." He reached for the gearshift, laughing.

Blake wasn't going to hear the end of this for a while.

• • •

Talia moved a stack of shirts to one of the display tables, the teal color contrasting nicely with the stack of rusty-orange ones beside it. She rubbed at her eyes before checking her watch. Three thirty? She'd been here all night, but the store was looking better than ever.

The glassware stood in an elegant line along the window. Children's gifts and toys rested on shelves in a corner that had some fun cushions on the floor so kids could sit down to read the books. This section was visible from the lobby doors, so children would be drawn to the store as soon as they entered the lodge. And where children went, parents—and their credit cards—followed.

She moved a stack of woolen blankets to a table along the back wall, beside the large collection of indigenous art. Myrtle had contracted with several Southern Paiute artisans to display their wares, but she hadn't moved the product onto the floor yet. No time like the present. And the jewelry and intricately woven baskets transformed that area.

Talia boxed up some cheaper souvenirs and banished them to the backroom. Myrtle had said she'd been keeping the low-quality tourist items on hand to please impulse buyers, but all it did was bring a tacky vibe to the merchandise. Better to go with quality items and local art pieces. Rooms in the lodge weren't cheap. The clientele could afford classier souvenirs, and there were plenty of trinket stores in town.

Stretching her arms above her head, Talia sighed. She'd move the food items over with the hiking sticks and maps, plus some near the register for quick purchases before visitors got out onto the trail.

There was more to do, but she'd made enough headway that Myrtle would see what Talia was aiming for. Hopefully she'd be pleased. Because if Talia had to put everything back, she'd break down in tears.

Snapping a few pictures, Talia gave the place a final once-over. She'd taken a few before beginning the work, but hopefully they would remain on her phone as the "before" shots, not reference images for going back to the same old same old.

After flattening the remaining cardboard cartons and hauling them to the storeroom, she grabbed her things and shut off the lights. Was it really worth going back to Pops's house for a few hours of sleep?

Probably not, but the sagging bed was calling her name.

Talia juggled the keys to lock the door behind her. She'd added Gammelfarmor's padlock to her key chain, and the weight was comfortable in her hand.

Halfway into the parking lot, she froze, dazzled by the incomprehensible array of stars glittering in the night sky. A half-moon cast its soft luminescence across the pavement, making it look like a silvery sea for Talia to cross. As a dark sky park, Zion prided itself on keeping light pollution to a minimum. Thankfully she had parked under a lamppost, and the downward glow created a comforting bubble of light around her Volvo. Talia clicked the remote and the car flashed its headlights in welcome.

Working here had been a joy so far. In California, she'd grown accustomed to waking every morning with either a tension headache or a rock in the pit of her stomach.

This summer would only be a sabbatical, though. It made no sense to waste her schooling and talents while her marketing skills atrophied. Eventually she'd have to start searching for another position.

But not today.

She got into the car and rested her head against the seat, gathering the energy to drive home.

Motion in the distance drew her eye. A man walked along the side of one of the lodge buildings, just under some of the guest-room windows. The beam of his flashlight lit the ground at his feet.

A security guard. Right? All she could see was his lower legs and dark shoes. Was he in uniform?

Talia reached over and locked the door. She'd never have sat unguarded like that back home.

The man directed his light at one of the windows, stepping closer to the building.

The sight sent a chill through her. He might be a guard—or possibly a maintenance worker answering an early-morning call. But he might also be up to no good. Were there families asleep in those rooms?

She started her engine and let it idle.

The bobbing light vanished as if the man had clicked it off or hidden it under his coat.

Her stomach tightened further, and she reached for her cell phone. It wouldn't get service here, but she was still close enough to the lodge to connect to their Wi-Fi. Should she call it in, or was she overreacting?

Talia bounced the phone in her hand for a minute before reaching for the gearshift. As she eased the car into reverse and backed from her spot, her headlights swept across the lot.

He was gone.

Biting her lip, Talia swiveled her head, trying for a glimpse of the stranger. He must have ducked around the far side of the building.

This is ridiculous. It's Zion, not Palo Alto.

She couldn't call 911 for a guy walking around in the dark, possibly stargazing like she'd been doing a few moments ago. It wasn't like she'd witnessed him breaking into vehicles or jimmying a door open. The lodge locked the outside doors at night, and guests could only enter using their room keys. If this guy was looking for trouble, there was no way he could get into the building. She'd mention the incident to the front desk in the morning.

Talia checked the clock on the dash.

It was already morning.

She turned the car toward home. A few hours of sleep and she'd start thinking sensibly again.

• • •

Before heading home after his night shift, Blake stopped in at the visitor center and took in the wide-open space decorated with beautiful photos of Zion and a 3-D model of the park. Even at this early hour, visitors drifted between the exhibits, their animated conversations promising an exciting day ahead. The hubbub and energy were a pleasant distraction after a week of working nights. There was something satisfying about seeing people starting out their days instead of keeping a watch on the few skulking about in the dark.

A long line of guests waited at the two stations. To his left, backcountry rangers advised on trail camps, permits, and weather conditions. In the center, interpreters at the main desk bowed their heads over maps with various hikers, pointing out trail options and fielding a steady stream of questions about the park. Katie's voice cut through the din as she laughed with someone about a raccoon encounter in the campground.

His eyes roamed the room a second time until he located Alder. Usually his friend was easy to pick out in a crowd due to his height. But right now, he balanced on one knee in front of a group of four wide-eyed children. He solemnly lifted one hand, and each child followed suit. The littlest couldn't even be old enough for kindergarten, yet her mouth scrunched in careful concentration.

Blake joined the group, not quite successful in hiding his grin. He knew Alder loved working with the kids almost more than he adored rattling on endlessly about geologic epochs.

His friend ignored him as he maintained an unblinking focus on his young charges. "After me, now. 'I am proud to be a Zion Junior Ranger.'"

"I am proud to be a Zion Junior Ranger."

Blake lifted his own hand, schooling his face into a serious expression. Vows were nothing to be scoffed at. He'd made several over the years. The first time, he'd stood trembling in front of the army recruiter who had changed his life. And then more recently at the Federal Law Enforcement Training Center in Georgia. And a few years ago, he'd taken a knee during the airborne division's chaplain-led Bible study and dedicated his life to God. All three promises had changed the course of his life in dramatic ways, but it was his faith walk that affected him the most deeply.

These kids might not understand the gravity of the pledge they were making, but Blake knew. After Alder said his piece, Blake joined the children in echoing, "I promise to help take care of and protect Zion National Park and all national parks."

The kids looked over with wide eyes. One of the boys frowned. "You're already a ranger."

"It's always a good reminder of what we stand for." Blake nodded to the little guy. "Listen to this last part. It's important."

Alder cast him a quick smile, then cleared his throat. "'I also promise . . .'"

They continued repeating, eventually working through the entire final vow of the junior ranger pledge: "to continue to explore, learn about, and respect the natural world wherever I go."

Without missing a beat, Alder replaced his flat hat and handed each of the children their small wooden badges. "Congratulations, everyone!" With a smirk he held one out to Blake. "Consider it a promotion. You can quit writing tickets and come do the fun stuff with us."

"Yeah, right." Blake placed a hand over his official badge. "My job is where the action is."

The little girl standing beside him clutched at his pant leg.

Instinctively, he rotated, careful to keep his firearm far from her reach. It was secure, but he still didn't like the idea of a child getting too close. He bent down so he could hear what she was saying to him.

She lifted the badge and pointed to the front of her purple T-shirt. "Can you help?"

"Sure." He glanced over at Alder, who was doing the same for the older boy while the kids' mother wrangled the preschooler.

He took a knee, examining the girl's purple T-shirt, which read "Hike Like a Girl." Blake awkwardly fastened the wooden badge in the center of one of the large glittery daisies, careful not to jab her with the pin.

She touched his badge. "Yours is pretty. My daddy has a gold one too."

The children's mom—her hair swept back into a messy ponytail—smiled at him with tired eyes. "Their dad is US Marine Corps Military Police. He's hiking the Narrows this morning, but we didn't think the kids were old enough to hike through the river."

"Wise choice." He stood, joining Alder as the family made their way toward the bookstore.

"Didn't expect to see you here." His friend grinned. "Don't you have some ringtails to chase?"

Word traveled fast. "That critter was clearly up to no good. If Noah hadn't interrupted me, I'd have had it detained and cuffed."

Alder chuckled. "Is this a social call, or did you need something?"

"You're doing the program in the campground amphitheater this evening, right?"

"Katie does on Thursdays. She's doing her reptile program tonight. It's always a popular one."

"Live ones?" The idea of Katie handling reptiles was amusing, but he'd learned quickly that her small frame hid a huge personality.

"A few. I can take over at the desk, if you need to speak to her," Alder said.

"It's not necessary. You can tell her later. Can we go in the back for a second?"

Alder's brows drew together, but he led the way. "What's up?"

Blake waited until the door closed before launching into his reason for coming. "During the night shift, I snagged a couple of yahoos for DUI and possession. I caught them just before the tunnel."

His friend whistled. "Have I mentioned that I'm really glad I don't have your job?"

"A few times, yeah," Blake said. "Evidently they spent part of last night at the campground with a larger group—pretty close to the amphitheater. I had a chat with the rest of the party, and they claimed they didn't know the other guys—that they'd only offered to share the campsite because everything was booked."

"Likely story."

"Right. But not much we can do other than keep an eye on them. I know interp is the last to know about this sort of thing."

"I appreciate that." Alder glanced toward the door, likely picturing his wife on the other side. "Maybe I should take tonight's program. Or go along, at least. Though I hate to leave the kids home alone. Chase is old enough to look after things, but—"

"I'm off tonight." Blake shrugged. "I wouldn't mind learning about snakes. The reptile kind, anyway. I've had enough of the human ones for a while."

The creeps he'd arrested had several packets of fentanyl in their truck, in addition to meth. He hated seeing drugs infiltrating places like Zion. But where humanity went, their problems followed.

Alder's shoulders relaxed. "Thanks. I appreciate it. Though Katie would argue that she can take care of herself."

"We want her focus to be on her talk, not on her personal safety or that of the campers."

"Right. And who knows? Maybe you'll learn a thing or two." Alder grinned.

"I'm sure you're right."

13

1951

"I'm sure you're right, Ranger Eriksson." Marshall Peterson pulled a pair of horn-rimmed glasses from his pocket and tapped his tablet of paper. "The story does seem far-fetched, but I need to rule it out before we can move on to other possibilities. I understand my inquiry was unwelcome news for you and your wife. I've read a bit about your situation, and I admire everything you've done for this child."

Henry relaxed a hair, settling into his seat. "I feel for those parents, truly. But I need to protect my family. I don't want my son to be turned into some sideshow for newspaper readers."

"I can appreciate that." He leaned back and spread his arms open. "So give me your take on the story. Why are you so convinced that your son and the Johnson baby are not one and the same?"

Henry winced. He hadn't known the family's name. It would've been easier on him if they'd remained nameless and faceless. "We did a full investigation after the baby was found. There was nothing to suggest he was a product of an abduction. He'd been well cared for and—"

"How did you know he was well cared for?" Peterson leaned forward.

Forcing his feelings aside, Henry shifted into work mode. "There were no signs of distress or abuse. No bruises, abrasions. He wasn't hypothermic."

"Dressed?"

"A diaper and wrapped in a section of blanket—one from Zion Lodge."

"And you know it was from the lodge, how?"

"We have a unique pattern. They're woven especially for the park."

"That wasn't printed in the newspaper story I read." The reporter made a soft humming sound, his gaze traveling to the small window. "He was in a hatbox, right? Isn't that a little small for an infant? Did you weigh the baby? Measure him?"

The words stopped Henry. "No. We were more concerned about getting him care and attempting to locate the mother." He should have weighed Billy. If the abducted newborn had been a grossly different weight, that could have stopped this nonsense cold. "He seemed small, though it had been some time since I handled an infant. My wife said he might have been born a few weeks early, though not so prematurely that his life was threatened."

Peterson uncapped a fountain pen and scribbled down some notes, his brow furrowing in thought.

Henry shifted on the chair. "The Johnson baby—was he born early?"

"Three weeks, yes, and undersized."

Henry's stomach sank. "Any noticeable marks? Birthmarks, moles, the like?"

The reporter ignored the question. "Tell me more about the box."

So that was how this was going to play out. "A leather carrying case, silklined. Fairly nondescript. The bellboy at the lodge told me he hauls identical ones to rooms on a daily basis. He couldn't say whether he'd handled this one."

"Do you still have it?"

"I do."

"Can I examine it?"

Henry sat back, thankful to finally have a card to play. "To what end?"

The man's eyes widened. "Come now, Ranger. There couldn't be any harm in me looking at the hatbox. I'm trying to bring peace to this poor family. Do you have a reason for stifling my investigation?" He slid a hand down his narrow tie. "Something you haven't told me?"

He never should have agreed to this interview. No matter what he did or said, the reporter was going to paint him as the bad guy. "I'm not resisting your inquiry. But the box is a piece of evidence, and I don't want every scrap of information we have plastered across the front page of *The Examiner*."

"I understand. But I need you to be up-front with me so we can put this case to rest. We can help each other here." He folded one ankle across his knee, a bright argyle sock poking out from under his cuff. "I'm sure you'd rather have me out of your hair."

He had that right. "Tell me more about the Johnsons. What do you know about them?"

The reporter bounced his foot. "This was their first baby. Richard Johnson is a banker, and his wife, Beatrice, is from a well-to-do family. They'd been married two years already and were eager for children. When Mrs. Johnson started having labor pains, they rushed to Holy Cross Hospital. Other than the baby being early, there were no complications. On the third day in the mother–baby wing, a nurse came into their room saying she needed to take the infant to the doctor for some routine checks. Mrs. Johnson handed him over without a second thought."

As any mother would. The story sickened Henry. What had this world come to? The most innocent and fragile among society should be protected, not stolen or abandoned. A chill raced over his skin. Had *both* horrors happened to Billy?

"When the child's father arrived for a visit, the baby had been gone for hours. Mrs. Johnson was in hysterics, but she couldn't get any of the staff to understand her. Mr. Johnson hurried down to the nursery, but no one there knew anything about it. His son was gone. That's when the alarm went out."

"And what have you got on this mysterious nurse?"

Peterson cocked his head. "You seriously haven't heard anything about this? It was in all the papers." He pulled a copy of *The Examiner* from his case and dropped it on the low table between them.

Henry left it where it fell. "I don't pay attention to that sort of thing. Plus, we had our hands full."

A sly smile crossed the man's face, his brown eyes narrowing. "So you did."

The change in tone was like sandpaper to Henry's nerves. "What exactly are you implying?"

The man pulled off his glasses and rested them on his knee. "Stay with me, now. A woman dressed like a nurse walks out of a hospital, a baby in her arms. She climbs into a getaway car, tucking the infant into a hatbox for safekeeping, and drives to the one place nobody would come looking—a national park. After a change of clothes, she'd resemble any other new mother."

Henry didn't like this line of supposition. "We didn't have any new mothers staying at the lodge. I asked."

"She's already proven to be a master of disguise."

"Let's say you're right." Henry tried to mitigate the growl in his voice. "She carts a newborn to Zion and takes a room at the lodge. Even if she manages to hide the fact that she's traveling alone with a fussy, undersized infant, why does she turn around and abandon the baby? Especially after all the risks she undertook to abduct it. It's preposterous. You might as well be writing a novel. This is pure—"

A loud knock on his office door startled both from their exchange.

Henry rose and crossed to the door, pulling it open. "I asked not to be disturbed."

"Henry, what's going on?" Mattie plunged her hands into the pockets of her uniform apron. "I just came from your house. Alma is in a state, but she won't tell me anything."

He worked to temper his irritation. "Mattie—Miss Simmons—I'm in an important meeting. I'll explain everything later."

Her red lips dipped into a pout. "Is something wrong with Billy? If he's sick, I deserve to know."

Deserved? "It's nothing like that. Everything will be fine." Henry sucked in a breath. How many times would he tell people in his life things were fine even when the world crashed in around him? "I'll be done pretty soon, and I'll check on Alma. You can go back to the lodge."

She placed both hands on her hips. "*Fine.*"

That word carried even more meaning when it came from a woman's mouth. Henry pressed the door closed, keeping one hand on the frame for a long moment before turning back to his guest.

Peterson was scribbling fast.

Henry's stomach turned. "What are you writing?"

The man didn't even bother to look up. "Oh, it's all falling into place."

• • •

Henry walked the reporter out to the Virgin River. He'd refused to let the man meet Billy and Alma, but there seemed little harm in allowing him to view the site. A layer of clouds had spread over the park, and the air felt heavy with the approaching storm. "We won't want to be down here long. The river's been known to flood even when it's not raining here in the canyon."

A fact he knew all too well.

"I understand. But I appreciate the tour." Peterson had a camera jammed under one arm and a briefcase clamped in the other hand.

"We had a few reporters down here when we first found . . . the baby. They seemed to like seeing where it happened."

Peterson grinned. "I can imagine. It's a good excuse to get out into this incredible place. I don't know how you handle spending any time in your dreary little office."

"I manage." Henry eased down the bank, watching for loose stones.

The man paused. "Are there snakes?"

"Probably." The only venomous one they'd found at Zion was the Great Basin rattlesnake, but Henry didn't mind letting the fellow sweat a bit. "Keep an eye out for the striped whip snake. They're tree climbers."

Peterson's pace slowed. "I'm not a fan of reptiles in general."

"Then maybe you should stay in *your* dreary little office."

"So the woman dumped the baby clear out here." The man's voice held a note of distaste. "With snakes and coyotes?"

Henry stopped and waited for him to catch up. "We're not far from the lodge and are right along a major footpath. It's not like she took it out into the wilderness to be consumed by wild animals. Though she could have."

Peterson didn't take his eyes off his feet until they reached the water's edge, the footbridge casting a shadow over the surface. "So why leave it here?"

Folding his arms, Henry watched the river flow past. "You'd have to ask her, I suppose."

"What about your investigation?" Peterson asked. "Any clues?"

The first droplets of rain pattered down. "Beyond what I've told you? Not really. We were working under the assumption that she was a desperate woman who didn't want to raise a child. I ride my horse past this spot every morning, so there's a possibility that the woman saw my uniform and decided I might be a safe choice."

Peterson shook his head, pulling a pen and notebook from his pocket. "A firehouse is safe. A hospital. A church. But a ranger in a national park?" He tapped the end against his chin before writing a few notes in his book. "And you accused me of reaching for far-fetched ideas. It seems more likely that the woman decided to be rid of her charge and found a convenient place to dispose of him. You came along just in time."

Henry turned to stare at the man. They came from different worlds, that much was certain. "Do you always think the worst of people?"

Peterson pulled his camera out from under his arm. "In my line of work, I often see the worst society has to offer."

And he was all of what—twenty-two years? At that age, Henry was slogging through Manila's alleys, trying to keep his head intact. He moved toward the bridge support, intent on staying out of Peterson's photographs.

The man aimed his lens at the water, a tight frown pulling at his lips. "But I do my best to put a hopeful twist on what I write. People are drawn in by salacious reports, but they like to leave with a sense that good wins over evil."

"So you're looking for a hopeful ending for the Johnsons? What does that make us—good or evil?" Henry braced one foot on a chunk of stone.

"To be determined, I suppose." Peterson swung the lens and snapped a shot toward Henry. "The heroic park ranger saves a newborn baby from the raging river and then raises the boy as his own. The story sort of writes itself."

Henry turned his head, the inscrutable focus of a lens catching him off guard.

The reporter clicked the shutter again. "But then, there's two sides to every story."

"Or more than two."

Peterson walked over to join him. "Is this the spot, then?"

The sound of the river rushing over the rocks echoed against the bridge. Henry gestured to a bit of rabbitbrush at their feet. "Right about here. It's not something I'm likely to forget anytime soon."

"Any footprints?"

"None that I noticed, though it's not unusual for guests to come down here to dip their toes in the water. It would be difficult to isolate the mother's prints from anyone else's."

"Difficult to isolate the *suspect's* prints, you mean." He crouched and pushed the reeds to the side, seemingly forgetting his earlier hesitance about snakes. "You don't know the person was the baby's mother."

"Yes." Henry chided himself. He was the investigator in charge of Billy's case. He shouldn't need to be schooled by some two-bit reporter. "I'm not sure what you're expecting to find, Peterson. It's been three years."

"You never know what you might find once you start digging around." The man stood, slinging the heavy camera over his shoulder. "In fact, I discovered that before you took this baby in, you and your wife had another child. I was sorry to read about your tragedy. A flood, is that right?"

Better to not give the reporter the satisfaction of seeing him react. Clearly that's what he was waiting for. "That's right."

"Here in Zion, yes?"

"If you've already read the articles, then I assume you already know the answer to that."

The man tipped his head. "My apologies. I prefer to confirm facts at the source rather than relying on what I read in small-town newspapers." He turned his attention to the river. "Was it also here in this spot?"

They needed to move away from the river before Henry gave in to the urge to shove this man into it. "Different spot. Same river. Which is why I said earlier that we shouldn't spend much time down here. With the storm breaking, this water can rise quickly." He turned to begin the short scramble back to the footpath.

Peterson followed in Henry's footsteps as if afraid of the ranger getting away without answering his questions. "It's an unusual situation. One baby lost, another found. What are the chances?" He grunted as he pushed his way up the last few steps to the path. "Astronomical, I'd say."

"'The Lord gave, and the Lord hath taken away.'" The words were never far from Henry's heart.

The man tipped his head, the pen lodged behind one ear. "Are you saying God gave you this baby? Because I was under the impression that a courtroom judge made that decision."

The hairs on the back of Henry's neck lifted. "I don't know if the Lord *gave* us Billy, exactly. But He called me to do the right thing by him."

"Billy—nice name." He smiled. "And if *Billy* turns out to be the Johnson baby?" The mist gathering around the tops of the cliffs had turned them shades of muted browns and grays.

Henry glared at the journalist. "We'll do whatever is best for him."

• • •

Alma held tight to her son's hand as they followed Henry along the path to the Canyon Overlook Trail. Billy had ridden on his father's shoulders for much of the walk up the steep stone steps, but now he was determined to walk on his own.

Her husband had seemed lost in his thoughts the past few weeks, ever since his interview with the reporter. So when Henry had recommended today's outing, she'd been quick to agree.

A tiny lizard scuttled across the path, coming to a stop under a clump of prickly pear cacti on the far side. Billy surged after it, but she held him back. "Remember, we look with our eyes." She allowed him to creep closer to the little creature. "Isn't he sweet?"

Billy crouched down on his chubby legs, his attention locked on the gray-striped creature. "It's a giz-gizzard."

"Liz-ard." She sounded it out for him. "He's a lizard. Didn't he move fast? God made them fast runners so they can escape other animals who might want to eat them."

"Giz-zard." Billy pointed a finger toward the tiny creature.

"Don't touch. We don't want to scare him. This is his home."

Henry appeared ahead of them, walking back their direction. "That's where I lost you."

She cast a warm smile at her husband. "We got distracted."

Billy looked at his father with a goofy smile. "Look at the gizzard, Pappa."

"I see it." Henry's eyes softened as he gazed at their son.

Billy had picked up the Swedish words for Mama and Daddy. Eventually he'd transition to *Mor* and *Far* like most children did as they matured, but she had no desire to hurry such things. Hearing his babyish words made Alma's heart sing.

A warmth crept through her as Henry crouched to observe the reptile with Billy, the pair of them chatting about Billy's favorite creatures. The two of them were made for each other. Billy may not be their flesh and blood, but there was little doubt that he belonged here with them.

The very idea that he might have been stolen from another couple . . . it sent a quiver through her stomach. She turned away and walked the last hundred feet or so to the viewpoint. A soft breeze laden with the scents of juniper and pine swept from the canyon below. She loved the sweet smell of this place. Leaning over the railing, she peered into the canyon, the small creek winding through a forested area. As the cliffsides rose from either side, the vegetation became increasingly sparse.

Henry joined her, Billy perched high on his shoulders.

She slid her hand into the crook of her husband's elbow and rested her head against his upper arm. The plaid shirt she'd made for him was soft against her cheek. "I'm glad you suggested coming here. It has been a long time since I visited this spot."

"I know it's one of your favorites. And Billy hadn't seen it yet."

As if cued by hearing his name, Billy bounced up and down while pointing at the view.

"I think he likes it." She squeezed Henry's elbow.

"We needed the distraction." His voice was gentle, as he'd always been, even when she'd spent month after month punishing him in her grief.

A crow circled past, its scolding drawing Alma's attention from the endless views. "Has there been more news, then?" She should have suspected that he'd invited her up here to soften a blow.

"Peterson's article came out this morning." Henry adjusted one of Billy's feet so the heel didn't continue whacking him in the same spot. He slid a folded section of newspaper from his shirt pocket. "There's nothing new in here, but . . ."

Her throat tightened at his hesitation. She took the newsprint and unfolded it. Henry's photo was featured prominently at the story's opening. The reporter had caught his rugged profile, square jaw and all, as he stood beside the Virgin River. She scanned the headline. *Foundling Rescued—Missing Johnson Baby?*

"What happens now?" She tightened her grip on the railing.

"The Johnsons have asked Sheriff Moody to obtain Billy's footprints. They will be compared against the ones collected in the maternity ward when the Johnson baby was born. It's a security measure they've been using at hospitals in recent years, mostly to prevent the accidental switching of babies."

"But he's three years old now. Surely his footprint would have changed."

"I would think so, too, but apparently they don't." He frowned, playing with Billy's booted foot as it thumped against his upper chest. "Just think. It could put all this hokum behind us. They'll find Billy's not their boy."

"He's ours." She'd keep telling herself that. Anything to scare off the chill that had descended the moment Sheriff Moody walked back into their lives. A new thought struck her. "What if . . ." She bit her lip. She hated to give voice to her concern.

Billy squirmed to get down, the view failing to hold the three-year-old's attention for more than a few minutes. Henry lifted him over his head and pulled him into the circle of his arms, nuzzling against the boy's stomach until he giggled. "Everything will be—"

"'Fine.' I know." She hated to question the man she loved. But she also didn't care for platitudes. "But what if—what if they match?" A lump formed in her throat. "Could the Johnsons claim him? It's been years. We're the only . . ." She placed a hand over Billy's ears. He was probably still too young to understand, but she still hated to discuss this in front of him. "We're all he knows. Surely the court would see that. Uprooting him now would be cruel." Alma fought to gain control of her quavering voice.

Henry backed away from the view before lowering Billy to the ground, keeping one of the boy's hands in his own firm grip. "I don't know, Alma. If those prints match, I think the court would side with the Johnsons. But they won't match. They can't."

With one last look at the expansive view spreading out below them, she sighed. *God, You made all this beauty. Surely You care about this child even more.*

"It will be fine." She whispered Henry's words into the juniper-scented wind. The breeze fluttered the newsprint in her hand as though the scrap were a bird wanting to take flight. If only she could release her fear as easily as she could let this paper float off into oblivion.

Alma pulled her hand back. Best not. There might be information here that could help them. Especially if she had to talk her little boy through a difficult transition.

The floodwaters had pulled one child from her arms. If she were to lose another, it would be on her own terms. Because right now she felt like the future was speeding at them faster than she could prepare for it.

14

Present Day

Talia pulled past Canyon Junction and reminded herself to watch the speedometer. Even though she and Blake were forming a friendship of sorts, she shouldn't test him or any of the other LEOs patrolling this section of the park. So when the shuttle bus flashed its turn signal, she slowed down to give it extra space.

Three hours of sleep would not be enough to get her through this day. The changes to the store had kept her buzzing for hours, tossing and turning in bed. Now every muscle in her back and arms ached. Moving things around had been so invigorating that she hadn't realized how much physical work she was doing. But her body certainly had. After years of sitting at a computer, her muscles were not accustomed to heavy lifting.

Myrtle had been at the shop since eight, but Talia hadn't received any panicked calls or curt texts about the remodel. Then again, three hours was plenty of time for Myrtle to get steamed up over the changes and start undoing everything. Talia really should have been there at opening so she could've explained her reasons for each shift in location.

Pulling into the parking area, Talia took cleansing breaths, holding each for four seconds before "releasing all tension from her core," as Sydney would say. But it wasn't working. If anything, Talia's heart rate had increased. She checked the clock before grabbing her bag and hopping out of the car.

She glanced over to where she'd spotted the mysterious figure last night, and her chest tightened. Pops would chide her for not calling someone, but what would she have said?

Maybe leaving a note at the front desk would suffice.

As Talia pushed through the lodge's front door, a hum of excited voices scattered all thoughts of nighttime creepers. A crowd of people—fifteen at least—wandered around the newly decorated store.

Myrtle shot her a crazed grin from the register. Six people stood in line to pay, and nearly every display had a cluster of customers surrounding it.

As soon as Talia stepped inside, a woman with a handful of T-shirts caught her arm. "Hey, do you have this in a medium? I need two."

"Let me check." Talia took the shirt from her hand and raced to the storeroom. Dropping her bag onto one of the stock shelves, she sorted through the extra shirts she'd put away last night. Hadn't she put five mediums out on the table? Talia snatched two more and returned to the customer.

"Should I take these to the register for you?" Talia's smile faltered as she glanced at the display table. At least half the T-shirts were gone. Had Myrtle been rearranging?

The woman snatched them from her hand. "No, I'll take them. I want to grab a few more things, but I saw someone else carrying around one of these and I wanted one too."

"Let me know if you need anything else." Talia scanned the store. Her relocations were all still . . . relocated. But they were in sore need of straightening. "I hope you're having a good visit to the park."

"Oh yes. We hiked Angels Landing yesterday and Emerald Pools the day before. But today we're going—"

"Excuse me—" A gray-haired man bumped into Talia's arm as he sidled around a group of children clustered about the stuffed animals and puppets. "I'm sorry. Oh, hey—do you carry calendars? I want to get one for my office."

The first customer had already melted into the crowd, so Talia walked the gentleman over to the books and calendars. While there, a hiker asked about walking sticks.

She spent the next two hours moving from one person to another, darting back to the storeroom to grab armfuls of merchandise to refill the emptying shelves.

After dropping another stack of shirts onto the table, she caught sight of Myrtle frantically waving her over. Talia quickly sorted the T-shirts into sizes and made her way to the register—still several people deep.

"Thank goodness, I've got to run to the ladies'. I'll be right back." She clutched Talia's upper arm. "Girl, you've done the impossible. This is insanity. I called Lauren and Jacob for backup. We're going to need help."

"Where did all these people come from? Is it a group tour?"

"It's been like this all morning. Everyone who walks in the door of the lodge has made a beeline for the store." With that, Myrtle scurried for the restroom.

The next hour passed in a rush as Talia rang up items as fast as the system would allow. By the time the other two workers arrived, they'd already logged more sales than all last week.

Myrtle was practically giddy, strutting around the store displays like a proud mother hen, showing off her favorite items and sending Jacob and Lauren running for extra stock whenever needed.

Sweat dripped down Talia's back as she worked the register. Eventually Lauren took over, freeing Talia to finally put away her bag. It was sitting on the now-emptied T-shirt shelf. At this rate, they'd have to reorder by the end of the day, not next week as planned.

Myrtle ducked in. "Talia, no hiding. We've got company."

"I'm not sure I can handle much more." Talia had been ignoring her sore muscles until now, but standing here in the relative quiet brought the stiffness rushing back. Even her brain seemed to be running on empty. What she really needed was coffee. About a gallon.

"Caffeine delivery." Blake's voice trailed inside the storeroom.

Myrtle tugged Blake into the small space. "When he walked past, I flagged him down and asked him to grab us each a latte and a scone." She pulled a cup from his cardboard carrier and handed it to Talia. "You've earned it, girlie."

Blake was out of uniform, wearing a simple gray T-shirt and shorts.

The warmth spread from the cup into Talia's palms, the room filling with the mingled scents of coffee and pastry. She scooted back so there was enough room for all three of them between the metal shelving units. "Are you off today, Blake?"

He nodded. "I just stopped in to pick up a book I've been eyeing. Didn't realize I'd be a witness to your wild success. Myrtle tells me this new layout was your doing."

Myrtle spread paper towels on one of the packing crates, opened the bag of scones, and set them out in a nice row. "It's been nuts ever since I unlocked the door this morning. You sprinkled fairy dust or something. As soon as people enter the lodge, they're sucked into the shop like they've stepped too close to a black hole."

Blake leaned on the shelving. "You watching sci-fi now?"

She shot him a withering look. "I was watching *Star Trek* long before you were born. Kids today think they invented the genre."

He raised his hands in surrender. "I had no idea you were a Trekkie."

Talia struggled to keep up. "This flood of sales is all because of the redesign?"

Myrtle beamed. "People are buying things I haven't been able to move in years."

Lifting the cup close to her nose, Talia let the spicy fragrance of chai sweep over her. "This is perfect. How did you know?"

"I asked at the café. They remember you." He took a sip from his own. "So you're some sort of organizing guru?"

Myrtle laced an arm around Talia. "Her grandfather is Swedish. Have you been to IKEA? Those people know how to design."

Talia reached for the scones, breaking off a piece and bringing it to her mouth. She hadn't realized how hungry she was until right now.

"You're Scandinavian?" His eyes latched onto her. "I wouldn't have guessed that."

She swept the crumbs from her lips, his scrutiny making her nervous. "My grandfather is. The other side of my family is a bit of a mish-mash. And my grandmother was Spanish. That's where I get my olive complexion."

Myrtle's focus alternated between the two of them. "Bill's father was a ranger here when I was a little girl. Both he and his wife came from Swedish immigrant families. Alma taught Scandinavian folk art at the lodge."

Talia took another bite of the scone, her memories mingling with the pastry's sweetness. Unlike Talia's lively Spanish grandmother, Gammelfarmor had always been quiet and reserved. But when Gammelfarmor smiled, Talia had felt a warmth that reached all the way to her toes.

Myrtle had already gone on to another topic, apparently oblivious to the stuffy air of the tight space. "What about you, Blake? Where are your people from?"

"Me?" His brows lifted. "No clue. My mom never talked about it. She was pretty busy. Single mom—for most of my childhood—usually working a couple of jobs at a time."

The words cut through Talia. "I bet she's proud of you."

His eyes flicked up to meet hers, a thousand unspoken emotions traveling through his eyes. "Sometimes, yes. Sometimes, no. Like anyone else, I suppose."

He hadn't mentioned a dad. Would her boss press him on that too?

Myrtle cupped her fingers around his arm. "Of course she's proud. And so are we." She reached out her other hand for Talia's. "Did you know that Blake served in Afghanistan with the Eighty-Second Airborne Division? You must have seen pictures of when our troops were guarding the Kabul airport from the Taliban and assisting with the airlift that saved so many?"

Talia caught her breath. "You were there?"

He took another gulp of his coffee, eyes down. "I was."

Myrtle squeezed Talia's hand, giving her a pointed look. "He's a hero."

• • •

Talia closed the front door and dropped her keys in the wooden bowl in the entry. Once again, she faced the choice: Up the stairs? Or down to her room? The thought of a hot shower and comfortable bed pulled at her, but it seemed rude to not go up and have dinner with Pops. Left to his devices, he'd microwave leftover pizza and probably guzzle some diet soda.

"Hey, Pops. I'm home." She climbed the steps.

Pops came in from the balcony, a partly empty jar of hummingbird food in his hand. He slid the glass door shut behind him. "Hey, kid. How was your day? Did Myrtle like the changes you made?"

"She loved them." Talia made a beeline for the kitchen, pulling out a cup and holding it under the tap. "We were packed the entire day. I had to order a rushed shipment so we'd have something to restock."

"That's great news."

She gulped down the water, the cool liquid filling every dry crack inside her. "I thought I'd throw together a salad and roast some seasoned chicken breasts in the air fryer. Does that sound good?"

"You're spoiling me. You're the one who's been on your feet all day—and most of the night. Point me in the right direction, and I'll do it. I bet you can talk this old dog through the process."

Her feet did ache. "All right." She plopped onto one of the tall stools at the island. "The chicken is marinating in the fridge. All you have to do is put it in and let it cook for ten minutes, then flip it and do another ten." She sat back, her muscles uncoiling a bit. If she wasn't careful, she'd fall asleep right here.

He pulled out the tray from the refrigerator. "I was worried about you being out so late yesterday."

I'm a grown woman. Should she remind him of that fact? "I'm sorry. I don't plan to make a habit of it."

"Those roads can be treacherous in the dark. I hope you were watching for wildlife."

"Of course, Pops. A fox did dart across in front of me. I haven't seen one for years."

He frowned at the air fryer's controls. "And I heard from Hal Martinson that there's been some questionable sorts hanging about the area. Drug busts, assaults, and such."

She sat forward, the memory of the shadowy figure banishing her weariness. "Drug busts?"

"Yep." The cooker chirped as he pressed buttons, his brow furrowing. "How does this work again?"

Talia slid off the stool and joined him at the counter. With a couple of presses, she got the chicken started. "Tell me more about this trouble."

"It's these ridiculous devices. I never did figure out that pressure cooker your grandmother loved so much. I'm thinking about giving it to the charity shop."

She couldn't help laughing. "It's not that bad, Pops. I can show you. But I was talking about the drug busts. What did you hear?"

He retrieved a head of romaine lettuce from the fridge and began cutting it up. "We had drunk drivers and pot busts in my day, but rarely the hard stuff. Now you hear it all the time. Hal said this last one was hauling fentanyl." He shot her a look. "Do you know what that is?"

"Yeah, of course." Her legs felt a little rubbery, so she sank onto the seat again. "I saw something weird at the lodge when I was leaving."

After telling Pops about the man she saw skulking around the building, his frown deepened. "You should have reported that, Talia."

"I know." Her stomach tightened. "I just wasn't sure about what I saw, and it was so late." She shook her head. "I even talked to one of the law enforcement rangers today, but things were so hectic, I didn't think to mention it." Had Blake taken part in the fentanyl bust? She'd heard it was dangerous to even touch the stuff.

"I'll give Hal a call. It was probably nothing, but he should be aware."

She took another sip of her water, embarrassed that she'd waited so long to report it. "Myrtle told me she remembered your mother. Did you and Myrtle grow up together?"

He chuckled. "That we did. She's a few years younger than me, but all the kids in the area played together and rode the school bus together. Myrtle's dad was the lodge manager for years." Pops shook his head. "Your gammelfarmor used to teach some of the girls—including Myrtle—how to paint. My mother was very talented. It's probably one of the reasons she approved of your grandma right off. They both had an artistic eye."

Talia got up and retrieved plates and cutlery for their meal. The beautiful Cordoba design on the plates made her smile. "Was it hard for you and Gran? You from a staunchly Scandinavian family, and her with Spanish roots?"

He checked the chicken with a thermometer, then slid it back in. "Not as hard as you'd think. We were both proud of our backgrounds, and our traditions didn't get in the way. We followed the same God, both loved nature and family." He shrugged. "What more do you need?"

As he dumped the chopped lettuce in a bowl, a distant expression stole over his face. "Of course we struggled a bit at first. She was boisterous and liked to talk about everything." He smirked at Talia. "Not unlike you. And my parents had always been quiet. Not a lot of hugging, crying, or yelling." He chuckled, shaking his head. "It took me a while to realize Camila wasn't ridiculously sensitive, she just needed to talk things out. And she needed me to do the same."

"And did you?"

"I did. And she learned that it took me time to come up with words. She used to say I was a think-first kind of fella. She was a talk-first-apologize-later kind of gal."

"That's where I get it, then." Talia set plates and napkins on the table. "I used to think I was more like you."

"You got the best of both of us, Tal. Your grandmother would say the same. And the best of your parents as well. Your father was more like me."

"That's true." She dished out the greens, adding some cherry tomatoes Pops must have plucked from the garden. They were still warm from the afternoon sunshine. "How much of that is genetics, do you think? Or is it more the way we're raised?"

He set the chicken breasts out on a cutting board to cool. "I don't rightly know. Maybe a combination of the two."

"Which of your parents were you most like?" She could remember her great-grandmother, but Pops's father had died before Talia was born.

"I never felt much like either of them, as much as I wanted to be. Didn't inherit your gammelfarmor's artistry or my far's good looks." He chuckled, digging in the drawer for a knife. "Or his aptitude for fixing things. He could repair anything, machine or animal. Even people, sometimes." He glanced at the table. "This is nice. A proper sit-down. Your grandma would be proud." His gaze faltered, and he lowered his eyes and folded his hands. "If you don't mind, I'll bless the food."

She dropped the salad tongs back into the bowl and bowed her head.

Pops's prayer was brief, but the emotion in his words made her feel like Gran and Mom, and all her relatives, were sitting there at the table with them, as if their conversation had thinned the boundary between earth and heaven. And the sense didn't pass even after he said amen and opened his eyes.

Talia reached for her water glass again, desperate for something to clear the cobwebs gathering in her throat.

"I'm glad your changes were well received. I always knew you were going to do great things, kid."

"It's a gift shop, Pops. Not curing cancer." Her voice cracked on the final word, and she clenched her fingers in her lap. That was a dumb thing to say.

His brows drew together. "'Do not despise these small beginnings, for the Lord rejoices to see the work begin.'"

"Right." Somehow she didn't think God intended for her to work at a gift shop the rest of her days. This wasn't a calling. It was a summer job. "I'm sorry. I appreciate your vote of confidence, really."

He nodded, reaching for a bottle of ranch dressing. "You don't need to apologize. I know this isn't your life dream, but there's a reason He drew you back to Zion after all these years."

"I needed a break. But I'll apply for jobs and be out of your hair before you know it."

"Take your time, Tal." He met her eyes. "Zion is a good place to seek truth. God's voice can be heard through the water and the stone. Be still and listen."

15

1951

ALMA'S HEADACHE WORSENED as she read through another of Marshall Peterson's articles. The man was relentless, and evidently his writings were now being picked up across the nation. Henry had received calls from newspapers as far away as Delaware. Everyone was looking for additional tidbits and requesting interviews. So far he'd ignored them, but that didn't stop journalists from inventing lurid details to fluff out their pieces.

This one was the worst yet. The reporter quoted anonymous sources who speculated that in a fit of insanity, Alma might have purposely drowned their first child and now claimed the Johnsons' baby was her own boy, somehow returned from the dead.

Her stomach twisted. Is this what people thought? She folded the article, running her finger along the creases. Billy was so different from Eddie. She couldn't imagine mistaking the two. Edward's baby-fine hair had been light in color and his blue eyes pale. Even as an infant, he never developed the chubby baby shape like so many others did, including Billy.

She and Henry had missed out on Eddie growing from infant to little boy, so they'd reveled in watching Billy's transformation day by day. His reddish-brown hair resembled their canyon—the colors subtly shifting with the light and the seasons. His eyes lost the initial steely blue, finally settling on hazel. And now his baby fat had melted into boyish muscles—ones that took him everywhere at a run.

Alma drew the wooden keepsake box closer along the table and opened the lid. It had traveled with them from Minnesota as a place for jewelry. Now she'd taken to adding the ever-expanding collection of newsprint. Henry would probably feed the articles to the stove, but she wanted a record of their pain, just in case.

When this blew over, she'd destroy the clippings. Billy never needed to know about his uncertain beginnings. Eventually, everyone would forget—except for her.

She added the new articles to the stack, her fingers brushing against the hard, metal padlock she'd tucked inside. Pulling it out, Alma turned it over, squinting at the imprint: *H-C-H.* Park Service locks were marked with *NPS.* What could *HCH* stand for? Perhaps the *H* stood for "Hotel" or "Harbor"?

The weight of the object in her palm sent a quiver through her arm. She'd tucked it into the box that first day, fully intending to show it to Henry, but in the urgency of getting the baby settled, it had slipped her mind. When she'd come upon it a few weeks later, the item no longer seemed important.

Now the brass piece mocked her.

Alma set it on top of the most recent article and sighed. Without its key, the brass lock was nothing but a paperweight and a sad reminder of what Billy had been through. He'd lost his mother, but he'd gained their love. Some of life's most tragic losses were heaped together with blessings, forming layers upon layers, like Zion's cliffs.

She reached for the box lid, the flowers she'd painted as a young girl smiling up at her with the blush of youth. Before she closed the container, a photo on the top clipping caught her eye. Beatrice Johnson held her infant on the day of his birth, the woman's sweet smile cutting into Alma's heart. Alma had spent so long staring at the baby, comparing it to the first photo they had of Billy, that she hadn't paid much attention to the new mother. Below the image, a tiny caption read *Roger Dale Johnson, born May 8, 1948, Holy Cross Hospital.*

Her eyes darted back to the padlock as the breath seeped from her lungs.

H-C-H.

She closed the lid.

• • •

Henry searched through the stack of papers for the campground report he'd received last week. He'd spent so much time fielding telephone calls lately that his work was stacking up. He could barely find the surface of his desk.

Now that Americans were traveling to the parks in record numbers, the days had grown longer and more chaotic. He needed to talk to the superintendent about adding a few men to their staff. They'd already hired an extra naturalist ranger down at Watchman. The campground was filling up faster every weekend with more visitors choosing to travel by automobile instead of train and bus.

He flipped through several more reports, his hand stopping on a reminder about an upcoming event at Zion Lodge.

The telephone jangled, nearly launching him from his chair. He'd gotten over much of his wartime jitters, but the stress of recent weeks had let some of it seep back in. He snatched the receiver before a second bell could shatter the silence. "Eriksson, here." His greeting was a bit gruffer than he'd intended.

There was a moment's pause before the person on the line began speaking. "Ranger Eriksson, I'm glad I reached you. It's Peter Wallace, editor with the *Sacramento Bee.* I was just reading about you and your wife on the AP wire and hoped you might have time to—"

"Mr. Wallace." Henry lowered his forehead into his palm. "I—"

"—about this abandoned infant. I am told the footprint evidence was inconclusive. Do you have any comment on that? How does it make you feel?"

Henry's stomach dropped. Inconclusive? How was that possible? And why did some newspaper editor in California know that before him? He cleared his throat. "I don't have a comment about it at this point. I'll need to read the full report." If he ever received it.

"Do you intend to meet with the Johnsons?" The man hardly took a breath. "I would like to send a reporter and a press photographer to document this historic meeting—"

"No. Absolutely not. My family is not entertainment for folks to discuss over the breakfast table."

"I understand your concern—"

A knock sounded from the door.

"To be frank, Mr. Wallace, I don't believe you do." Heat surged up Henry's collar, and he did his best to temper his voice. "There have been a dozen calls already this morning."

Another knock sounded just as Mattie poked her head around the door, a large bear claw Danish balanced on a plate. She spotted him at the desk and offered a big smile.

"I have work to do, but you people continue interrupting with your constant badgering requests." Henry nodded to her before swiveling his chair toward the window, clamping the receiver against his shoulder. "I have no intention of speaking to any of you. No photographers or reporters are welcome here." If any arrived, he'd be sorely tempted to drop them down the nearest slot canyon and see if they could find their way out.

The smell of coffee drew his attention just as Mattie set a steaming cup on his desk. Whatever had he and Alma done to deserve her?

As the editor continued chattering, Henry clamped his palm over the mouthpiece and lowered it to his chest. "Mattie, you're a lifesaver. You didn't need to do this."

"Fred told me what was going on, and I thought it might help." She scowled at the phone. "Have you really gotten that many calls?"

"It's constant. And they won't take no for an answer." He reached for the cup.

"Give it to me." She waggled her fingers toward the telephone. "I used to fill in at the switchboard in my father's office."

Henry hesitated for a moment. But how much damage could she do? With a sigh, he passed her the receiver.

Mattie perched on the corner of the desk and twisted the phone cord between her fingers. "Pardon me," she said into the handset, her voice even brighter than usual. "This is Ranger Eriksson's secretary. I'm afraid he had to step out for an emergency." With a pointed glance at Henry, she motioned toward the door with her head. "Now, Mr. Wallace, what can I do to help?"

Henry didn't need a second push. He hurried around the far side of the desk, gulped down a few swallows of the coffee, and picked up the napkin-wrapped pastry.

Mattie covered the mouthpiece. "I'm due back at the lodge in two hours. I'll see to the phones until then. Get out of here."

He snatched his Stetson from the hook and ducked through the door. Several years ago he'd had the idea to slip the cheerful young woman a couple of bucks in exchange for looking in on his wife, but he hadn't anticipated that Mattie would take it as a lifetime appointment. Now she watched over the entire family.

Best investment he'd ever made.

• • •

"Ah, Mrs. Eriksson. So good to see you." Elmer Dawson hurried out from behind the lodge's desk waving a small greeting card. "I received a thank-you letter from the Clark family. Mrs. Clark wanted me to inform you that your class has inspired her to paint flowers all over her kitchen cupboards. And something about doing the piano next?" He took her bag of painting supplies.

"How sweet of her to write." Alma hurried after the fast-paced man. His light step and chipper attitude tickled her. He was a whole different man ever since he'd succeeded in wooing—and then marrying—Mattie's roommate, Irene. Mr. Dawson had even taken to calling Irene the Little Missus as if he feared someone would forget their relationship. Over a year had passed since their wedding, but his giddiness hadn't faded an iota.

"Where exactly are we going?" She struggled to keep up. "I thought I was meeting Sue in the front courtyard?"

"Haven't you heard?" His voice trailed behind him. "The movie crew arrives today. I don't want the two of you detracting from the scene as they drive up."

How flattering. Alma tied her painting apron around her waist. "The same crew that came three years ago?" She hadn't paid much attention back then, as absorbed as she was in her own grief.

"Some of them are returning, yes. Our staff is quite excited." He led her onto the back porch, where Sue had already set up her crafting tables with basket materials for the first session. "I'm sure glad Irene agreed to marry me when she did. I remember all the girls were quite smitten with Mr. Legend the last go round."

"And how is Irene? Mattie tells me she's expecting. Congratulations." She offered the man a warm smile. Mr. Dawson had been a confirmed bachelor, pushing forty, when the two had wed. He must have nearly given up hope of raising a family of his own.

"She is pleased as punch. We both are." He plopped her bag on top of a table, completely ignoring the other woman's things.

Sue frowned but quickly shifted her supplies so the manager wouldn't accidentally knock one of the Paiute baskets to the stone porch.

"I'm trying to convince her to stay off her feet as much as possible, but she's such a hardworking girl. Hardly a moment goes by when she's not fussing over me. I believe she's a little nervous. Perhaps you could pay her a visit, Mrs. Eriksson?"

"I'll try to do that. Though Mattie might be more welcome. I barely know Irene."

He cleared his throat. "I think it would be good for her to get to know more of the married ladies around here. The maids will all be busy with the movie crew arriving today. And I don't want the Little Missus upset by all the activity and gossip."

As Mr. Dawson hurried off, Alma greeted her friend and claimed the seat beside her. "A movie crew. Did you hear that?"

The woman's lip curved in a slight smile. "About a hundred times already this morning. You'd think they bathed in gold dust from the way Mr. Dawson speaks of them." Sue handed Alma a half-finished basket. In between sessions, she'd been teaching Alma her weaving skills in exchange for some of Alma's painting techniques. "Does his wife appreciate being called the Little Missus?"

Alma couldn't help rolling her eyes. "I just hope she doesn't call him Big Mister. I don't think I could keep from laughing. But I'm glad they're happy."

Several minutes later, they were both immersed in their weaving.

Sue turned the willow stems in her graceful fingers. "I heard about what's happening with your little boy."

"I believe the whole nation has." Alma sighed. "And everyone has an opinion."

When her friend said nothing else, a heaviness took hold in Alma's chest. "I'm sorry. I didn't mean that as it sounded. I'm just so weary."

"I understand." Sue laid down her project and placed a hand on Alma's wrist. "You have a mother's heart, and you don't want to see your son hurt."

The gentle touch unraveled Alma's defenses. "I'm really lost. I was so sure God had brought Billy to us. I never dreamed . . ." Her throat grew thick. "I don't understand what He's doing."

"Have you asked Him?"

Shifting in her seat, Alma lifted her eyes to the sandstone cliffs, the rusty reds, pinks, and browns echoed in the project in front of her. "Yes. I've told Him that we want Billy here, in Zion. But I also want His will to be done."

"You just hope it's the same as your will."

Alma dropped her eyes to the table. "Yes."

Her friend picked up a strand that had been softening in a tray of water. "It is good that you seek His will. But He's a loving papa. He wants to hear everything that is on your heart."

"Then what?"

Sue took her time finishing the design. After a long moment, she smiled, turning to Alma. "Then you wait. Be still. He knows where your son belongs—here in Mukuntuweap with you and your husband or farther away with someone else. Listen to Him speak. His voice is everywhere—in the stone, in the wind. And especially in the water. But you know that." She winked.

"'He leadeth me beside the still waters.'" She spoke the words softly.

"That He does."

Alma reached for the basket. "Your work is beautiful, Sue. Thank you for letting me learn from you."

The woman smiled. "We learn from each other." She reached for another willow stem. "Now, tell me more about these movie stars."

16

Present Day

HE HADN'T REALIZED Katie was a star. Blake walked around the back side of the campground amphitheater, surveying the enthusiastic crowd that had gathered to hear Katie's "Reptiles of Zion" talk. A rowdy bunch of kids took up the front row, eager to get close to the action. Parents and other campers sat farther back. Were they distancing themselves from the topic or from their children? Hard to say.

Katie was in her element. Rather than reciting dry facts about the various species, she wove in funny stories and enough gross trivia to keep the eager boys in the crowd interested. He would need to ask her about the blood-throwing lizard later tonight, because that was about the most disgusting thing he'd ever heard.

Maybe that was the real reason parents were sitting farther back.

So far he hadn't noticed anyone suspicious in the area. In fact, this was about as wholesome a group as he could imagine. Katie had interviewed the crowd a bit during the warm-up, and it sounded like a large contingent of the families were part of a homeschooling co-op, here on a joint educational and team-building trip.

Slipping out the back, he walked through the campground, taking in the mixture of RVs and tents occupying the nearby loop. Some of these rigs must've cost more than a house. He'd driven a lot of vehicles during his years in the service, but nothing quite as luxurious and cumbersome as these.

On the far side of the loop sat a short converted bus, its white paint dotted with stickers from various locations. The campers had spread towels over the picnic table and a Starlink dish perched on the roof. When he and Noah had visited earlier, the owners—a young couple—insisted they didn't know the two guys arrested on drug charges and regretted letting them crash for the night. They welcomed the rangers to look around their *skoolie*, as they called it. The man even threw open all the doors and hatches without being asked, almost like he was giving a tour.

If anything, they were *too* accommodating.

Then again, if the couple were guilty of something, Blake figured they would have taken off right away. They were booked through the end of the week.

The RV looked dark now, the occupants apparently out for the evening.

Blake hadn't seriously thought drug dealers would show up at Katie's program when he'd warned Alder—but he also knew the interp crew. Friendly, optimistic, and just trusting enough to make him nervous.

LEOs, on the other hand . . . While they were trained to be positive and approachable, wariness and caution were key too. Those were the traits that kept everyone safe. Someone needed to run the possible scenarios and stay ahead of potential dangers.

But for right now, he needed to remember that he was off duty. The uniform carried a level of respect—that, and the duty belt loaded with protective weaponry and first aid supplies. Walking the loop in a T-shirt and shorts, he felt strangely exposed. He'd met with a ranger special agent earlier at the EOC, and he knew they often dressed down to not distract from their investigations. At one time he'd considered applying to the Investigative Services Branch, but after wearing a uniform for so much of his life, he wasn't sure how to work without one.

A roar of laughter and squeals from the amphitheater caught Blake's attention, and he moved to where he could see the action while still keeping an eye on the camping area.

Katie was in her element, carrying around a six-foot gopher snake for people to pet as she rattled off reasons why the snakes were important to the ecology of the park.

He smiled and turned back to survey the campground.

A man walked along the loop with his hood up over a ball cap and his eyes glued to the phone in his hand.

Something in the guy's demeanor set Blake's nerves on edge. Determined to remain under the radar, Blake started forward but veered to the right as if on his way to the restroom.

Even with his hunched posture, the person's lean athletic build was obvious. Likely a runner. Or a climber. Whenever someone wore a hood on a warm day, alarms blared in Blake's mind. Usually it turned out to be nothing, but he'd learned to trust his instincts—even if lately they'd only pointed him toward wildlife and an intriguing woman working in the gift shop.

The man stopped near the bus before stripping off the sweatshirt and cap and running a hand over his head. The unkempt hairstyle and cleft jaw seemed familiar somehow.

Blake stopped at the water fountain outside the bathhouse and fumbled with the screw cap of his Nalgene bottle. If he worked this right, he could stand here for several minutes without looking stalker-ish.

The guy rapped on the bus's door. Shielding his eyes with his hands, he leaned in close to the window. After a long moment, he turned around, scanning the campground as if searching for the occupants. His eyes lit on Blake.

Recognition hit Blake with a jolt—it was one of the concession employees he'd spoken to outside the dormitory. And the man obviously had a connection with the folks from site B12. Ducking his head, Blake snatched a drink from the fountain and berated himself for making eye contact.

The climber yanked the ball cap low over his forehead before turning on his heel and hurrying the opposite direction.

For just a minute, Blake considered following him. But maybe it'd be better to play it low-key. The guy hadn't done anything, and there was no need to lay out his suspicions before he knew what they were dealing with.

Closing the lid of his water bottle, Blake turned back toward the amphitheater.

After all, he knew where the man lived.

• • •

Talia snapped down the lid of her reusable coffee cup and added it to the side pocket of her backpack. Her lunch walks had only deepened her craving to get back on the trail, so today she'd driven into the park several hours before her shift, intent on catching sunrise at the Canyon Overlook. She'd been working here almost a month, and it felt like the days were slipping away. She wanted to take every single opportunity Zion presented before she had to return to corporate life.

After locking her car, she dropped the keys into her coat pocket. The weight of Gammelfarmor's lock had become like a familiar friend, and Talia patted the bulge on her hip. Pops had said this was his mother's favorite spot in the park. Carrying something of Alma Eriksson's on this walk seemed fitting. Clicking on her headlamp, Talia headed up the trail. From what she read, it was less than a mile and fairly flat after an initial uphill section. The silence of the morning pressed in against Talia, and she shivered. She really needed to line up some hiking buddies, because hiking alone never felt like the safest option. Who knew what kind of wild animals lurked around—or questionable humans for that matter. Then again, there hadn't been any cars in the parking area.

She wasn't sure if that made her feel better or worse.

She had met quite a few park employees but no one she really clicked with, except for a certain good-looking ranger. Myrtle didn't hike anymore, and most of the other concession workers were college kids and international students who'd already made their own friendships. She was the oddity.

Talia crouched to retie her bootlace, the light from her lamp bouncing around the rocky outcropping beside her. She switched it off. The sky was starting to brighten in anticipation of the sun cresting the cliffs in the distance. She hurried the last section, eager to snap a few photos with her phone. Maybe she should text Jasmine and see if she and Drew wanted to do some hiking at Zion. Last she'd heard, they were exploring British Columbia on their way up the Alaska Highway. But maybe after that?

Blake's face wandered back into her mind. They'd had several fun conversations at the lodge. How awkward would it be to invite him hiking? He'd be the ultimate tour guide.

The thought sent a wave of heat swelling in her chest. She'd had her head buried in either school or work for so long that she never got much experience asking guys out. Her one college boyfriend had developed out of a series of group study sessions that eventually turned into private tutoring. Had she ever asked Holden out? Or vice versa? It seemed like they had just settled into a relationship without really going through the expected steps.

Her toe caught a rock in the trail, and she narrowly avoided face-planting into the dirt. She steadied herself, feeling her pulse speed up. *Yeah, definitely need a hiking buddy.*

Fingers of colored light were reaching into the canyon as she approached the overlook fence. The layers of rock glowed, deep purple and gray slowly transforming into brilliant reds and oranges as the light fanned across the surfaces like the touch of a paintbrush.

Talia drew in a deep breath, her chest aching with the beauty spreading before her. Tears blurred her vision, and she reached up to dab them away, not wanting to miss a second. Did this majesty happen every day? Or had God set this up, just for her?

"New every morning."

What had Pops said? She needed to listen for God's voice. Of course, he'd also suggested she was a talker, like her grandmother. Listening had always been harder for Talia. Especially since it involved being still and quiet—two things that had always eluded her. But maybe she was finally learning.

The verse referred to God's mercy, not the sunrise. But perhaps the dawn served as a reminder of this truth. He created the rocks and the morning sun, so surely He could use them to speak to her heart. Goose bumps lifted on her arms. She'd come here for a new start, and this might be the first time she really sensed His kindness all the way down to her toes. After all, He was the God of second chances. Of new beginnings. "Thank You, Lord. Thank You."

An army of birds sang a welcome to the morning sun, and she wished she could join them. But her voice was more akin to a crow's. Instead, she lifted a hand, palm out, as if the rays of light could paint her with the same glow they did the cliff faces. When she leaned against the fence, the phone in her pocket bumped against her leg. Talia sighed and fished out the device, knowing full well the view deserved more than a screen could offer. Even so, she switched the camera into selfie mode, smiled, and tapped the shutter.

She'd added several Zion photos to her social media feed in the past weeks, but every time she did, she couldn't help thinking of her coworkers slaving away in their offices and cubicles. What did they think when they saw these snapshots? Did they feel sorry for her because of her lost job, or jealous that she was living in this beautiful place?

Talia might just keep this photo to herself. Because it didn't matter what they thought. She was here for her own reasons, and God had shown up in a mighty way.

Now she could check *Sunrise at Canyon Overlook* off her list. The rest of the must-do items would have to wait for another day. Once she'd ticked all those boxes, maybe she'd feel ready to jump back into office life.

• • •

Blake brushed a hand down the front of his vest as he walked into the lodge. He forced himself to scan the entire lobby before allowing his gaze to shift to the gift shop. How many times could he *accidentally* run into Talia before she grew suspicious of his intentions? But even he didn't understand why he kept stopping by. She just had a way of pulling him off course.

Talia stood at the register, marking something on a pink clipboard. She'd pulled back some of her hair, but the rest fell wild and untamed to her shoulders.

No matter how much he chided himself, Blake headed in her direction. "Good morning."

Talia glanced up, the stitch between her brows vanishing and a bright smile easing her features. "Hey there. I was just thinking about you."

That made two of them. "I'm flattered. What did I do to deserve that?"

She smiled. "I went out to the Canyon Overlook this morning for sunrise, but afterward I realized that it's probably not the best idea for me to be hiking alone. As you succinctly pointed out once before—I don't want to be number ten."

"The one who actually goes missing?"

"Exactly."

He leaned on the counter, strangely touched by her remembering an offhand comment from weeks ago. "I never recommend anyone hike alone. But I'm guilty of doing it myself on occasion. Sometimes it's tough to get friends' schedules to align."

She fiddled with the clipboard, bringing it up to her chest like a shield. "I wondered— Would you— Are you . . ." A touch of color spread through her cheeks. "I mean, I'm sure you have plenty of buddies to hike with, but . . ."

A jolt of electricity shot through him. Was she asking him out? "You're looking for a hiking partner?"

Her shoulders seemed to relax. "Yes. That's it. A hiking partner. Or if you knew someone else who might be interested?"

So *not* asking him out. He felt the air leak out of his chest just a bit. Still, a day hiking with Talia was intriguing to say the least. "Did you have a trail in mind?"

A grin spread across her face. "I have a list." She moved from behind the register and darted toward the backroom. "Myrtle, I'll be right back."

The older woman came over to join him. "I was trying to be discreet. That sounded like an important conversation between you two."

He chuckled. "Not so much."

She adjusted her reading glasses as if she were conducting a military inspection. "Time's a-wasting, Ranger Mitchell. In case you haven't noticed, I've been trying to stay out of your way."

He folded his arms. "Out of my way for what?"

"She's single. You're single. I don't think it takes a rocket scientist to figure it out."

Talia chose that moment to reappear, waving her half sheet of paper. "Here it is. I've been doing my research, and these are the top ten must-see spots in Zion. I intend to hit all of them."

"Oh, child." Myrtle clucked her tongue. "Life is what happens when you're busy making lists." She turned on her heel and headed for the backroom. "I'm on my break!"

Talia spread the list out on the counter. "See, here's the Canyon Overlook. I've already ticked that one off."

The handwritten list was so perfectly spaced, it could have been done by a computer. "Fancy. You've got checkboxes and everything."

She shrugged. "I like marking things off. It makes me feel accomplished."

He bent his head to read the remaining items. "The Narrows, Emerald Pools, Checkerboard Mesa, Walter's Wiggles, Angels Landing—well, those two usually go together."

"But it gives me two boxes to tick."

"I see that. Isn't that cheating?"

"Don't question the system." She read the final ones aloud to him. "Watchman, Kolob Arch, and a slot canyon."

He wrinkled his brow. "Any slot canyon?"

She chewed her lower lip. "Well, I haven't done any canyoneering. I put that last and gave it two boxes because I'll have to find someone to teach me how it's done. I never learned to rappel, and I'm sure there's other safety stuff I'd need to figure out. It might be out of my reach."

And just like that, his spirits soared. "I could do that."

"You know how to do it?"

Should he point out how many times he'd rappelled from helicopters during Air Assault School? "Yeah, you could say that. And I've got a couple of friends who'd probably like to come along. Katie is really good at teaching stuff."

Something flickered through Talia's expression, and she looked back down at the list. "We can work up to that, right? I mean, I'm not asking you to haul me into a slot canyon on day one."

"Sure." Day one suggested a day two and three. Was she asking him to accompany her on all these adventures? "What are your days off?"

"Myrtle told me she's redoing the schedule. I could probably put in a request, but as the new person, I might not get them."

"Whatever you do, don't ask for weekends. You'll get laughed out of here."

She smiled. "Even I know better than that. I'll see if I can arrange my shifts to match. Are you sure you're willing to do this? You can tell me no. It won't hurt my feelings."

Yeah, that wasn't happening. "Sounds fun." He shrugged. "What do I have to do in my free time except laundry and grocery shopping?"

Her forehead scrunched. "I could help with some of that. You know, in exchange for your being my tour guide and all."

The idea of having Talia Eriksson wash his dirty socks made his skin crawl. "That's not necessary. You make it sound like I'm doing you a favor. I want to go hiking too. If anything, you're giving me incentive to get out there." He tapped her sheet of paper. "We've got boxes to tick."

She grinned. "Yes, we do."

17

1951

ALMA CLUTCHED THE small basket to her chest as she walked the path from the lodge toward the women's dormitory where the maids lived. The chill of the morning had given way to luxurious heat that spilled through Alma, from the top of her straw hat down to her toes. Henry had told her the story of Mattie taking over his office phone and putting the reporters back on their heels. He was like a new man, all smiles and swooping Billy up and tossing him into the air like he hadn't done for weeks.

She'd wanted to thank Mattie for a while—not just for this, but for everything. This woven basket wasn't much in comparison to all that her friend had done for them over the past few years, but maybe it was a start.

Alma stepped inside and peered down the long corridor. Mattie had visited her little house hundreds of times over the years, but Alma had only been to this building on a few occasions. She headed straight for unit number 5 and knocked firmly.

The door opened a crack, and it was Irene's face that peeked out. Her eyes widened at the sight of Alma on the threshold—or at least, they widened as far as puffy, tearstained eyes could.

"I-I'm sorry. I must have the wrong room." Alma fumbled with her words, checking the number. "I'm looking for Mattie."

"She's here. And I was just leaving, anyway." Irene dabbed a tissue at her nose. "If you'll excuse me." She hurried down the hall like she had better places to be.

Mattie appeared in the doorway and called out after her former roommate: "I'm glad you stopped by, Irene."

Alma studied the woman's retreating form. "Is everything all right?"

"Oh, you know." Mattie rolled her eyes. "Marriage, pregnancy, all that. I think it's getting to her. She used to hate living in the dorm, but we still see her here pretty often—like she misses it."

Mr. Dawson had asked her to check in on his expectant wife. Maybe she'd stop by and see her later. Alma remembered the gift in her hands. "I'm sorry to drop in unannounced, but I wanted to bring this over for you."

Mattie's mouth fell open. "For me?" She waved Alma inside her small room. "Whatever for?"

Afternoon sunlight filtered in the small window, creating a bright square of light on the rag rug beside Mattie's bed. A stack of novels stood on a bedside table with a lipstick-smudged glass.

"This couldn't begin to repay you for all the kindness you've shown me over the years, but I thought it might be a small token of my appreciation." Alma set the basket in the windowsill, the traditional Southern Paiute design she'd learned from Sue looking at home against the Zion scenery. It had felt good to stretch her creative wings and try something new.

"Alma, it's beautiful!" Mattie crouched to examine the basket. "It's far too nice for someone like me."

"Don't be silly. You have been a loyal friend for years—far better than I deserved."

The maid sprang up and wrapped her arms around Alma's shoulders, pulling her tight to her chest. "There's no repaying anything. I love you and Billy. Watching you emerge from your shell in the past few years has brought me so much joy."

As the two women sat down to visit, Alma glanced toward the door where Irene had departed. "It seems you are drawn to people who are hurting. Do you often have tearful maids pouring their hearts out to you?"

Mattie's gaze faltered. "Irene and I have been friends since high school. We applied to the Utah Parks Company together. Most of the staff is new, but she and I have been here a few years now. You understand how it gets. We know each other's secrets and all that."

Alma lowered her eyes, studying the edge of her homemade skirt. She didn't know. She and Henry had married young, and while he was off at war, she'd stayed with her family. "I admire your independence—all of you who work at the lodge. Was it frightening to leave home and come to such a place all alone?"

Mattie sat back in her chair. "We were both new that first summer. I'd already experienced some life before coming here. But she was a good Mormon girl, and she wasn't accustomed to all the dances and parties the staff throw. I think the high life here got to her at first. And some of the guests—well, you can imagine."

Alma shook her head. "I don't understand."

Mattie's brows stitched together, and she reached for a pair of pearl clip-on earrings that were resting in a dish on the side table. "Most of them are really sweet, but there's always those who try to take . . . liberties." Her nose wrinkled. "Men who think we maids should offer more services."

"That's— You're not serious."

The clasp on the earrings clicked as Mattie fiddled with it. "We watch out for one another. And Mrs. Whyte is good about reporting guests who get too demanding."

"I should hope so."

"She's also fierce about firing staff who put themselves in compromising situations."

Alma managed a nod. She had a couple of years on Mattie, but with her sheltered life, she hadn't realized what was happening right under her nose. "And you—you've had guests who—"

"Oh sure. You get used to it, though. But this movie crew." She shook her head. "I guess I'm getting jaded. I was here the first time they came—that was right after I started work. All the girls are starry-eyed, but I've been trying to warn them." She leaned forward. "On their last visit, one of the guys in particular—he was a bit . . ." She clamped her lips tight, glancing toward the window where Alma's gift sat. She sighed. "*Forceful* might be the right word for it. I was disappointed to see him return."

"One of the movie stars?" A stone settled in Alma's gut. "Was it Gary Legend?"

A knock at the door startled them both.

Another of the housekeepers popped her head in. "Mattie, I grabbed a newspaper for you out of one of the cabins. There's a juicy—" Her eyes fixed on Alma. "Oh!"

Mattie jumped up and hurried to the door. "An advertisement? I'm so glad. I need to go to the market later. I hope there are coupons." She grabbed the paper and waved her friend out of the room with a cheery thanks.

Alma stood, her heartbeat racing. "If it's another one of those trashy articles about Henry and me, I'd like to see it."

"It's just some—"

"Let me read it." She held out a hand.

Her friend pressed the newspaper to her stomach. "More senseless tittle-tattle. I'm trying to stay on top of it so you and Henry don't have to deal with this nonsense."

"I don't think hiding it from me is going to save us any heartache. I'd rather know what people are saying about us than be left wondering." She wasn't sure that was true, but it sounded brave. God knew where Billy belonged—isn't that what Sue had just told her? Be still and trust the Lord.

Mattie sighed and handed it over.

Scanning through the headlines, it didn't take long to locate the article. *Park Ranger's Wife Guilty of Infanticide and Abduction?* Alma's breath stuttered as she sank down in the chair. "Infanticide? How could they say such a thing?"

Mattie laid her hands on Alma's shoulders. "They're spilling lies to sell more papers. Nobody believes it."

Alma lifted her eyes to meet her friend's. "Everyone will believe it. It's in black and white for all to read." She refocused on the article, reading the demonized account of what she'd supposedly done to her son. "'Temporary insanity led a woman to murder her own child, sacrificing him to the hungry waters of the Virgin River. Less than a year later, dressed in a nurse's uniform, Eriksson stole a newborn from Salt Lake's Holy Cross Hospital and spirited it away to Zion National Park, declaring it to be her own son raised from the dead. Now the true parents are fighting back—before she can drown this child too.'"

Nausea spilled through her. "This is—"

"Claptrap. Slander. Gobbledygook." Mattie tore the paper from her hands. "I'm going to call and give them a piece of my mind. They're in cahoots with that Peterson fellow. I'll show them insanity."

"Where would they get such a scandalous idea?" The grotesque twisting of the truth had created a horror story that would have Mary Shelley and Franz Kafka quaking in their boots.

"Leave it with me," Mattie insisted. "I'll talk to them. Come on, let's get out of here. You don't want to face Billy and Henry looking like that." Mattie slid her hand around Alma's arm and helped her to her feet.

• • •

The iconic sandstone cliffs provided an epic background for a Hollywood Western, and as Henry approached, he couldn't help picturing how it might appear on a big screen. In Technicolor. Watchman and Bridge Mountains framed the scene beneath the blue sky, a couple of towering cumulus clouds boiling up behind them. He'd need to keep an eye on those.

The fact that several folks milled about the area, some resting in chairs arranged under umbrellas, suggested that they weren't shooting anything at the moment. Henry guided Duck along the edge of the wash.

The director, Mr. Bernard Dixon, lifted a hand to shade his eyes and then walked over to where Henry stood. "We're all set here, Ranger. You sure you don't want to join us? You'd be a fine addition to the chase scene. Your mount is a handsome specimen."

Henry dismounted, patting Duck on the neck. "He's a good one. But no, I've had my fill of cameras lately."

The man had removed his coat and now folded his arms across his chest. "I heard something about that. Seems like you're getting more press attention than our stars. Watch out, they might get jealous."

Taking off his hat, Henry swiped a wrist across his forehead. "I'm here to talk to one of your actors. I heard some rumors I'd like to squelch."

Mr. Dixon smirked. "Rumors are what this industry runs on, Eriksson. It keeps folks interested between pictures. But we do try to control which ones are flying around at any given moment. Is there something I can help with?"

"I'd like to speak with Gary Legend."

The director quirked a brow. "You and everyone else around here. He's a hot commodity since his last two films with Ann Margaret. Before I allow this, I'd like to know the topic at hand."

Before he allowed it? The words rubbed Henry like sand. "May I remind you that I'm not a fan looking for autographs. I have a responsibility to this park and the people who visit and work here. I don't believe I need your permission."

"Of course, of course." Mr. Dixon dropped his arms to his side, opening both palms. "I meant no disrespect. Only, I'm in control of Mr. Legend's schedule. Is this a legal issue?"

"It could become one if I'm not allowed to speak to him. Privately." He replaced his hat, tipping it against the sun's glare.

The man huffed. "I hope it won't take long. We're at the mercy of the weather here. I'll send Legend over." He strode back to the cluster of cameras and chairs.

Henry watched the two pillars of clouds billowing up behind Bridge Mountain. He'd need to post something at the ranger station warning visitors of the flash flood danger. Typically folks wanted to climb for the best views, but you never knew when someone would get the idea to explore one of the smaller canyons.

Gary Legend sauntered toward him, his fringed buckskin vest and tall Stetson transforming him into an Old West sheriff. A thick coating of pancake makeup made him appear to have spent years under the blistering sun. "Ranger, I heard you was a-lookin' for me."

The fake Western drawl burrowed under Henry's skin. Did Legend intend to stay in character for this entire interview? "I appreciate you taking a minute from your busy schedule to meet with me."

"What seems to be the problem?" He slid his hands through his belt loops, just above the low-slung six-shooter.

Giving Duck a final pat, Henry looked the man in the eye. "I heard some disturbing rumors about how you treated the housekeeping staff the last time you were here. Evidently some of the girls are afraid to enter your room if there's a chance you might be present."

The actor chuckled. "Ranger, that was three years ago. I came here for a job, and that's what I did. I don't remember any trouble. But rumors tend to follow me wherever I go, no matter what I do or don't do. I assure you, I'm a married man now." He winked. "I've heard a few rumors about you as well."

Henry gritted his teeth. "The accounts came from someone I trust, so I'm inclined to believe them. I'm aware it's ancient history, legally, but I wanted you to know that *I know*. Any complaints from the staff will come straight to me. And I'll shut this picture down and escort you out of the park, if I need to."

Legend touched the tin badge on his chest and smirked. "You'd do that to a fellow officer of the law?"

"Try me."

• • •

Alma swiped a dampened washcloth over Billy's face, removing the last traces of supper as the boy squirmed from her grip. "Bath for you later, you little prairie dog," she called after him as he scurried from the kitchen.

Henry folded his napkin and sat back. "I can't believe how much he packed away tonight. He used to eat like a bird."

"He's a growing boy." Alma picked up the empty plates and carried them to the sink. "Josie said her boys are eating them out of house and home."

"Her boys are teenagers. Billy's only three." He rose from the table and walked to the cabinet. "Do you want some coffee?"

"I can do that." She wiped her hands on her apron.

"You haven't even eaten yet." He grabbed her hand and pulled her close. "You were so busy making sure Billy and I both ate that you hardly took a bite. Are you feeling well?"

His tender touch sent a wash of fatigue through her, the words from the newspaper story clinging to her mind like a bit of lint. She melted into his embrace, letting her cheek come to rest against his shoulder. "I'm not hungry. Just weary. Bone weary."

He slid his hands up her back, hooking a thumb into her apron ties. "Me too. Let's get him to bed early tonight, shall we?"

"I'm hoping the warm bath will help settle him down."

"Sit for a few minutes. I'll make the coffee and then we'll gang up on the kid and rustle him into bed."

She sighed, not wanting to let go of her husband. Maybe she could just lean on him all evening. "All right. But no sugar in mine. We're running low, and I want to bake a cake tomorrow for Mattie's birthday."

"Always putting others first. That's my girl."

As she sat down, the tension that had held her upright for the past few hours seeped out through her toes. Coffee was her only hope of making it until bedtime.

Henry filled the percolator and placed it on the burner as he filled her in regarding his visit with Gary Legend. "The man's trouble. He claims to have mended his ways, but I can't say as I believe him."

"My mother used to say you could pour perfume on a polecat, but he'd still stink."

"I told him I'd be keeping an eye on him, but he didn't seem concerned. I think the man is accustomed to an audience."

She closed her eyes. "Probably so."

A rapping on the door jerked her back to alertness. She moved to rise.

Henry waved her to stay where she was. "I'll get it. It's probably George. I asked him to come get me if there were any problems in the campground tonight. Fred is down with influenza. So much for an early night."

As he swung the door open, a man stood on the step, a short woman hovering behind him. "Ranger Eriksson?"

"Yes?" Henry stepped through the door and pulled it shut behind him, blocking Alma's view.

Alma rose, quickly untied her apron, and ran a hand over her hair. They didn't often have guests who weren't Park Service. She turned off the coffee before inching the curtain aside to spy out the window.

The woman clung to the man's elbow, a checked silk scarf covering her hair. He sported a dark brown suit, his fedora pushed back to reveal a round face with a mustache.

The voices were too low for her to hear, so she moved closer to the door, peering out the crisscross windows of the Dutch door.

Henry's shoulders were so stiff she could see muscles in the sides of his neck. His voice rose. "You shouldn't have come. I don't want my family disturbed."

The woman touched the man's arm and spoke quietly to him, her face turning toward the house.

Alma dropped the curtain as if it were hot to the touch. The Johnsons. She recognized Mrs. Johnson from her photo in *The Examiner.* Sliding her hands along the counter, Alma tried to steady her breathing.

"I'm sorry for what you've gone through, but our son is not your child. If I thought he was, even for a moment, it'd be a different story." Her husband's voice softened. "We lost a baby too. Did you know that?"

She closed her eyes, thankful Henry had intercepted the couple. She wasn't sure she could face the poor lady—a mother with empty arms—so like she had once been. Alma drew one hand to her chest, pressing against the seed of sorrow that still lived there. God had helped her walk out of the darkness, but this poor woman?

"He leadeth me beside the still waters." The verse filtered through her thoughts.

"Lord, what is it You want from me?" After a shaky breath, she whispered a few more lines of the psalm to quiet her fears. "'The Lord is my shepherd; I shall not want. He maketh me to lie down in green pastures: he leadeth me beside the still waters.'" She swallowed hard, closing her eyes again to picture the Virgin River flowing through the heart of the canyon. They weren't green pastures, but it was the place God had sealed in her heart.

"'Thou preparest a table before me in the presence of mine enemies . . .'" The words stalled on her tongue. *A table.*

The Johnsons were not her enemy. The fact settled into her soul like a whisper. Mrs. Johnson was a grieving mother.

Straightening, Alma grasped the doorknob, cold against her fingertips. She eased the door open and took three steps to stand behind her husband. She touched his back. "Henry, let them come in."

18

Present Day

Talia pressed her palms against the tops of her thighs, fighting to catch her breath. They hadn't gone far on Watchman Trail, but the first segment was a long climb. At least Blake had pulled some distance ahead, so he wasn't there to witness her humiliation. The summer sunshine beat on her back, turning her cute black T-shirt into a steam oven. So much for this stuff wicking away moisture. Apparently any fabric had its limits. Lots of women hiked in sports bras and spandex shorts, but she wasn't ready for anyone to see that much of her. Especially Blake.

He trotted down the hill toward her. "You okay? I looked back and you were gone."

"Just trying to find where I stashed my energy." She tried to ignore the droplet of sweat charting a path down her spine. "Evidently desk life doesn't prepare you for hiking adventures."

He reached over to her pack and slid the water bottle from the side pouch. "Drink. It's hot today, and you're losing water faster than you're putting it in."

So he's aware I'm a sweaty mess. Perfect. She uncapped the bottle and took a sip. The water soothed her throat, dusty dry from the panting she'd been doing. As she stood in the shade of a twisted juniper tree, she waited for her pulse to slow. "If I can't handle this, maybe I should reevaluate my list. I had this trail marked as easy. What will I do on Angels Landing?"

He smiled, running a hand over the back of his neck. "You take it slow and keep putting one foot in front of the other. I haven't done that one yet, but I hear it's more of a mind game than anything. You afraid of heights?"

She plucked the back of her shirt away from her skin, letting a whiff of fresh air cool the area. "Not too bad. You?"

"Not since I fast lined out of my first Black Hawk."

She guzzled another drink. "Right. I forgot who I was dealing with." She shook her head. "That's intense. I must look like a weakling." She capped the bottle and slid it into her pack.

Blake followed her up the path. "Like I said, it's a mind game. Your brain concocts all these reasons you shouldn't do something, but you power through. Once you check the safety, of course. I'm not stupid."

"I'm glad to hear it"—she dug her hiking boot against the stony path, pushing herself up the last stretch—"since you said you'd teach me canyoneering. Unless today has changed your mind."

He adjusted his ball cap. "Not at all. You can handle it. You've got ranger DNA, after all. And what was it Myrtle was saying—Swedish organizational skills?"

She turned and surveyed the path ahead. It seemed to be flattening out, even if there was still a long way to go to the viewpoint. But maybe she'd be able to hike and talk at the same time rather than gasping for breath every few steps. "I think that was an IKEA joke. But what do I know?"

"The Swedes were Vikings, right? That means you're tough. Your people probably looted and pillaged my people, wherever they were from."

"You really don't know what your heritage is? That seems so odd to me." Talia sidestepped a loose rock.

"It might be fun to find out someday. I've thought about doing one of those DNA tests. I hear they're pretty accurate."

"Maybe you're a Viking too. Or a Spartan? Some kind of warrior people."

"Aztec? Mongol?"

A snake rustled through the brush next to Talia's feet, and she jumped back a few steps, halting just before she slammed into Blake. The touch of his hand against the small of her back kicked her pulse up faster than the reptile ever could.

"Just a gopher snake. Nothing to worry about." His voice held a note of laughter.

"I know, it just startled me." She faced him, the closeness sending a quiver through her gut. *Get it together, Talia. This isn't a date.* "I'm not afraid of snakes. Pops taught me all about Utah reptiles when I was a kid. He's fascinated by them."

"You should hear my friend Katie talk about lizards. It gave me a nightmare or two."

He'd mentioned that name before. Girlfriend? A tickle lodged in her throat.

"Oh yeah? She's into both climbing and lizards?" There was no competing with a woman like that. Not that she wanted to.

"She's an interpretive ranger. She and Alder work at the visitor center."

"And Alder is?"

He grinned. "Her husband. All-around geology geek and father of three."

The surge of joy that coursed through her was humiliating. Obviously she'd lost her mind. "Oh, nice. And that's who we're going to go canyoneering with?"

"You said you wanted to meet people. They're my people. Friends and landlords, all rolled into one." He gestured up the trail. "We're almost there. The trail to the right will get us to the lookout."

She focused on the path, doing her best to rein in her senses. She'd come to Zion to reset her life, not throw herself at ex-military law enforcement rangers. Jasmine would have a field day with this.

As they approached the viewpoint, the canyon opened up below them, stealing Talia's breath—in a good way this time. "That's the visitor center down there, isn't it? And the campground. I've never seen it from above."

"I thought you spent a lot of days here when you were a kid."

"I did, but we didn't hike much. I remember riding horses with Pops along the Sand Bench Trail, and we always hiked the Riverside Walk out toward the Narrows. I think I've been to Scout Lookout, but I was pretty young."

They chose a good place to sit and fell silent as they enjoyed the view. The Watchman rose to the south, the triangular peak standing near the entrance to the park and Springdale beyond. "I love how green it is down along the river. It's like a ribbon of trees cutting through the desert."

He pulled a granola bar from his bag. "Looks peaceful from here. You can't see the thousands of people streaming through that entrance station complete with demands, problems, and careless ways."

The troubled look on his face held her attention. "That's a sad thought. How about 'all those people who are about to experience the best day of their lives'?"

He grimaced. "That's why I get jealous of Alder and Katie sometimes. They experience our visitors' favorite moments—cute little junior rangers, people petting a lizard for the first time, a camper excited to head out on the trail. I tend to get the opposite: people in crisis, breaking laws, causing trouble." Blake offered her a hesitant smile. "Not always. But it seems to happen more and more."

"Like your big drug bust? Everyone's saying you're quite the hero."

"Just a couple of idiots. Then we've got numerous reports of someone lurking outside the staff dormitory."

"Would that be the same creeper I saw hanging around the lodge?"

He met her eyes. "I heard about that. It's possible. Someone I interviewed regarding the case turned up at the campground, with another suspicious group—related to the bust."

She flicked a rock out from under her leg. "So creeper guy and the drug traffickers might be connected? Makes sense. Do you think there are drug issues among the lodge staff?"

He tipped his head back, gazing up toward the blue sky. "People are always using. My fear is someone is selling."

"Not good."

"Typically folks fly through this park. We deal with them for a day or two, not for weeks on end. So most of our investigations are cut-and-dried, not ongoing. Plus, the Park Service has the Investigative Services Branch—special agents—for that."

"You've called them?" Talia studied Blake's furrowed brow. She should be soaking in the view, but his brooding demeanor was infinitely distracting.

"With the exception of the drug bust, everything is conjecture." He shrugged. "We have no signs of continued illegal activity. No more complaints at the lodge, the campers have moved on—life seems to be back to normal."

She leaned forward, fighting the desire to rub a hand across his stiff shoulders. "So why do you still have that worried expression on your face?"

Blake scrubbed both palms over his face as if to wipe it away. And it worked—to a degree. "I don't know. I'm probably looking for trouble that isn't there. But let's call it a hunch."

"Pops says we should always trust our instincts. And he was a ranger here for years."

"I'd like to meet him sometime. I've heard stories."

She fiddled with the strap on her daypack. Did she dare? "Come by for dinner tonight. He enjoys swapping ranger stories."

A chipmunk scuttled through the juniper bush nearby, popping his head out at the word *dinner*.

Blake frowned. "I couldn't just show up like that. It seems rude."

"We're low-key. And Pops would love it." *So would I.*

He pushed to his feet, wandering a few steps away. "Maybe next week after we hike Angels Landing? I told Alder's son I'd help him with a homework project tonight after I got back."

Hopefully she hadn't scared him off. She slid her hands down the tired muscles in her legs. "Okay, but you're just giving him time to come up with more stories."

Blake grinned. "Maybe by then, I'll have a few of my own."

She stood, brushing the dirt from her rear end. "Be careful what you wish for."

• • •

A week later, Talia slid her damp palms along the heavy chain helping her navigate the narrow rock ledge leading to Angels Landing. The sweat dotting her brow wasn't just from the exertion.

The ragged edge of the cliff seemed to be mere inches from her lug-soled hiking boots. She turned her eyes back to the metal links in her hand and reminded herself that they were bolted to the rock. As long as she kept a good hold and didn't look down, she would be fine.

The fact that she'd been reading a copy of *Death in Zion National Park* during her last coffee break probably didn't help. Eighteen people had died on this trail from taking a bad step. It was a good thing she'd gotten that heart condition repaired when she was younger. A fainting spell here could be lethal.

"Why am I doing this again?" Her voice trembled nearly as bad as her calves.

"Because it's on your list," Blake answered from somewhere far ahead.

"That list is going to be the death of me."

A man cleared his throat loudly behind her. "Do you mind if I go past?"

She tried not to notice the sheer drop-off on both sides of the trail as she glanced back at the athletic-looking dude creeping up on her. The watercolor design of Arches National Park on his spandex compression shirt made her stomach sink. ZetaWear had released the new line even though Lissa's scathing reports were causing waves in the industry.

Talia turned her eyes away. "Is there enough space?"

"No problemo." He sauntered up like the incline was nothing more than a treadmill. As his shoulder bumped hers, she ducked her head, overpowered by the mingled odors of sweat, Old Spice, and coconut-scented sunblock.

As soon as he made his way along the narrow trail, she kept her focus on the dusty toes of her hikers rather than the mind-numbing abyss on either side. Every muscle in her legs was screaming to sit down, just to crouch here on the edge of the world and let everyone pass by.

Instead of a check mark next to *Angels Landing*, she'd draw a line through it. Just like she'd done with her career.

"You okay?" Blake's voice came from a distance.

"Just c-catching my breath." Her vision frayed around the edges like a scrap of loosely woven silk. She didn't dare lift her head.

His footsteps shuffled along the trail. He must be backtracking. "We can turn around if the trail's too much."

"Never." The word jumped from her mouth before she even stopped to consider the possibilities.

"Tal." His hand touched hers, settling on top of her fingers. "You've been hunkered down here for five minutes."

Hearing him use her grandfather's pet name brought up a well of emotion. "I didn't realize it had been that long." She sneaked a peek under her arm at the trail behind her. A group of three women waited, obviously not daring to pass on the narrow stretch. "I'm holding up the line."

Blake rubbed his thumb along her pale knuckles, devoid of color from gripping the metal for so long. "Don't worry about them. Take your time." He bent low to meet her eyes. "Look at me."

Talia didn't even remember squatting down. She blinked back tears, rubbing her arm against her cheek before focusing on his face. He hadn't shaved this morning, a few coppery bristles catching glints of the morning sun. How could a man with dark hair have red whiskers in his beard? Her fingers tingled with a sudden desire to touch them. The distraction was enough to ease a bit of the tension from her arms.

He quirked a smile, as if aware of the stupid turn of her thoughts. "A few deep breaths and you'll feel better."

"They're waiting on me."

"It's all right. Breathe."

She did, watching the rise and fall of his chest.

Blake took a water bottle from his hip and uncapped it. "Here, take a sip."

"I have my own." Not that she dared reach for it. Freeing one hand from the links, she accepted the metal canister from him and choked down a mouthful of water before handing it back.

He casually returned it to his side pocket like they had all the time in the world. "Now, do you want to go forward—or back?" Blake's green eyes held flecks of gold too. How had she never noticed that? He held out a hand to her. "No judgment."

She took it, the coolness from the water bottle still lingering in his palm. For a moment, she imagined what it would feel like pressed gently against her cheek. "Forward. Always forward."

"Gotta check that box." He smiled.

She straightened up, the dizzying sensation of being farther from the ground forcing her to draw another deep breath. "Something like that."

Over his shoulder, the breadth of Zion spread before her—the Temple of Sinawava, the Three Patriarchs, the Watchman, the Great White Throne. She'd seen them all, but never from this lofty perch. Early in the park's history, someone had joked that "only an angel could land here." She could see why.

"We're almost there. Keep your eyes on my back. That will prevent you from looking where you shouldn't." He turned and started up the path.

She glued her focus to his charcoal-gray shirt, her eyes tracing where the fabric clung to the curve of his spine. Polyester and cotton blend, most likely. Moisture-wicking and UV protectant. Talia forced her feet to follow his. One step at a time.

The tension in her legs and arms eased as she settled into a rhythm. Hand over hand along the chain. The solid surface beneath her feet and the gentle breeze lifting the edges of her hair almost made her feel like she was back in California walking by the bay instead of maneuvering a narrow fin of rock almost fifteen hundred feet in the air. If she didn't think about the gaping chasm, she could imagine it was any other trail. There was plenty of space to choose her steps. Patches of sagebrush clung to the cliffsides below.

Thirty minutes later, they reached the end of the trail, the rocky outcropping feeling more like a platform than the knife-edge she'd been traversing earlier. Her heart steadied. "We did it."

He smacked her shoulder like she was one of the guys. "Great job. You should be proud."

Talia flexed her fingers and shook them out, the stranglehold she'd used on the chain catching up to her. "I didn't think I was scared of heights, but that was brutal."

"A lot of people turn back."

She retrieved her phone from her bag and pointed it at the view. "What about you? I guess after jumping out of airplanes, that was probably anticlimactic."

He ran a hand through his cropped hair. "There were a few moments when it seemed a bit sketchy. Intentionally jumping with a chute is different from accidentally stumbling off a cliff."

She turned the camera toward him, catching his profile against the mind-blowing view. "You're just saying that to be nice, aren't you?"

"Not completely." He caught sight of her lens and laughed. "This great view and you're taking pictures of me?"

"I'll want to remember the guy who got me to the top. I'd still be cowering on the edge if it weren't for you."

He shook his head and reached for her phone. "Let me get one of you. You conquered your own fears. I just distracted you long enough for you to remember why you were up here."

"Stupidity?"

He lifted the phone, aiming the lens at her. "An overwhelming drive to succeed."

• • •

Blake followed Talia up the steps to her grandfather's home, wishing he'd had time for a quick shower before meeting her grandfather. After the Angels Landing hike, they'd stopped at his apartment just long enough for him to grab a clean shirt. But even with that, he felt ill prepared to meet the former chief ranger that everyone spoke of in near-reverent tones.

"You're sure he doesn't mind me coming?"

Her airy laugh set him at ease better than any words she could say. "I already told you, he's excited. Stop worrying. You're jumpier than I was on the trail." She pulled the large clip from her hair, letting the reddish-brown locks tumble down her back.

"People skills aren't my forte. Look at our first meeting."

She turned the doorknob and pushed through the large double-door entry. "I'm the one who decided to veer around a bus full of visitors. You were focused on your job."

Unfortunately, he'd been unable to focus on anything but her ever since. From the moment he'd met Talia, he'd been like a marshmallow in a s'more—soft, gooey, and completely melting whenever she was near.

He probably shouldn't lead off with that when he met Bill Eriksson.

Blake followed her up the heavily carpeted stairs to the living room, running a quick hand down his rumpled shirt. It might be sweat-free, but unfortunately not wrinkle-free.

"Hey, Pops, we're here." She paused halfway up, stopping to rub a hand down her thigh. "Oh, man, my legs still hurt from that climb. I wonder what they're going to feel like tomorrow."

"The more you keep moving, the less stiff you'll be," Blake offered before instantly regretting the words. One of the few times he'd seen his sister in recent years, she'd chided him about giving unsolicited advice. *Mansplaining*, she called it. It had been like a splash of ice water to the face. "I'm pretty sore, too, now that you mention it."

She shot a playful glance back at him, one brow arched. "Liar."

An older gentleman stepped from the kitchen, a dripping glass in his hand. "There you are. I was wondering if I'd have to call the cavalry out for you two."

"We made a quick stop." Talia waved Blake forward. "Pops, this is the friend I was telling you about—Blake Mitchell. Blake, my pops, Bill Eriksson."

Blake extended a hand. "It's an honor, sir. I've heard so much about you."

The man gripped his hand with more strength than Blake would have expected for someone his age. "I'm always pleased to meet a fellow ranger. Hal tells me you're fitting in just fine. He's excited to have you on the crew. Pull up a chair. I was thinking about turning on the game."

Talia smiled. "Don't get too wrapped up in baseball, Pops. We're going to eat soon." She turned to Blake. "I'll give the two of you a minute to get acquainted while I change. I'll be right back." With that, she descended the steps toward the lower level.

Blake followed the retired ranger into the kitchen, eyeing the platter of cold cuts sitting on the counter. He'd only downed a granola bar on the hike, and his stomach had been reminding him of the fact for the past hour.

"So how was Angels Landing? Lots of people today?" The man's easy smile immediately put Blake at ease.

"Not too bad. The permit system is keeping it to a reasonable number. It still bottlenecks in some places, but I hear it used to be a lot worse."

Bill leaned against the counter and took a sip from his water glass. "It didn't used to be that way. But with the arrival of the internet, it got busier every season until it was unbearable. We had people trying to head up there in flip-flops. I know the permits are a pain, but better that than disasters." He pulled another glass from the cupboard. "What are you drinking? I've got soda, water, juice . . ."

"Water would be great."

"Water and ice are in the fridge door. And here's a plate of snacks. You two have to be famished after that hike." Talia's grandfather held the glass out to him. "I had to do a body recovery from that route once. That's something you don't soon forget."

A few minutes later they both settled into recliners near the television.

The seat sucked Blake in like a hug from a good friend. He settled the plate on his knee. "How many years were you at Zion?"

"Depends what you mean." Eriksson chuckled. "I was born there, so it's been my whole life, really. But I started working as a seasonal when I was seventeen. Moved through the ranks over the years." He took a piece of cheese from the plate on the side table. "I tried out a few other parks—Yosemite, Rainier, Rocky Mountain. But this is home, and it kept calling me back."

"Myrtle told me you two were childhood friends."

He laughed. "You could say that. Or you could say that Myrtle puppy-dogged around me and my friends like an annoying little sister. As much as we tried to run her off, she was determined to insert herself. Of course, that became less of an issue when we all hit a certain age. She and Ralph paired off early on and that was that. A few of my buddies regretted not being nicer to her when we were younger."

"But not you?" Blake glanced toward the stairway. Talia was taking quite a while, and pretty soon he'd run out of safe topics.

"Nah, didn't have the patience for that nonsense. Not until I met Camila." He gestured toward her portrait on the mantel. "No looking back after that. She was the one God had set out for me."

Blake studied the photograph. A young Bill gazed adoringly at the dark-haired beauty ensconced in his arms. It'd be nice to have that sort of certainty about a life partner. So far Blake questioned every choice he'd made in life. He took another sip of water. He didn't know Mr. Eriksson well enough to ask how one attained that level of assurance.

Bill muted the television before glancing back toward where Talia had disappeared. "And I'm a firm believer in not awakening love until it's time, if you get my meaning."

Blake's scalp prickled. Was he so transparent? "I assure you, sir. We're just friends."

The man smirked and picked up a handful of potato chips. "I'm not sure my granddaughter feels the same. I haven't seen her light up like that for anyone."

The ice in Blake's cup chilled his fingers. He swirled the cubes around and contemplated getting up for a refill. "Be that as it may, I have no—" The sound of footsteps on the stairs made him scramble for words. "I am happy to have a hiking buddy. It's been good to get out on the trail a little more consistently."

Talia appeared right on cue. Somehow in fewer than ten minutes she'd transformed herself from sweat-stained hiker into fashion model. The summery dress hugged her curves, and her hair had been pulled back into a neat ponytail. She hesitated at the top of the stairs for a moment, her gaze latching onto him.

An odd shifting sensation in the vicinity of his heart caught him off guard. Hiking buddy. Sure. One didn't get a rush of heat in one's chest when spotting a friend. He needed to nail down how he felt about Talia before he lost all control. "H-hey there." Should he get up? Though prying himself out of this recliner might take more coordination than he could muster right now.

The older man chuckled again. "Come join us, Tal. We've got snacks and drinks ready here."

She wrinkled her nose. "I was going to put some burgers on the grill."

He waved her to the spot next to Blake. "I'll get 'em on in a little bit. But your friend there looked like he was going to faint from hunger. I thought it best to start with some appetizers."

Talia wandered over and pulled a gift from behind her back. "Myrtle told me today is your birthday."

Blake scooted forward on the seat. "You didn't need to do that."

"It's kind of silly, so don't get your hopes up. A conversation we had the other day made me think about it. But after it arrived, I almost talked myself out of giving it to you." A touch of color appeared on her cheeks. She placed the small package on the table beside him. "If you don't want it, I'll understand."

Could she get any cuter? He picked up the gift, the box hardly weighing anything at all. "I'm touched. Katie and Alder got donuts this morning, but that's the only gift I've received."

Her brows pulled down. "What about your family?"

He fiddled with the curly tuft of ribbons sprouting from the center of the package. "My mom's been pretty busy, and my sister—well, she's a bit of a mess. She texted me. I'm surprised she remembered with everything that's going on with her."

She plopped onto the love seat beside his chair. "Now I wish I'd gotten you something better. This is low-key nerdy."

"Nerdy is my favorite. I'm sure I'll love it." He felt the smile pulling at his lips. "Should I open it now or wait for later?"

"Home run!" Bill Eriksson blasted through the tension in the room with his shout toward the ancient television set. "Did anyone see that?"

Talia laughed, shaking her head. "Just you, Pops." She turned back to Blake. "Open it. I'm going to fill a plate. I'm starved too. Can I get you anything while I'm up?"

"I'm good, thanks."

She brushed past him on her way to the kitchen, her leg gently bumping his knee. It sent a wave of electricity up his thigh. Oh, yeah. He was a goner.

Thankfully, her grandfather was locked onto the game.

Focusing on the gift, Blake slid a finger under the tape. When was the last time he'd received a real birthday gift? Christmas, sure, but birthday? It had probably been a couple of years. He hadn't realized how pathetic that seemed until just now. The paper parted to reveal a small rectangular box that seemed slightly medical in nature. He flipped it over just as she walked back into the room.

He read the label. "'Find your ancestry'?"

"I know, I know. It's dumb." She sat, clutching a plate of cheese and crackers. "We were talking about our backgrounds, and you said something about a DNA test. I looked into it, and I thought it sounded like fun. I bought one for me too."

He met her gaze. "But you know everything about your history, don't you?"

"Sure, but I want to see the percentages. I figure I must be at least twenty-five percent Scandinavian. And then a good chunk of Spanish from my grandmother. And my mom has some German heritage. But you said you don't know your heritage. I hope you'll think it will be an interesting experiment." Her voice lifted at the end like she questioned her sanity. "Though I realize now that it probably sounds weird. You don't have to take the test. Or you can take it and not tell me anything." She tugged at the end of her ponytail like it was a lifeline. "Now you know how quirky I can be. Good time to run."

He sat back, clutching the box. "I think it's sweet. I love it."

"We'll see if you feel the same after you have to fill a tube with spit." She smirked.

Blake skimmed over the instructions on the back of the package.

"And we get the results online? What if it says I'm part human, part alien?"

"That would explain a few things." She popped a cheese square in her mouth. "Like how you can walk along the edge of a cliff without breaking a sweat."

19

1951

ALMA CLAMPED BOTH hands around the coffee urn to try to still the tremor in her grip as she poured the steaming liquid into cups. Mr. and Mrs. Johnson had come a long way to sit in her kitchen. She had no idea how this conversation might go. In many ways, she was walking in the middle of a desert in the pitch black. How would they find their way through this evening?

Lord, be our light.

Henry placed the cups and sugar bowl on the tray. "Is Billy asleep?" He kept his voice low.

"No. He's playing in his room." She glanced up at her husband, his eyes meeting hers. "Will they want to see him?"

"I imagine they do. I don't like this, Alma. You should have let me send them on their way."

She laid a hand on his arm, leaning close to his shoulder. "They're just like us, when Edward was taken."

The couple sat on the little settee, facing away from her. The woman's brown hair was styled simply, fastened back in a silk scarf. The man's hair was lighter, his skin fair.

"They have questions. So do we. Maybe it's best that we talk to them out here rather than continuing to let the newspapers spin worse and worse stories about us all."

He nodded, putting a hand on her back and pulling her close. "You're right. They're not the enemy. But we can't let them sway us either. Billy is our son, and there is nothing linking their son to ours."

She closed her eyes, leaning into Henry's strength as she always did. "I should take them the refreshments. They've had a long day on the road."

Alma picked up the heavy tray and carried it over to the low table in front of their guests while Henry retrieved their two kitchen chairs so they could sit across from the couple.

Mr. Johnson cleared his throat. "I've spent the past several weeks imagining what I'd say if we had a chance to meet. But now that we're all sitting here together, I find I'm at a loss for words."

His wife slid her small hand into his. "You are very kind to invite us in." Her eyes roamed the room. "Your home is lovely."

Alma tipped a small stream of milk into Henry's coffee and then again into her own. "It's small, but we like it. The Park Service has been good to us."

"We saw some of the countryside as we drove in," Mr. Johnson said. "It's quite stunning. I can see why the government set it aside."

"But it must be a harsh place to live," his wife added. A stitch formed between her eyes. "Lonely."

Henry lifted his chin. "Not at all. We have a wonderful community here. The rangers and their wives look out for each other. There are several families who live nearby. And the guests at the lodge come and go. Plus we're not far from Springdale."

"What about school? Church?" she asked, fiddling with the button on the pocket of her dress.

Alma studied the woman's clothing—an especially fine fabric in a stylish new cut. Did she put on her Sunday best for this meeting, or was this how she always dressed? "There's a bus that takes the children to school in the morning, and it brings them home in the afternoon. Not that our—our Billy is old enough for that yet. And we attend church in Springdale every Lord's Day."

The woman didn't seem impressed. She shifted on the seat, glancing toward the dinette, where Alma had painted a long row of flowers along the top edge.

Henry took a sip of his coffee. "I think we should clear the air a bit. Why don't you tell us why you're here."

Mr. Johnson gave him a curt nod. "I know it must seem quite rude to show up unannounced. But Mr. Peterson told us you would likely refuse a meeting."

"He was right about that," Henry said.

Alma wrapped her fingers around the cup, her racing heart making it difficult to concentrate.

"I felt it important for us to see each other face-to-face." Mr. Johnson's fingers drummed a steady rhythm on his knee. "We opted to come in secret to prevent any newspaper interference. As much as I appreciate Mr. Peterson's discovering you folks, I realize he's only in this for the newspaper sales." He scooted forward, placing both hands on the edge of the seat cushion. "We only care about finding our son."

"Mamma? Mamma?" Billy's voice carried into the room just ahead of him.

Jumping to her feet, Alma moved to intercept their child.

He appeared at the edge of the room, half of his hair standing on end. With one hand, he dragged his blankie over the floorboards while his opposite fist scrubbed at his eyes. "Mamma?"

The Johnsons rose as one, Mr. Johnson placing his hand on his wife's shoulder.

Alma lifted Billy to her hip. "It's past your bedtime."

Henry must have followed her because he now stood directly between his family and the Johnsons.

Alma's heart steadied at the sight of her protective husband. But only God could protect them, and for some reason He'd seen fit to allow this. She moved to Henry's side, close to his arm. "Billy, these are our guests, Mr. and Mrs. Johnson. Can you say hello?"

He bundled the blanket up under his elbow and buried his head against Alma's neck, peeping out at them.

Tears formed on Mrs. Johnson's lower lids. "Hello, Billy. I'm happy to meet you."

When Billy didn't reply, Alma rubbed his back, so warm and inviting to the touch. The weight of him in her arms drove every fear from her heart. "Mr. and Mrs. Johnson have a little boy about your age, but they haven't been able to see him in a very long time."

Henry turned to the Johnsons. "Why don't we all sit down. I'd like to hear more of your story."

An hour later, Alma laid Billy in his trundle bed and tucked his blanket around his sleeping form. Her back ached from holding his sleeping weight for so long as they talked, but she hadn't had the heart to put him down until now. Beatrice Johnson stood in the doorway watching them. "He's precious, Mrs. Eriksson. So precious."

Alma ran fingers along his cheek. "I thank the Lord for him every day."

Mrs. Johnson moved closer. "We need to leave soon." Her voice was hesitant and soft. "Would you mind if I kissed him good night? He'll never know of course. But I will."

Backing a few steps, Alma nodded.

The woman wiped tears from her eyes as she crouched beside the bed. "Sleep well, Billy. May the angels protect you through the night." She placed a kiss on his forehead, sweeping the soft hair back with her fingers. As she rose, the tears fell afresh, and the woman pressed shaking hands to her lips as if to prevent any sound from escaping.

Ignoring her own tears, Alma wrapped her arms around Mrs. Johnson's shoulders.

• • •

Henry buttoned up his shirt, the tension of the previous night's visit lingering in the muscles of his neck and back. The Johnsons hadn't made any demands and had departed for a hotel room in Springdale with plans to return to Salt Lake that morning. No one even knew of their visit outside of he and Alma and whoever had given them directions to their house. Hopefully this was the first step to life getting back to normal.

Alma appeared in the doorway, the belt of her housedress pulled tight around her middle. His wife had lost weight in the past few weeks, something he hated to see. After Eddie had died, she'd nearly wasted to nothing, so frail he feared a strong wind could blow her away. He couldn't let that happen again. Maybe he'd talk to Mattie about staying with Billy so he could take Alma out for a special dinner in town. He'd spoon-feed her if need be, like she had done so many times for their son.

"Henry, I need to talk to you."

The quaver in her voice sent a chill through him. "What is it?"

She walked over to the dresser, her feet sliding along the floor like she was dragging herself. "There's something I haven't told you. I should have mentioned it long before now . . ."

What was it his mother used to say? *"It never rains but it pours."* He sat on the edge of the bed. "Yes?"

Alma pulled open a drawer and drew out her jewelry box.

Henry hadn't seen it in years. She'd long ago put it away, saying there was no need for such things here. On rare occasions, she'd pin on her mother's brooch, but that was it.

She opened the lid, pushing a few small baubles to one side until her fingers closed around something. Turning to him, her eyes were puffy. "I found this the day you discovered Billy by the river. It was in the hatbox." She extended her hand, a small brass padlock sitting square in her palm.

"When I found . . ." His words dissolved on his tongue as she placed the item in his hand. "That was years ago, Alma."

"I know." She shook her head, brushing a few strands of hair from her face. "I meant to show you right away, but everything was so busy at first, I never found the right moment. And then . . ." She glanced heavenward. "I didn't want anything to get in the way. It was wrong. I know that." She placed both palms to either side of her chin, pressing fingers against her temples.

He stared down at the strange item, rolling it over in his grip. "I looked through the hatbox carefully."

"It was hidden in the lining. I'm not sure if it had been placed there intentionally or fallen in and gotten lost. There was a tear in one of the seams."

Holding it up to the sunlight streaming in the east window, he read the markings. "H-C-H."

She sank down onto the mattress beside him, clasping his elbow. "It was wrong of me to hide it. I was just afraid."

He slid an arm behind her and pulled her close. "I'm not sure what good it'll do now."

Alma tightened her grip on his upper arm. "Henry, you don't think . . . H-C-H?"

"I don't know what you mean."

She tucked her lower lip between her teeth for a moment. "You don't think it might be Holy Cross Hospital?"

Henry's mouth went dry as sandstone. He closed the lock in his fist. "No."

• • •

The lock weighed down Henry's shirt pocket, thumping against his chest as he walked—a heart beating on the outside of his body. What was he supposed to do with this thing? He'd closed the investigation years ago. He couldn't reopen it because of a chunk of metal that might be completely meaningless.

Only, it didn't feel meaningless. The moment Alma had placed it in his hand, the brass warm from her fingers, his pulse had kicked into overdrive. He could almost picture a woman sliding it into the hatbox's lining as a way to later identify her infant.

She held the key.

He'd searched the hatbox and had even gone so far as to shake out the blanket Billy had been wrapped up in, hoping for a letter—a clue—anything that might identify the child's mother and why she made the choice she did.

His first son had ended up in the water by accident. Billy had been placed there with intention, like Moses in the bulrushes. He'd never shaken that image from his mind. Moses was saved by the pharaoh's daughter and raised in the palace, only to come back as a mighty messenger for God's people.

Had he placed too much stock in the biblical allusion? Had Billy instead been stolen from his mother's arms and hidden here for some nefarious reason? Henry pressed his hand against his pocket, his strides slowing as he approached headquarters.

He lifted his gaze, staring across the river toward the cliffs beyond. Sometimes their little world here at Zion seemed so self-contained it was easy to forget that there was an entire country outside of their canyon. Cities and people, states and nations. Personal tragedies and world wars. He closed his eyes, willing his pulse to slow. This place was a refuge of peace. It was little wonder the first settlers named it Zion. The park's beauty rivaled any temple or cathedral. *"Thou art my rock and my fortress."*

Unlocking the door, he headed for his office, turning the lights on as he made his way down the hall. The day ahead looked to be slow, nothing his staff couldn't handle. He'd leave a note on Fred's desk asking him to check in on the film crew. So far Legend seemed to be true to his word. Henry hadn't received any negative reports about the man. Hopefully either the gossip was meaningless or married life had set the fellow on a better path.

A light rapping on the doorframe caught his attention. Mattie stood in the doorway, her face pale. "Good morning, Henry. I thought you should know Irene Dawson had her baby last night. She had a rough go of it, and she and Elmer are at the hospital in St. George."

He sank down into his chair, the pen still clamped in his fingers. "Will she be all right?"

"Elmer—Mr. Dawson—telephoned this morning. It was touch and go, but she pulled through."

"And the baby?"

"A little girl. I could hear her squalling clear through the telephone line. They've named her Myrtle."

"We should send flowers. How long will they be away, do you think?"

Mattie smiled. "I already ordered the bouquet. I hope you don't mind."

"You're a gem." He chuckled. "When are you going to give up pillow plumping and come to work for me? I'd hire you in a heartbeat."

She crossed the floor and stood in front of his desk. "If you're serious, I'd love that."

"Oh, I'm certain." He should have done it earlier. "Let me put the paperwork in and get approval from the superintendent." He dug into his pocket. "Hey, have you ever seen this? Alma just gave it to me. Apparently it was in the lining of the hatbox where we found Billy."

Mattie's posture stiffened. "No. Why would I have seen it?"

He studied her. "I thought maybe Alma had shown you. For some reason she hid it from me." He pointed to the imprint on the lock face. "She's concerned H-C-H might stand for Holy Cross Hospital."

"The hospital where the baby was stolen?" Her eyes widened. "That's preposterous."

"Normally, I'd agree with you. But we met with the Johnsons last night and—"

She backed a few steps. "Why would you do that?"

He stood, uncertain of Mattie's reaction. Another case of women acting in ways that made no sense to him. "They showed up. I couldn't toss them out on their ears. Or rather, *I* could, but Alma wouldn't hear of it."

She clutched handfuls of her skirt. "I should go make sure she's all right. And tell her about Irene."

He added a few more lines to the note and dropped it on Fred's desk, moving a paperweight on top of it. "Good. That's a sound idea. And tell her I'm going to be gone for a couple of days."

"Can I say why?"

"I'd rather you didn't. Not right away, anyway." He lifted his hat from the hook. "I'm going to Salt Lake City. If I can get someone at the hospital to assure me it's not one of theirs, I can put her mind at ease."

20

Present Day

Blake leaned against the counter as the young woman steamed the milk for his order. He skimmed his memory for her name. Melsomething. Melanie? Melissa? His gaze drifted across the cafe until it locked onto a familiar figure cleaning a corner table. The sight jarred him to attention.

The girl slid the two cups over to him, her smile bright. "So you're picking up coffee for Talia again. Are you two *together*?"

"No." He nearly dropped his travel mug but managed to save it and the to-go cup he'd ordered for Talia. "Just friends."

"Good." She folded her arms across her chest. "Several of us would be bummed if that were the case."

Several? Maybe he shouldn't be coming in quite so often. Digging for his wallet, Blake gestured toward the busboy. "What's that guy's name?"

She leaned to see past him. "That's Ethan. He's usually in the kitchen, but they've got him working double duty. We're short-staffed."

"Thanks." He tucked an extra dollar in the tip cup. "I hope you have a good day today."

"It's always better when you stop by."

He lifted his coffee in a gesture of thanks.

Ethan had made it to the last bank of tables, his wet cloth making quick work of the surface. Either he was more industrious than the usual busboys, or he was hurrying to get off the floor and back into the obscurity of the kitchen.

Blake made a detour so he could cut off the guy's exit path. "Hey, Ethan. It's good to see you again."

The young man straightened, the basin of dirty dishes rattling in his grip. He moved it to the waiting cart. "Have we met?" A lock of brown hair fell over his eyes, and he brushed it back with a tattooed arm.

The intricate mountain design caught Blake's eye. One of the popular climbing walls at Yosemite—El Capitan? Something like that.

"I had a little chat with you and two of your coworkers outside the Cottonwood dorm a month back."

Ethan shrugged and gave the table another unnecessary wipe. "I talk to a lot of people. But if you say so."

"And I'm pretty sure I saw you down at Watchman Campground last week."

"That a crime?"

This guy was clearly on the defensive. "Not at all. I was just curious. You've got your own place here, so I didn't know why you'd be hanging out at the campground."

"I had some friends staying over."

"At the site I was keeping an eye on."

Ethan blinked, then looked away. "Why?"

"Want to tell me how you know them?" This was a sorry excuse for an interview. He was fishing without any bait.

Thankfully Ethan took the hook anyway. He set down the washcloth. "I don't, actually. A buddy told me they'd been asking around about climbing guides, and I thought maybe I could pick up a few bucks." He tipped his head toward the kitchen. "This gig hardly pays anything, and they siphon money off our checks for lodging and the mandatory meal plan. The vegan offerings are lame. I end up having to buy groceries in town anyway."

That might be a good reason to supplement his income with drug money. The smell of bacon and eggs hung heavy in the air. Blake grabbed a sip of his coffee. "Did the campers hire you?"

Ethan gripped the cart's handle. "Would I tell you if they did?"

He couldn't resist the chuckle. At least the man was honest. "Not if you're smart. You must know Zion doesn't allow guides or outfitters in the park."

"I didn't take the job anyway. They were talking about doing Kolob Canyons out through the Narrows. That's a two-day trip. Besides, I'm more of a free climber. I've done a few canyons, but it's not really my scene."

"Did you hear if they found someone?"

Ethan met his gaze. "How would I know? I haven't seen them since."

More lies. Blake studied the wiry young man. "Nice tat. Yosemite? You do any free climbing there?"

The guy tugged at the cuff of his shirt, rolling it down over the artwork. "Yeah, sure. I'm a grad student in anthropology at Texas A&M, but I took the year off to travel. I got this job so I could explore Zion." He rolled his eyes. "Didn't realize they were going to work me over sixty hours a week."

"Doesn't leave much time for climbing."

"No, man. If I do this again, I'm bringing my van so I can cook my own meals." He glanced back toward the kitchen. "Look, dude, I gotta get to work."

"Of course." Blake stepped out of his path. "One last thing. The guy and girl I saw you with before. Are they students too?"

His eyes narrowed. "Don't remember. Might be."

After thanking Ethan, Blake headed for the door, giving Melanie—or whatever her name was—a quick wave on his way out.

• • •

Talia sat at her favorite bench, picking through the remains of her lunch and gazing up at Angels Landing high above the canyon floor.

Several weeks had passed since the hike, and Blake had hardly had time for lunch, much less another hiking adventure. So now her folded list moldered away at the bottom of her pack, and she'd returned to boring days working the counter at the gift shop.

He'd texted her earlier, asking if she was free at lunchtime, but she'd been sitting for twenty minutes already and he'd yet to show. She bounced her leg, chiding herself for feeling stood up. It's not like he was her boyfriend or anything.

Plus, in his line of work, interruptions were commonplace.

She crumpled her sandwich bag and stuffed it into her lunch cooler. Who was she to complain? This was a beautiful place to wait.

Patience had never been her strength. She pulled out her phone but avoided the tempting email she'd spotted in her inbox this morning.

Jasmine had been on her to post more selfies. A shot with the lodge in the background would be a nice change of pace. Her feed was dominated with shots of glorious red rocks recently.

Lifting her arm, she held the screen out and pointed it back at herself. *Ugh.* She'd never get used to this. Tucking some loose hair behind her ear, she managed a mysterious Mona Lisa smile. She could caption it *Waiting for Mr. Right*. No, scratch that. No girl wants to be left waiting.

A familiar uniform showed up in the background, and she yanked her hand down, twisting on her seat.

"Sorry I'm late." Blake extended his arm with a peace offering in hand.

"Mmm." She closed her fingers around the steaming cup. "Forgiven."

"Wow, you're easy." He winced. "I mean—"

"Easy to buy off?" She loved seeing him flustered. "Easygoing?"

"That's it."

She laughed. "I don't think anyone has called me easygoing, ever. Not once. But maybe Zion is getting to me."

He dropped onto the bench beside her. "It has a way of doing that. Hey, did you get an email this morning?"

Her breath caught. "Yes. I take it you did too?"

"I did. But since you bought me the test, I didn't want to open it without you." He drew out his phone. "Since we took the test together and all."

"Spitting in a tube hardly makes for a glamorous date." The words spilled out unbidden.

He glanced up from his phone.

A wash of heat swept up her neck. "Not a date-date. Just two friends . . . um . . ." What had she done? She couldn't seem to look away.

The smile started at the corners of his mouth and spread from there. He reached over and placed his hand on hers. "It's the best time I've ever had spitting in a tube with anyone. Our second date better include dinner."

The gentle touch sent her pulse racing. "Deal." Of course they'd had dinner on that night too, but who was she to quibble?

They sat there for a long moment, eyes locked.

He squeezed her hand. "So should we open these emails now, or are we going to wait until dinner?"

She laughed. Blake had a gift for breaking the tension. "Let's do it now. Then we can celebrate with Italian food or Mexican food—whatever wins out in your pedigree."

"Now that sounds good." He winked and released her fingers. "What does Swedish cuisine consist of? Other than meatballs?"

"I need to make my gammelfarmor's favorite *renskavsgryta* for you someday. She told me back home it was made with reindeer, but she used venison."

"Your people eat Rudolph?" A smile accompanied his mocking tone.

"It's tough to find in Utah."

He shook his head and lifted his phone. "Come on, Italy. Don't fail me now." Blake tapped a few times to open the results.

She scooted closer on the bench so she could see the screen, the proximity of his arm an added benefit.

A map and pie charts appeared on the tiny screen. He grinned. "I have some Swedish too. A whopping five percent. Maybe we're distantly related."

She pointed to the map of Europe. "You've got a bunch more from Scotland and England. Twenty percent and fifteen percent. And five from Indigenous Mexico and more from Brazil. Then look—Nigeria and Morocco. That's fun."

"No Italian at all." He frowned. "Does that mean I have to trade my pasta in for haggis?"

"Let's not get crazy. How about fish and chips?"

He pointed to her phone. "Your turn. You know about the Swedish from your grandpa, but who knows what other surprises you might be harboring."

"I doubt it's as interesting as yours. I'm as white bread as they come." She clicked open the email and found the link to her test results. Opening the file, she stared down at the world map, the smattering of countries not making sense. England. Spain. France. A few others.

A chill raced along Talia's skin and lifted the hairs on the back of her neck. "This isn't right." Scandinavia was blank.

He leaned closer, peering over her shoulder. "Did they get you mixed up with someone else?"

She scrolled through the report, double-checking her name. "Maybe? Do they make mistakes like that?"

"Mistakes happen all the time. I don't know why this would be any different."

She clicked on a link marked "View DNA matches." Among the names that popped up for extended family, she recognized a few. "Here's my cousin Elijah, and his dad. And my mom's aunt." Her stomach tightened.

"I wouldn't worry too much about it. Maybe they didn't get a good enough sample. I'm sure it's an error."

She pressed a hand to her mouth, unable to look away from the list of names. Maternal cousins. None of the names on the other side seemed familiar. "Or . . ." Her throat squeezed at the possibilities. "Or my dad isn't . . . my dad."

Blake fell silent, and he laid a hand on Talia's shoulder.

She leaned against him, no longer able to focus on the screen. Her mom had always been her rock—quick to laugh and transparent with everyone. Talia's dad had often joked that Mom was an open book.

Maybe this was the one thing she never saw fit to share.

• • •

Talia let herself in the front door, dropping her bag against the coat-tree. "Hiya, Pops! I'll be up in a bit. I'm going to change first."

"Welcome home." His voice filtered down the stairs.

Home. Family. An antique robin's-egg-blue table decorated with painted flowers sat on the front landing. Dread sank into the pit of Talia's stomach. What if she didn't belong here? Pops would likely wave it off like nothing had changed. But if she weren't her father's daughter—an Eriksson by birth—it would shake everything she'd ever believed to be true about herself.

It wasn't about losing her Scandinavian heritage, even though that had been the first thing to slam into her when she opened the DNA results.

The sound of the television filtered down the stairway, and she could picture Pops kicked back in his easy chair, dozing in the face of world news. Her dad, her grandfather—they were *her* world.

She ambled down the stairs, the cozy basement wrapping its arms around her as it had since she was a little girl. The smell of the dusty books and the pool table shoved in the corner spoke of home. Talia traded her work polo for a soft T-shirt and a pair of jeans so worn they were practically falling apart. The perfect match for her mood.

She collapsed into the dented cushions of the dumpy sectional, curling her knees up to her stomach. Why did this bother her so much?

She was the same person she was yesterday. A stupid spit test couldn't change that.

Talia pulled out her phone and opened her photo app, scrolling back to the last time her family had been all together at Christmas, just weeks before her mother died. She studied her dad's smiling face, mentally comparing it with her own. Talia's brothers were perfect matches for Dad. Yet she was her mother's doppelgänger—a near carbon copy.

The realization settled into her chest like the marker they'd placed on Mom's grave.

I'm the only one who doesn't look like Dad.

She lowered the device to the cushion, pinching the bridge of her nose to prevent the tears that gathered behind her eyes.

Call Dad. Just call him and ask.

Her family had always prided themselves on being open about the truth. But what would she say? *"Hey, Dad—did Mom cheat on you? Am I the product of a fling? Or maybe a sperm donor?"*

A mantel clock on the far bookshelf ticked rhythmically. Talia drew the tiny padlock out of her pocket and ran her fingers over the patina. Knowing it had belonged to her great-grandmother was what made it special. But why had Gammelfarmor kept a lock that didn't have a key?

This confusing DNA mess felt a bit the same—a lock without a key.

Talia sat up and clicked on her dad's number.

It rang three times before he picked up. "Talia? So good to hear from you. How are things at Mukuntuweap?"

She pressed a hand against the ache settling in her chest. "It's good, Dad. Beautiful. A friend and I hiked Angels Landing a while ago."

He made an odd sound in his throat. "I'm kind of glad I didn't know that ahead of time. That route scared the tar out of me when your mom and I did it twenty years ago. Now you know why I didn't become a ranger like my dad."

She leaned forward and pressed the shaft of the lock to her forehead, pondering how to broach the uncomfortable topic. "How's work?"

"Boring. Yours?"

"Good. Good." This conversation was going nowhere fast.

"Your grandfather told me you brought a boy home to meet him."

She sputtered a laugh. "A boy?"

"A man, then. Anything serious?"

"Too early to say." She set the brass lock on the arm of the sofa and stood, wandering over to the shelves that held a collection of labeled cardboard boxes. Toys, tools, records, cassette tapes. Why did Pops keep all this stuff? She should help him sort through it.

"You're quiet tonight. Something on your mind?" Her father's voice held an edge of concern. "Do I need to come take care of some guy problems for you?"

"Nothing like that." She bit her lip, running her fingers over the crates. "I bought a DNA test for my—my friend. As a birthday gift. And I took one too."

"Like those ones they advertise on TV? I think your mom's brother was into that stuff—Uncle Jeff. He's the genealogist in the family."

"I thought mine would be pretty boring. You know, all Swedish and stuff."

"Well, my dad is Swedish, but my mom's parents were Spanish. And your mom always said she was a Heinz 57. Probably some Scottish-Irish and German mixed with a bunch of other stuff. Jeff would know more."

The last box in the row didn't have a label on the side. She shifted it to see if there was one on the end. A yellowed strip of masking tape slid loose and fluttered to the floor. She bent down and picked it up. *Alma Eriksson, Springdale Retirement Home.*

"But Dad, the weird thing is this—the test didn't show any Scandinavian heritage at all." She tucked the tape on top of the box.

"You should be at least a quarter."

"That's what I thought." She sat down on the edge of her bed, her throat tightening. So her father didn't know. "Is there any reason that I wouldn't come up as Swedish?"

He went quiet. "I might have to chew on that for a while, Tal. Nothing jumps to mind. You're not adopted, if that's what you're thinking."

It might be easier if she had. Tal clicked open the report again, switching through to the family connections. "I can see some of Mom's relatives on here. Uncle Jeff, Cousin Mike, and a few others."

"It shows you that?" His voice sounded tight.

Maybe he did know something. Now Talia had to decide how hard to press. "It lists other people who have taken the same test and opted in to seeing family connections. So it doesn't show everything. There are a lot of names here I don't recognize. The app doesn't say the exact connections. It just makes guesses based on the amount of shared DNA."

"Talia, I feel like you're trying *not* to say something. What is it you're asking?"

She took a deep breath, steeling herself for what she might learn when she opened Pandora's box. "Is there a chance that . . . that Mom . . . that you're not . . ."

The laughter bursting through the phone made her pull the speaker back from her head. "Tal, no. Is that what's got you all wound up?"

She let go of her breath, sinking back down onto the bed. "You're sure?"

"I was there, honey."

"Yeah, but—"

"Tal, I'm serious. *I was there.* Both when you were born and when you were conceived. I won't say more than that. But trust me on this, kiddo. I am one hundred percent sure. Two hundred percent. Your mother could no more cheat on me than she could strap on ballet slippers and dance *Swan Lake.*"

Talia flopped back against the mattress, covering her eyes with her free hand. "Oh, I'm so relieved."

"I bet she's rolling on the floor of heaven in hysterics right now because we're discussing this."

Sitting up, Talia grabbed her pillow and squeezed it against her midsection. "Then what is going on? Did they make a mistake? I mean, they use this kind of data in crime labs. You'd think you could trust the results."

"I don't know what to tell you. Maybe I'm the child of the milkman."

"Don't joke about such things. I just fell down a rabbit hole of believing Mom was some sort of floozy. To think of Gran doing such things? That's more than I can handle."

"Does it even matter?" His voice softened, taking her back to being a little girl safe in her daddy's lap. "We're talking ancient history now. I mean, I don't like the idea either. You're talking *my* mom here."

"But Pops is Swedish, right? I mean, they used to talk about it all the time. Gammelfarmor used to sing to me in Swedish when I was a little girl. You don't make that stuff up. I was just telling Blake how she fed us reindeer stew."

"Blake, eh? Is that the guy?"

She bit her lip. "Don't make a big deal about it. We're still figuring it out."

He sighed. "Those early days are fun. I still remember my first date with your mom. I took her to see Journey in concert. What a show."

Talia closed her eyes, trying to picture her mom with eighties blue-frosted eye shadow and her dad with—well—hair. "This may all be nothing. But I'm seeing him tonight, so I'd better get cleaned up."

"I'm glad you called, Tal. And whatever you do . . ." He cleared his throat. "Don't stop be-lie-vin'." He wailed the words in a half-decent Steve Perry imitation.

She groaned. "Yeah, Dad. You too."

21

Salt Lake City, Utah
1951

Henry stared up at the imposing building, the sharp angles of its redbrick masonry cold and lifeless compared with Zion's water-shaped sandstone. The street noise echoing off the building threatened to dredge up memories of Manila, but he shook away the odd sensation and dug into his pocket for the lock. Had Alma really pressed it into his hand just this morning? It felt like days had passed, the brass mechanism focusing all his uncertainties into something that fit into the palm of his hand.

He lifted the padlock to catch the light, comparing the initials on its brass surface to the name of the hospital, hoping against hope they'd somehow changed during the long drive to Utah's capital city.

This place might hold the secrets to his son's first days.

He closed his fingers over the lock and squeezed. Hidden away in a drawer, the small object would have haunted his thoughts until the pressure turned him inside out. Better to learn the truth and have this over with.

He'd spent the journey riffling through options. *H* might stand for *hospital* as they feared. But it could also be *hostel*, *hotel*, *harbor*. Even a children's home. That one had given him pause. Was there a children's home that began with the letter *H*? Hope Children's Home. Houston Children's Home.

Forcing himself forward, Henry climbed the stone steps to the front door. Once inside, he ignored the flurry of activity and went directly to the front desk.

The nun studied him through gold-rimmed spectacles. "May I be of some assistance, sir?"

He fumbled in his pocket. "I have a rather unusual question for you."

Her brows peaked, nearly disappearing under her pristine white wimple. "I've served at hospitals for many years now. I highly doubt you can surprise me."

Tempted as he was to challenge the sister's assertion with his bizarre story, he chose the easy route. "Your years of experience might be helpful in this case. I was given this padlock as part of an investigation." He slid the brass piece across the counter. "Based on the engraving, I'm curious if it originally belonged to the hospital. Do you recognize it, by chance?"

The nun picked up the object and turned it over in her fingers. "It's quite small. I can't say as I've seen anything like it here. It looks more like a post office box lock, or perhaps something for a safe deposit box."

The tension that had been growing in Henry's back eased a notch or two. "Very possible. Does the hospital have anything like that? Perhaps for a patient's belongings?"

"We do." She handed it back to him. "But I'm not familiar with the process. I suppose you could speak with one of the janitors. They could take you down to see the storeroom where we keep such items."

Henry returned the lock to his pocket and listened as the nun detailed the route to the janitorial department. Walking down the long white corridors, he couldn't help but touch the spot on his biceps where the shrapnel scar cut across like a streak of lightning. He'd spent only two days in the military hospital, but it was an impression that would likely stay with him for a lifetime, embedded like a fossil in the layers of his life.

A bank of glass windows to the right brought him to a standstill. The row of tiny bassinets each held a swaddled infant. He paused, placing a hand against the glass. As secure as the place seemed, there had been a wolf among the lambs—waiting to snatch a child from its mother's arms.

Henry closed his eyes. The sight of the innocent children was more than his heart could bear. Was no place safe? First Eddie, then Billy.

No. The thought pricked. Not Billy. It had been the Johnsons' baby. He couldn't allow himself to succumb to the newspapers' conclusions.

"One of those yours?" A grizzled-looking older man pushed a mop bucket along the white tile floor, his gray hair tucked up under a flatcap.

"Um, no." Henry turned away from the glass. "No, but I have one at home. It brings back memories."

"They sure don't stay small, do they?" The man chuckled. "The next thing you know, they're trotting out the door."

"So true." Henry scrambled to refocus on his mission. "Have you worked here long?"

"Going on ten years now. Name's Herb Mason." The man reached out his hand.

Ten years should be enough for his query. Henry shook the janitor's hand and introduced himself. After pulling out the padlock, he held it out. "Does this look familiar to you at all? Is there a chance it belonged to Holy Cross?"

Herb plucked it from Henry's palm. "Oh, indeed." A smile deepened the wrinkles to either side of his eyes. "That's from the nurses' locker room. Not the one the sisters use, mind you. But the students from the nursing school. They have cabinets there where they store their coats and pocketbooks and such." He handed it back.

Henry's knees grew weak, and he swallowed hard. "You're sure."

"Abso-tootly. But they changed them a while ago, so now they're gun-metal gray. This one's five years old, at least. Probably more. They were all discarded and exchanged for the new style a few years back."

"Discarded?" His mind raced. "So they could be anywhere now."

"A lot of folks took them home. I've got a couple somewhere. Not sure what to do with them, though. They're not big enough to use for a chain lock. Might work on a steamer trunk or something like that. You got the key?"

"No, I'm afraid not. It was— Someone gave it to me." Best leave Alma and Billy out of this. The story was disappearing from the papers, he didn't need to stir the gossip mill. "I was just trying to figure out where it might have come from. The initials led me here."

"Yes, that's one of ours, for certain. Do you want to see the room?" He waved an arm. "I can show you what the new ones look like."

Henry glanced back at the rows of infants. "No, I don't think that's necessary. Wouldn't want to upset any student nurses."

"Come on. It's empty right now. I'll just give you a quick peek." Herb stashed his bucket in a corner and sauntered down the hall, a noticeable limp-shuffle in his step. He stopped at a narrow door at the end of the hall. He rapped hard before cracking it open. "Maintenance. Anyone home?"

The room remained silent.

He swung the door wide and beckoned Henry to follow. The sparse room was lined with tall metal cabinets and folding chairs. A few coats hung over the backs of the seats, and a lone pair of pumps sat under a vanity dresser topped with a large mirror. "That's where the girls do their primping. The staff likes them to look pretty."

Henry took a few hesitant steps inside, the mingled scent of hair spray and perfume a sure sign he didn't belong in this domain. A single silver lock hung from each cabinet handle. After walking over to the closest one, he tipped the small apparatus for a clearer view. His stomach sank. The stamped design, *H-C-H*, was unmistakable.

• • •

Alma hoisted Billy higher on her hip as she stormed into the ranger station. "Where is my husband?"

George jumped up from behind Henry's desk, his face flushing. "Mrs. Eriksson? I was just about to lock up for the night."

She didn't pause in the doorway but marched up to Sue's husband, fueled by the tension bubbling in her chest. "I assumed Henry was here all day, but then Mattie tells me he left on patrol this morning and might not return until tomorrow or later? He'd never do that without speaking to me first—unless there was some sort of emergency."

Billy squirmed down her side until he managed to get his feet on the floor. Without a moment's hesitation, he raced over to the low shelf where his pappa kept a stack of bird and reptile books.

Alma refocused her attention on George. "So?"

The ranger swallowed, his Adam's apple bobbing in his throat. "I'm sorry, Alma. I don't know. He left a note saying there was a personal emergency and he'd be away for a couple of days."

A personal emergency. A shudder started at the base of Alma's spine and worked its way upward. He'd seemed fine when he left this morning. Even considering the trauma of the night before and then the bomb she'd dropped on him this morning with the hidden padlock. Had he been more upset than he'd let on?

She walked to the window, gazing out at the darkening sky. "What else did he say?"

George pushed in Henry's chair and came out from behind the desk. "Only that I should keep an eye on things while he was gone." He stopped a few feet behind Alma. "Is there something I should be aware of? Are you—are you both all right? I know things have been hard—"

Alma swung around and pinned him with a glare. "Hard? *Hard*? Try having your name splashed across the newspapers saying you killed your son and stole a baby from a hardworking couple. Then you can talk to me about hard."

Billy looked up from the book he'd spread open on the floor, his little hazel eyes rounding. "Mamma?"

Regret sluiced through her. She hurried to her son and crouched beside him. "I'm sorry, Billy. I didn't mean to yell."

George cleared his throat. "Alma, you know Sue and I are here for you. Whatever you need."

"I need my husband."

Footsteps sounded in the doorway. "I know where he is." Mattie's voice was calm. "He asked me not to tell you because he knew you'd worry."

Alma pulled Billy into her lap, the boy clinging to her neck. "He went after the Johnsons, didn't he?" A clawing sensation tore at her ribs just above her heart. The peace God had given her last night was fading fast, replaced by a mounting dread.

She'd take Billy and run, like she should have done with Eddie. Run for higher ground.

Mattie shook her head. "It's not like that."

The telephone on Henry's desk rang, the harsh bell tearing through the silence in the office. Mattie crossed the floor and picked up the receiver. "Ranger Eriksson's office, Mathilda speaking."

A moment later she placed a palm over the receiver. "Alma, it's him."

Alma got to her feet as Billy scrambled back to his books.

"Henry, Alma is here. Would you like to speak to her?" Mattie asked.

There was no way Alma was giving him a choice. She snatched the handset from Mattie's grip, pressing it to her ear. "Henry, where are you?" The shrill note in her voice hurt her own ears. Alma took a breath. "You frightened me."

"*Jag är så ledsen, älskling.*"

His gentle apology cut through the ropes of fear that bound her heart and sent tears flowing down her cheeks. Since moving away from their families, they didn't often speak Swedish anymore. But occasionally the language of her youth expressed things English never could.

"Where are you?"

"I'm in Salt Lake City. I thought . . ." His sigh carried across the miles. "I thought I could clear your mind in regard to the padlock."

"You drove all that way?" Her throat tightened, and she focused on their son, happily turning pages while searching for his favorite illustrations.

"I can't talk long, Alma. But I wanted to let George know—well, *you* really—I'm on my way back."

"What did you learn?"

He hesitated. "You were right. It likely belonged to a student nurse at Holy Cross Hospital, though it wouldn't have been in use when Billy was born. The janitor said they were replaced, and these older ones were discarded after staff had taken any they wanted to keep."

She sank down into her husband's chair, the words sinking deep into her soul as she stared down at their son. *Wanted. Taken. Discarded.*

"Henry," she whispered, her throat not allowing more. "Come home."

22

Present Day

Pops sat in the Adirondack chair on the back porch, his nose wrinkled as he stared at the printout of Talia's DNA heritage in his hand. "I can't make heads nor tails of this. You're saying it doesn't show any Swedish at all?"

Talia crouched beside him and pointed at the colored sections of the map. "That's what I don't understand. There's Spain—from Gran. And all these other countries. But nothing out of Scandinavia."

He shoved it back at her. "It's a mistake. My parents were both children of Swedish immigrants. So you're probably about a quarter."

She folded the paper into a square. "It also shows links to various other people who have done the same test. I saw my mom's brother Jeff and his son Mike. While Blake and I were at dinner last night, we searched through the names a little more and I found one of my Eriksson cousins, Justin."

"Tom's son. You spent your date looking at our family tree?"

Talia tapped on the screen, opening the app. "Not the whole time." Enough of it to put a damper on things, though. Blake had probably been counting the seconds until he could go home.

"Blake seems like a good guy." Pops tipped his head to the side, studying her. "You like him. I can tell."

She tried not to blush, but her cheeks were out of her control. "Never thought I'd be into a park ranger. But he does remind me a bit of you."

Pops grunted as he reached for his can of Diet Pepsi. "Maybe that's what scares me."

"You don't mean that." She scrolled back to the cousin match she and Blake had identified last night. "You were impressed with him. I could see it in your face. But I don't think it can go anywhere. Myrtle has asked me to stay on at the gift shop into the fall, but even so, it means I only have a couple more months here. And I really should start sending out applications before the fashion world forgets who I am."

"Oh, Talia." He clucked his tongue. "You're always in such a hurry. The question isn't whether the corporate world has forgotten you—it's what does God have planned for you?"

She lowered herself into the neighboring chair, where Gran always used to sit. "And you think God wants me to stay here and work in the gift shop for the rest of my life? That might be a waste of my MBA."

"Nothing is wasted in God's kingdom. Maybe He brought you here to meet Blake. You won't know unless you spend some time listening to Him instead of racing toward your future."

The idea rattled her more deeply than she cared to admit. She hadn't dated anyone seriously since college. "Don't book the church yet, Pops. I barely know the man." Sure, her heart pounded whenever he met her eyes, but somehow that didn't seem enough to rearrange her whole life.

She tapped the screen once more. "Okay, this is what I wanted to show you. This is Justin's file." Talia lifted the screen so Pops could view the brightly colored map.

"You can see other people's DNA? Nothing is private anymore." Her grandfather scowled at the device.

"Only those who've opted in and are a match with me."

He jabbed a fingertip at the map. "He's got Sweden, Norway, *and* Denmark all lit up. But I think your Aunt Joan—Justin's mom—said she had some Scandinavian roots too."

She sat back, staring down at the app. Her cousin showed only eight percent Scandinavian, five from Sweden. By her simple calculations, he should also be around a quarter, but maybe the tests weren't that accurate. She'd read on the website that since inheritance is random, people didn't always receive the expected amounts from each region. So the math was rarely as simple as anticipated.

Maybe that's all this came down to. That she was nothing but a mathematical anomaly.

Still—there was a huge difference between unexpected amounts and . . . *zero*. Something wasn't clicking.

Talia switched off her phone. At least she knew her dad was really her dad. Justin wouldn't have shown up as a match if her initial fears had been true.

She stared out the window to where the setting sun illuminated the sandstone cliffs in the distance. These rock formations weren't quite as grand as the ones inside the park, but they were still breathtaking. Layers upon layers of colors, like the many strands of DNA making up every cell in the human body. She'd started this to help Blake learn about his heritage. She hadn't expected it to put her family history into question.

So she wasn't Swedish. It wasn't that big of a deal. Blake had gone his whole life not knowing his ancestry. Last night at dinner, he'd given her a puzzled look. "Why does it matter? It doesn't change who you are."

But he'd missed the point. Pops and Gran. Her gammelfarmor, Alma. Pops's stories of *Gammelfarfar* Henry. The threads connecting her to these lovely people were fraying.

There was no way she could explain her pain to someone who didn't seem to care about family. She'd swallowed the protests and put away her phone, choosing to focus on enjoying their time together.

But the knowledge was like a rash that wouldn't stop itching. Somewhere her family tree had broken down, and she needed an explanation.

• • •

Blake pressed the wooden staff down into the water, finding purchase on the big slippery rocks as he sloshed his hiking boots through the current. He'd been told about the Narrows trail, but this was the first time he'd actually walked it.

"This is insane." Talia's voice echoed through the canyon.

Blake turned to check on her. The canyon walls pressed in on either side of the river, leaving no place to walk but right along the riverbed.

About fifteen feet back, she stood thigh-deep in the flowing water. She clung to her walking stick with both hands as a grin lit up her face. "This is so much fun," she called to him, the sound barely audible. She'd fastened her reddish-brown hair up in some kind of knot, but locks had already fallen loose and dangled around her face. Her leggings and hoodie were sodden, but it didn't seem to be dampening her joy.

His heart squeezed at the sight of her smile. They hadn't been out again since their fish and chips dinner a few weeks ago had sent them spiraling back into the friend zone. He wasn't sure what exactly had gone wrong, but she'd made it pretty clear that her interest in him had fizzled. It was probably just as well.

Unfortunately, his heart had refused to let go of its fascination with this amazing woman. Without even realizing it, she already owned a piece of him. One of these days she'd disappear back to her real life and he'd be stuck like gum to the bottom of her shoe.

The cliff walls loomed close overhead, the dark, rusty browns seeming almost otherworldly, like he and Talia had found themselves on a planet ruled by water and stone. The sound of the current echoed off the wet walls, and thousands of feet up, a smear of blue sky provided the filtered light they needed to see where they were going.

Talia lifted her knees high with each step, finally catching up to him.

He gestured to her soggy sweatshirt. "Did you go for a swim?"

"I tripped. Again. Nearly went face-first this time. But I think I've got my sea legs now. Or should I call them my river legs?" She touched the clear pouch dangling from a lanyard around her neck. "Good thing I have this, or my phone would be ruined."

He waved her ahead of him, preferring to enjoy this adventure through her eyes rather than lead the way. He placed his waterlogged boots with care so as not to turn an ankle on the basketball-sized rocks washed smooth by the river's flow.

She might joke about being a klutz, but Talia moved with the grace of a dancer, even in this uncertain terrain. Keeping a grip on the wooden pole, she tipped her head back to study the rock face.

The sight stole the breath from his lungs. How could anyone look so strong and yet fragile at the same time? Talia Eriksson was stunning.

He slid a hand inside the collar of his shirt and pulled his phone from its own waterproof pouch. The vivid colors in front of him were almost too much to be believed, Talia's safety-yellow dry bag and blue hoodie standing in stark contrast to the striated sandstone that blocked much of the sunlight. On the small screen, Talia resembled an intrepid explorer dwarfed by the massive cliffs pushing in from both sides. He clicked several shots.

Blake had rarely bothered with photos over the years, but his phone was now littered with pictures of Talia as she worked her way through her Zion bucket list. These would be the best of the lot.

He tapped an icon, sending the photo to Favorites. Then he must have swiped the wrong direction, because a photo from Kabul popped up instead.

A knot formed in his belly. The image was so ingrained in his memory, he hardly needed to inspect it, yet he couldn't look away. Buddies stood on either side of Blake, their arms wrapped about each other's shoulders. *The night before the blast.*

The air had crackled with tension that day. He'd been on guard duty along the pockmarked wall, keeping watch over the facility, his brothers-in-arms, and the civilians gathering around the outside of the airport, many of them hoping to escape before the Taliban completed their takeover of the city.

"Take her. Take her—I beg you!" A man hoisted a baby girl toward the American soldiers. The air reeked of dust, smoke, and desperation—mingled odors that haunted him to this day.

Blake clicked the memory off with the phone screen and shoved the device back into the pouch, sliding the clamp that sealed it away from potential damage. If only there were such things for people.

Talia glanced over her shoulder at him, her face practically glowing. "Are you taking pictures?"

He tucked the pouch under his shirt and started her direction. They'd been in the river for a few hours already, leaving the hordes of other tourists back in the early stretches. A couple of college girls had passed them at lunchtime, but now it felt like he and Talia were the only two people in the world.

The tension that had gripped him when he saw the photograph loosened its claws as the cold water and the unusual scenery worked to drag him back to the present.

"I should be taking more pictures, but I'm worried I'll drop my phone," she said.

"I just got one of you. I'll text it to you later."

"Oh, great." Talia wrinkled her nose. "My wet backside."

Blake managed to bite his tongue before making a joke that might embarrass her. As much as he liked seeing her blush, he should be on good behavior. After their last date, he'd assumed she'd written him off for good.

One of the boulders shifted under his boot, and he grabbed onto his staff with both hands. Maybe this wasn't a good place to get lost in his thoughts.

"I'm glad to see it's not just me fighting to keep my footing," she called to him.

"You seem to be enjoying it, though."

"This is the coolest thing I've ever done—by a long shot." A glowing smile spread across her features.

"I assume you're talking about the hike, not the temperature."

"The water's cold, yes. But just"—she gestured toward the sheer walls on either side of them—"the incredible beauty of this place. To think a couple of months ago, the highlight of my day was stopping by the coffee shop and getting to work early, before the day's hubbub."

"Do you miss it?"

She lowered her eyes, as if searching the stream for her answer. "Sometimes. I liked marketing, even if I didn't care for the office atmosphere and their fake ideas of team building. I was good at what I did. I could see it making a difference to the company's bottom line. That's a heady feeling."

"Nothing wrong with that."

"I don't know." Her nose wrinkled. "I spent a lot of energy figuring out how to convince people to buy stuff they didn't need. And then learning our products might be harmful?" She shook her head. "Some of that's on me. You know what I mean?"

"You weren't aware of it."

"I should have been." She repositioned her stick and started forward again.

He walked by her side so they could still hear each other. "You need a company that sells a better product. One you can believe in."

"That's a rare find in the fashion world." She paused for a long moment, her eyes taking on a faraway look. "I've read up on some companies using all-natural fibers. Merino wool, organic cotton, other plant fibers—even recycled materials. But there are only a handful of small outfits doing that, and they fold as fast as they open. The big ones dabbling in it are usually just doing it for the PR, not because they truly care. It comes down to money, as always."

"You could start your own."

She shook her head. "I'm a marketer, not a manufacturer. But sometimes I wonder if I could help some of these small artisans who—"

A bird darted in front of them, skimming along the rippled surface before flitting back up the canyon.

Talia laughed, her joy echoing around the enclosed space as it might in an elegant concert hall. "Did you see that? Like a little feathered fighter jet."

"I did." He probably wouldn't have paid the bird much notice, but seeing it alongside Talia made it far more interesting. Her passion for nature made everything come alive—not unlike someone else he knew. "Hey, I'm meeting up with Katie and Alder for dinner tonight. You should come."

Her brows rose. "Really?"

Yeah, that probably sounded like he was inviting her on a double date, and she was now thinking of a million excuses to bow out. "I think you'd hit it off. But if you're tired and want to go home, it's no biggie."

She tipped her head, a smile toying at her lips. "No, I want to meet them. You talk about them a lot."

He probably did. He'd never spent time around a family that actually worked.

"Besides"—she slid her phone from its pouch—"I assumed after I was so distracted on our last outing, you wouldn't want to hang out again. Except for our hiking adventures. I knew you wouldn't let your hiking buddy down." She tipped her phone up, aiming the lens toward him.

Blake tightened his grip on the walking stick, the rocks suddenly feeling even more unsteady. "Are you kidding me?"

She lowered her camera. "Yeah, I mean, I was on my phone the whole time and going on and on about my family. I could understand if you decided to cut your losses. I know family isn't as big of a deal to you—"

"It *is* a big deal." He shook his head, hoping the movement would rattle his thoughts back into place. "It's a huge deal. Just because my family was messed up doesn't mean I don't care about them. Or that I don't want a big family of my own someday."

Her eyes widened.

And maybe that was a step too far. No wonder he was such a failure in the dating department. He either said too little or came on too strong.

But if she'd been frightened off, there was little evidence of it in her face. Instead she stepped closer and touched his arm. "I'll do better this time."

If she did any better, he'd have to marry the girl. Blake adjusted his arm so her fingers slid down into his palm. They were like ice, and he closed his hand around them. "You're doing fine."

Her smile could have lit the canyon.

Man, he was falling for this woman, hard, and there was no parachute that could save him if it went south. But at this moment, he didn't much care.

She laced her fingers with his and took an additional step to close the already small gap between them. "Good, then."

The sensation of her skin against his kicked his heart into high gear, and he fought the urge to throw down the walking stick and pull her into his arms—something he'd wanted to do since practically the first day they'd met. Instead, not wanting to risk the unsteady surface, he released his grip and slid his hand around her back. The world's most painfully slow embrace.

When she repositioned her feet and nestled her arm around his waist just under his loose jacket, her icy touch against his side sent an answering rush of heat through him.

She stared up at him with unwavering brown eyes. "How are you so warm?"

"I'm going to have to plead the fifth on that."

Her lips lifted into a smile that made him want to test and see if they were cold too.

Instead, he lowered his head enough to place a kiss on the top of her head.

Talia wrapped her other arm around him, lifting her head so his lips trailed down along her temple. Her walking stick pressed against his shoulder blade, but he wasn't going to complain.

Her hair smelled faintly like wildflowers, and his fingers ached to run through the sweet strands. Blake's pulse ratcheted up. *Not here.* All other sensations faded, an overwhelming desire to kiss her rushing in to take their place. He wanted to claim her for his own, right here in the middle of the river's flow. "Talia," he whispered against her hair. "Are you just getting warm, or can I kiss you?"

Talia's shoulders bounced lightly, as if she offered a soft laugh. She lifted her chin so her cheekbone slid against his jaw. "Both. And I hope you do."

He didn't ask twice. Closing the distance, he covered her mouth with his, the soft warmth of her lips surprising him.

She met his kiss with one of her own, her fingers bunching the back of his coat against his spine.

He longed to caress her face, to savor every inch, but one hand was claimed by his walking stick and the other anchored at her waist. So instead, he let his mouth linger, following her lips in an effort to draw out the moment as much as he could. Who knew when—or if—he'd get another chance. With the tip of his nose, he trailed a slow path along her jaw, memorizing the warm scent of her skin.

Talia uttered a soft little sigh.

Her reaction only made him want to dive in for more, but he managed to hold himself in check. If they stood still much longer, they were going to lose all their body heat to the river—as impossible as that felt right now. He retreated a few inches, studying her closed eyes and parted lips. *This woman is beautiful.* He cleared his throat. "We should probably keep moving."

The corners of her mouth tilted upward even before she opened her eyes. "I know. But wow. I'm adding this to my bucket list just so I can check it off."

The rasp in her voice sent an odd jolt of pleasure through him. "I'm here to serve."

• • •

Talia followed Blake into the small house. Ever since Blake had mentioned her meeting Alder and Katie, a nervous tic had taken up residence in her stomach. Since he wasn't close to his family, this might be the next best thing in his mind. If the couple didn't approve of her, today's kiss might be the last.

And she definitely wanted more of those.

Her mind battled with her heart ever since the moment their lips had met. So many things in her life were up in the air. Maybe if she'd still been safely employed, her life unfolding in front of her, then she'd have felt comfortable adding a dating relationship. But now? She didn't even know where she'd be in a couple of months. She'd come here to reset and relax. Not to fall in love.

But her heart had other ideas.

And kissing him felt so very . . . right.

Pops might have a point. Maybe she needed to take this to God and spend more time listening. With her work schedule, she'd only made it to church a couple of Sundays since arriving in Springdale, but she loved the little congregation. Pastor Garcia taught mostly through stories, weaving tales that illuminated the Scriptures, opening Talia's eyes to aspects of the gospel she'd never spent much time thinking about. Quite a few of the park staff attended there as well, though not very many of the seasonal concession staff. That was part of the trouble with working tourist hours—one rarely had a free weekend.

Her youth group leaders had always taught her to "guard her heart." Yet no one had ever explained how to do that and for how long. Surely being guarded didn't mean pushing someone away out of fear. While establishing her career, she'd steered clear of the distractions of dating. Now that work no longer stood in the way, uncertainty still lingered. Would there ever be a perfect moment?

"I think they're out back." Blake extended a hand to her, and she laced her fingers with his as if they'd been doing it for years, not hours.

Falling in love with Blake would be so ridiculously easy. But what happened when she was ready to get back to normal life?

He led the way through the cozy living room and to the sliding doors leading out to a small patio.

A petite woman stood at the grill, flipping burgers and large portobellos as she watched her husband and three kids kicking a soccer ball around the backyard.

She turned and cast them a huge smile. "There you are."

Blake squeezed Talia's hand and dropped it, stepping a little away from her to go greet their hostess. "I'm sorry we're late. The Narrows took longer than I anticipated. We were having too much fun to rush." He winked at Talia before turning back to Katie. "Katie, I've told you about Talia."

Katie placed an oven mitt–clad hand on his back. "You have. Welcome, Talia. I'm so happy to meet you." She gestured to the yard. "Those four troublemakers belong to me. The tall one is my husband, Alder, and the kids are Chase, Amelia, and Emma."

Alder pried himself loose from the two girls, who seemed to be intent on tackling him, and made his way over. "Am I glad to see you. These three seem to think three-on-one is a fair game. I need backup." He stretched his hand out to Talia. "Hey, Talia. I know your grandpa. Great guy."

"Thanks." She shook the man's hand. "He is one of the best."

Blake lowered his head to Talia. "You mind if I go join the game for a few minutes?"

"Of course not."

With that, Blake and Alder took off, each swooping up one of the girls and running a lap with their prisoners while Chase juggled the soccer ball on his own.

Katie smirked. "Don't worry, they'll tire out soon."

"I'm surprised Blake isn't already wiped out after today's hike." Talia walked closer to the barbecue, the scent of the grilling meat making her stomach gurgle with anticipation. "Can I help with anything?"

"It's all ready. I just saved the meat until last so it would be hot when we got around to eating." She lifted a spatula, her gaze centering on Talia. "I'm glad Blake invited you. He's talked a lot about you—and he's not a big talker. So I'm glad to meet the woman who's managed to get him to open up."

Warmth flooded through Talia. "He's been such a help this summer. I had this list of things I wanted to see at Zion, and he's jumped in with both feet. We're most of the way through it already. I may have to add a few more items or we're going to run out of things to do."

Katie laughed. "It's impossible to run out of adventures around Zion. You could stay a lifetime and barely scratch the surface. Just ask your granddad."

"I suppose that's true." Talia eyed the food hungrily. "What about you? How long have you and Alder worked here?"

"Just a couple of years." Katie flipped the burger patties and removed the mushrooms to a waiting platter. "We were at Yosemite before this. But Alder is obsessed with Utah geology, so we'll probably hang around as long as the NPS will have us."

She and Talia discussed some of their favorite hikes, getting to know each other as the men romped around the yard with the children. Ten minutes later, they were all sitting down at a glass-topped patio table, a blue-and-white umbrella blocking some of the sun. The kids had their own little picnic table in the corner of the yard, and other than popping over for more food, largely stayed there.

"This is great." Talia added lettuce and pickle to her burger. "I'm starving."

Alder reached into a bag of chips and added a handful to his plate. "How was the Narrows hike?"

Talia met Blake's eyes, but the amused lift of his brow scattered any hope of a sensible answer.

Katie sat forward. "Oooh, this looks good. Spill the tea."

Blake took Talia's hand under the table. "Let us keep a few secrets. I'll just say, it was a very interesting hike."

Alder chuckled. "Good enough."

His wife glared at him. "For you, maybe."

Their son popped over and snatched one of the chip bags. "Do you mind if I take this?"

"Only if you share with your sisters." Katie turned back to Talia. "Blake told us about the DNA test you bought for him. That sounds like fun. I've been thinking about getting some for Alder and me."

Talia shifted on her lawn chair. "It's been a bit more surprising than I anticipated. I thought I had a clear picture of my family tree, but it seems like there have been some misconceptions along the way." She squeezed Blake's hand. "But I don't want to bore you all with that."

"I find it fascinating." Alder helped himself to some water from the pitcher. "This science is opening up new avenues of research into the human genome. And then for families—nothing will be secret anymore. Adoptions will be revealed, secret siblings, abducted children. You can't hide that kind of stuff anymore. And police are using it to bust open decades-old crimes. That's how they found the Golden State Killer."

"Alder." Katie's voice held a note of warning as she glanced over at the kids. "Let's keep this light, shall we?"

Talia set her burger on her plate, her appetite fading. "I don't think my family contains that level of drama. Or at least, I hope not. But there's a missing chapter somewhere that I can't seem to figure out. I know my grandfather is of Swedish heritage, and yet my DNA doesn't show any."

Katie's eyes widened. "Are you adopted?"

Blake cleared his throat. "Talia, you don't need to talk about this if you don't want to. But my friends are total science geeks. They might be able to help you figure this out."

Alder lifted his glass. "Geeks and proud, right, Katie?"

That earned a huge smile and nod from his wife. "I took several college courses in genetics. I'd love to take a look—unless you'd rather keep this private."

Talia scooted forward in her seat. "I've got nothing to hide. And I want some answers."

Blake turned to his friends. "We've already determined she's not adopted. The DNA results identified positive matches on both sides of her family tree."

Katie wiped her fingers on a napkin. "Then the issue is further back. Is Bill Eriksson your paternal or maternal grandfather?"

"He's my dad's father."

"Have you confirmed the link between your father and your grandpa, then? Maybe your dad was adopted or . . ."

"Or he isn't Pops's son. I've wondered about that. My grandmother's Spanish heritage shows up in my chart, though now I'm questioning everything."

Alder squinted as if he were trying to picture the links. "That would be Bill's wife?"

"Yes." Talia stood to grab a can of soda from the cooler sitting nearby.

"I need to graph this out on paper." Katie sprang up and hurried inside after supplies.

Blake joined Talia by the cooler, reaching into the icy water to get one for himself. "I can rein them in if you get uncomfortable at any point."

She dried her fingers on her pant leg before reaching out to squeeze his arm. "You don't have to protect me, but I appreciate the sentiment. If you get bored of all this talk, we can change the subject." The last thing she wanted was to ruin another date by talking too much about her family.

He took her hand and placed a kiss on her temple. "As much as I'd like to have you to myself right now, I'm pleased you're hitting it off."

The touch of his lips against her skin chased away her anxious thoughts. She was going to like this new phase of their relationship, even though she was determined to keep things low-key.

Katie was already mapping the family tree in colorful washable markers that she'd probably borrowed from their kids. "Here's what we've got." She pointed to Talia's name written at the bottom of the page in bright purple letters. The faint scent of grape candy floated in the evening air. "Let's fill it in, shall we?"

Uncapping another of the scented markers—cherry this time—Talia filled in her parents' names and her siblings. Her heart stuttered as she wrote her mother's name in its corresponding box. What she wouldn't give to call her mom and pour out everything that had happened in the past few months. From ZetaWear to Zion, the DNA mess and . . . she glanced over at Blake, her heart rising. Mom would have adored Blake. There was little doubt in her mind.

The corners of his mouth tilted up as he met her eyes.

Pulling out her phone, she opened the Heritage app and added some of the information she'd confirmed on there. Cousins, uncles, aunts. Seeing it in black and white—or purple, pink, and red in this case—made this all seem more approachable. Talia had made a similar diagram back in grade school that was decorated like a real tree with spreading branches. But she'd never realized that some of the branches might not be connected. She uncapped the green marker and added her Great-Aunt Annika, Pops's little sister, and her progeny. None of them were listed on the DNA report.

Katie tapped on Pops's name. "It really looks like everything points to this spot."

Talia's stomach tightened. That's what she'd feared. The idea that she might not be related to her beloved pops sent a trickle of unease through her soul. He'd always been her biggest cheerleader. A simple DNA test wouldn't change that—right?

"It could be an earlier generation, before your grandfather," Alder added.

Blake had gone quiet through the discussion. He seemed to be studying her, as if trying to understand the depth of her emotion on the topic. She couldn't help him with that. She didn't understand it herself. Her throat thickened.

Katie reached a hand across the table and placed it on Talia's wrist. "It'll be okay. It won't change anything."

Talia managed a nod, but a seed of doubt had taken root the moment she'd opened the results.

Moving her hand back to the paper, Katie pointed at Great-Aunt Annika and her children. "How well do you know these cousins? Is there a chance any of them have done one of these Heritage tests?"

"We spent every Christmas together for years. We practically grew up together."

Blake crossed an ankle over his knee and rubbed a muscle in his calf. "Wouldn't they have shown up as matches? My test gave me a long list of names of second, third, and fourth cousins. None of whom I know."

Alder raised his brows. "I think that's what Katie's getting at." He turned to his wife as if to confirm.

She nodded, jumping up from the table and coming around behind Talia. "Exactly." She ran a finger down that branch of the tree. "Anyone along here who's taken a test should be your genetic match. It's very possible none of them have tested, but if they have—"

"They'd show up here." Talia scrolled through the list of names from her results. "Mark Lehmann, Carly Stilts, Jacob Johnson, Elizabeth Johnson, Michaela Seeger—some of them seem vaguely familiar, but they're all like third to fourth cousins. I don't know them. I don't see any of Annika's children or grandchildren. So if they're not genetically related, then . . . what?"

"Then Annika is not your pops's biological sister."

Alder took another handful of chips. "You could ask your grandfather to do a test. That would give us a lot more information to work with here, wouldn't it?"

Katie stared at the paper. "Sure, but I don't think he needs to. If you could get the results from any one of these cousins, you could backtrack through their matches to see if Annika was related to these two." She pointed at Talia's great-grandparents.

Talia selected a raspberry marker and filled in the slots. *Alma and Henry Eriksson*. "If she's related, but Pops is not . . ." Silence descended over their little circle, the sound of the kids' chatter a pleasant hum in the distance. Talia dropped the writing instrument back into the wooden basket. "Then Pops isn't who he thinks he is."

And neither was she.

23

1951

BILLY NAPPED IN the center of their bed, one arm thrown over his sweaty forehead. Alma sat on the edge of the mattress, the damp cloth in her hand warming in the afternoon heat. Her son's sudden fever had caught her by surprise, but it explained the mood he'd been in since last night. Fitful, grumpy, anxious—almost mirroring her own. She'd blamed her low spirits on the uncertainty and had assumed he was picking up on their fear. But Billy's fussiness came from a much more organic source.

In a way, having him come down sick was an odd relief. Something new for her to obsess over instead of the constant fear that the Johnsons—or more likely Sheriff Moody—would appear on her doorstep to collect Billy. Her son. Their son. Her stomach tightened. Her heart had finally begun to grasp the truth. He might be both their sons.

A cruel joke. That's what the past three years had been.

Alma ran a finger down Billy's sleeve, the clean shirt a replacement for the one he'd ruined with the last bout of nausea. If only life could be reset as easily. Her thoughts had traveled back to little Eddie often in the past few days since Henry had returned from Salt Lake with the news.

Her firstborn would have been almost five now. Maybe learning his letters and his colors. She imagined Henry coming home leading a chubby pony, intent on teaching Eddie to ride.

She rocked slightly on the bed, the ache in her chest needing some sort of release, like the valve on her pressure cooker. Leaning forward, she rested the damp cloth on Billy's forehead. Billy would never know his brother.

And soon, he might forget her as well.

The sound of the front door opening brought Alma to her feet. She walked out to the kitchen, the sight of her husband removing his hat and placing it on the hook bringing a flurry of strange emotions in her chest. "Mattie told you?"

He nodded, jaw set. "How is he? Should I telephone the doctor?"

"It's just a little tummy upset and a fever. No reason for concern." She kept her voice light, though a tiny quiver likely betrayed her. "He was playing with Sue's girls, and they've been sick too."

He ducked his head into the bedroom for a long moment before backing out and turning toward her. "I don't like it when he's ill."

She placed a hand on her hip. "Neither do I, especially when I was cleaning up his bed. I lost my own breakfast after that."

"Are you coming down with it too?" He placed a gentle hand against her forehead.

"No. Just the smell—you know how it is. Sympathy sickness." She shooed away the thought before her stomach was reminded of the situation. "Is that the only reason you came home?" Alma picked up her empty water glass and placed it on the drainboard.

The corners of his mouth lifted. "Can't I sneak home to see my lovely wife?"

"Nice try. I know you too well for that."

He leaned against the stove and folded his arms over his chest, the smile vanishing like a wisp of fog. "I've had a call from Marshall Peterson."

That name struck a nerve, sending every hair on Alma's arms to attention. She snatched a wet dishrag and wiped the counters even though she'd already scrubbed them this morning. "Trying to rake up more dirt, I'm sure."

"He caught wind of my trip."

She dropped the cloth into the sink, staring down into the basin.

"I didn't give him any information, but I'm sure it's a matter of time before he sniffs it out."

"I should have pitched that lock in the garbage years ago." She dried her hands on her apron, wringing the cotton between her fingers.

Henry came up behind her and slid both arms around her midsection, resting his chin against the nape of her neck. "You don't mean that." His breath tickled her skin.

"I at least should have told you about it."

He didn't respond, merely held her close, his arms a barrier against the fears accosting them both. The fresh scent of his aftershave was as gentle as a kiss. "It will be fine. Whatever happens, the Lord is with us."

• • •

Henry entered the lodge, his blood pressure rising. Two new reports of Gary Legend's behavior had made it to his office, thanks to Mattie. He should have hired her long ago. She was better than a bloodhound.

Elmer Dawson glanced up from the register, a pen tucked behind his ear. "Ranger Eriksson. I wish I could say I am surprised to see you."

"Where is he?"

The manager sighed. "Irene told me too. Please, Henry—we have a lot riding on these bookings for the crew. Don't go in there like a rattlesnake that's already been stepped on once or twice."

Henry laid his palms on the counter and leaned in, bracing one foot behind him. "If you're aware of how the man's been abusing your staff, how come you haven't intervened yourself?"

Elmer bristled, his narrow shoulders rising a few inches. "I've spoken with the director. I've also warned the girls to stay clear of the man, and to clean his cabin only when he is on set. But not all of them listen." He lifted both hands. "I imagine some of them fall for his malarkey about getting them into pictures."

"I'm throwing him out. Out of this lodge. Out of the park." Acid curled up Henry's throat. "If I could throw him out of the state, I'd do that as well."

Elmer's frown softened and he made his way around the counter to stand at Henry's side. "Why does this bother you so much? So a few girls get a lesson in life's hard knocks. He hasn't committed any crimes, best I can tell. Those women need to take some of the responsibility."

If Dawson didn't step back, Henry would grab his collar and shake him. "Those women are our responsibility. We're the ones who rolled out the welcome mat for these Hollywood people."

"Irene told me what you and Alma are going through, Henry. She's very concerned for you both. Motherhood has made her very sensitive to these sorts of things." The man ran a hand along his slender mustache. "Maybe that's coloring your view of what's going on here? Legend hasn't hurt anyone. He made a few girls cry, but that's no reason to bring this whole picture to a standstill."

Henry bit back the growl that threatened to emanate from his throat. "Where is he?"

Elmer sighed. "In the restaurant."

It only took Henry a minute to launch himself up the stairway to the eatery. The director sat at a table by the window, his arm languidly draped around the leading lady and a lit cigarette dangling from his fingers.

Across from them, Gary Legend gripped a bundle of typed sheets, his fist tight around the crumpled pages. He waved it at Bernard Dixon like he was scolding a puppy that peed on the floor. "I won't say that line. I'll be a laughingstock. What sort of hero begs the woman not to leave him?"

"You should have read the script before you took the part, Legend." Dixon shook his head slowly.

"She can walk out—I don't want to change the ending. Just my character's reaction to it. How about, 'Baby, leaving me is the worst mistake you'll ever make.' Or 'Baby, you'll never find another cowboy like me.'"

Henry took a moment to shove down the revulsion he had for the man. He needed every ounce of professionalism to make this work. He could probably use a few acting lessons himself. With a deep breath, he approached the table. "We've got a problem."

All three instantly focused on him, Dixon pulling his arm back to his lap and stubbing the cigarette out in a waiting ashtray.

Legend stood, quick to put his lanky frame to work for him. "What might that be?"

Henry did his best to match the man's posture, if not his height. "I informed you that if I received complaints, I'd come looking for you."

The actress tapped fingernails against her water glass. "Gary, have you been a bad boy? I suppose we should expect it by now."

Legend shook his head. "I haven't done anything out of character."

Exactly what Henry feared. "I want you out of here. Our staff are not your playthings."

"Hold it, hold it." Dixon stood and placed himself between Henry and the star of his production. "Gary's only got one more scene to shoot, then I'll have my driver take him to the airport. But not before then."

Legend bristled. "A girl spouts a few lies, and I get kicked to the curb?"

Dixon pressed the script pages against the man's chest. "Learn the line, deliver it, and get out. I'm fed up with you."

Legend's brows drew low, shadowing his eyes. "I'm not the problem here."

Dixon laid a hand on Ms. Reel's shoulder. "If you want to work on any more of my pictures, you'll do as your told."

The actor snorted and tossed the script aside. "I'll see you on set."

Henry watched him depart. "I'll be glad when we see the back of him."

"No more than me." The director sighed. "His ego's bigger than this canyon." He turned to face Henry. "He'll be out by sunset."

24

Present Day

THE HEADLIGHTS PIERCED the darkness as Blake steered his SUV through the lodge parking lot. He dropped his hat onto the seat and breathed out a long sigh. This night had not been boring. After responding to noise complaints at the campground, he and Noah broke up two fights and took one guy in for drug possession and disorderly conduct.

He'd gone back to double-check that everything had settled down only to get another call about a party spinning out of control in the concession staff dormitory.

Evidently Ethan and his roommate had been charging his climbing buddies a fee to crash on his floor, and one of them had harassed a female employee in the hall.

Blake gripped the steering wheel and ran a hand over his eyes. How many of these "suspicious individual" reports were college kids looking for a night's stay? Another staff member said Ethan had even sneaked friends into empty lodge rooms, which might also explain what Talia saw that night.

The sun would rise soon, and that meant that most of the troublemakers would be sleeping it off while the serious hikers hit the trails with early permits for Angels Landing or canyoneering expeditions. A big part of him wished he were joining them, but his bed was calling.

These night shifts were killing him. He swiped a hand over his eyes and steered in the direction of the Emergency Operations Center. There was still a little time on the clock, but he needed to write up the reports of tonight's arrest.

Blake parked the vehicle and stretched. After this, he'd head home and grab a few hours' sleep before trying to catch Talia during her lunch break. More effective than an energy drink, the thought of seeing Talia again brought him to full wakefulness. Ever since their hike in the Narrows, the floodgates had opened in his heart and she now consumed almost every waking thought—and a good portion of his non-awake ones too.

He grabbed his hat and hopped out, locking the vehicle behind him.

He and Talia had shared a few more kisses since that day, but not with the same wild abandon of the first time. She seemed to be holding back, as if she battled some inner doubts about him or their future together. She hadn't said much more about her return to corporate America, but he knew it must be weighing on her.

After Blake's lifelong habit of bailing on relationships before commitment ever became a conversation, this was new territory for him. But no matter how much he tried to remain detached and prepare himself for her inevitable departure, his heart refused to cooperate. He'd been trained to retreat and regroup when a situation went south, but he knew in his gut there'd be no doing that with Talia. He was all in.

And when she decided to return to her executive life? He'd be back where he started. Alone and unhappy.

The morning air smelled fresh and sweet, a light breeze picking up. He took in a deep breath, savoring the sage and juniper goodness as it flooded through his system. That would have to hold him until he got done with his reports. He headed inside and beelined for the cubicles the enforcement rangers shared.

The chief ranger came out of his office and leaned on the half wall. "Rough night?"

"The usual. You're in early." Blake checked his watch. This building was typically pretty quiet until at least seven, and it hadn't even reached five yet.

"Yeah, I've got a stack of overdue reports. I thought I'd get here early and knock them out before other people started clamoring for my attention." He folded his arms across his chest. "Think about that the next time you're complaining about breaking up fights. You could be spending your days filing reports and attending meetings."

The irony that Blake had only stopped in to file a report wasn't lost on him. "Yes, sir. I'm grateful, sir."

Hal chuckled. "At ease, soldier. That wasn't a test." He headed for the coffeepot sitting to Blake's right and pulled out the filter basket. "I hear you're dating Eriksson's granddaughter. Gutsy move. You met him yet?"

Blake forced himself to relax. "I had dinner with him and Talia last month. He seems like a nice guy."

Hal dumped a scoopful of grounds into the machine, then added a second one for good measure. "The Virgin River runs in his bloodstream. In all the Erikssons'. Talia's new here—and not part of the ranger staff—but I imagine if anyone had the sense that you treated her badly . . ."

"I understand. We're taking it slow."

"Good man." Hal frowned at the machine, his hand hovering over the bag of coffee. "What do you think, one more?"

"Depends how strong you want it."

The chief dropped in another scoop. He turned on the machine and leaned back against the counter. "Bill was my chief when I was in your position. He used to complain about writing these annual reports too. Said his father had written them before him." He shook his head. "Sometimes I question whether I'm worthy to follow in their footsteps."

"The fact you're in here before 0500 speaks pretty well of you, I think."

"Or it means the job has gotten infinitely more complex. I like reading through my predecessors' reports. There was one where Eriksson's father described a whole day on the trail checking telephone cables. A ranger stringing phone lines. Can you just imagine?"

Blake opened a day-old box of peanut butter cookies sitting on the counter and claimed one for his breakfast. "You can still access those old reports?"

"This is the government. Nothing is ever thrown away. Some are online, but pretty much all of them are in the archive."

"I might have to check that out. I bet Talia would be interested as well."

The chief wiped a few crumbs from his beard. "Maybe someday you'll be reading my reports there too. But only if I stop procrastinating and get my rear end in the chair." Grabbing a cookie, he headed for his office.

The coffeepot glugged painfully dark liquid into the glass carafe. Blake left his cup on the desk. Better not risk it. The night had been long enough.

• • •

Later that day, Talia slid a thick book of bound papers closer along the wooden table, leafing through the pages with gloved hands. "This is incredible." She kept her voice low, the archive seeming like a place one should whisper out of respect for the billions of memories housed within its walls. "Look—1945 and 1946. That's around when my great-grandfather started here. And 1948. That's the year Pops was born."

Blake leaned in, one hand on each of her shoulders.

Her skin couldn't help but react to the warmth from his touch, the pleasant distraction rippling through her. With some regret, she refocused her attention on the pages. "I love this old typewriter font. I used to play with Pops's old one when I was a kid. I wonder what happened to that?"

"Maybe it's in a box somewhere around here. You wouldn't believe the stuff they've saved."

She smiled, the idea of the old Royal typewriter taking up space on a shelf making her strangely happy. "Here's Gammelfarfar's first report."

Blake pulled out the chair beside her and dropped into it. "Far-Far? Is that some kind of nickname?"

She glanced up from the yellowing page. "It's Swedish for *grandpa*—paternal grandpa. Maternal grandpa would be *Morfar*. *Far* means 'father,' so *Farfar* is 'father's-father,' essentially. And technically, Henry is my great-grandfather, so *gammelfarfar*." The Swedish words from her childhood sent a pang through her heart. She wasn't even Swedish. The Heritage test had proven that. She pressed a hand to her collarbone, trying to push back the sense of loss creeping over her. "He passed away before I was born."

"What does he say?"

She skimmed over the reports. "Pretty basic stuff. Patrolling, road reports. Car accident—a woman was killed when she was thrown from her vehicle during a crash. Thank goodness for seat belts, right?" Flipping through a few more pages, she located the month of Pops's birth. It likely wouldn't be mentioned in an official report, but it would be fun to get a copy to show Pops what his dad was doing during that time. No paternal leave in those days.

She skimmed over the words, her attention zeroing in on the word *infant*. Talia sucked in a quick breath.

"What?" Blake leaned close.

"'Abandoned infant discovered under footbridge near Zion Lodge.'" A sudden coldness spread through her like she'd just dunked her feet back into the Virgin River. If Blake hadn't been standing directly behind her chair, she'd have slid back from the startling revelation. "A baby left all by itself. That is awful. Why would someone leave a baby out next to a river?"

He sat on the wooden chair beside her. "Desperate people do desperate things."

She skimmed through the few lines that followed. "He didn't write much about it other than investigations were unsuccessful in locating the child's mother and the baby was transferred into state custody."

Blake reached for the book, then drew his hand back. "When's your grandfather's birthday?"

"May eighth—the same as mine." The gravity of what he'd insinuated settled on her. She turned back to the report, sliding her finger up to the date. "May fifteenth."

• • •

Pops stared down at the photocopy, his brow furrowed.

Talia switched on the kitchen light to make it easier for him to read at this late hour. Her stomach had been in knots since she and Blake had stumbled onto the troubling information in the archive. For a moment, she'd considered closing the book and never speaking of it again. Pops hadn't asked her to dig into their DNA or drag aging family secrets out into the open.

But once she knew the truth, it seemed wrong to hide it away again. She'd only been home a few minutes and still juggled her car keys in her fist. The vintage padlock felt warm in her grip. Its U-shaped shackle had been lodged in the brass body for countless decades, much like this family story. How many other mysteries had her great-grandparents taken to the grave? Stumbling over this bit of information had felt like a key finally sliding into place.

The crinkles around her grandfather's hazel eyes deepened as he read the report his father had typed back in 1948. Pops had been staring at the document for a good five minutes now, even though the section about the abandoned baby was only a few lines long.

A crawly sensation raced across Talia's skin. "I'm sorry. I know this must come as a shock."

Pops took a few steps across the kitchen and lowered himself to one of the barstools. "I can't believe I never saw this before."

"There's nothing saying that it's . . ." She scrambled for words. "Maybe it's coincidental. But it did happen about a week after your birthday, according to Gammelfarfar's words."

He pulled off his readers. "My parents never said anything. I mean, quiet adoptions were commonplace back then, but this?" Pops shook his head. "The Swedes are known for being private and reserved—never drawing attention to themselves. My parents fit that stereotype to a T. If this is true—if it's me—then . . ." He ran a hand across his thinning hair. "Talia, I don't know what to say. I'm perplexed."

Talia filled a cup with ice water and handed it to him. She'd never seen Pops flustered. "Did you ever suspect anything?"

He drew it close to his chest without bothering to take a drink. "I don't know. I suppose I felt different, but what child doesn't? I don't resemble them. None of that led me to believe I wasn't their son. I guess I have a lot of questions."

So did she. More than she wanted to burden him with. Talia put her arms around her grandfather. "Even if you weren't their biological son, they loved you. I have no doubt of that. And selfishly, I'm glad we're still related. I was a little afraid that silly DNA test was going to say we weren't."

He hugged her back, his blue flannel shirt soft against her skin. "Tal, you'll always be my grandgirl. Even if the test had come back different."

Pops went to bed early, so Talia retreated to the basement. She'd been staying away from social media the past few weeks. Comparing her life with others' had become a bad habit, and she'd added it to her list of things she wanted to tackle this year. She should probably check her email on occasion, though.

Flopping on the bed, she rolled to her side and opened her laptop.

It only took a few clicks to access her email account and start sifting through the useless junk. A couple of gossip-laden messages from Sydney, a newsletter from Lissa's watchdog organization, an alumni newsletter, and countless other meaningless missives. She continued scrolling through, separating the good stuff from the junk, filing a few to read later and dumping the rest. Her finger stopped on an email from HustleHip Activewear. Her pulse picked up as if she were back on the trail with Blake. Just yesterday she'd read an article about this Phoenix-based company. They were an up-and-coming brand featuring some renewable fibers in their products.

Talia held her breath and clicked open the message.

> Dear Ms. Eriksson,
>
> We received your name and contact information from Jasmine Michaels. We are currently seeking a creative and highly experienced marketing director to assist in developing a solid brand foundation for our forward-thinking company.

A surge of electricity rushed through Talia's body. She launched to a sitting position, jostling the computer. She hadn't applied for any positions, but here one had come looking for her. She pressed two fingers to her lips as she read through the job announcement. The company had been producing urban hip-hop wear, but they were shifting gears to step into the health-conscious fitness clothing market. A major rebrand.

Her fingertips tingled. It would be an incredible opportunity, and the kind of project she could sink her skills into. Skimming down to the bottom of the announcement, she focused on the pay range and drew another quick breath. It was more money than she'd ever dreamed of making.

Talia set the computer to the side and drew her knees up to her chest, wrapping both arms around her lower legs.

The light flickered overhead, not powerful enough to chase away the shadows lurking in the corners of the room. She closed her eyes and tried to picture herself in an office in Phoenix, a pumpkin spice latte in one hand as she worked on the next big project. It was the stuff dreams were made of . . .

But so were red sandstone cliffs, sunrises, and a very special park ranger.

25

1951

"'THE LORD IS my shepherd; I shall not want.'" Alma recited the words as she and Billy walked the path along the river, the Fremont cottonwoods swaying in the breeze. She held on to her son's hand but kept her grip light. He didn't need to know the rhythm her heart was beating inside of her. Today would have been Eddie's birthday, and the memories were so close she could almost touch them with her fingers.

"'He maketh me to lie down in green pastures: he leadeth me beside the still waters.'" The trickling sounds of the Virgin River washed over her, and as she drew in a deep breath, the faint smell of damp earth lingered in the air.

Billy pulled away from her grip, running ahead a few steps and stopping in that adorable little boy crouch—like a frog on a lily pad—to examine a flower next to the trail. "Mamma, look see!"

"Isn't that pretty?" She bent for a better look as commanded. He could probably ask her to go and explore the moon's craters with him and she would comply. Some of the other rangers' wives had commented on her attentiveness and mentioned she and Henry might be spoiling the boy, but she didn't care. Every moment of his young life was precious, and she didn't want to miss a single one.

She laid a hand on her stomach. When she'd first missed her cycle, she'd assumed it was nothing but the nerves. But the days had stretched to weeks.

"The Lord gave, and the Lord hath taken away; blessed be the name of the Lord."

She'd never gotten comfortable with that line from Job, especially considering all that followed in his life. But it was hard to hear the water flowing past and not think on it. The Lord had used the river to take Eddie. And it had also been the place where they found Billy. What part would it play in this babe's life?

Billy got up and jogged down the path, eager for his next find.

Fader Vår, I will trust Thee. It's not easy, but I will trust.

The Lord had been hard at work, not just in her womb but in her soul. When Henry had told her that the Johnsons were requesting another meeting, she'd agreed. A few months ago she couldn't have imagined the unexplainable peace that now flowed from deep inside of her. Even though her heart quivered like a flower in a breeze, her soul was a deep-rooted tree. The Lord was at work, and who was she to get in His way?

"Alma!" Her husband's voice carried down the trail from the direction she'd come.

Turning, Alma cupped a hand over her eyes. "There you are. I thought maybe you were called out."

He jogged toward them, his ranger hat gripped in his hand. "Just running late."

Billy had been clambering over a fallen limb and now sat on top of it with a huge smile on his face. "Look at me, Pappa."

Fine lines fanned out from the corners of Henry's eyes. After pressing a kiss to Alma's cheek, he took a minute to admire his son's climbing prowess. "You got yourself all the way up there? You look like an owl sitting on his perch."

She'd yet to tell Henry about the life growing inside her. It still felt too new, too fragile. But maybe, after all they'd been through, it always would. "I'm glad you could get away."

"Me too. The movie crew is packing up today. I'll breathe a lot easier when they're gone."

"But then there will be something else. Other troublesome guests, another rockfall." Her eyes turned toward the river. "Another flood."

"That's life, I suppose." He lifted Billy from the limb, then set him back on his Buster Browns.

"It is. And life brings good things too."

"It does at that," he said.

She took his hand as they continued walking, trailing after Billy as he explored. Laying her opposite forearm across her body, she touched his wrist. "Good things like friendships, first loves, weddings." She paused. "Babies."

He squeezed her fingers and moved his arm around her waist, drawing her close so their hips bumped as they walked. "It does me good to hear you speak with such contentedness. Especially with what I have to tell you."

Her throat tightened, choking off the news she was about to share.

"The Johnsons aren't coming alone on Thursday."

She sighed. "They're not bringing that newspaperman, are they? I thought they agreed we needed to remain quiet about all this."

"No." The deepening shadows around his eyes spoke volumes. "Alma, I'm not sure how to say this."

She stopped, her feet no longer willing to walk this path.

He turned, taking both of her hands. His Adam's apple bounced just above his collar and the knot of his forest-green tie. "They've hired an attorney."

• • •

The formal office with its glossy cherrywood furniture seemed out of place for this part of Utah. Henry had never imagined he and Alma would need a lawyer for anything beyond drafting his last will and testament, but he'd also never dreamed someone would try to take their son. He stopped just inside the doorway as the attorney pulled out a seat for Alma at the long table. Fighting an insane desire to loosen his tie, Henry claimed the chair beside his wife. He reached over and laid his hand on top of hers.

She rotated her cold fingers to latch onto his grip as if he were the only thing keeping her afloat. She'd long been a lifeline for him, in truth. God had called them to serve one another, though their abilities of doing so had been sorely tested over the years.

Mr. Wilson took a seat at the head of the table, adjacent to Henry. "I'm glad you folks could come in early. I wanted to have an opportunity to discuss your case before we meet with the other parties."

Case. Parties. The words tolled like bells. With the exception of Billy's adoption proceeding, Henry had always been on the outside of legal matters—the arresting officer, in some cases. Never an interested party. He cleared his throat. "And we're thankful you were available to help us walk through this."

The man's graying eyebrows drew low over a pair of gold-rimmed spectacles. "It's an unusual situation, and that's what I specialize in. I've been in semiretirement, but it's cases like these that keep me coming back—much to my wife's dismay." He chuckled.

Alma sat as still as a stone chimney, her large eyes locked on the attorney.

Henry rubbed his thumb along the back of her hand. Typically he wasn't a man given to displays of affection, but the pallor of his wife's skin sent a deep tremor through his soul. She might not survive the loss of another child. He'd known that when she first laid claim to Billy, but he'd never pictured it would happen like this. "What do you think our chances are?"

Mr. Wilson opened the folder, leafing through the small collection of documents hidden within. "The Johnsons have no proof the child—"

"Billy." Alma's voice cracked. "His name is Billy. William Eriksson. Our son."

The attorney smiled. "Good, good. You're right to point that out,

Mrs. Eriksson." He cleared his throat. "If we go to court, we will want to use Billy's name from the get-go and as often as we can get away with. It might help solidify the judge's attitude that Billy's not just some charge of the state to be placed."

Charge of the state? Henry's stomach rolled. "The state granted us adoption rights almost two years ago. Could they really rescind that now?"

Mr. Wilson raised a hand as if to halt the flood of questions he knew were coming. "Let's not get ahead of ourselves. I'll get to that in a moment." He uncapped a fountain pen and placed it on a clean pad of paper beside him. "William—Billy—is your son, according to the State of Utah. And the Johnsons have not made any assertion that either of you were in any way connected to the abduction of their child in Salt Lake City."

Henry sat back in his seat, the air leaking from his lungs. "Of course not."

"The media have made some ridiculous claims, but I want you to be assured that none of that will have play in the courtroom."

"We will have to go to court, then," Henry said.

His wife's soft but quick intake of breath was like a thorn to his heart.

The attorney picked up his pen and fiddled it between his knuckled fingers. "It seems likely, yes. But if we come to an agreement first, we might be able to avoid that outcome. Please, bear with me. I have more to say before we get to that fork in the road."

Henry nodded as Alma's hand slid tighter into his grasp.

"The problem as I see it," Mr. Wilson continued, "is that the Johnsons have compiled a rather alarming amount of circumstantial evidence suggesting Billy may actually be their child. Enough to convince a prominent Salt Lake City attorney to petition the state to reopen the case. That could put your adoption decree in jeopardy." He paused, allowing that truth to sink in. "Their hesitance to do this before now was that no one had been able to connect the dots. They were recently made aware of your visit to Holy Cross Hospital. A nurse there informed the police that you were seen on the premises, making inquiries regarding a piece of hospital equipment that had come into your possession." He met Henry's eyes. "Is this accurate?"

Henry's stomach sank. "Yes."

"May I ask how you obtained this item?" Mr. Wilson pointed his pen toward Henry. "And please, be truthful. I'm on your side, but I can't help you if you lie to me."

Once again, his actions had doomed his family. From the moment Alma placed that padlock in his hand, he'd known that the item held power over them in some odd way. He swallowed, hoping to moisten his dry mouth. "It was found in the hatbox alongside the baby." He glanced at Alma, her eyes downcast. "My wife wasn't aware of its significance. Neither of us were. It was only after we met the Johnsons that we realized the engraved initials might refer to Holy Cross."

Mr. Wilson blew out a long breath, his fingers drumming a dirgelike rhythm on the table.

Henry sat forward. "But we don't know how it got there. It might be unrelated. The janitor said there were hundreds disposed of when the hospital switched to a modern version."

"Do you still have it?"

It had ridden around in Henry's pocket ever since, a shackle on his heart. He retrieved the lock and slid it across the table to the attorney.

Wilson picked it up and adjusted his glasses as he squinted at the letters imprinted on the weathered brass. "And the hospital positively identified this as one of their own?"

"Yes."

Sighing, the attorney made some notes on his pad. "That does complicate matters. I can see why they requested a hearing. And I assume, since we're here, you had no further luck in identifying a suspect in the local area."

"No." With each of these questions, a little more hope emptied out of Henry's heart.

His wife's eyes remained fixed on the table as if the discussion had caused her to withdraw into herself once more. The touch of her hand was his tenuous link to her heart. Once again, he was failing her. He hadn't been at her side the day the flood swept her and Eddie into the river, and these past few nights, his dreams had been laced with images of reaching for Alma's hand in the swirling, debris-laden water, only now it was Billy she clutched to her chest. *Lord, have mercy. Please. I beg You. You're a father too.*

Mr. Wilson rubbed fingers over his cheekbone, studying the document in front of him. "It's a weak link for them. And yet it's something. Your own claim to the child is merely the order from the State of Utah."

"We found him." Alma's voice was flat. "I know that means nothing to the eyes of the law, but we've raised him. We're all Billy knows. We are his mamma and pappa."

"I'm aware of that, Mrs. Eriksson." The attorney's voice was gentle. "And hopefully the judge will take that into account. But it doesn't overrule the Johnsons' claim. I should warn you—if this goes before a judge, it could be a long and painful procedure. Every aspect of your lives will be fair game. Your marriage, your work, your home." He drew a hand down his mouth and chin. "Even your oldest child's death."

The room started to spin slowly. Henry splayed fingers on the tabletop. "That was a horrific accident."

"On top of that"—the attorney plowed forward, turning one of the typed pages—"Mr. Johnson is a prominent banker in Salt Lake City—well-respected and better connected. A member of multiple service organizations. A descendant of a pioneer family. And if we end up in court, it would likely be in Salt Lake."

"What does that mean?" Henry asked.

"It won't help you if I mince words, so I'm going to lay it out there.

In cases like this, it can come down to splitting hairs for the judge." Mr. Wilson met their eyes. "He'll be asking himself, What is better for the child? To live in the wilds of a national park afflicted by flash floods and rattlesnakes and brought up by a park ranger who doesn't even own a home? Or to be raised by a wealthy couple in the heart of one of America's most prosperous cities, where he'll have access to the best education?"

"Billy should be with his mother," Alma inserted.

"The trouble is, Mrs. Eriksson—we don't really know who that is."

Alma's hand slid from Henry's grasp.

• • •

Still waters don't always mean an easy swim.

Alma sat on the edge of her bed, gazing out the small window that faced Lady Mountain. She unfastened her hairnet and unwound one of the curlers holding her hair tight against her head. All night, as she'd tossed and turned, they'd dug against her scalp like so many grasping claws.

Henry shifted under the covers, the sheets rustling in protest of his motion. "You're awake early." His voice was low and gravelly, as if it hadn't yet joined him in wakefulness. "Is Billy still asleep?"

"Yes." Their son had yet to make a peep, but she knew what she'd find if she went in to check on him. He always slept sprawled across his small bed like a mountain lion draped over a tree limb. Sue had promised to send over their extra single bed as soon as they shuffled their kids into the new bunks.

The thought brought an all-too-familiar lump to Alma's throat. She yanked several more hairpins, desperate for relief from something—anything.

Billy might not need the new mattress. Once again, they'd be hiding things away and trying to forget. Forget the life that God had imprinted on their hearts.

She touched her stomach where the new life grew. *Why now?*

The bedsprings creaked as Henry's arms came around her. The warmth of his skin was shocking in the early morning chill, and she leaned into his grasp.

"Come back under the covers," he whispered into her shoulder. "You're freezing."

Alma freed the rest of the curlers and ran her fingers through the loose strands. Lying down would ruin her efforts, but what did it matter? No one expected her to be Betty Grable. Not here. Not now.

She slid her bare legs back under the bedding and scooched close to Henry's side. The only safe place. "I didn't sleep."

"I know." His fingers ran circles along the back of her nightgown. "I didn't much myself."

She hesitated, holding her breath for a long moment. It was no good keeping the news for a better moment. "I need to tell you something."

Her husband's hand stilled, and he drew back a few inches, taking his warmth with him. "Is there more?"

More? The word played like a discordant note. "What do you mean?"

"The lock?"

"No. This isn't . . . that."

His muscles relaxed.

She'd mangled his trust keeping that secret. "There's going to be another baby."

He pulled his arms free and sat up. "What are you saying? Another baby where?"

She took his hand and drew it back to herself, placing it on her abdomen.

In the colored light of dawn, his face softened. "You're expecting?" He pulled her to him. "Alma . . ."

She moistened her lips. None of this had come out like she'd hoped, but then, what did? "I know the timing is awful."

He crushed her to his chest. "Shh, *min älskling*. This is a blessing. An unexpected blessing."

With her ear pressed against him, the sound of his rapid heartbeat flooded over her. She rubbed a hand across her midsection, the thought of a life growing there suddenly feeling more real than ever now that Henry knew the truth.

"You'll need to take care of yourself." He mumbled the words into her hair. "No more lifting. Get more sleep."

A smile tugged at her lips. Her husband—always the protector. Always trying to step into God's shoes. Watching over her. Eddie. Billy. And now this little one.

How much weight could one man's shoulders bear? The Lord had given him a good heart. She'd never doubted that, even in the midst of her mind-numbing grief.

Her mind wandered to Beatrice Johnson. She'd barely had a chance to hold her son.

My son.

Her fingers curled inward against Henry's chest.

He covered her hand with one of his own. "What's wrong?"

Alma drew in a shuddering breath. "Billy."

Henry stayed motionless, her fingers sandwiched between his palm and his body. "What about him?"

"I think . . ." Her throat tightened. Saying the words aloud would tear at the threads holding her together. Fragile, uneven stitches that had been added the day she first laid eyes on Billy, wrapped her arms around the little body, and taken him into her heart. And their home. "I think he belongs with them." Her voice trembled. "We have no right to hold him here, if he is their son."

"He is *our* son."

"I believe God placed us here 'for such a time as this.' The Lord knew he would need us. And we would need him."

Henry rolled toward her. "What are you saying—we no longer need him?"

"Never." She took a shaky breath. "Never. But I think the Lord is telling me . . . it's not about us."

He gripped her side. "What the attorney was saying about our living situation—he's gotten to you. The fact that we live in government housing in a wild place—"

"Henry, no." She lifted her fingers to his lips, the shadows around his eyes breaking something deep inside of her. "We could be living in a tent in the middle of the desert, and I wouldn't care. We have enough love to raise dozens of children. Billy loves us and our home. He's never known otherwise, and I don't think he'd be better off because the Johnsons have more money or better schools."

"Then I don't understand." He rolled back to stare up at the ceiling.

He didn't seem to *want* to understand. Frankly, neither did she. Alma pressed a gentle kiss to her husband's upper arm, the corded muscles quivering beneath her lips. These same arms that had held her while she cried. Had bounced Eddie while he fussed with colic. Had held Billy's hand while they walked along the bank of the Virgin River. "What do you think we should do?"

"Alma." His voice was soft, barely stirring the early morning air. "That court hearing . . . it'll be torture. A public spectacle. Us against them. But I would walk through fire for him. You know that."

"I do. As would I."

"But then, I think of Billy being dragged through all of that. His name would be on everyone's lips." He swallowed. "We both heard the attorney. The evidence—such that it is—it's in the Johnsons' favor."

She trailed fingers down his arm, treasuring the warmth of his skin against hers. "Where's Solomon when we need him?"

He wove his fingers through hers, lifting her knuckles to his lips. "So what are we saying?"

"Going to court . . . might not be the best choice. For any of us."

26

Present Day

Blake settled onto the plush sofa at the Erikssons' home, exhausted from a long night shift followed by a hike around Checkerboard Mesa with Talia. Their days off hadn't coordinated lately, so he'd happily sacrificed a few hours of rest in order to hang out with her. A good exchange if anyone asked him.

They'd taken their time exploring the fascinating landscape near the park's eastern entrance, where the red rock cliffs gave way to the lighter-colored sandstone laced with a crisscrossing pattern of vertical and horizontal cracks. The stone had radiated the sunlight back up at their faces, and the stinging heat in Blake's neck and face suggested the beginnings of a sunburn.

Talia sat next to him with a cup of tea in one hand and her laptop in the other. "Lissa James messaged me the link to a website that might offer more information on my grandfather's birth."

He picked up the glass of ice water from the coffee table, hoping the chill would revive him. "That's your social media influencer friend?" Talia had been a little withdrawn during today's walk, but she'd talked a bit about her old life in marketing, and he was doing his best to keep up. Whenever she mentioned her career, an ache settled in the back of his throat. She was missing her old life. He could feel it in his gut.

They'd grown closer over the past several weeks, and he'd even managed to open up to her a little about his own past. Mostly his time in

Afghanistan and the Federal Law Enforcement Training Center. He didn't want to burden her with his childhood. Not yet. Maybe never.

"No, she's the journalist who clued me in to the problems at Zeta. We've been texting ever since. She's been keeping me up to date with the fashion industry." She turned back to the computer, the glow of the screen illuminating a slight downturn of her lips. "I knew she was an ace at research, so I sent her a message about—about what we found."

Blake slid an arm behind her shoulder, like a teenager at a movie, pleased when Talia nestled into his side. The warmth of her body against his was intoxicating. He laid his head back against the cushion and closed his eyes, the flowery scent of her hair filling his senses. If he sat here too long, he might drift off, and he didn't want her to think he was bored. He forced his eyes open.

Talia folded her knees up underneath herself, as flexible as a yoga master, and created a platform for her computer. "She said you can search all sorts of old newspapers with just a few clicks. Do you mind if I do a quick search?"

With her snuggled up against him, she could be defusing a bomb and he wouldn't care. "No, go right ahead." He stifled a yawn.

A frown flitted across her face. "Blake, you haven't slept at all—have you? I should take you home."

"No, I'm fine." He ran his fingers along her upper arm, relishing the touch of her long hair draped over his knuckles. "There's no place I'd rather be."

She leaned over and pressed a kiss to his cheek. "You're too sweet. If this gets to be too much, let me know. Or just close your eyes."

Sweet. Yeah. No one had ever called him that. He let his eyelids slump. He wouldn't sleep, but he also wouldn't mind resting for a few minutes.

The sound of her typing and clicking had nearly lulled him into slumberland when she sat upright, dumping his head from her shoulder.

He jolted to attention. "What—what is it?"

"I found it. There's an article about Pops—I mean, about the baby abandoned in the park."

"Seriously?" He wiped his eyes. "From 1948?"

She pointed a finger at the screen. "'Park Ranger Seeks Mother of Abandoned Infant.'"

"Read it to me." He shook off the sleepiness.

Talia shifted, opening the laptop wider. "'Zion Rangers said the trail had gone cold in their search for the mother of a foundling baby discovered near a river in the national park.'" She shook her head. "*Trail* gone cold. I'm sure the reporter was quite proud of that line. 'Thankfully, Park Ranger Henry Eriksson rescued the infant before it succumbed to exposure or became food for the local coyotes and bobcats known to frequent the area.'" Talia touched fingers to her mouth. "I hadn't even thought of that."

"It wouldn't be the safest place to leave a child." Of all the crimes Blake had investigated since starting with the Park Service, he couldn't imagine being faced with one like this. "It does make you wonder what the mother was thinking."

She turned back to the screen. "'The foundling, which is estimated to be about a week old, was wrapped in a wool blanket and tucked into a leather hatbox. Sheriff Albert Moody who delivered the baby to the hospital in St. George reported that the child was in good condition and there was no note or any other identification included in the container.'"

"A week old." Blake reached for his glass and took another sip, still struggling to shake off the cobwebs of sleep. "I always think of abandoned babies being newly born. But someone took care of this one for a week before leaving him behind. That means he could have been born outside the park."

"Does that make a difference?" Talia asked.

"It would complicate the search, that's for sure. If the baby had been birthed at the lodge, guests might have heard or seen something.

There might be evidence left behind. But if he was born in Springdale or farther afield?" He shrugged. "Then the possibilities are endless. Anyone could have driven in and deposited the baby there. That's probably why the mother was never found."

"But why there? I've heard stories of children being left at hospitals and church doorsteps. But a national park? That's harsh."

No harsher than thrusting your child into the hands of an American soldier. The desperation in that father's eyes was forever burned in Blake's memory. He reclaimed his arm from behind Talia's shoulders and slid forward on the seat, legs itching to move. "No safe haven laws in those days. I'm sure the mother was desperate. Maybe not in her right mind."

Something flickered across Talia's face. "The mother."

Blake stopped, studying her odd expression. "What about her?"

"I hadn't really stopped to think about her. If Pops was that baby, then his mother . . ." A faraway look stole into Talia's brown eyes.

"She's your great-grandmother."

"She could have had other children. Pops might have family he's never known."

"And so do you."

Talia pulled her arms tight around her middle, staring at the computer screen as if she could force the article to give her additional information. "That's a strange feeling. Do you think we could find them?"

Blake walked to the fireplace hearth, where a line of small, framed portraits stood. A long-legged girl in pigtails was but a glimpse of the woman Talia would become, and there she was surrounded by countless siblings, cousins, aunts, and uncles. She'd been raised among a big family. He'd never understand how that felt. "I imagine some of those names on your Heritage report are connected to this."

She scooped up her phone from the table and opened the app. "You're right, I'm sure." Standing, she headed for the kitchen. "I'm starved. I'll be able to process this better with some food in my system. Do you want a sandwich?" Standing in the doorway, she opened a green bag of chips and popped one in her mouth.

"I wouldn't turn one down. Can I help?"

"No, I've got it." She turned and headed for the refrigerator. "You should sit down and close your eyes again. It was fun hearing you snore."

"I don't snore." He followed her into the kitchen, came up behind her, and wrapped both arms around her middle. "And you don't need to cook. I could take you out to dinner."

"Oh, you snore all right. And this isn't cooking. I'm slapping some mayo and turkey on bread. You might get a leaf of lettuce if you're lucky." She rotated in his arms and leaned in for a kiss, gently massaging her fingertips down his spine.

The salty taste of her lips sent energy zipping through him. No way he was sleeping now. He groaned and pulled her closer. "You taste like sour cream and onion. If I wasn't hungry before, I am now." Blake captured her mouth for a deeper kiss. He needed to get a hold of himself. As tired as he was, he wouldn't be making good decisions. He gave her one more kiss—softer this time—then stepped back. "I think food might be wise."

She tipped her head, a grin spreading across her face. "All right. But you better go sit down, otherwise I can't concentrate on sandwiches."

Grabbing a handful of chips, he forced himself to retreat to the sofa. That woman was going to drive him mad. In all the right ways.

The computer sat open on the table in front of him. "Do you mind if I scan for more articles?"

"Sure. Let me know if you find anything."

He pulled the laptop close and examined the website. Her previous search hadn't been saved, from what he could tell. He typed *Baby found Zion National Park* into the form and watched as the site sorted through potential hits. A list of twenty-one separate articles came up.

Blake rubbed a hand over his chin. Maybe he should have entered the year. Talia had located only a few articles.

The dates caught his eye. 1951. There couldn't have been a second baby. Why was this being regurgitated in newspapers three years later? Blake clicked open one of the articles. *Zion Foundling—Abducted Salt Lake Baby?* He squinted at the blurry type of the old newspaper.

A notification popped up in the screen's top right corner, pulling his attention from the page.

> New Message: HustleHip Activewear
> Subject: Job offer. Let's talk.

Blake's stomach dropped. He glanced toward the kitchen, but Talia was still quiet. Had she received the same notification on her phone?

The window vanished as quickly as it had appeared. Just as well. It hadn't been meant for him. Blake took a deep breath to clear his mind. He'd known she was only here for the season, and yet he'd still managed to lose the grip on his heart. Time to reel it back in.

He directed his eyes back to the website and tried to focus. The article remained open, and he skimmed through the words.

> Authorities are comparing inked footprints of the famed Zion foundling to see if he might indeed be the missing Johnson baby, abducted from his mother's arms at Holy Cross Hospital.

So there had been some leads, after all. The trail might have been cold in 1948, but someone heated it up in 1951. "I found something you might want to see," he called to Talia.

"Be right there." Her voice was soft, like she'd already traveled some distance from him.

He rubbed a hand across his chin as he read through the other headlines. They came from as far away as New York. That couldn't be right.

Opening another to check, he tipped the screen so he could read it more easily. *Ranger's Wife Kills Son, Steals Another.* Blake almost dropped the computer.

"You're a lucky man." Talia appeared with two plates and the bag of chips. "I found Swiss cheese too. These are going to be better than I'd hoped." Her eyes locked on Blake, and she froze. "What's wrong?"

He closed the laptop. "I'm not sure we can trust this data. Newspapers are known to embellish stories."

She lowered herself to the sofa and laid the dishes on the coffee table. "What did you find?"

Blake blew out a long breath, all thoughts of job offers—and food—gone. "Something you're not going to like."

• • •

Talia swept the shards of broken glass into the dustpan, careful to check the nearby surfaces for stray pieces.

"I'm so sorry." The hiker shrugged off his pack, nearly catching a second display of blown-glass sculptures with the tips of his trekking poles.

"It was only two shot glasses. It looks worse than it is." She eyed his large pack. "Maybe you should take that out to the lobby, though."

"I'll do that right now, and then come back in to pay for the cups. I'm so embarrassed. My legs are jelly after that hike." He swung the bag onto his shoulder—miraculously missing any more items—and made his way out.

The throbbing in Talia's temples deepened to a viselike grip as she bent down and plucked a tiny sliver from the edge of a basket holding stuffed animals. She needed to shake them out. Scooping up the wicker container, she clipped the shelf and sent the glasses rattling against one another, the one on the end spilling onto the floor and adding to the mess.

She bit her tongue before putting voice to the words that collected on the back of her tongue. The basket of plush animals flopped to the ground at her feet, scattering fuzzy critters across the floor. She pressed both palms against her eyes. "I can't. I just can't."

A hand touched her back. "Talia?" Myrtle's voice was low and soothing. "Take a breath, girl."

If she didn't blink her eyes quickly, they were going to fill with tears. That corner of the gift shop had grown strangely quiet considering the crush of people who had swarmed through the displays all morning. Maybe she'd frightened them off.

"You're acting like your dog just died and your best friend ran off with your man." Myrtle's hand rubbed circles in the small of Talia's back.

"You've been listening to too much country music." Talia bent down and retrieved the basket, flinging the park creatures back into their home one by one.

"Leave it. I'll send Mark over to clean up." Myrtle gripped Talia's elbow. "You're in no shape to be doing this." She steered Talia toward the door. "Hey, Lauren—we're taking our fifteen."

"Together?" Talia asked. "Isn't that against the rules?"

"I'm the boss. I make the rules." The older woman rolled her eyes. "Come on, fresh air or caffeine? Which is more critical?"

"Air sounds good."

Talia followed her boss out the front doors and down the sidewalk toward the parking area. She expected Myrtle to steer her toward a bench, but the older woman kept a brisk pace and marched them both across the road and toward the corrals and the river. She slowed just enough for Talia to come up beside her. "There now. I thought it best to get you away from the guests before you snapped and started pelting them with souvenir mugs."

"I wasn't that bad." Talia rubbed at her forehead, willing the tension to ease.

"It isn't Blake, is it? If that idiot dumped you, I'll—"

"Blake and I are fine. Better than fine, actually." Talia shot her a look, mildly amused that Myrtle would take her side after all her shameless flirting. "Idiot—really? What happened to 'American hero'?"

Myrtle's penciled brows lifted, nearly disappearing into the gray curls that lined her forehead. "I'm rather fond of the both of you. I'd hate to have to choose. So what's bothering you, then?"

They continued walking, enjoying an easier pace now. Talia jammed a hand into her pocket, her fingers closing over Gammelfarmor's padlock. She and Pops had talked late into the night about the articles she and Blake had found online. She'd eliminated some of the worst ones as lies, but a handful of others had intriguing information. As best as she could tell, her great-grandparents had lost a child about a year before finding the abandoned baby. Though he was initially taken into state custody, they had petitioned for custody and that had been granted. This seemed to support the idea that Pops was the baby found in the hatbox.

Wherever the information led, it didn't solve her other problem. "I received a job offer."

Myrtle stopped walking, her eyes locking onto Talia. "I didn't know you were applying for other positions."

"I wasn't. I'd planned to wait until the end of my season and then reassess what I want to do with the rest of my life."

The older woman pressed her lips together, looking like someone doing a duck-face selfie.

Talia pushed out a noisy breath. "It came from one of my company's competitors. They heard why I was fired, and they're starting a new line of cleaner activewear and want to bring me on to promote it." The ache in her head intensified, the tension spreading to her neck muscles. "I don't know what to do."

"Do you want to work for this company?"

Talia stood on the footbridge, her eyes drawn to the flowing current of the river below them. "I don't know. I think they just contacted me to rub it in Zeta's face. When I first got fired, I might have embraced that idea. But now?" She sighed.

"Now you don't want anything to do with their posturing?"

"I came here because I wanted to sort things out, but honestly, I feel more confused than ever. I'd be a fool to turn this down. It's more money than I ever dreamed of making." Sweat broke out between Talia's shoulder blades. "But leaving right now? I've done nothing here but create chaos in my grandfather's life—making him question everything he knew about himself. Then I just walk out on him?"

"I ran into Bill yesterday at the grocery store. He told me some of what you found." Her voice lowered. "It sounds like you've been digging in the family graveyard—unearthing stuff that family intended to keep buried." She gripped the handrail.

"That was never my intention." Talia's heart sank even lower. "But once I started tugging on that loose thread, things just started unraveling."

"That's how these things usually go."

"And then there's Blake." Even saying his name made the emotions well up in her chest like a bubbling spring. How her heart yearned for that man. Could she honestly walk away from him now? Phoenix was closer than Palo Alto, but still distant enough to make a relationship feel just out of reach.

"Better than fine, you said." Myrtle smiled. "Oh, to be young and stupid again."

"I've made a pro-con list for the job. But none of it makes sense. If I don't take this job"—she swallowed, her throat growing thick with emotion—"there might not be another. But I'm not even sure I want another." An incredulous laugh burst from her mouth. "That sounds so crazy. I mean, I have to get another job. I can't work in the gift shop forever. I even sat down to write out a list of goals, but I honestly didn't know where to start."

"You and your never-ending lists." Myrtle laughed, her cackle swept away on the breeze. "Child, you are just like this river."

The assertion stopped Talia cold. "What do you mean? Deep? Shallow?"

"You're always in a *rush*. Your thoughts are consumed by the future. All you can see is the headlong plunge to the ocean, and when the earth gets in your way, you just"—she made a chopping motion with her arm—"slice your way through it. Splashing over waterfalls, digging through canyons, washing away anything that gets in your way."

The words burrowed into Talia's heart. "Is it wrong to have goals? Dreams?"

"Not a bit." Myrtle leaned on the railing, gazing down at the swirling water below them. "But if you're not careful, you miss all the good stuff along the way." She gestured at a leaf spinning a few circles in the current before being carried off. "Imagine that's you."

Talia watched as the leaf cascaded over a few rocks on its way. "Okay. So I was water, but now I'm a—"

"Listen to me." Myrtle locked eyes with Talia. "I've got a few years of experience, and I might have something you need to hear."

"I'm sorry." Talia stilled. She'd never been good at accepting criticism, and she could feel it coming at her like a storm. "Go on."

Her boss turned to stare at the stream, the leaf already disappearing into the distance. She fell silent, her fingers gripping and releasing the edge.

Remorse crept through Talia. Had she missed her chance to hear the woman's advice? Right now she could use every bit of wisdom anyone had to offer. Job, relationship, family, goals. It was all a muddle in her mind.

After a few minutes, Myrtle turned her face skyward as if begging God for assistance. She breathed out a long exhale. "Imagine you're that leaf. You're spinning your way down the river, excited about how far you've traveled and how far you have to go. All you want is to get to the ocean."

Talia let her lids fall closed, determined to listen with an open mind.

"The current grabs you, and you're flying—racing past rocks and roots, dodging fallen branches like they're nothing. You want to see what's around the next bend, and the next, and the one after that. But in your hurry"—her voice grew soft as she slowed her words—"you never see this."

At the touch of her friend's hand, Talia opened her eyes.

Myrtle stretched out her other arm, gesturing to the massive cliffs on either side of them.

The brilliant reds and oranges of the sandstone nearly stole Talia's breath as they gleamed in the morning light. "I'd hate that."

Myrtle squeezed her wrist. "You are the water, Talia. God is the rock. Don't be so quick to pass Him by."

The sting of tears blurred Talia's view of the river as fragments of Bible verses she'd learned as a child flooded her heart. *The Lord is my rock, and my fortress. The rock of my salvation. The rock of my refuge.* How many times had she read these words in the Psalms but never really thought about what they meant?

Her friend wasn't done. "And when the disciples were terrified of the storm, do you remember what Jesus said to the water?"

All Talia could manage was a headshake. Her voice had vanished somewhere downstream with the leaf.

The older woman slid her arm around Talia's waist. "He said, '*Be still.*'"

• • •

"On rappel!" Talia gripped the brake line and tried not to think about the quiver in her legs, hidden beneath the neoprene of her rented wet suit. Her heart pounded as she backed toward the yawning chasm. Putting canyoneering on her Zion to-do list had been an impulsive decision. But as usual, once it made it onto paper, her brain was unwilling to let it go. And seeing Blake's eyes light up when he read it had sealed the deal.

"We've got you, Talia. You can do this," Katie called up, her face set. The woman had birthed three children and climbed four of Colorado's fourteener peaks. If that wasn't reason to trust, Talia wasn't sure what was.

Lord, help me. Backing over the edge into nothingness would take every bit of mind-over-matter guts she had. She gripped the rope with gloved hands, one in front and one behind her back as Blake had shown her.

"You're doing great, Tal. Step of faith." His voice echoed below her, the familiar sound slowing her pulse.

Over dinner last night, she'd told him about the job offer from HustleHip Activewear, and he'd responded with the steady support and confidence she'd come to expect from him. Had there been the tiniest scrap of uncertainty in his forest-green eyes, she might have gone straight home and dashed off a regretful email to the clothing company.

"I won't stand in your way, Tal," he'd said. "I respect you too much for that. If this is your dream job, I think you should take it."

Was it her dream job?

She stood on a precipice—in more ways than one.

Her breaths came fast. One scuffing step after another, she lowered herself over the edge, silencing the self-preservation instincts screaming in her head. Once past the lip, the steady grip of the rope and harness became more obvious. She leaned into them, walking her boots against the sandstone cliff. A squeal burst from her lips. "I'm doing it!"

"Slow and steady," Blake reminded from below.

She followed his recommendation, letting the line advance through her fingers.

"Look confident. I'm getting video." The teasing tone in his voice broke the tension.

She laughed, twisting to see him over her shoulder. "No you're not.

My backside? Why are you always taking pictures from behind me?" Maybe she didn't want to know the answer to that.

"You're going to want to remember this. There's nothing like the first rappel."

Talia refocused on the rock face, placing the soles of her feet against the sandstone. She'd need to ask Blake later about his first rappel experience. He so rarely spoke of his years in the army. Even after all these months, he'd only shared a handful of stories. His life was like a series of closed doors, memories packed away in storage compartments where they could no longer hurt him—his childhood, his family, his service time. As much as she'd love to peek behind those doors, she didn't want to push. And if she moved to Phoenix, the memory of her might be relegated to one more locked compartment. The thought landed hard.

She touched down on the slot canyon floor to find him waiting for her. "I did it!"

"You did." He grinned. "Now, don't forget . . ."

Talia gasped and looked up toward the ledge. "Off rappel," she called.

"Belay off," Katie said behind her. "Great job, Talia."

"What a surge of adrenaline." Talia fumbled with the clips and carabiners as her breathing slowed to a manageable level. "How many more rappels do we have?"

"Just a couple today. This is an easy canyon to get you acclimated." Blake reached down and helped her sort the equipment. "This one here." His fingers brushed against her own.

"I've got it." She reset the rope for Alder like she'd been shown earlier. "But you should double-check me."

"I am." He bent over her shoulder. "Everything's good."

Alder was the last to descend the short run, bounding down the cliff like he'd been doing it all his life. "This is such an incredible example of erosional downcutting. I can't believe Chase is missing out."

"He's thirteen, Alder. Girls trump geology." His wife stood back, coiling the rope.

"That's blasphemy." Alder shook his head. "Geology rocks."

The horrible joke landed flat on the canyon floor. Katie shot a look at the other two. "You see what I have to deal with? Prehistoric humor."

Talia smiled at the couple's teasing.

Blake gathered the bags. "Let's move along. We want to get out of the slot before eleven. I don't like the sound of the afternoon forecast."

"You're kidding, right?" Talia adjusted the laces on one of her boots. "I checked it—it said maybe a five percent chance of precipitation later today. That's practically nothing."

Katie took a quick sip from her water bottle. "You don't want to be in a slot canyon if there's *any* chance of rain. I had it drilled into my head by my climbing instructor. 'See a cloud in the sky, there's a chance you could die.'"

Talia glanced up at the ribbon of blue. "It looks good, though."

Blake bumped her arm. "That's why we need to keep moving. We want to be out of here before anything changes. Rain anywhere in the drainage—miles away, even—will funnel into these slots before it begins to fall here."

"And after this next drop, there's no turnaround," Katie added. "Only forward. We could shimmy back up this one, but not the next. At least, not easily or quickly."

Shimmying up sounded far too technical for her. She could run for miles, but her upper arm strength had always been poor. "Okay. I'm ready." She checked her zipped pocket for the lump of her cell phone. She wanted to get a few pictures of the next rappel. They'd planned for Alder to go first on this stretch, and she'd follow, leaving Blake and Katie bringing up the rear. Maybe she'd get video of Blake's tail coming down that line. It would only be fair.

Alder led the way through the narrowing canyon, the sandstone walls pressing closer together the farther they progressed. He pointed up to the undulating curves in the walls. "You can tell this was shaped by water."

The canyon floor grew increasingly narrow until Talia found herself walking with a hand on either wall as she traversed clumps of stone and debris in the gap. "How often do you get down here?"

"We only do a couple of canyons each year. Our work schedules aren't very conducive to trip planning. I'm glad we could squeeze this in." He glanced up toward the strip of sky above them, like he'd done multiple times in the past ten minutes.

Talia followed his line of sight. The blue seemed to be leaching away like a well-worn pair of denim jeans. *Only five percent chance.* Her stomach fluttered. The image of water flowing through this gap chilled her.

"Watch the pothole." He pointed ahead to a circular dip that held murky water. "This one's just a puddle, but they're often far deeper than they appear. You don't want to go into one if you don't have to. It's not unheard of to get stuck in one of these holes with no way to extricate yourself." Alder braced a hand against one wall and his feet on the other to edge his way across. "Eventually we'll have to slosh through some water, but you always want to keep an eye on these depressions."

Blake caught up behind her. "Don't worry. We're not going to let anything happen." His soothing voice eased the tension growing in her chest. "But you need to know all the hazards."

She took a deep breath, placing her hands where Alder had. "It's better to know. I don't want to do something stupid that puts everyone at risk."

With a few more minutes of walking, the canyon opened out again, the wash littered with scrubby bushes and rocks. Talia breathed deep, the claustrophobic sensation drifting away on the morning breeze. "We're not done already?"

"Not at all," Alder said. "That was just the first stretch. Some people skip over it to get to the good stuff, but Katie and I thought it would be a good practice run to show you guys what we're in for. We hike for a bit in the open, then drop into the next slot."

Laughter caught Talia's attention, and she studied the rock formations jutting upward just to the left of them. A group of hikers were scrambling along on the jagged edges, laughing and talking. They wore helmets and harnesses but seemed to be having fun exploring the side wall of the canyon through this section. One guy crouched low, reaching his arm into a small rockfall and pulling something out, turning it in his fingers before reaching in again.

"Blake." She laid a hand on his arm. "What are they doing?"

He turned, his eyes following her line of sight. "That's the guy from the concession staff. Ethan." Blake's brow furrowed. "I figured he'd been fired after the last incident."

Katie came up beside them. "They shouldn't be over there. The cryptobiotic soils are super fragile. It's not good to walk on them. It's better to stick to the wash."

"He pulled something out of that hole." Talia's stomach muscles tightened. "And his buddy over there is digging around too. What do you suppose they're looking for?"

The climber bent down and pushed something into the cavern, stopping to wipe his palms against his pants afterward.

Blake stiffened. "I've been suspicious he's been supplying drugs to the concession staff. He let us search his car and apartment, but we didn't come up with anything."

Alder unhooked his helmet and ran a hand over his hair. "You think he could be hiding a stash out here? That seems like a lot of trouble."

"It does. I'm sure there would be easier places to hide something."

Ethan held up his phone as if grabbing a few photos. As he turned, his gaze found their group, and his eyes widened. Jamming the phone into his pack, he hurried after his friends, dislodging a couple of rocks as he scrambled down the slope.

"Well, that didn't look at all guilty." Katie chuckled. "He's definitely up to no good."

"Yeah, I don't like it," Blake said. "They're headed in for the second pitch. We're going to be following them the whole way through. We should have used this opportunity to get ahead of them, but I'd also like to get a look at whatever he was so focused on."

A layer of thin clouds was spreading across the sky. Alder frowned. "Do we have time? It might take us a while to get all the way over there. And then finish the canyon."

Katie fiddled with her harness. "We could check it out and then backtrack, not finish the slot today. The weather is suspect anyway. And with a beginner in tow, it'll slow us down." She glanced at Talia. "No offense."

A prickle raced across Talia's arms. "I understand. I don't want to put anyone at risk."

Blake slid an arm behind her back, his fingers settling on the harness wrapped around her waist. "No, we're here. I think we should finish what we started. I can check that out another day."

"Don't be silly." Talia placed a hand on her hip. "What if that guy comes back and cleans out his stash? You'll have missed your chance." She shook her head. "My list can wait. Or I can tear it up." She jutted her chin. *Look at me, growing.*

Blake chuckled. "Let's not get crazy."

Alder stepped forward. "I'll take Talia down the next rappel. You and Katie are fast. Run, check it out, then catch up to us. Or walk around and meet us at the canyon mouth. It's not far." He checked the sky again. "But we need to decide now."

Blake turned to Talia. "Would you be comfortable with that?"

Doing the slot canyon without Blake drained some of the joy out of the experience, but she didn't want him to know that. "Yes. But hurry. I want to celebrate when we get to the other end." Ignoring the fact that Katie and Alder were watching, she stood on tiptoes and pressed her lips to Blake's.

He pulled her close for a second, longer kiss. "You got it."

Katie elbowed her husband. "See—girls before geology. You could take some romance lessons from those two."

Alder bent down and placed a kiss on her cheek. "You know I love you more than all the rocks in the world."

She tipped her head. "Even rhyolite?"

"Even obsidian." He grinned. "You and Blake go sniff out the secret stash. I'm going to entertain Talia with the geologic history of Zion and the Colorado Plateau."

Talia adjusted the straps on her pack. "Can't wait. I want to be able to give your whole ranger talk when we're done."

• • •

Blake chose his steps carefully as he and Katie traversed the wash toward where they'd seen the group gathered. It was farther than he'd calculated, and they'd had to pick their way over rubble and cacti.

"We need to veer west a bit," Katie called out from behind him.

"Why's that?" He glanced back the way they'd come. Talia and Alder had already vanished down into the slot, and regret poured through him like a waterfall.

"Look at the cryptobiotic soil crust." She caught up and gestured to the dirt in front of them. "That stuff takes decades to form, and our boots will destroy it."

Heat gathered in his chest. More delays. "How do you suggest we get over there?"

Katie pointed with a flat palm. "We can head over to the outcropping and then work our way along the slickrock, staying out of the most fragile bits."

He groaned. That route would take three times as long, but so would standing here and arguing with the biologist. "All right. Lead the way, but let's move fast." This day was getting infinitely complex. He hated the idea of Talia doing the slot without him, but not as much as asking her to postpone. Alder's recommendation made sense, but this detour meant he and Katie wouldn't be able to catch up.

"The clouds are pushing in faster than the weather service predicted." He pulled off his helmet and attached it to his harness.

Katie chose her steps with care. "They're going to get wet, but they should be all right, as long as they keep moving. Alder knows what he's doing."

Blake kept an eye on the horizon as they continued on their way, the sinking sensation in the pit of his stomach growing deeper by the moment. Streaks in the distant sky suggested it was already raining in the far reaches of the watershed, and that water would head their way soon. This detour had better be worth their while.

Easing along the slickrock ate up precious minutes, the uncertain footing forcing them to proceed slowly or risk a fall. He edged his foot along a narrow ledge of the outcropping, keeping his lug-soled boots from damaging the soil below.

Several yards in front of him, Katie yelped, her voice ringing through the narrow canyon.

Blake dropped from the wall, his feet finding purchase on the rough ground as he sprinted to her side. "What—what's wrong?"

Her brows pinched, and she shot him a motherly glare. "Blake!"

His heart pounded. "I thought you were in trouble."

"I'm not—it's nothing like that." She scowled down at his feet. "Take a few steps this way. At least that will put you in the area that the other group already disturbed."

He complied. "What happened? Why did you cry out?"

She pointed to nearby markings on a section of the cliff face. "It's a glyph wall. Look." Katie lowered herself off the outcropping. "It's a nice collection too."

The simple designs were scattered along the rock face. Spirals, concentric circles, animals, and even handprints—like an ancient people reaching out across the ages. A shiver ran up his back. "Did you know this was here?"

"I don't think the Park Service knows this is here. I'm friends with the cultural director, and she's taken me to see several other archaeologically significant sites in the park. But she never mentioned one being here." Katie tipped her head back to study the designs reaching higher up on the wall. "It's remarkable."

"How old are we talking?"

"I'm no expert on this sort of thing." She shook her head. "Give me a lizard or a Utah pine, and I can detail out its life cycle, but not human stuff. But very, very old. The Southern Paiute and several other tribes in the area are believed to be their descendants."

Blake studied the odd designs. "It almost looks like a map." He pointed to some lines moving from one spiral to another. "Maybe a river?"

"Possibly." She walked a short distance, keeping her boots on rock wherever possible. "There are the little caverns the guy was messing with."

Some shadowy depressions in the side of the cliff lay just beyond them. Blake followed, keeping his feet to the same path. As they approached, he pulled a headlamp from his pocket and shone the light into the opening. Nothing seemed unnatural, and thankfully nothing snakelike. Pushing closer, he stepped up on the rock outcropping for a better view. The light illuminated fragments of red clay.

After slipping on a glove, he drew one of the pieces out. "What's this look like to you?"

Katie stepped closer, her mouth dropping open. "Pot shards. Artifacts." She waved both hands in front of her. "Put it back. Don't disturb anything else."

He crouched and angled the item back into the gap. "So, not drugs."

"Drugs?" She clamped both hands on her hips. "You've got a serious case of tunnel vision, Blake. It's an important archaeological site, and those guys were tromping all over it. Possibly looting."

Tunnel vision. The words stung. His commanding officer in Afghanistan had pointed out the same on his performance evaluation. *"Once Mitchell gets his focus set on something, he struggles to pivot to the right or the left. Good for following orders but could one day put him or his fellow soldiers at risk."*

Shoving the memory back into its own safe cavern, Blake shook off the dig. "I'll grab a couple of photos, and then we can intercept that group on the other side—make sure they don't take anything."

A low rumble crawled across the canyon. Blake scanned the sky as the knot in his belly tightened.

The color had faded from Katie's face. "Was that . . ."

He hopped down to stand next to her. "Thunder."

• • •

The deep rumble sounded like the growling of the earth's stomach. Talia placed a hand on either side of the crevice and glanced back at Alder.

His jaw was set, the helmet casting shadows over his eyes. He gave her a curt nod as if to affirm what they'd both heard. "Keep going. It's all we can do at this point."

She pressed her lips together. Nowhere to go but forward. And fast. To pass another pothole, she turned sideways to creep through a narrow spot, the rock walls feeling like they were ready to close in at any moment, like that trash compactor scene in *Star Wars*. "I-I think you should lead." Pressing her back against the sandstone, she made enough space for Alder to get past.

They'd been moving at a steady pace so far. He'd talked her through the rappel, and then, as they walked, he'd explained the geologic history of the area—from inland seas creating layers of sandy mud lined with countless tiny marine fossils, to the uplift that followed, and then to the river shaping the canyon in which they traveled. She'd soaked in his knowledge, content to listen as he explained the red and orange world into which they'd descended. How many people got to enjoy an educational tour while adventuring? It almost made up for not having Blake at her side.

Almost.

But about ten minutes ago, Alder had fallen silent. The absence of chatter had curled into Talia's chest like a serpent. She doubted he was out of information. It was more like the hush that fell over the land before . . .

Now that she understood, the knowledge struck her with terror. "They said five percent chance."

"Do you want the scientific explanation of what a five percent chance of precipitation really means?"

For once she didn't. The beautiful curving stone with light filtering down into the gap that had once seemed so gripping and beautiful now felt imposing. *Carved by the force of running water.* She'd seen videos of flash floods, water flushing through at high speeds and sweeping everything in its path. No chance to swim because of the churning, debris-laden current. Her knees grew rubbery as she stumbled over the rocks underfoot. "How much farther do we have to go?"

"We've still got one short belay, then the final stretch. We're going to get wet; it's just a question of how wet."

"No going back." Isn't that what Blake had said? Talia glanced up at the smooth walls of the slot. "If it gets bad, what do we do? Climb? We have a rope."

"Just hurry. We should be fine."

His voice sounded more strained than "fine."

A second rumble echoed around them, the sky above darkening to a charcoal gray. "And maybe pray," Alder added.

She grabbed onto the suggestion as if it were a belay line. Following her guide through the curving passage, Talia did her best to quiet her soul. *Lord. Lord. Please watch over us. You know we're down here.*

Something pattered onto her helmet, drawing her attention away from her feet. When she tipped her head back, a fat raindrop splashed over her forehead and into her right eye. Another followed, hitting the tip of her nose and sliding down. This wasn't going to be a gentle shower. Within minutes, the temperature had plummeted and the droplets had transformed into needles of ice pinging against her helmet. This was the answer to her prayer?

The sound of voices ahead speared her with hope. Maybe someone had come to assist them? Perhaps Blake and Katie had realized their situation and worked their way into the slot from the opposite side. Something.

Alder stopped so fast she nearly collided with his back.

She adjusted her harness. "What—are we at the rappel?"

"Yeah, but the other group is there."

She placed her hands on Alder's pack and rose up on her toes to peer over his shoulder. The man in the rear shrugged at them. "Sorry, bro. Our rope got hung up. We're almost through."

"Need help?" Alder's voice was low.

"Nah. We got it." He seemed to study them for a long minute. "Where's the rest of your group?"

Talia touched Alder's arm, thankful that she wasn't down here alone. There was something off about this guy. "They're behind us." The passage bent around behind her, so he wouldn't know any better.

"I saw you watching us over on the slickrock. We were just exploring." He curled his hands inward, gripping his arms across his thin frame. "Nothing more than that."

"All we care about is getting out of here before this becomes a torrent." Alder glanced up at the sky. "You should really get down that rope and rejoin your group."

Small streams of water were filtering over the edge of the slot and draining down on top of them, like a myriad of tiny waterfalls springing to life.

A distant call of a woman's voice rang through the slot. "Ethan—come on. We gotta go."

He twitched his mouth to one side. "I know what your ranger buddy is thinking, but he's so far off it's not even funny. We're not running drugs. We're just searching the park for—"

"Ethan!" The girl's voice shook. "Where are you?"

"Chill, would you!" he snapped.

Alder moved forward. "Look, dude. If you're not going to get moving, we're going to have to pass you. At this moment, I don't care what you've been up to. I just want to get my friend out of here and make sure I see my wife and kids tonight."

The guy narrowed his eyes and lazily nodded his head, backing up with his arms spread. "Sure, man. Whatever." He took up his line and clipped the carabiner to his harness.

Talia backed up a step, giving Alder room to maneuver, but the motion put her directly under one of the downspouts. The water cascaded off her helmet and down her shoulders, its icy fingers penetrating the neckline of her wet suit and down her back.

The floor of the canyon was already several inches deep in water. "How far down does this rappel go? It must already be full of water down there." The ground seemed to shift under her feet.

He turned to meet her face-to-face, his eyes nearly invisible behind his droplet-spattered glasses. "You can swim, right?"

"Sure—but—"

"Let's just focus on that for now. It's going to be a cold swim. We don't have far to go before the canyon opens out again. Aim for the left and scramble out. You don't want to get swept downstream."

"I-I'll follow you."

"Talia." He yanked off his glasses, his brown eyes shadowed in the dim light, water splattering off the front edge of his helmet. "Whatever happens, you get out."

"I—"

A shout from below finished their conversation for them. "You're all clear. We're heading out."

"I'm going first, but you need to be right behind me. Be careful, but no hesitating. Got it? I'll belay you at the bottom, just as an extra precaution. Rappelling with flow can be disconcerting."

She swallowed, but her mouth was too dry to answer, despite all the water falling around them. Talia nodded, her heart racing. This wasn't the trip she'd signed up for. "I'll be all right."

He squeezed her hand. "We'll have to embellish the story a bit for Blake and Katie. Water up to our chins and all that."

"Whatever you say."

Alder threaded the rope, fastening the webbing with a practiced hand.

Talia brought her wet fists up to her mouth and blew on them, hoping to wake the tips of her numb fingers. The wet suit helped keep the heat in around her core, but she'd be glad to get back to the car and put on some dry clothes.

"All right. Here goes nothing. On rappel." Alder flashed a smile and a wink. "Nothing like seeing a little geomorphology in action."

"I don't want to be part of the geological story, if you don't mind." She breathed over her fingers again as he backed over the ledge, gripping the brake line to slow his descent.

Talia placed a cold hand against the dripping rock and stared down into the chute where her friend had disappeared into the murky shadows. The water sloshing through the passage obscured any other sounds. She waited a minute before calling down to him. "Alder? You make it?"

A faint answer floated up to her, but she couldn't make out the words. "I can't hear you," she called back, her stomach beginning to ache with the tension. Had he said "Belay on"? The water pulled at her body, nearly dragging her to the edge. Rushing, she hooked into the line before it became less of a rappel and more of a water cannon. She adjusted the clamps, then rechecked her work, her clumsy fingers trembling as she touched each connection. Backing toward the edge, she took a deep breath and closed her eyes. *Lord, Blake called this a step of faith. I didn't realize how true that would become.*

Even with the water pulling at her body, her knees didn't want to cooperate. For just a moment, Talia considered hunkering down right here. The water would be deeper in the next section. Deeper and darker. How much worse would it get? Her legs trembled, refusing the final step. *I have to do this.* The image of Pops waiting for her at home—and Dad, her siblings. Her tiny nephew, cutest little guy in the world.

And Blake. Blake was waiting, probably going nuts out there.

Talia took a deep breath, gripped the wet line, and then eased over the edge before starting down the slick sandstone. Water poured from the lip, cascading along her arms and shoulders, and dragging her faster than she could control. The last few feet sped past, and she landed rear first in the pool below, water surging up over her head and filling her eyes and ears. It took every bit of strength she had to pull herself to the surface with the slick line. The current spun her about, and she held on with one arm, flailing with the other. Where was Alder?

She kicked hard, freeing herself from the whirling pool even as her rope tried to drag her back in. Reaching down for her harness, she yanked at the carabiner. She had to get loose, or she'd get sucked under again. "Alder? Alder!"

He was nowhere to be seen.

27

1951

Alma struggled alone in the dark water, the current hauling her downstream—away from their group, away from their home. Away from Henry. She must have hit her head when she'd gone in, because her hand came away bloody when she touched it.

The baby—where was her baby?

She thrashed about, trying to see over the branches dragged along in the river's cruel flow. The tree limbs pressed against her, crushing her arms to her sides. Had she been holding Eddie, or did one of the other women have him?

She wrapped her fingers around a bough and kicked hard.

Strong hands shook her. "Alma, you're all right. You're safe." Henry's voice cut through the haze threatening to pull her under. "Wake up. You're here with me."

She gave two more kicks before surrendering to his embrace, her pulse racing. "Where is he?" Her voice was but a whimper, like a little girl lost.

He drew her close. "You're safe—just dreaming. It's not real."

But it was. More real than it had been even that day. The water tugged at her still, its cold tentacles grasping at her legs, her torso, even as she allowed her husband to gather her into his arms. The silty taste lingered in her mouth. "Where—"

"Quiet now, or you'll wake him. Billy's all right."

Billy. Alma's heart slowed. "I-I was back there. In the water."

"I know." He nuzzled against her head. "You haven't dreamed that in ages."

The first rays of morning light filtered through the bedroom curtains. Her throat closed. "Billy. He's going today." She almost couldn't push the words out.

"Yes." He slid his hands behind her waist. "Yes, he is."

She brushed fingers against his face, finding moisture on Henry's cheeks. "What have we done?"

He didn't answer, just held her close. "What needed to happen."

A child lost.

A child found.

Alma burrowed her head against her husband's neck, the familiar scent of him pushing away the last vestiges of the nightmare. She pressed a gentle kiss to his jaw, damp and salty from his tears.

He laid a palm on her stomach, only slightly rounded from the little one who grew there. Would this baby provide solace, or forever be a reminder of the two sons they'd lost?

Mattie's words from that first day Billy had shown up in their lives floated back through her memory. "'God has a plan,'" Alma whispered against Henry's ear.

He pulled back a hair. "I wish I understood what it was."

"Me too."

• • •

Three hours later, she stood over the little case they'd purchased at the department store and folded the last of Billy's shirts into neat squares. The Johnsons would buy him new clothes, probably. Crisp white shirts and adorable little sailor suits. Shoes that didn't pinch his toes. She lifted the sturdy brown boots that had carried him down so many trails in search of his beloved lizards and snakes. They wouldn't fit for much longer, but she'd still cleaned and polished them for the trip. She pressed them to her face, the scent of the worn leather filling her heart.

New shoes. New parents.

She wiped away a tear and pressed a kiss on the toe of each boot before tucking them into the case next to his favorite blanket and toys. "I should have bought a bigger case. A trunk, maybe. I don't want him missing his belongings." *Missing us.*

Henry walked into the room, Billy on his hip. "You heard what Mr. Wilson said. The Johnsons are wealthy. They will want to buy him new things."

With a nod, she closed the lid. The one thing she wanted to send with her son the most wouldn't fit in the confines of a piece of luggage.

Their love.

Billy seemed content to be cuddled this morning, almost as if he sensed the minutes ticking away. At his young age, he likely wouldn't even remember them. The thought choked her, but she gulped down the emotion. Tears could come later. These precious moments needed to be happy and calm.

Henry placed a hand on her shoulder. "Remember that day you walked into my office and demanded to take him home with you? I thought you were crazy."

She managed a weak laugh. "I know."

"Do you regret that decision?" His eyes were warm and gentle as his fingers kneaded her shoulder.

She placed her palm against Billy's back. "Never." She met her husband's gaze again. "Do you?"

"Best thing we ever did." He blew a slow breath from between his lips. "But today might be the hardest thing we will ever do."

She leaned against his arm, the three of them standing quietly in the little bedroom until a light tap sounded from the front door. Alma buried her forehead against Henry's arm. Too soon.

"That would be them." Henry said. "Do you want to take Billy?"

"Yes." She pulled her elbows close to her sides. "But if I do, I might not be able to let go."

"All right." He reached down and squeezed her hand before walking out of the room, toting Billy on his hip.

She followed on his heels, willing her heart to beat at a normal rhythm.

Mr. Wilson stood on the small porch, his fine suit looking out of place here in the park. He gave them a nod. "I'd say good morning, but I'm sure the sentiment would sound a little hollow about now." His eyes traveled to Billy. "He's ready?"

"I forgot to bring his case." Alma touched her husband's arm. "Don't let him go until I'm there."

"Don't worry. I won't cross the threshold without you. We're doing this together, or not at all."

She raced back to the room and closed her fingers around the case's handle and suddenly thought of the hatbox, crammed into the back of their closet. Billy had come to her with all his belongings in a box, and he was leaving much the same way. But now, instead of being motherless, he had two. Two women who loved him. Two pappas. She lifted the suitcase, set her chin, and walked back to her husband's side. "I've got it. Let's go."

• • •

Henry sized up the couple standing next to the large Ford Packard. Mrs. Johnson stood frozen beside the oversized vehicle as her husband paced up and down the path in front of the Eriksson's small house. They looked even more distraught than he and Alma.

Billy squirmed in his grip for the first time all morning. "Down," he whimpered. "Down." He pushed against his father's hands.

Henry's heart seized. This might be his last chance to hold his son, and he'd selfishly hoped to place the boy straight into Mrs. Johnson's arms with a minimum of fuss. This was going to be hard on everyone, but more so if Billy decided to protest or run to his mother—to Alma.

His wife's strength through this ordeal had taken him by surprise, but every woman had her limits. Pushing away a crying, clinging Billy would be too much to ask of her.

The boy pulled his arms to his sides and attempted to slide from Henry's grip like a greased pig at a county fair.

After a quick juggle, Henry set him on his feet and held tight to his hand.

Billy stopped still, his eyes locked on the two people facing him. Alma had dressed the boy in freshly ironed short pants and a white shirt. He looked like a schoolboy ready for his first day, not a child facing the biggest change of his short life. He tucked a finger into his mouth and pressed himself against Henry's knee.

Alma came up beside him and crouched down, her yellow dress flapping gently in the breeze. "Billy, you remember Mr. and Mrs. Johnson."

The boy shoved away from Henry and threw himself at his mother's chest, colliding with her like a bighorn ram. "No!"

Alma's face drained of color as she closed her eyes and rubbed two fingers on Billy's back instead of closing her arms around him. "Don't they have a lovely, big car? Why don't we go see it?"

The attorney stood to one side, pulling his spectacles from his face and wiping the lenses with a white handkerchief. "We should try not to draw this out. It will be harder on everyone."

Mr. Johnson thrust his chest out and started toward them.

"Wait." Henry stuck his hand out like he was stopping automobiles on the canyon highway. After taking a deep breath, he bent over and tugged Billy's hands loose from Alma's sleeves, trying not to look at his wife's eyes.

Alma uttered a short sob, but she clamped her lips shut. Leaning forward, she took both of Billy's reaching hands and placed a kiss on each one, front and back. "*Vi älskar dig*, Billy. We love you."

Henry's throat ached as he lifted his son and carried him toward the waiting car. "It will be all right, Billy. You'll see. God will go with you, and so will our love."

"What are you doing?" Mattie appeared at the far end of the walk. She clutched her pocketbook to her stomach. "What's happening here?" She hurried toward them.

He raised his hand, palm outward. "Mattie, it's none of your—"

"Stop this. Whatever is going on, you need to stop." She sprinted toward Henry, colliding with him and Billy before they could reach the Johnsons.

He jerked back, heat flushing through his body. And here he'd thought Alma would be the emotional one. "We've decided this is for the best."

"You don't . . ." Her eyes darted to Alma. "He's not their child, Alma." She jabbed a pointing finger toward the Johnsons. Turning on her heel, she glared at the waiting couple. "He's *not* your child."

Billy started squirming again, his whimpers building into a full-blown wail. He stiffened his legs, kicking Henry hard in the ribs. "Down! I want Mamma."

Henry's jaw ached, his clenched teeth doing little to stem the tide of his own torment. He sidestepped the hysterical woman and carried his son toward the waiting car.

Mattie grabbed hold of his elbow, her fingers like the talons of a hawk.

Alma appeared at her side. "Mattie, you're frightening Billy. Don't make this harder, please."

Splotches of color appeared in Mattie's cheeks as she swung toward Alma. "You're supposed to protect him. You promised."

Henry stopped just short of Richard Johnson's outstretched hands, the tone in Mattie's voice piercing through the turmoil today had wrought. He turned, Billy still thrashing in his arm. "What do you mean?"

"When I brought him to you, you promised." Tears streamed down Mattie's face, her makeup smudged and running. "You promised."

Alma clutched her friend's sleeve. "You didn't bring him, Mattie. I took him from Henry's office." She slid an arm around her, as if Mattie were the hysterical mother in need of consolation. "You're confused."

Henry's heart pounded as the images coalesced. *The mother in need of consolation.* "Mattie, were you . . ." His throat closed around the words. No, he'd seen Mattie that day and many of the days before and after. She couldn't be.

Mattie shook free of Alma's hand. "I'm his mother. Not that woman." She shot the Johnsons a look of fury. "Go home. I'm not letting you take him."

The color faded from Alma's face. "Mattie . . ."

The attorney stepped forward; his brow furrowed. "Young lady, you're saying that you're the boy's mother? Do you have proof?"

"Proof?" Mattie's mouth dropped open. "Billy was born here, not in Salt Lake City. I-I'm the one who placed him under the bridge." She swung about and jabbed a finger into Henry's chest. "I stayed in the rushes nearby, just to make sure you would find him. He'd be safe with you and Alma—I knew that."

Mr. Johnson sputtered. "She's lying. We've already made the connection between the boy and Holy Cross Hospital."

She straightened. "I started out as a nursing student at Holy Cross, but I learned quickly that I couldn't handle the sight of blood." She swung around to face Henry. "It should be in my file. You can ask Mrs. Whyte."

Sweat dampened Henry's shirt where he still clamped Billy to his side, and the more Mattie spoke, the weaker his arm grew.

Billy slid from his grip and darted back to Alma, throwing himself into her arms.

She drew him in, cuddling the boy to her chest and under her chin, both arms crossed behind his back like a shield. "Mattie, why didn't you say something before?"

The young woman's chest rose and fell like her lungs couldn't gather enough air to sustain her. "I-I wanted to be near him. If you knew . . ."

Alma reached out a trembling hand and cupped her friend's face. "You silly girl."

Henry's mind reeled, still feeling one step behind. "You're Billy's—"

Beatrice Johnson's cry was guttural and heart-wrenching, cutting through the confusion. He turned to see the woman's husband draw her into an embrace just before her knees crumpled. Mr. Johnson eased her into the Packard.

Henry stood in the center of this melee, numb. When the attorney extended a hand to him, Henry shook it out of reflex.

Mr. Wilson's grim face was belied by the twinkle in his eye. "I think we're done here. For now, at least. I'll contact the Johnsons' attorney and explain what transpired. I have an inkling that they won't pursue it any further."

The world seemed to shift about in slow motion. The Packard pulled away, and Alma hugged Mattie as the two women followed Billy into the house.

Henry stood frozen, the eye of the storm, his mind refusing to accept what had just happened. The Johnsons' vehicle drove into the distance—without his son.

28

Present Day

IN THE DARKNESS, Talia somehow unclamped the rope with her numb fingers, allowing it to spiral free from its bolt. In an instant, the pressure on her harness released and the water closed over her head.

She flailed with both arms and legs, tumbling through the murky depths until her shoulder slammed into the sandstone wall and her head emerged. Gulping in air, she flattened her palms against the wall, desperate for a handhold, but her fingers slid helplessly against the smooth stone.

Before she could try again, the current spun her about and carried her down along the crevice. She kicked hard, and her foot bashed against rocks—either the ground or the wall, she couldn't tell. Colliding with the wall again, she managed to grab onto a small outcropping and slow her momentum.

Lord, please help me.

The icy water spilled over her face, and she fought to keep her gasping mouth above the current. A roar filled her ears as the sound bounced around the narrow slot.

Talia's fingers loosened, and she repositioned her hand, cupping it against the wall. If she lost her hold, any breath she managed might be her last. Her shoulders and arms trembled with exertion as she labored against the stream's force. Kicking hard, she tried to push herself higher, but her chin fell back under the surface.

Something slammed against the back of her helmet, knocking her loose from the wall and sending her spiraling down the passage like a pool ball heading for the corner pocket. The large object pressed against her in the current, and instinctively Talia grabbed for it, her fingers closing around the rough surface of a tree limb. Hefting her arm over the top, she pulled herself far enough above the torrent to grab a few gulps of precious air. The branch trundled a little further before wedging against the stone wall.

Talia laid her head against the rough surface, using the moment to catch her breath even as the water pulled at her legs. She closed her eyes, putting all her ebbing strength into holding on. Any moment the flow would yank her loose. Weakness spread through her muscles and sinews as they gave way to the biting cold.

Hold on. Just hold on.

The echoes sounded different from when she first plunged into the pool. Talia forced her eyes open and tipped her head back to stare upward. Her view of the sky had widened, the canyon opening out like a gaping seam. Rocks and vegetation lined the banks.

Somehow she'd made it out of the slot, but the river had deposited her somewhere downstream. She must have been fighting too hard to keep her head above water to even notice. What had Alder said—swim to the left?

Alder.

Black spots danced in front of her eyes. What had happened to him? Had he been sucked down into the whirlpool or dragged far downstream? Her throat clogged as if all the water she'd swallowed had pooled in her chest. "Alder?" she croaked. Coughing a few times, she finally managed to free her voice. "Alder! Are you out there?"

No one answered. Nothing but the sound of water gurgling and slapping up against her. She adjusted her grip, trying to look back the way she'd come. *Lord, please let him be alive.*

The branch shifted with her movement, jogging loose and rotating enough to reenter the current.

Talia yelped, gripping onto her new friend with all her strength and kicking her feet like she'd done as a child in the YMCA pool.

After traveling a few yards, the limb jammed up against a boulder wedged along the sandstone wall. The stop was so sudden she nearly lost her grasp on the rough wood. Talia dug her nails into the wet surface. She couldn't stay in the water much longer and hope to ever emerge. Wedging herself between the log and the boulder, she jammed her knee between the two and rested one of her arms.

"Be still." Myrtle's voice echoed through Talia's chest, softly at first behind the sound of the water, but coming clearer the more she reached for her friend's words. Talia closed her eyes again, imagining herself standing at the footbridge, Myrtle by her side.

"Child, you are just like this river . . . You are the water . . . God is the rock."

Talia slid her fingers across the boulder, its cold, hard surface speaking of strength and age.

"You remember what He said to the water?"

Talia's teeth chattered, and she lowered her forehead to the stone. "What?"

"He said, 'Be still.'"

• • •

Blake slid down the rock slope on his heels, the rain splattering up from the slick surface. This storm had blown in at a ridiculous speed. They'd no sooner heard the distant rolls of thunder than the first raindrops pelted down, but he knew that the water falling around them wasn't nearly as worrying as how much may have fallen in the distance, now rushing toward Talia and Alder like an oncoming train.

"They must have gotten done before it started." Katie's voice sounded behind him. She'd repeated herself three times now, each instance a little more high-pitched than the one before it. "Alder is quick with the ropes—especially with it just being the two of them. They should already be out."

If Alder and Talia were done, they'd be dashing for the car—and Blake had yet to see anyone. Not even the group that had gone in before them. He didn't like it. "Do we get cell service out here?"

"I don't know, maybe a little."

He had his radio in his glove box, but doubling back would eat up precious minutes. Right now, all he wanted was to lay eyes on Talia and Alder. He'd been a fool to let them go alone with poor weather rolling in. It only took one delay on a rappel to bring their forward momentum to a halt, and Talia wouldn't have been much help. If the rope got caught, or Alder was hurt . . . if Talia was hurt? His throat tightened.

They'd be forced to wait for help. And being stuck in a slot during a flash flood meant certain death.

His foot slipped, and he stumbled down the incline, barely catching himself from plunging headfirst into the ravine.

"Slow down," Katie ordered. "If you get hurt—so help me—I'll throttle you. We haven't got time for carelessness."

They didn't have time for arguing either. He cast a quick glance to make sure she was still on his heels.

The frown that darkened her face rivaled the storm.

"You're right." Of course she was. If he broke his leg, he couldn't help anyone. Blake forced his breathing to slow and proceeded a little more carefully toward the mouth of the canyon. The group of three climbers huddled under a rock outcropping, and the sight gave him a rush of energy. "Look." He gestured toward them.

"What about Alder and Talia?" Katie's voice crackled with emotion.

"Let's find out." He grabbed Katie's arm to help her over a pile of boulders, releasing it just as quickly as she surged forward. So much for slowing down.

"Where are they?" Her words grew shrill as she approached the trio. "Where's our group?"

The woman in the group shot Ethan a sour face. "We had a little trouble on the final rappel, so it slowed everyone down. But they were *right* behind us."

Ethan pulled off his helmet, crushing fingers against his forehead. "We barely got out ourselves. The water rose crazy fast. I tried to go back, but I didn't get very far. I don't know where they went."

Katie pressed both hands to her lips.

Blake pushed past them toward the canyon mouth, the churning water rushing through the riverbed at a breakneck pace. "Talia? Alder?" He plunged in, getting waist deep before the flow knocked his feet from under him. Battling against the current, he dragged himself to the side. Were they still in there, or had they been swept downstream? Neither option sounded promising.

Scooting on her rear down the slope, Katie joined him on the narrow bank. "What do you think happened?"

His mind was already plowing through the options, but each seemed more gruesome than the last. "Hopefully they found high ground."

The wetness on her cheeks might have been rain, but it seemed unlikely. "There is no high ground in that last stretch. It's a clean chute up to this point."

"We need backup—search and rescue." He thrust his keys toward her. "Go to my car and radio for help. I'm heading downstream. They may be hung up somewhere and waiting for rescue."

"Don't you dare give me orders," she snapped. "I'm coming with you. We already made a mistake by splitting up."

Her subtle accusation pierced his heart. His poor judgment had led them here.

Ethan scrambled closer, his thin face darkened by shadows. "I'll do it." He held out his hands.

Blake nodded and tossed his keys up to the young man. "Black Subaru parked just up the road." Suspect or not, it didn't really matter at this moment.

"I saw it." He spun and dashed toward the road, the slick rock barely slowing his pace.

Turning back to the waterway, Blake scanned the rocks for any sign of life—a rope, a pack, anything. But it had all been washed clean. He picked his way along the bank.

Katie hurried after him. "Blake, we've got to find them."

"That's the plan." He strove to push confidence into his tone, but the thought of facing Talia's grandfather with the news had kicked off a whirlpool in his gut.

I should have told her I loved her.

He'd realized the depth of his feelings weeks ago, but fear had stolen the words. Last night, when she'd shared the news about her incredible job offer, it had cemented his decision that the truth should remain unspoken. He wanted her to stay. He needed her to stay. And he loved her more than he had any right to.

But if he told her the truth, and she left anyway . . .

Coward.

Life was fragile and fleeting. A bomb could steal a friend in the span of a single heartbeat. No one knew that more than him.

The memories flooded in like the water sweeping downstream. The father thrusting his baby up toward Blake on the wall. *"Take her—please! It's not safe for her here."* Without stopping to consider the implications, Blake's free hand had closed around the bundle, the warm, squirmy child locking eyes with the American soldier. Instead of squalling in fear, trust spilled out from her young gaze. Helplessness? Or simply surrendered to the will of her father?

Blake had passed the child to a marine behind him, and in that second it took to turn, the baby's father had melted into the crowd.

Father, please. Talia and Alder are in Your hands, not mine.

Blake came to a standstill on a large boulder overlooking the water. "Talia!" he shouted.

No answer.

29

1951

ALMA LEANED AGAINST the kitchen counter, waiting for the teapot to boil as Mattie sat staring at the kitchen table, bouncing her knees. *Billy's mother?* Alma pulled tea bags from the canister, trying to remember back to the day he'd arrived in her life. Mattie had been there—as trim and smiley as ever.

None of this made sense.

But the Johnsons had left, and Henry stood out front speaking to Mr. Wilson. Her heart had flown aloft and scattered like so many wildflower seeds carried on the breeze.

Billy came out of the bedroom, his hands full of colorful blocks. "Build, Mamma."

"You go ahead, Billy. Mamma and Mattie are going to have tea."

Mattie looked like she needed something stronger. If she bounced the knee any faster, she might drill a hole in the floor.

Alma carried the cups over to the table. She had a thousand questions but couldn't bring herself to ask a single one. She was too busy reliving the past three years.

"I'm sorry." Mattie's voice sounded ragged.

Alma slid into the seat opposite her, studying the drawn expression. "For not telling us you're . . ." She glanced down at her son playing on the floor.

"*You* are Billy's mother." Mattie met her gaze for the first time since they'd come inside. "You always will be. You can't let those people take him."

Those people. The words jolted Alma. "We didn't want to put Billy through a court hearing, especially since it seemed like—like he could very well be theirs. The lock—"

"Was mine." Mattie shut her eyes so tightly wrinkles formed on her brow. "It must have slid into the lining somehow when I was traveling."

"I wish you'd said something." Alma shook her head slowly. Mattie had been by her side the day she'd brought Billy home. And nearly every day since. "You hid it so well."

"People see what they want to see." She took a sip, then reached for the sugar bowl.

Henry came in from the porch, rubbing his arm absently. "Mr. Wilson has gone back to the office to sort out the details. He almost seemed tickled with how things turned out." He pulled a water glass from the cupboard.

"I made tea, Henry," Alma said.

"I'll join you in a moment." He stared out the window above the sink, his shoulders hanging low.

Mattie's knee began to bounce again. "Maybe I should go."

He turned, leaving the glass on the counter. "Not yet. I need the truth." Henry folded his arms. "What was that performance out there?"

She blanched. "Performance?"

"Henry." Alma's thoughts scrambled. "What are you—"

"Mattie couldn't be the mother." His jaw set. "I'm rather surprised the attorney didn't see through her charade."

Mattie pushed up to her feet, wavering on her slingback shoes. "Why would you say such a thing?"

"You weren't pregnant, Mattie. You never missed a day of work. How could you possibly have given birth, hidden it from everyone, and shown up for every single shift?"

"I-I— How do you know that?" Mattie pressed both hands to her mouth, likely getting lipstick on her cotton gloves.

He lifted his chin and stared at the ceiling as if it might provide answers. "I asked your supervisor on the first day of the investigation."

Alma's stomach lurched to her throat. Billy might belong with the Johnsons after all. She'd never be able to endure that scene a second time. Her heart couldn't take it. "Mattie?"

Henry cleared his throat. "In fact, Mrs. Whyte said you picked up shifts for several of the girls who were down with the flu. So somehow you managed to double your workload, become a mom, and abandon your child all over the course of a single week?"

Mattie sat back down, both arms wrapped around her midsection.

Billy knocked over the tower of blocks and chortled. He moved to his hands and knees, pushing one around the floor like a train.

"He doesn't belong to the Johnsons." Mattie shook her head. "I chose you. You and Alma."

The room spun, slowly. Alma gripped the table edge. "Did you give birth to him? Are you the mother?"

"You are his mother." Mattie repeated.

The words sank in. Alma leaned forward. "You placed him in the hatbox, but someone else gave birth to him." She reached across the table and laid a hand on Mattie's sleeve. "Is that it?"

The young woman didn't look up. "Yes. But it doesn't matter. Let them think it was me."

Henry choked. "It *does* matter."

At the sharp sound, Billy stopped mid-chug. After jumping to his feet, he hurried over and grabbed onto Henry's legs.

Henry lifted Billy into his arms. He waited a moment before speaking again, and this time his voice remained steady. "Mattie, if you lied about that, what else did you lie about? Is any of it true? The hatbox—the lock? You knew what you needed to say to cast doubt on the entire situation. But your story is full of holes."

Mattie squared her shoulders, fire flashing in her eyes. "I was there. I watched you tuck the box under your arm and carry it away, leading your horse by hand. I was even close enough to hear what you said."

He tipped his head. "And what was that?"

"'A child lost. A child found.'"

30

Present Day

THE PULL OF the water against her legs seemed to be losing strength. That or she'd grown fatally numb. Talia kept her cheek against the wet stone, one arm wrapped around the branch, the other jammed in a crevice below the boulder.

Tipping her face upward, she studied the outcropping just above her head. If she could get a hold of that, she might be able to climb onto the bank. Talia loosened her grip on the rock and stretched her fingers upward, grasping the protruding shelf like the lip of a swimming pool. Was there any strength left in her arms? After hoisting herself up a few inches, she braced her foot against the stream bank. Bit by bit, she wriggled out of the channel, shimmying onto the gravel like a seal.

Falling back against the solid ground, she closed her eyes and let the tears flow down her temples. Tremors rippled outward from her chest to her fingertips. A sob clung to the inside of her throat, and she placed an icy-cold palm against her lips. No one was around to hear, but it seemed a stupid moment to break down, now that she was safe.

"You are the river, carving and cutting your way to the sea. Rushing along and never seeing all the beauty around you."

The sun's rays caressed Talia's chilled skin, allowing some of the feeling to creep back into her fingers. She pushed up to her elbows, scooting backward to get her lower legs and feet clear of the stream.

Watching the water rush past, her throat grew thick. Alder was still out there somewhere. She needed to get on her feet and look for him, but every muscle trembled. Her legs might not even support her. Exhaustion pressed her down, and she curled on her side, splaying her fingers over the warm surface like a lizard soaking up the sunlight.

Be still.

The words felt like they'd become part of her bloodstream, flowing through her body and steadying her from within. She let the stones support her head, their strength—His strength—becoming part of her as well. *"The Lord is my rock, and my fortress, and my deliverer."*

Blake—he was out there somewhere, probably tearing the canyon apart looking for them.

He'd stepped into her life when she needed a steady presence—a friend. But somewhere along the way, he'd become so much more. Something her heart ached for. And that need had frightened her.

The realization rose slowly, like the first light of dawn spilling over the landscape. She loved him. His kindness, his laugh, his fierce protectiveness—she loved all of it.

She didn't want to leave this place. Blake. Pops. Myrtle. And she certainly didn't want to go back to sitting at a desk, focusing on convincing people to purchase clothes they didn't need. If she were going to market clothes, she wanted to be sure they were worthwhile. Quality fabrics like organic cottons and wools and garments produced by individuals who were paid fairly for their labor. Artisans, not sweatshop workers.

Could she do that? Create her own company?

Talia stood up on wobbly legs, bracing one hand against the cliff face. The bank had expanded a bit since she'd crawled out onto it—a sure sign the water was receding. She could now walk alongside the channel.

Her heart reached out for Alder. Was he trapped in that pool back in the slot canyon? "Alder? Can you hear me?"

She strained her ears to listen beyond the ripples of the water and the whispering wind. Was that an answering cry in the distance or simply wishful thinking? Alder had a wife and three kids who needed him. If she could help—

"Here . . ." The faint voice carried on the wind, kicking Talia's pulse into overdrive. She pushed forward, picking her way across the stones and around the woody debris washed down by the floodwaters.

"Alder?"

"Y-yes." He sounded closer now.

Hopefully he wasn't on the far bank. Even though the flood was receding rapidly, she had no desire to plunge back into its depths.

A flash of yellow caught her eye in a tangle of broken tree limbs up ahead—the sleeve of Alder's wet suit. She rushed to his side, blinking back tears as she wrenched a branch loose.

"Careful—I'm in a bad way." His voice cracked.

Talia dropped to her knees. "I'm so glad to see you."

"Likewise." He reached a hand to her.

She caught it and pressed it between both of hers, his skin icelike. "Where are you injured?"

He tipped his head toward the opposite arm, the shoulder hanging at an odd angle. "Arm—shoulder. Got smashed against the wall on the rappel, and I heard it . . ." He grimaced. "Heard it crack."

She'd washed up on a fairly sunny bank, but Alder was in the shade—his legs still submerged. His blue-tinged lips were trembling even as he struggled to get a breath. He'd been in the frigid water far too long.

She pulled the rest of the debris loose, casting it aside. "I need to get you out of the stream. Do you think you can stand?"

He blew out a breath and coughed. "Yeah. I can't feel my feet . . . but I assume they're still there."

"I can assure you, they are. And if your sense of humor is intact, I'd say that's a positive sign." She moved around behind him, sliding her hand under his good arm.

"C-c-can't lose that." Alder's teeth chattered. He braced himself against her, and somehow they managed to get him on his feet, leaning heavily on her side. He cupped a palm under his elbow, supporting the broken arm as they picked their way over to the bank. "Talia, I'm sorry."

"What do you have to be sorry about?"

"I had no b-business . . ." His brows knit, and he turned his face away. "Blake and Katie have more rappel experience. My pride—it got in the way. It can be tough having a wife who's better at—well—everything."

"You didn't know what was going to happen. I can't imagine what they would have done differently." She helped him over to a flat area of rock warmed by the sunshine.

Alder squeezed his eyes shut as he slowly lowered himself to the ground. "I don't know. Maybe nothing." He groaned, pulling the arm closer to his chest. "But if you had died back there, I doubt either of them would have forgiven me."

"I'm the one who protested when you guys considered canceling. If anyone's to blame, it's me."

He rested his head on his hand, his face resembling wet clay. "Just give me a few minutes. Then we can go find the others."

She studied him. "Maybe I should go for help."

"Don't. I can walk. I just . . ." He swallowed hard. "Turn around."

"Why?"

"I'm going to be sick."

She crouched beside him, resting a hand on his back. "I'm not squeamish."

He choked and gagged, his face contorting with pain as the heaves jostled his arm and shoulder. Grabbing a quick breath, he unlatched his helmet and cast it aside.

The sight of blood over his right ear set Talia's heart racing again. She touched his hair. "Alder, you have a head injury."

"I what?" He reached up a hand and tested his scalp. "Oh, that's nothing. The helmet took the brunt of it. I got a little too up close and personal with a chunk of rock. Hazards of being a geologist."

She sat back. "It looks deep. You're going to need stitches."

He offered a crooked smile. "They can give me all the stitches they want. I'm just happy we both made it out of that river."

• • •

Blake shoved past shrubby junipers and sage along the wash, straining his ears for sounds besides the rushing water and his own ragged breathing. From Ethan's description, Talia and Alder had been caught in the most unforgiving stretch when the canyon overflowed. He and Katie had already traversed the area above the slot, calling down into the depths and hoping to hear a reply that suggested one or both had found higher ground.

The only voices to echo back had been their own.

If they'd been washed downstream, they could end up anywhere—in any condition.

Shoving down his turmoil of emotions, he focused on what needed to be done. Hopefully Ethan had succeeded in alerting emergency services, but from the violence of that fast-moving storm, it was likely that they were already stretched thin across the park.

Other than occasionally shouting out Alder's and Talia's names, Katie had gone quiet. Her initial questions and suppositions had been like claws to his heart, but her silence was far worse. Her ashen face made her look like a drowning victim herself. If they found Alder dead, would she ever recover? Raising three children while living the NPS life was tough, but doing it as a single mom seemed almost impossible.

If Alder died, she may not even want to continue here.

Would he? As hard as he tried to push away the dark thoughts, they soaked into every crack of his psyche. One more failure. One more lost friend. Another crushed family.

But this time, it burrowed deeply into his soul. *Talia.*

As the sun baked down, he'd shucked off the top portion of his suit, leaving it to dangle about his waist.

Just last week, he'd helped Talia pick out a wet suit at the outfitter in town, pointing out the features that would keep her warm when they got to the wet portions of the canyon. But even that wouldn't protect her for long in the chilled floodwaters. A knot twisted in his stomach as he considered the options: head trauma, crush injuries, drowning, being pinned under debris . . . The more time that passed, the lower the chances of finding them alive.

"Talia!" His voice had grown hoarse.

He stopped, scanning the wash in both directions.

Katie caught up, wheezing for breath as if her throat were so tight it wouldn't let the air pass. "Alder!" Her voice croaked out, just loud enough to carry over the water.

Just because they didn't answer didn't mean they weren't there. Somewhere. As gruesome as the thought was, he turned his eyes to the river. The turbulent water was beginning to slow. He feared what it might reveal.

Picking their way along the side of the channel, they searched every debris raft and crevice.

Lord, help us find them. I might be a failure, but You are not.

Straightening, Katie grabbed his arm and pointed across the stream. "What's that, over there?"

He turned to look. A blue line was tangled in some rocks on the far side of the stream, trailing under the surface. His stomach dropped. "Stay here." He pushed one hand in front of her.

She followed him to the water's edge.

The cold water splashed up over Blake's waist as he struggled against the current.

His heart hammered as he closed his fingers around the nylon line. Was there a body on the other end—somewhere below the surface? He choked back the thought. Either way, they needed to know.

The line was taut and cold between his fingers. He gave it a tug and the resistance didn't bode well. "Katie, turn around."

She pressed a fist to her mouth but stayed put.

The rope might as well have been attached to his heart. "Lord, please. Don't let this be what I think it is."

He pulled it a little harder, then slid his grip down the cord and under the surface. It disappeared under a pile of rocks. With one good yank, it came loose.

Blake lost his footing and sat down hard in the water. No body. "Thank You, Lord. Thank You."

Katie shrieked. "It's not? You're sure?"

"No, just snagged in some rubble." The cold water rushed over him, and for a moment he was back at Fort Bragg, stepping into the baptismal. If only today would bring the same peace. "Let's keep going." This didn't mean Talia and Alder were alive, but it restored an element of hope. And he'd take any hope God had to offer them just now.

He pushed up to his feet, then walked the stream like he and Talia had done in the Narrows. "Talia! Alder!"

Katie echoed his call from the far bank.

They continued on for some distance before a sound caught his attention. He glanced toward Katie, who had stopped her forward momentum, her eyes locked downstream from him. "Do you see something?"

"No, I . . ." Her brow furrowed. Katie cupped her hands around her mouth. "Alder!"

Blake turned his head slightly, finally catching the sound. A faint word.

"Here!" Talia's voice. "We're here!"

Katie whooped, and she sprinted along the rocky bank.

His throat was too thick to answer. Instead, he plowed through the water and up onto the dry ground. The channel bent slightly to the north and after he'd clambered over a pile of rocks and brush, the sight of Talia—standing on her own two feet—almost brought him to his knees. Alder sat nearby, one arm cradled against his ribs.

Blake forced his rubbery legs forward until he reached Talia and gathered her into his arms. The warmth of her skin against his seemed fleetingly unreal. As she trembled in his grasp, he drew back to study her face. "I can't believe you're alive. Are you hurt?"

She shook her head. "No, but Alder—"

"Good to see you too, buddy," Alder said. "Now I know where I rate."

The teasing tone in his friend's voice filled Blake with relief. But the drying blood on Alder's head and the awkward angle of his shoulder tempered Blake's response. "Your head—"

Alder twisted away from Blake's probing hand. "It's nothing." Staring toward his wife, Alder's eyes went wide. "Katie, don't—"

Before he could get another word out, she'd plunged into the stream, staggering against the strong current. She obviously was determined not to be left out of this reunion.

Blake hurried over and helped her cross. As capable as Katie was, the last thing he needed was another friend swept downstream.

After trudging onto the bank, Katie rushed toward her husband. She grabbed his good arm and laid her other hand on his thigh. "Thank you for not being dead."

"I'm rather thankful, myself." He brushed tears from her cheek before drawing her close.

Blake made his way back to Talia and gave her a good head-to-toe survey. "Are you really all right?"

She laced her fingers with his. "I'm battered and exhausted, but otherwise fine."

He squeezed her hand, lifting it to his mouth to plant a kiss on her knuckles. The way their hands fit together would never fail to impress him. He'd come far too close to losing that forever.

She leaned into him, her body heavy against his. Her fatigue was evident in her stance.

"Do you think you can walk out of here?" he asked.

"Yeah, but I'm not sure about Alder."

Alder was already on his feet, cradling his arm. "I'm not waiting around for a ride. I'd prefer to make it back to the car under my own power."

"Wait a minute." Blake reached for Talia's harness. "Slip this off and we'll make a sling for Alder's arm."

Talia seemed more than happy to shimmy out of the wet straps, and between him and Katie, they managed to strap Alder's arm against his ribs.

Blake took hold of Talia's hand, delaying her even as Katie and Alder set out upstream. "Let's give them a minute. Katie's pretty shook up."

"I think we all are." Talia leaned heavily against his side. "He was pretty woozy when I found him, but he's been steadily improving ever since. It must have been shock."

"We'll get him checked out. Both of you, actually." He turned to her.

"I'm fine." She shook her head, running a hand through her hair. "And I think I can mark canyoneering off my list."

"Yeah?" He couldn't resist the smile pulling at his lips. "What's next? Skydiving? Bungee jumping?"

She slid an arm around his waist. "I think I'll stick to hiking." Turning to catch his eye, she flashed him an unsteady smile. "But I did decide one thing today."

His heart shifted. "Oh?"

"I'm turning down the job in Phoenix. I want to stay here. For a while, at least."

The sun's rays were beating down on them, catching the reddish highlights in her brown hair and turning them golden. He couldn't resist combing his fingers through the drying strands. "Why is that?"

She lowered her eyes. "I think the water helped me carve away all the useless ambition and stuff I didn't really want—leaving behind only what actually matters" She smiled, her chin quivering slightly. "You.

Pops. Myrtle. My family." Talia gestured to the area around them. "This beautiful world. I want to see more of it, not be locked in some urban office building. And"—she met his gaze—"I want a career I can be proud of. I'm going to start my own small business selling natural-fiber clothing."

He resisted scooping her up in his arms. As bruised as she was, it probably wouldn't be welcome. But he leaned in and covered her mouth with his, lingering there for a long moment. "I can get behind that. But you might need another list."

She kissed him back, the touch of her lips sending shivers through his body. "No more lists. Just life."

• • •

The floodwaters must have carried every last bit of Talia's energy downstream because by the time they made it back to the road, her legs and feet felt like they belonged to someone else. She planned to strip out of this wet suit and curl up in the old picnic blanket she knew Blake kept in the trunk of his car. The blazing sun had thawed her slightly, but the chill of the water seemed to be clinging to her bones.

He'd mentioned taking her to the emergency room to get checked out, but all she really wanted to do was sleep. And take a shower. She wasn't sure in which order. Could one sleep in the shower?

As they emerged on the side of the road, several ranger vehicles parked alongside Blake's vehicle, and a group of people milled about. Ethan and his two friends stood with a team dressed in search-and-rescue gear. Pops split from the crowd and jogged toward them, Myrtle trailing him like an aged shadow. "Talia! Blake! You about gave this old man a heart attack."

Talia nearly fell into her grandfather's outstretched arms. "I'm sorry, Pops. I didn't mean to frighten you."

Myrtle frowned, grabbing Blake around the middle and squeezing him tight. "When that storm rolled in, I thought there might be trouble. Then when I heard the report on the radio, I called Bill straightaway. I knew he'd want to be here. Me too—though I wasn't sure what I could do to help."

The tremor in her friend's voice brought tears to Talia's eyes. "Thank you. We're all right. It was a wild ride, but we're safe."

Pops shook his head, cupping his fingers around her face. "I'm so relieved. Of all the rescues I went on in my career, I would never want one to be my own granddaughter."

"It's my fault, sir," Blake said. "We had a delay, and everything went downhill from there."

Her grandfather clasped Blake's arm. "You got her out, though. For that, I'm glad."

Blake ran a hand across the back of his neck. "She got herself out. I'm just as thankful as you."

Talia was too weary to add any more, so she let Blake and Pops walk her over to the EMTs for a quick assessment. After a flurry of medical checks and a long list of things to watch out for, they released her to go home.

Blake finally escorted her back to the car, but before he could close the door, Myrtle leaned in and caught hold of her hands. "Talia, I was praying something fierce. I knew He'd bring you through the waters."

Through the waters. "Thank you. He sure did." Talia closed her palm around her friend's fingers.

Ethan had intercepted Blake before he had a chance to climb into the driver's seat. Talia couldn't hear their conversation through the windshield, but seeing Blake squeeze the other man's shoulder caught her by surprise.

She turned her attention back to Myrtle. "What you said before—about me being like the river—"

"Oh, don't you listen to this crazy old woman. I didn't mean like destructive floodwaters."

"No . . ." Talia took a quick breath. "You were right. I *am* like the river—or I was. He is our rock. Your words helped me sort through some things while I was waiting for the flood to subside. Don't ever take them back, please."

A huge smile crossed her lined face, and she stroked Talia's arm. "Well, good, then. I'm glad. And honey"—she leaned close, lowering her voice—"I have some other things to tell you. Things I should have shared ages ago. When you're feeling stronger."

"I'll take all the wisdom you have to share."

Myrtle's smile faltered, but she patted Talia's knee as she withdrew and closed the door.

Blake climbed into the driver's seat. "It's just us. Alder and Katie went with the ambulance."

"What's going on with that Ethan guy? Did you find a drug stash?"

He plugged his phone into a charger. "No, I was way off base. Katie and I found an archaeological site there—a wall covered with incredible glyphs. The crevices contained some artifacts. We didn't spend long searching, though, because we were worried about you and Alder."

Blake glanced out the window toward the group of climbers, now busy talking with a pair of rangers. "You know, Ethan had told me a while back that he was an anthropology student. What he didn't say was that he and a couple of his friends have been scouring the park, trying to find undiscovered sites to feature in his thesis."

Talia frowned. "Why wouldn't he tell you that?"

"The Park Service is protective of those locations, for obvious reasons. Maybe he was concerned that if he found something, he'd lose access. He insists they weren't stealing artifacts and were being very careful. They didn't intend any harm—especially to you and Alder. He feels awful about what happened."

She latched her seat belt. "So what happens to him now?"

"There will be an investigation. But someone else will be in charge. I'm too connected to the case now."

Yawning, Talia laid her head back and let her eyes drift shut. At the soft touch of Blake's hand on her cheek, she opened them again.

He was staring over at her, his expression serious.

"What?" She lifted her head. "Is there something else?"

"No." He shook his head and offered a soft smile. "I'm just thanking God for keeping you both safe."

Her heart swelled. She took his hand, running a thumb along his wrist. "I kept thinking of you while I was clinging to that rock."

His brows drew together. "Me?"

The emotions spilling through her were nothing like the torturous floodwaters. They were gentle and warm, filling every inch of her soul. "I love you, Blake. I never told you, and I don't know if you—"

He closed the distance between them and brushed her lips with his own. "I love you too. More than you will ever know."

Her breath hitched, tears blurring her vision. She cupped his face with both hands, drawing him back to her lips before nuzzling his rough jawline. "It shouldn't take something like this to make me say it. But I was scared to admit it to myself."

"So was I."

She smiled as his breath tickled the side of her face. "We're a good match, then."

"As much as I'd like to continue this"—he gave her hand a quick squeeze—"we should get you home."

Talia dropped her head back again, turning to stare out the window as Blake steered the car onto the highway. The beautiful cliffsides of Zion Canyon glowed in the late afternoon sun. She could spend a lifetime soaking in that view.

31

1951

HENRY PACED THE living room floor, Billy cuddled to his chest. The child grew heavier as he relaxed toward sleep.

Mattie and Alma still sat at the table, sorting out the bits and pieces of Mattie's story.

He wasn't sure whether he should be thanking the woman or shaking her. She'd lied to the Johnsons and to the attorney. She'd lied to him. What parts of her story were true, and which were total rubbish? It was so muddled he no longer trusted his own instincts.

Obviously, she had played a part in Billy's appearance by the river, but she'd also confessed to not giving birth to him. The inconsistencies and half-truths smelled worse than a road-killed skunk.

Billy laid his cheek against Henry's shoulder, his fingers playing with the pocket flap on his pappa's shirt.

Henry's throat ached, and he pressed his arms tighter around the boy. Billy would be staying where he belonged. He could thank Mattie for that, at least.

Alma's voice lifted. "Tell us who the mother is. You owe us that. I don't want to be looking at every woman I pass and thinking, 'Is that her?' Or wondering who else is going to lay claim to our child."

"She won't." Mattie sighed. "She's built a new life for herself, and she knows Billy is happy and safe."

"But you still won't tell us?" Henry asked.

"I promised not to. Her husband wouldn't understand."

"She's married?" Alma's brows knit as if she was sorting through every married couple she knew.

Mattie rose to her feet. "I've said too much already. But please—don't let Billy go. He's yours. He belongs here."

Henry rubbed circles on his son's back, the dead weight in his arms suggesting Billy had dozed off. "Mattie, I'm sorry about your vow, but we *need* to know."

She reached for her pocketbook and clamped it under her arm. "Why?"

How had she missed this? Was she really that naive? "Because the Johnsons could argue that you're the kidnapper."

Her eyes widened, and she sat down hard. "Why would anyone think that?"

He walked over to the table and stood beside his wife. "You have connections to the hospital where the Johnsons' baby was taken, don't you?"

"From three years before. I was working here by then. What could they say?"

He ticked the points off on his fingers. "Your friend had lost a child, and you were determined to assuage her grief. You had intimate knowledge of Holy Cross Hospital—the schedules, the exits, and where the uniforms are stored. Dressed as a nurse, you walked in and stole the Johnsons' baby before anyone was the wiser. Then you placed the baby where the grieving couple would find it. Years later, when your plan was discovered, you lied to cover it up."

After blinking several times, Mattie turned to Alma. "You don't believe that, do you?"

Alma shook her head. "We don't." She bit her lip and glanced at Henry. "Do we?"

He thought about it for a moment, doing his best to weigh each fact objectively. "No, but I'm not the investigator on the Johnsons' case. And once they realize you lied about being the mother, it's going to cast you in a very bad light."

She pushed fingers into her hair. "I had to do something. I couldn't let them spirit Billy away."

"You need to tell us everything," Henry insisted. "It's the only way I can protect you—and Billy."

"Henry, I can't do that." Mattie let her head rest against the back of the chair, staring up at the ceiling. After a long moment, she sat up and locked eyes with him. "Here's what I can tell you—there are other people who know what happened. Other witnesses."

Henry yanked out one of the chairs and sat. He'd been investigating this for years. How many people around him knew the truth? "They can attest that you're not a kidnapper?"

"Yes." She lowered her jaw. "Speak to Mrs. Whyte."

• • •

The head housekeeper stood outside the women's dormitory, a mop handle gripped between both hands. "I'm not sorry. I take care of my girls."

Henry spread his arms. "You've known—all these years? Back when I was here interviewing all the maids and waitresses?"

"Of course I knew." Mrs. Whyte folded her arms. "I helped her deliver the boy."

Her words hit Henry like a slap. "*You* delivered the baby. *Mattie* hid him by the river. *I* discovered him there. We're missing one person in this equation. Who gave birth to him? Does she still work here?"

"No. She doesn't. And that's all I'm going to say." The woman gave a slow shake of her head. "Ranger Eriksson, *go home*. Enjoy your family. Your son is a beautiful gift from God."

He breathed out a long, noisy exhale and shifted his focus to the tops of the Fremont cottonwoods, their branches raised in worship of their creator. "I'm Billy's father—I'll continue to believe the heavenly Father brought the boy into our lives. But I'm not sure I can rest until I know more." He swallowed.

Ask her. A final question swirled in his gut like the churning current of the Virgin River. The one thing he'd been terrified of asking Mattie. A truth he and Alma had never discussed. He'd saved it for God, but the Almighty had been silent on the topic. At least until now.

The housekeeper pressed her hands into the pockets of her apron. "What is it you want to know, Ranger?"

The hairs on Henry's arms prickled. He scrubbed a palm over his face. "Do you know who the father is?"

She closed her eyes, her chest rising and falling in a deep breath. "I do."

"Did you promise him anonymity as well?"

Mrs. Whyte shook her head. "I did not. But I'm not sure the answer will bring you any peace. It certainly hasn't to anyone else around here."

"I'm Billy's father. That won't change. But if the man works in this park, I need to be aware of the fact." Even putting voice to the fear that had plagued him so long made his mouth go dry. The thought that the man who'd sired his son could be walking the same trails, watching from afar—it had haunted Henry's dreams. "I won't rest until I know. If that means I have to ask every single woman who has worked in this park, I will." He pointed toward the lodge. "Starting with the women who worked here in 1948. I was discreet when I conducted my first investigation. I see little need to continue that now."

Gripping the handle of the cart, Mrs. Whyte began rolling it toward the lodge. "Walk with me, Ranger Eriksson."

He obliged. "Would you like me to take that for you?"

"And give the younger maids the idea that I'm too old for this job? Heavens no."

After a few minutes, she turned to study Henry as they walked. "You've met him. But he doesn't work here. At least, he doesn't now."

Relief spilled through Henry like cool water. "I'm not a fan of riddles."

"You remember the movie they filmed here back in 1947?"

Henry stopped in his tracks. "Gary Legend."

She turned and looked at him, surprise in her face. "No. What makes you say that?"

His breath hitched. "No?"

A smile crossed her lips, making her appear years younger. "Don't believe everything you hear in the rumor mill. I'd think you'd know that by now. Most of the talk about Gary Legend was concocted by the crew to uphold his reputation. Gary was completely besotted with his wife. Any bravado he put on was merely an act."

"Then give that man an award. He had me buffaloed." He ran a hand down his shirtfront. "Who was it, then?"

"The man who gave Legend the old heave-ho when he started making problems for him on the set. The director."

"Dixon?"

"That's what I'm told."

Henry thought back through his interactions with the man. "He had a relationship with one of your staff?"

She wrinkled her nose. "I'm not sure I would put it quite like that. He pretty much bamboozled the girl into thinking he'd take her away from here. Make her into a movie star." She gripped the handle of the cart with a little extra oomph. "He pulled that trick with more than one of our girls. Tried the same nonsense when they came back this year."

"I wish you'd told me," Henry said.

She offered him a bemused smile. "I couldn't really do that, now could I? You and Mrs. Eriksson had already opened your arms to the little boy. If I brought you the story, you'd have put all the pieces together. So I looked after the man myself. Cleaned his room, brought his meals, kept an eye on his comings and goings."

"That must have been a lot of work. I can't imagine he's an easy person to please."

Mrs. Whyte stopped the cart in front of one of the cabins. "Oh, I had some fun with it. Short-sheeted his bed, dumped salt in his coffee, filled his shoes with Jerusalem crickets—that sort of thing. Basically made his life miserable."

"He deserves worse." Henry lifted out the bucket of cleaning supplies before Mrs. Whyte could protest. It sounded like he owed her this much.

She put her hands on her hips. "You don't read the Hollywood gossip magazines, do you?"

"No, why?"

"The man was run down outside his Hollywood mansion last month by a jealous husband." She took the bucket from Henry's hand. "A tragic ending for a tragic life." She shook her head. "But you can rest assured—he's never coming after your son. Billy is safe. You and Mrs. Eriksson can trust in that."

The stiffness in his limbs ebbed away. He reached out and touched Mrs. Whyte's arm. "Thank you for telling me the truth. And thank you for looking after the woman who gave birth to our son—whoever she is. If she ever needs anything . . ."

"I know where to find you."

• • •

Alma adjusted the newborn on her lap so Billy could see her little face. Seeing her two children together brought a flutter of joy to her chest. "What do you think of her, Billy? This is your sister—Annika."

He stared down at her and tipped his head as if trying to decide what to make of the wrinkled little creature. "She's small."

"So were you, my love."

Billy screwed up his face. "Like that?"

Henry walked into the room, a tray balanced on his arm. "You were even smaller, buddy. Annika is a giant compared to you."

Their son folded both arms over his striped shirt. "I'm big."

"Now you are," Alma said. Annika had been with them only a few hours, and the sibling rivalry had already begun. She and Henry were going to need to spend a lot of time in prayer if they were going to stay ahead of these two.

Henry nudged Billy. "Shall we show Mor what we made?"

Billy jumped up onto his knees, making the mattress shake. "We made breakfast. I helped."

"Oh, goodness. And I'm so hungry too." She smiled, adjusting Annika's blanket so her beautiful little face was easier to see. Three hours old, and she already looked completely different from either of her brothers. Give her a few years and she'd be chasing Billy down the trail.

Setting the tray down on the bedspread, Henry reached for his daughter. "The children and I are going to go outside and get some fresh air. That way you can eat your breakfast and get some rest. You deserve it."

Alma's heart jumped. "Outside—already? Are you sure?"

He grinned, bending down to place a kiss on her forehead. "Annika is a park ranger's daughter. She'll need to get used to the big, beautiful world—right, Billy?"

Billy scrambled off the bed, heading for the door. "I'll find a lizard for her."

Alma laughed, picking up a slice of toast. "Don't go too far."

"We won't." Henry lifted the baby's hand to wave at her mamma. "We're just going to introduce her to Zion Canyon. I'm pretty sure she's going to love it."

32

Present Day

Myrtle's pink sofa was pure mid-century modern, and Talia happily claimed one end of it. The fragrance of lemon-scented furniture polish almost obscured the remnants of cigarette smoke lingering in the cushions and drapes. Myrtle must have kicked the habit long ago, but some things took forever to fade. Pops sat down beside Talia while Blake settled into a high-backed wing chair.

Even though everyone was still full from the wonderful meal, Myrtle passed around dessert plates topped with slices of chocolate cake. "I've been wanting to show you something, Bill. Talia will be interested too. She's told me a bit about the family genealogy she's been working on, and I think I can help." She brushed crumbs from her hands as she traipsed over to a set of built-in bookcases on either side of her fireplace.

Sliding out a large binder, she pulled it to her chest before walking back to the sofa and setting it on the low coffee table. "This belonged to my mother, Irene Dawson. As you know, Bill, she worked at the lodge for several years before marrying my father. She had a bit of a reputation as a gossip, I'm afraid." She smiled. "I know what you're going to say . . . runs in the family, right?"

Pops chuckled. "I would never accuse you of such things, Myrtle."

Blake raised his eyebrows as if to say, *I might.*

Talia scooted forward to get a better look at the scrapbook. "May I?"

Myrtle spread her hands. "Be my guest. I should have shown you long ago, but I wasn't sure how you'd feel about me knowing what I did."

"Now you've got me curious," Pops said.

Talia opened the cover. The first page was lined with newspaper clippings about the foundling discovered at Zion National Park. She glanced at Myrtle. "You knew about this?"

"I think a lot of the older folks at Zion knew. The ones from our parents' generation, anyway. But no one said anything. Adoption wasn't discussed as much in those days."

"Why would your mother keep these?" Talia flipped to another page, filled with more articles.

"I think that will become clear as you read further. It did for me." She set her plate to the side, the dessert untouched. "I found this in the back of a closet after my mother passed away. I wasn't sure what to do with it. It felt wrong to discard what amounted to a piece of history. But I wasn't sure showing you was the wisest choice either." She blew out a long breath. "Would you want to know this sort of thing about yourself? Or is it better to live in blissful ignorance?"

Pops rested his hands on his knees. "I don't blame you. We've uncovered a right can of worms. But it's probably better that the truth is brought to light. My parents are gone, so it won't affect them. And I'm pretty set in my ways. It's too late to rewrite my life story."

Talia flipped through more pages. The handwritten dates showed that a couple of years had passed, and the articles turned darker in tone, discussing the missing Johnson baby and the possible connections to Zion and Pops. She pointed a finger at one yellowed piece of newsprint. "This is the one Blake found online. It mentions Pops's older brother who was lost in a flood."

The words sent a chill through her, sweeping her back to her own experience in the water. "Poor Gammelfarmor. I can't imagine how she felt losing a child in that situation. The flash flood was horrific for me, and I didn't have a baby to worry about."

Pops cleared his throat, looking over Talia's shoulder. "She didn't speak of it much, but I know she thought of him often. She and Far always said my sister and I were a great comfort to them. Not when we were bickering, mind you." He shook his head. "Annika had a talent for getting under my skin."

Talia paused on the next page before reading the headline to her grandfather. "Zion baby proves not to be missing Salt Lake infant." She exhaled, the tension in her heart easing. "I guess the Johnsons on my family tree aren't long-lost relatives."

Blake stirred. "Well, they are related to you, but not through these Johnsons. It's a pretty common name."

"I hated thinking that the poor family never found their missing baby, and how it might have been Pops." Skimming the article, she stopped. "It says here that a woman named Mathilda Simmons claimed to be the lost mother." She turned to her grandfather. "Why does that name seem familiar?"

"Mattie was a family friend." He cocked his head as if trying to understand. "She's my mother?"

Myrtle grimaced. "Keep turning pages."

Talia flipped the leaf. A childhood photo of Pops was fastened to the paper with little corner tabs. Beside it was another clipping listing the local spelling bee winners from 1959. At the top was a picture of Pops standing next to two grinning girls, all three holding certificates.

Pops frowned. "I remember that. Mor made me wear a starched collar. I wasn't happy."

"But you were so cute." Talia ran a finger over the picture, her scalp prickling. Myrtle's mother had kept all this information about another family's child. Who would do that? The unease gathering in her stomach kept her turning pages. More clippings followed. Sports scores, awards, and Pops's high school graduation. His and Gran's wedding announcement.

She sat back, leaving the book open on the table. "Your mom kept all of this?"

"She did." Myrtle shrugged. "I thought it was bizarre too. It goes on—articles of when Bill was hired at the park. Promotions. Baby announcements."

Pops scrubbed a hand over his face. "It's starting to sound like, maybe, she's my . . . Irene Dawson was my mother?"

Myrtle exhaled slowly, as if she'd been holding that pent-up breath for years. "I don't know for sure. But it's the only thing that makes sense to me. She and Dad raised five kids. I was the oldest. She and Mattie were good friends. Roommates, I think. So either Mattie was your mother, and my mom was just oddly fascinated. Or my mother was also yours—and Mattie was covering for her. I think the latter seems more likely, don't you?"

Talia set down her plate, pondering the implications. "That would make Pops your brother."

Pops fell silent, taking a moment to process this new information.

"Half brother," Myrtle added.

Blake leaned forward. "And Talia would be your great-niece."

Myrtle's lips stretched into a wavering smile. "I've always thought of the both of you as family—even if I couldn't tell you. I'm sorry I kept it secret all this time." Myrtle rose and collected the dishes. "It's a lot to take in. I'll go wash up, and give you all a chance to talk."

"Myrtle." Pops stood. "I'm glad to know, even if there's still some doubt. I had wonderful parents. And as odd as it may sound, I appreciate that my birth mother—if it was Irene—could still love me from afar. I'm only sorry that she's gone, and I can't tell her so." He opened his arms to his friend. "And having you as another sister is an unexpected blessing. Nothing could make me happier."

"My dear Bill." Myrtle stepped into the embrace, closing her arms around his back. "I'm not sure what made Mom and Mattie put you out there for Henry Eriksson to find, but I'm confident of one thing. God had a hand in it. He always does."

Talia started to close the book, but a small brown envelope fell from the back cover and landed in her lap. "What's this?" She lifted it for Myrtle to see.

"It was taped inside. I guess the adhesive must have given out after all these years." Myrtle smiled. "I opened it once. It contains a tiny key, but there's no explanation of what it belongs to."

With trembling fingers, Talia opened the flap and let the brass key slide into her palm. Her breath caught. "I think I know." She dug into her pocket and pulled out her key chain. As everyone leaned in to watch, Talia inserted the key into the vintage padlock. After she wiggled it a bit, the shackle clicked open.

Talia lifted her eyes to meet her grandfather's. "Irene must have known you had the lock. Why else would she keep the key with all these other mementos? Do you think maybe she planned to show it to you someday? To prove her story?"

Myrtle squeezed Pops's arm. "She tucked it away, like a prayer nestled in a mother's heart."

He nodded. "It's not for us to know. It was between her and the Lord."

• • •

As Talia and Blake strolled toward the footbridge, she zipped the front of her coat, tucking her gloved hands into her pockets. The December day had been chilly, and now with the sun sinking low in the sky, the temperature promised to drop even more. But it didn't mean she wanted their walk to end.

"My family is growing. Since Myrtle took the test two months ago, my app keeps adding new Dawsons to my tree. She bought sets for all her siblings, and several of their children jumped on board too." She fiddled with the tiny padlock deep in her pocket. "When I received the results from my test, I thought I was losing family, not gaining it."

Blake caught her arm and turned her toward him. "Who wouldn't want to be a part of your family?"

"I wish we could have learned more about yours. That's why we started this, after all."

He pulled her close. "I'm content. I have you. And I'm honorary uncle to Alder and Katie's kids. That's more family than I've ever had before. Plus, my mom is coming for Christmas in a couple of weeks, remember? I'm hoping she and I can find some common ground. Start fresh."

"I can't wait to meet her." She shook her head. "It's a good beginning, I suppose."

He caught her chin, leaning forward to place a kiss on her warm lips. "Someday I'd love to have a big family too. Assuming I can find a soulmate who's interested in such things."

"Hmm." She nuzzled into his cheek, placing a line of kisses along his jaw. "How's that search going?"

"I'm pretty sure I've found her. But I've got a few more boxes to check before we can get to work on that big family." He squeezed her hand, nudging something solid into her palm. "Let's start with this one."

Her fingers closed around a small box. "What's this? Tell me I don't have to spit in a tube again."

Blake grinned and folded his larger hands over hers. "Don't look yet. I want to do this right."

Her breath caught as Blake lowered himself to one knee on the snow-covered bridge. "Talia Eriksson, the day I pulled you over and made you late for work was one of the best days of my life. It was the first step in falling in love with you." He kissed her fingers. "And that love has grown a little more during every coffee break, lunch, and walk. And then on epic hikes and our unusual first date."

"Ahh—that was the spitting."

He grinned. "Yes, ma'am." His brow creased, the smile fading as fast as it had flickered to life. "And when I thought I'd lost you, I knew my life would forever feel incomplete."

Her throat tightened. If he didn't finish soon, she wouldn't have a voice left. "Can I say yes now?"

Blake raised a brow. "I haven't asked anything yet."

"Sorry. I'm working on being a better listener, but I've got a ways to go." She blinked back tears.

He ducked his head for a moment as if to hide a smile, then lifted his chin to stare up into her eyes. "Talia Eriksson—I'm not sure this is on your list—but will you marry me?"

"Yes, of course I will." She bent to kiss him.

He intercepted her, tugging her down to sit on his knee as their lips met.

"I think she said yes!" Myrtle's voice echoed across the river, followed by the laughter of several more people. She and Pops appeared from hiding spots on the far side of the bridge.

Talia bounced to her feet and extended her hand to Blake, forgetting for a moment that she was holding on to a box. She rescued the velvet case before it could land in the snow. Opening it, she saw the golden glint of a vintage ring with a small diamond nestled in an art deco band. "Oh, Blake, it's gorgeous."

"I thought you'd like it. It's beautiful and unique, like you." He slid it out and placed it on her finger. "Plus, your grandfather approved when I showed it to him. He says you have an 'old soul.' I'm not sure what that means, but I was happy to receive his blessing."

More friends popped out from various hiding places around the bridge. Alder and Katie and their three kids were joined by several of the law enforcement rangers, plus the whole crew from the gift shop. Myrtle must have locked the doors.

Pops walked over and shook Blake's hand. "Welcome to the family."

Talia gave her grandfather a hug. "I'm so glad you were here for this, Pops."

"I wouldn't have missed it for the world." He hugged her tight. "My best granddaughter getting engaged on the very bridge where her great-grandfather found me? It might have taken a few generations, but the Erikssons have come full circle."

She slid her arm around Blake's waist, relishing his warmth on this chilly day. He pulled her away from the gathered crowd and together they walked to the center of the bridge. Talia leaned against his side, gazing at the Virgin River and the view beyond. The same river that had carved this canyon had left its indelible mark on her family. From the very beginning, God had used the water's steady, unrelenting flow to shape her life, but it had taken until now for her to learn to slow down and enjoy the view.

Blake stroked his hand down her back. "The sun will be setting soon. Should we stay and enjoy it?"

"Absolutely." She tipped her head so she could look up into his eyes. "And then endless sunrises to come."

Acknowledgments

LIKE THE TIMELESS work of water on rock, this book bears the imprint of those who shaped it along the way.

My dear husband, Steve, explored Zion with me—walking many of the same trails that Talia and Blake experience in *Through Water and Stone*. He even took one for the team by hiking Angels Landing alone (I'm terrified of heights) and sharing every vivid detail with me afterward. Thank you for always being my hero.

My two adult kids have become my personal experts on twenty-something attitudes and slang. You can thank them for the fact that my modern-day characters don't sound like they're taking part in a historical drama.

Thank you to my agent, Rachel Kent, who encouraged me countless times through the writing of this novel. You're the best!

I'm eternally grateful to the awesome staff of editors and marketers at Kregel Publications: Rachel Kirsch, Catherine DeVries, Janyre Tromp, Lindsay Danielson, Emily Irish, Mark Rice, Sarah Cross, and so many others. Thank you for your commitment to bringing great books to readers. I've loved working with you all.

I owe a debt of gratitude to my critique group: Heidi Gaul, Christina Suzann Nelson, Amy Earls, and Don White. I treasure our friendships! Thank you for making me look good.

And finally, thank you to the rangers at Zion National Park. I'm sure you must have gotten tired of me coming to you with "just one more question." You always greeted me with enthusiastic smiles and patient answers. Zion has one of the best ranger staffs I've ever had the joy of getting to know. You should be very proud.

Author's Note

HELLO READERS!

I hope you enjoyed exploring Zion National Park in *Through Water and Stone.*

With each of my national park novels, my goal has been to capture not just the scenery but the spirit of a remarkable place. Here are a few things you should know about Zion and the writing of this book.

The Footbridge

The pedestrian bridge over the Virgin River near the Zion Lodge features prominently from the first page of this novel all the way through to the end. If you've been to the park in the past year or two, you might realize that the bridge has been closed for repairs. For the sake of story, I've omitted this fact. The park administration could not give me a reopening date, and maybe—I hope!—it'll be repaired by your next visit.

What's in a Name?

Before 1850, the area now known as Zion National Park was inhabited by the Southern Paiute tribe. They referred to the land as Mukuntuweap, usually translated as "straight canyon." President William Howard Taft officially designated the area Mukuntuweap National Monument in 1909. Mormon settlers had referred to the canyon by the name Zion, or Little Zion. In 1918, the acting director of the National Park Service,

Henry Albright, decided the Paiute name might deter visitors and officially changed the park's name to Zion.

Baby Footprints?

Were baby footprints really used for security in the 1940s? Yes! I found newspaper articles about the "new" science of using infant footprints for identification as early as 1920. By the 1940s, many hospitals—including those in Salt Lake City—had implemented the new security measure. Unfortunately, very few abducted infants were ever successfully identified by this technique.

Flash Floods and Rockfalls—Oh My!

Yes, Zion is prone to both flash floods and rockfalls. While my husband and I were visiting in November 2023, a massive rockfall occurred at Weeping Rock. While we didn't witness the event, we were on the shuttle bus that drove through the dust cloud to rescue a large group of hikers. Thankfully no one was hurt. It's events like these that remind us how nature is constantly changing and that *wilderness* contains the word *wild* for a reason.

According to the NPS, Zion experiences an average of one to two flash floods per year. One of the deadliest incidents occurred in 2015 when a team of seven canyoneers perished after getting caught in the Keyhole Canyon during a sudden rainstorm.

Which Slot Canyon Did Talia, Blake, Alder, and Katie Explore?

Rather than describing a specific location, I decided to create a fictional slot canyon for the characters' adventure. The conditions in Zion's slot canyons can vary quite a bit from day to day, so I didn't want a reader to be disappointed if my description did not match their experience. The petroglyph wall is also fictional, though it was loosely inspired by Petroglyph Canyon, a site located about 2.5 miles east of the Zion–Mount Carmel Tunnel on Highway 9.

Author's Note

Thank you for taking the time to step into this story and walk alongside these characters. Your presence as a reader brings these pages to life, and I'm deeply grateful for your time, imagination, and heart. I hope this journey has touched you in some way, just as your support means the world to me.

Blessings!
Karen Barnett

About the Author

Karen Barnett is the award-winning author of ten novels, including *When Stone Wings Fly*, *Where Trees Touch the Sky*, and the Vintage National Parks novels. A former national park ranger, she's also a hobby photographer and enjoys teaching writing workshops with both Cascade Christian Writers and West Coast Christian Writers. She and her family live in Albany, Oregon. Visit Karen online at karenbarnettbooks.com.